HE WOULD HAVE HER . . . OR NO OTHER

"You've fired three governesses over a seven-day period? Then why do you wish to hire me, my lord?" Alexandra asked.

"Desperation, Miss Gallant. And because you possess something none of the other governesses had," Lucien answered.

"And what am I possesed of, my lord?"

He stood. When she didn't attempt to flee, he made his way around the desk to sit on the front edge. "It's very simple. Since I set eyes on you, I've had the strongest desire to pull the clips out of your golden hair, peel you out of that ridiculously prim gown, and cover your naked skin with hot, slow kisses."

Alexandra's mouth dropped open.

"And inspiring me, Miss Gallant, " he continued, "is not an easy task."

Avon Books by
Suzanne Enoch

A Touch of Minx
Twice the Temptation
Sins of a Duke
Billionaires Prefer Blondes
Something Sinful
Lady Rogue
Don't Look Down
An Invitation to Sin
Flirting with Danger
Sin and Sensibility
England's Perfect Hero
London's Perfect Scoundrel
The Rake
A Matter of Scandal
Meet Me at Midnight
Reforming a Rake
Taming Rafe

SUZANNE ENOCH

With This Ring

Reforming A Rake

AVON BOOKS
An Imprint of HarperCollins*Publishers*

This is a work of fiction. Names, characters, places, and incidents are products of the author's imagination or are used fictitiously and are not to be construed as real. Any resemblance to actual events, locales, organizations, or persons, living or dead, is entirely coincidental.

AVON BOOKS
An Imprint of HarperCollins*Publishers*
10 East 53rd Street
New York, New York 10022-5299

Inside cover author photo by Cheryl Byrne
Library of Congress Catalog Card Number: 99-96438
ISBN: 0-380-80916-8
www.avonromance.com

First Avon Books paperback printing: March 2000

Printed in the U.S.A.

10 9

For Kay Kerby
Carol Zukoski
Helen Kinsey
Jim Drummond

You taught, you inspired, and you shared
your enjoyment of learning, literature, and life.
All my love and gratitude to you—
my teachers

Chapter 1

Lucien Balfour, the Sixth Earl of Kilcairn Abbey, leaned against one of the marble pillars at the front entry of Balfour House and watched the storm clouds gather overhead. " 'By the pricking of my thumbs,' " he murmured, puffing on his cigar, " 'something wicked this way comes.' "

Though an ominously darkening sky hung over the west side of London, that particular storm was not the one that concerned Lucien Balfour. A larger tempest was galloping toward him: he was about to welcome Satan's handmaiden and her mother into his house.

Behind him, the front door opened on well-oiled hinges. Lucien glanced skyward as a long boom of thunder rolled across the rooftops of Mayfair. "What is it, Wimbole?"

"You asked me to inform you at the hour of three, my lord," the butler answered in his usual monotone. "The clock has just struck."

Lucien took another drag of his cheroot, letting the smoke curl from his mouth and be snatched away by the stiffening breeze. "Make certain the study windows are closed against the rain, and provide Mr. Mullins with a glass of whiskey. I imagine he'll be needing it shortly."

"Very good, my lord." The door clicked shut again.

Rain began plopping onto the shallow granite steps before him just as a coach clattered onto Grosvenor Street and turned toward the mansion. Lucien took one last, long draw on his cigar, snuffed it out against the pillar, and cast it aside with an oath. The demons had splendid timing.

The front door opened again and Wimbole, flanked by a half dozen liveried footmen, appeared at his elbow just as the great black monstrosity of a coach rocked to a halt at the foot of the steps. A second vehicle, less ostentatious than the first, stopped behind.

As Wimbole and his troops marched forward, Mr. Mullins took the butler's vacated position on the portico. "My lord, I must again commend you on your attention to familial duty."

Lucien glanced at the solicitor. "Two people signed a piece of paper before their deaths, and I am left with the results. Don't commend me for getting trapped into something I've simply been unable to avoid."

"Even so, my lord . . ." The smaller man trailed off as the coach's first occupant emerged into the light drizzle. "My goodness," he choked.

"Goodness has nothing to do with it," Lucien murmured.

Fiona Delacroix stepped out onto the drive and with a flick of her gloved fingers beckoned to Wimbole for her walking cane. She didn't seem to notice the rain, but given the size of the hat perched on her bright red—orange—hair, she likely would have no idea of the downpour until the weight of the water capsized her.

"Lucien!" She gathered her voluminous pink skirts and marched forward as he descended the steps to meet her. "How like you to wait until the last possible moment to send for us. I'd begun to think you meant for us to rot in mournful solitude all summer!"

Mountains of luggage began sailing off the roofs of both coaches and into the arms of the waiting footmen. Lucien spared the heap one look, noting that he'd have to give over another room simply for female wardrobe, before he took her gloved hand and bowed over it. "Aunt Fiona. I trust the journey from Dorsetshire was a pleasant one?"

"It was not! You know how traveling upsets my nerves. If not for my dear, dear Rose, I don't know how I should have managed." She swung her rotund, schooner-topped form around to face the carriage again. "Rose! Come out of there! You remember your cousin Lucien, don't you, my sweet?"

"I'm not coming out, Mother," echoed from the bowels of the cavernous vehicle.

Aunt Fiona's smile became more radiant. "Of course you are, my dear. Your cousin is waiting."

"But it's raining."

The smile faltered. "Only a little."

"It will ruin my dress."

Lucien's determined good humor began to crumble a little. His uncle's damned will did not in any way obligate him to catch pneumonia.

"Rose . . ." his aunt trilled again.

"Oh, very well."

The incarnation of hell on earth—as he'd thought of her since their last meeting, when she'd been seven and throwing a screaming, stamping tantrum at being denied a pony ride—emerged from the coach. She stepped down amid a cloud of pink lace and ruffles that perfectly complemented her mother's frothy gown.

Rose Delacroix curtsied, the blond curls that framed her face bobbing in pert unison. "My lord," she breathed, rising and batting her long lashes at him.

"Cousin Rose," Lucien responded, suppressing a shudder at the horrifying thought that some of his gender would find her angelic appearance attractive. With her great puffy sleeves and feathered frills she looked more like some ungainly bird than an angel. "You both look colorful this afternoon. Shall we go inside, out of the rain?"

"It's silk and taffeta," Aunt Fiona crooned, fluffing up one of her daughter's drooping wings. "They cost twelve pounds each, and came directly from Paris."

"And flamingos come directly from Africa."

The comment was a mild one, for him, but as he turned to usher Rose toward the steps, her blue eyes filled with tears. Lucien stifled an annoyed sigh. Sometimes one's memories remained perfectly accurate, despite the passage of time.

"He doesn't like my gown, Mama," she wailed, her lower lip trembling. "And Miss Brookhollow said it was the very thing!"

Lucien had meant to behave himself, at least for today. So much for his good intentions. "Who is Miss Brookhollow?"

"Rose's governess. She came highly recommended."

"By whom—circus performers?"

"Mama!"

"Good God," Lucien muttered, wincing. "Wimbole, get their things inside." He returned his attention to his aunt. "Does all your attire match so . . . vividly?"

"Lucien, I will not tolerate your insulting us five

minutes after we've arrived! Dear Oscar would never tolerate such cruelty!"

"Dear Uncle Oscar is dead, Aunt Fiona. And as you well know, he and my father conspired to see that you would end up here in that eventuality."

" 'Conspired?' " Aunt Fiona repeated, in an ascending voice that could shatter crystal. "This is your familial obligation! Your duty!"

"Which is precisely why you are here." He climbed the steps unaccompanied since they seemed content to stand about bellowing in the rain. "And only until she"—and he jabbed a finger in his soggy cousin's direction — "is married. Then you can be someone else's familial obligation and duty."

"Lucien!"

He glanced at his sobbing cousin again. "Would this same Miss Brookhollow be the one who has taught you everything necessary to ensure your success in society?"

"Yes! Of course!"

"Splendid. Mr. Mullins!"

The solicitor emerged from behind one of the marble pillars. "Yes, my lord?"

"I assume our dear Miss Brookhollow is cowering in the second coach. Give her twenty pounds and the directions to the nearest spectacle shop, and send her on her way. I want a posting in the *London Times*. Advertise for a finishing companion for my lovely cousin. Immediately. Someone knowledgeable in music, French, Latin, fashion, and—"

"How dare you, Kilcairn!" Aunt Fiona snarled.

"—and etiquette. Have them apply in person to this address. No names. I bloody well don't want the world at large to know that my cousin has the appearance of a poodle and the style of a milkmaid. No one in his right mind would want to be leg-shackled to either animal."

Mr. Mullins bowed. "At once, my lord."

Lucien left the screeching females behind and strode into the house. That had certainly deteriorated nicely. The headache with which he'd awakened resumed with a vengeance. He should have had Wimbole pour him a whiskey, as well.

At the top of the stairs he paused, leaning his wet backside against the mahogany railing. A series of paintings covered the opposite wall, part of the vast portrait gallery in the Great Hall at Kilcairn Abbey. Two of them, hung several yards from one another, bore black ribbons across their top right corners. One was a passing likeness of Oscar Delacroix, his mother's half brother. He'd barely known the man and had liked him even less, and after a brief moment Lucien turned his attention to the nearer portrait.

His cousin James Balfour had died a little over a year ago, so Lucien should have had Wimbole remove the ribbon by now. The mourning band served as a reminder, though, of exactly what sort of predicament James had left him in.

"Damnation," he murmured without heat. His nearest male relation, James would have—and should have—inherited Kilcairn Abbey. His young, headstrong cousin's thirst for adventure, though, had collided fatally with Napoleon Bonaparte's quest for power. As the inheritance now stood, once the weepy pink confection downstairs was married, her offspring would have the Balfour titles, lands, and wealth. But after setting eyes on her again, Lucien was of no mind to allow that to happen.

And so the inconsiderate mortality of all his male relations had effectively trapped him into taking the one road down which he'd sworn never to venture. The Earl of Kilcairn Abbey needed a legitimate heir—and so, by logical if unfortunate extension, he needed a wife. But before he could begin that task, he needed to conclude his obligation to Rose Delacroix and her mother with all possible haste.

Alexandra Beatrice Gallant stepped down from the London hack she'd hired and straightened her pelisse. The blue morning dress was the most conservative one she owned, and the high neck scratched at her. Uncomfortable or not, though, she'd been on enough interviews over the past five years to know that a conservative appearance and manner did wonders for one's employment prospects. And at the moment she needed all the help that she could get.

Shakespeare, her white Skye terrier and most faithful companion, jumped down beside her. Without a backward glance, the hack driver turned his coach back out into the light midday traffic. Alexandra looked up and down Grosvenor Street. "So this is Mayfair," she mused, eyeing the staid facades of the massive homes.

Though she'd taken positions with landed gentry and minor nobility in the past, nothing compared with this. Gilded Mayfair, the favorite haunt of England's wealthiest and highest born, bore little resemblance to the rest of noisy, crowded, dirty London. From the hack's window she'd spied numerous pleasant walking paths for her and Shakespeare to explore in Hyde Park. Finding employment in Mayfair could have definite benefits, provided the young lady and her mother weren't completely reclusive.

She pulled the folded newspaper advertisement from her pocket and read the address once more, then tugged on the terrier's leash and strolled up the street. "Come along, Shakes."

This would be her second interview of the day, and the ninth of the week, with one more prospect in Cheapside remaining. If no one wanted to hire her in London by the end of the week, she'd have to use her scanty savings to go up north. Perhaps they had never heard of her in Yorkshire. Lately, though, she'd had the sinking feeling that every household, or at least those needing a governess or a companion, knew every blasted detail of her life—and the best she had come to expect was a polite refusal to offer her employment.

"Ah, here we are, twenty-five." Alexandra paused to survey the mammoth town house that stood at the far end of a short, curving drive. What seemed like half a hundred windows peered toward the street and overlooked the small, simple garden on the east side. The house was bordered by a carriage run to the west, and not much distinguished it from the other splendid houses with which it shared the way. So far, so good.

Taking a deep breath, she walked up the carriage drive around to the back of the house and climbed the three steps to the rear entry. Before she could even rap on the door, it swung open.

"Good afternoon." A tall, thin man dressed in impeccable gold and black livery dating from the height of George III's reign stood just inside the kitchen entry and gazed at her. The dusting of silver at his temples served as an exclamation point to his dignity. "I presume you are here in answer to the advertisement?"

"Yes, I—"

"This way, miss."

Without even a glance at Shakespeare, the butler turned on his heel. Alexandra followed him through the huge kitchen, down two long intersecting hallways, and into a large, spacious study tucked beneath a winding staircase of carved mahogany. She took in the scattered, tasteful paintings by artists as celebrated as Lawrence and Gainsborough, the ornate Far Eastern carvings in ivory and flawless ebony wood, and the gold-inlaid cornice running along the top of the walls. Tasteful, elegant, interesting, and very well appointed, the house seemed curiously unfeminine for the residence of a young lady and her mother.

"Wait here, miss."

Alexandra nodded, absorbed in her observations. Shakespeare found an interesting scent beside the massive mahogany desk, while she approached the fireplace to warm her hands. A carved elephant stood guard on the mantel, and tentatively she touched its smooth, ebony leg.

Footsteps padded down the stairs that curved above her head. With a start she abandoned the hearth and seated herself in the chair placed opposite the desk. A moment later, the door opened. Alexandra affixed her best look of professional yet sincere interest on her face, ready to begin her well-rehearsed speech about her experience and mostly impeccable references, and looked up. And then forgot everything she'd been about to say.

He stood in the doorway, gazing at her. At first all she took in were his eyes—a fine light gray beneath dark, sardonic brows. Gradually the rest of him sank into her senses. Tall, with dark hair curling at his collar and an athlete's lean build, he had a French aristocrat's high cheekbones and arrogant, shamelessly sensual mouth. He remained where he was, unmoving, for several long seconds.

"You're here for the governess position?" he asked in a deep, cultured drawl.

"I . . ." Alexandra nodded, shivering a little as the sound of his voice resonated down her spine in electrifying spirals. "I am."

"You're hired."

Chapter 2

She blinked blue-green eyes as deep as the sea. "Hired?"

Lucien closed the door, an unfamiliar agitation tugging at his nerves. *Good God, she was delicious.* "Yes, hired. When can you begin?"

"But . . . you haven't seen my references, and you don't know my qualifications—or even my name."

Given her conservative attire and very upright posture, telling her just how arousing he found her obvious qualifications might run her off. A movement caught his attention, and he glanced down to see a small white terrier snuffling under his desk. Lucien lifted an eyebrow. "Yours?"

She tugged on the leash, and the animal returned to her side and sat. "Yes. He's quite well behaved, I assure you."

Grateful for any distraction that would give him a moment to recover his usual calm veneer, Lucien stepped around the small white beast and took a seat at the mahogany desk. "You don't need to assure me of anything.

You already have the job, Miss . . . What is your name?"

"Gallant. Alexandra Beatrice Gallant."

"A very upright name, Miss Gallant."

Miss Gallant blushed, the color rising prettily in her cream-colored cheeks. "Thank you, sir." Abruptly she looked down at her large reticule and pulled out a thin stack of papers. "My references," she said, holding them out to him.

He leaned forward and took them, his fingers brushing against the soft white kidskin of her glove. "If you insist." Lucien set them down without looking at them, preferring to keep his gaze on the tall, elegant goddess sitting before him.

She gestured at the papers. "I do insist. Don't you wish to examine them before you offer me a position?"

He could think of several positions he'd like to offer her. "I'd rather examine you."

Her blush deepened. "Beg . . . beg pardon?"

She was genuinely naive, he decided. And she had absolutely no idea who he was, thank God. "Everyone's references are perfect, or they wouldn't offer them. Ergo, they are useless. I prefer to go to the source." He cupped his chin in his hand and smiled, hoping he didn't look as predatory as he felt. "Tell me about yourself, Miss Gallant."

She smoothed her skirt, the motion practical and at the same time very feminine. "Of course. I have served in various governess and companion positions over the past five years, sir. I am considered more than competent." She lifted her chin, obviously launching into a rehearsed speech. "In fact, young ladies are a special favorite of mine. I—"

"Hm. I prefer mine to have a little more maturity."

"You . . . I beg your pardon?"

"How old are you, Miss Gallant?"

She eyed him, the beginnings of suspicion touching her gaze. "I am four and twenty."

He would have guessed a year or two younger, but that was likely because the skin of her cheeks looked soft and unblemished as any babe's. "Continue your presentation."

"Your advertisement mentioned a seventeen-year-old girl. Your sister, might I presume?"

"Good God, no." He scowled, annoyed out of his lust—temporarily. "I am cousin to the demon, and that is as close as I care to get."

She didn't seem offended by his blunt speech, but paused, waiting, no doubt, for him to explain. If she wanted to know something, though, she could ask. She'd been in his employ for five minutes already, and still she insisted on going through this damned silly interview nonsense.

"Perhaps," she resumed a moment later, "you might elaborate? And might I know your name? There was no mention in the advertisement. I don't know how to address you, sir."

He drew a slow breath. Well, she was bound to find out eventually. Miss Gallant didn't seem to have much missish nonsense about her, but now he'd find out for certain. "Lucien Balfour," he said. "Lord Kilcairn."

Her fine cheeks paled. "As in the Earl of Kilcairn Abbey?"

He kept the mild expression on his face, although his instincts urged him to spring for the door to bar her exit. "You've heard of me."

Alexandra Gallant cleared her throat and tugged her little white dog closer. "Yes, I have heard of you." She reached for her papers and stood. "I apologize if I misunderstood your advertisement, my lord, but I must tell you . . . you must know it sounded quite . . . Good day, my lord."

Lucien's eyes lowered to her slim, rounded backside as she fled for the door. "I don't generally advertise for mistresses in the *London Times,* if that is your concern, Miss Gallant," he said in the same dry tone. "Though I shall give you another point or two for name recognition and your expression of genuine horror, if you wish. Not the best I've seen, but certainly passable."

Miss Gallant stopped her retreat and turned around. " 'Passable?' "

At least he'd kept her attention. "I had one fat old bag in here last week who fainted when she realized who I was. It took Wimbole and two of my sturdiest footmen to drag her out." He leaned forward, folding his long fingers together on the desk. "The position is a legitimate one, and it pays extremely well. However, if you plan on succumbing to faints and vapors at the mention of my name, please do go. Posthaste."

"I have never fainted in my life," she declared, once more lifting her proud chin. "Nor would I be so foolish as to do so in your presence."

"Ah," he murmured, a smile curving his lips again. He couldn't recall enjoying himself so much in days. "You think I might simply lift your skirts and have my way with you while you lie unconscious on the floor?"

The lovely blush returned to her countenance. "I have heard worse said about you, my lord."

Lucien shook his head. "There's no fun in coitus unless both parties are coherent enough to enjoy the experience. Are you turning down the position, then? It pays twenty quid a month, if that interests you." Or more, if it didn't.

She balled her fists, wrinkling her neat stack of references. "My lord, this is preposterous!" she exclaimed. "You know nothing about me!"

"I know a great deal about you," he returned, and gestured at her vacated chair. "Shall we continue?"

She squared her shoulders and seated herself again with her reticule on her lap, no doubt to speed her escape if it became necessary. "What do you know of me, then?"

"I know you have exquisite eyes. What color would you call them?"

Those same eyes looked at him dubiously for several seconds. "I . . . hardly think the color of my eyes has anything to do with my competence as a governess and a companion."

"Hm. Almost blue, but not quite," he mused, ignoring her protest. "And not quite green, either. Not serpentine, or emerald. Turquoise, I think."

"I see you know your rocks and minerals, my lord," she broke in, lowering her gaze and making a show of untangling her dog's leash. "May we return to the nature of the position?"

"And what of your hair?" he continued, unruffled. "A bronze, only lighter. Like burnt sunlight." Lucien tilted his head at her. "Yes, that's a fine description; or spun gold, perhaps. More standard, but not quite as accurate."

"My lord," Miss Gallant burst out, "what of my employment?"

Lucien gestured for her papers again, and after a hesitation she returned them to him. "My aunt and my cousin are presently living under my roof," he began, perusing her references, though he didn't give a damn what they might say, "until such time as my cousin marries. I require someone to look after them, and to put a coat of polish on my cousin—a heavy coat of polish. I've hired three governesses for her already, and lost the last one yesterday morning."

"It must devastate her, to have lost so many companions."

"I hired the first one a week ago. I doubt she remembers their names, if she had the mental capacity to learn them in the first place."

Her look became more speculative and less wary. "You've hired three governesses over a seven-day period."

"Yes, I have. Damned waste of time. Which is why I've decided to try a different tack." A tack that he'd decided upon only since he had set eyes on her five minutes ago, but she didn't need to know that.

"Ah."

"I'll make this very clear, Miss Gallant. My aunt is Satan, and my cousin Rose is the incarnation of hell on earth," he stated. "My uncle's will—and a clause in my sire's—requires that I see her married, and married well, unless I wish to support her for life. Any of those other old bags could have taught her Latin—some of them were probably children during the reign of Caesar."

Her lips twitched. "Why me then, my lord?"

He raised his assessment of her once again. Curious, and with wits enough to have a sense of humor, though he'd sensed that already. "Desperation. And because you are possessed of what none of the others were."

Miss Gallant sat looking at him, her little dog at her feet and her large reticule in her lap. Someday he'd find out why she'd answered his advertisement rather than the other half a hundred that had run in the newspaper that day.

"And what am I possessed of, my lord?"

Lucien stood. When she didn't attempt to flee, he made his way around to sit on the front edge of his desk. "It's very simple. Since I've set eyes on you, I've had the very strong desire to pull the clips out of your spun-gold hair, peel you out of that ridiculously prim gown, and cover your naked skin with hot, slow kisses."

Her mouth dropped open.

"And inspiring me, Miss Gallant," he continued when she didn't lose consciousness, "is not an easy task."

"Because of your years spent in the pursuit of decadence and debauchery, I presume?" she ventured, her voice shaking a little.

"Precisely. And it is that inspirational quality I wish you to attempt to pass on to my cousin. She is not likely to snag anyone with her wit or refinement."

Her turquoise eyes fixed on his face, Miss Gallant stood and slipped around the back of her chair, her reticule hefted in her arms in what he presumed to be a threatening manner. "I can't believe you could possibly be serious. Therefore, I must presume that you are playing some sort of game with—"

"I am completely serious. And as I have said, I will pay you very well for your instruction."

She drew herself upright. "Perhaps you should have advertised for a mistress after all, my lord."

He gave her a sour look. "That would have accomplished nothing. One doesn't *marry* a mistress."

Miss Gallant backed a few steps toward the door. "Lord Kilcairn, I instruct young ladies in etiquette, language, literature, music, and the arts. I believe the art of seduction to be *your* forte. I cannot—I will not—assist you in that area. If that is what you require, I suggest you look elsewhere."

Lucien sighed, wondering if Alexandra Gallant had

any idea how very well he was behaving himself, considering he had no intention of letting her out of his sight. "You continue to insist on a damned inquisition, then. *Parlez-vous français*?"

"*Oui. Je me recevu l'ducation plus premier,*" she answered immediately.

"Where were you educated, then?" he shot back at her.

"At Miss Grenville's Academy. I was considered an excellent student."

"Translate. *'Dum nos fata sinunt oculos satiemus amore.'* "

She didn't even hesitate. " 'While the fates allow us, let us fill our eyes with love.' "

Lucien lifted an eyebrow. "Latin, as well, Miss Gallant. I imagine you *were* an excellent student."

"As were you, apparently."

He nodded, noting the surprise in her voice. "Some rakes do read. And I find your qualifications—all of your qualifications—acceptable. At the risk of repeating myself, you're hired."

Self-assured and undeniably arrogant, the Earl of Kilcairn Abbey sat back against his desk and folded his arms across his broad chest, eyeing her expectantly. Alexandra disdained fluttering; it seemed an obvious refuge for the weak-minded. Yet, as she gazed into the light gray eyes of Lucien Balfour and heard him announce that he wanted to strip her naked and kiss her, she felt distinctly fluttery. And horrified—because "fluttering" hardly began to describe the breathless rush Lord Kilcairn's words began inside her. Heaven knew she'd never had an actual rake in pursuit before. She'd never even seen a rake before today.

"My lord," she said, as diplomatically as she knew

how, "in all fairness, before you offer me such a . . . generous post, I think you need to know something more about me."

"I know all I need to know."

Alexandra gestured at her recommendations. "Even so, I have to make you aware that I do not have a letter from my last employer." When he didn't interrupt that pronouncement, she took a deep breath and tried to continue in a calm, reasonable tone. "I do have a letter from Lady Victoria Fontaine attesting to my character."

"You're acquainted with the Vixen?"

Oh, dear. Victoria's mother had warned the silly thing that she was well on her way to notoriety. "I tutored her for a time. She's a dear friend."

He opened his mouth, then evidently changed his mind about what he'd intended to say. "What is the difficulty, then?"

"My last employer was Lady Welkins, of Lincolnshire." There. She'd said it.

His gaze sharpened. "You're the chit who lifted her heels for Welkins and gave him an apoplexy."

Alexandra blanched. In six months she'd never heard the accusation put so bluntly. "You are mistaken, my lord. I did nothing of the sort. Lord Welkins had some kind of attack without any prompting on my part."

"Why did you leave the household, then?"

With effort she kept her voice steady. "Lady Welkins dismissed me."

The earl studied her countenance for so long that she wondered what he must be looking for, and what he saw there. "That was six months ago," he said finally. "What have you done since then?"

"I've looked for employment, my lord."

He straightened, lifting her papers from his desk, and

came forward. As the earl reached her, he held them out to her. "Thank you for your honesty."

Alexandra blinked back an unexpected desire to cry. If someone with as tainted a reputation as Kilcairn wouldn't hire her, no one would. Ever. "Thank you for your consideration," she returned, taking her recommendations back and stuffing them into her reticule. Her few remaining friends had told her she was stupid and naive to be so honest about her disaster with Lord and Lady Welkins, but she couldn't bear the idea of being dismissed after she'd begun employment somewhere.

"When can you begin?"

"I—Begin?"

Kilcairn tilted her chin up with his fingertips. "I told you, I know all I need to know."

For a bare moment, Alexandra thought he meant to kiss her. She looked directly into his eyes; she had to, with him standing so close and touching her like that. "I'm staying with a friend in Derbyshire."

He nodded, running the backs of his fingers softly down her throat as he released her. "I'll have my coach sent around front for you. Will two footmen be enough to transport your things?"

"Two . . ." Alexandra closed her mouth. This was going far too fast, like a whirlwind in a storm. But for whatever reason, she didn't want it to sweep by her. "Two will be more than enough."

"Good." The earl reached down and took her hand, bringing it slowly to his lips. She could feel the warmth of his touch even through the thin barrier of her gloves. "I'll see you this evening, then."

"My lord, I think it's only fair that I tell you I will tutor your cousin to the best of my ability," she said stoutly, trying to ignore the knowing smile and the light in the gray eyes watching her so closely. "Nothing more."

He brushed his lips against her knuckles again. "I wouldn't wager on that, Miss Gallant."

Lady Victoria Fontaine pushed the lace curtains to one side and looked down at the drive. "You mean to say that is *Lucien Balfour's* coach?"

Alexandra nodded and continued folding items into a trunk.

"The Earl of Kilcairn Abbey."

"Yes."

"But . . ."

"But what, Vixen?"

Alexandra's hostess glanced at the coach again, then released the curtains. "Well, I was just going to say that for someone so determined to stay clear of scandal," she continued, beginning to laugh, "you're certainly doing a poor job of it."

"I realize that." Never would she be able to explain why, in God's name, she had accepted the post. Nor why she was in such a hurry to pack her things and return to Balfour House. A heat, a fever almost, ran just under her skin and urged her to begin her employment before one could change one's mind. Whether that one was Lord Kilcairn or herself, she didn't know. "I'm glad you find it so amusing, Victoria."

In truth, under different circumstances she would probably have found it amusing herself. She'd met men as arrogant and self-assured as Kilcairn before. She knew men who assumed they were going to get their way by virtue of being, who mowed down everyone and everything in their path without realizing or caring whom they might be humiliating—and they annoyed her in the extreme. Yet now, after a fifteen-minute interview with a prime example of their kind, nervous, jittery anticipation to return for more made her clumsy and restless and shivery.

But it certainly wasn't anticipation of his promised kisses. *Naked* kisses, for heaven's sake. What nonsense!

Upon her return to Balfour House she would reiterate that tutoring his niece and serving as companion to his aunt was *all* she intended on doing, and that if he had something more nefarious in mind, he'd best forget it at once. That would settle her—to make absolutely certain he knew the rules and meant to abide by them. If he didn't, she would simply decline the position and leave.

That, however, didn't explain why she was bothering to pack.

"I don't find it amusing. Really." Victoria leaned down to scratch Shakespeare behind the ears. "Just stay here, Lex. It's much safer."

"I've stretched your parents' kindness to the limits, Vixen. I can't impose on them any longer."

"It's not an imposition," Vixen insisted, plunking herself down on the bed. "They *like* you."

"They used to," Alexandra amended without bitterness. "Now I'm a difficulty and an embarrassment, and no doubt a poor influence on you. You'll be heading for London in a few weeks, and they certainly won't want someone of my reputation hanging about you then."

Victoria smiled. "I am perfectly capable of causing trouble without your influence. But as for—"

"But nothing." Alexandra closed the trunk and hurried over to toss her toilette items into a hatbox. "I will make my own way, Vixen. I don't have the luxury of fortune and family that you do, and I can't just sit about being idle and wait for someone to rescue me."

"But Lord Kilcairn?"

She'd been trying to avoid that point, though he seemed to have become lodged in her thoughts the instant she'd set eyes on him. And it wasn't simply because he was the most beautiful, compelling, masculine being she'd ever seen. "He's the only one who's even *offered* employment in the past six months."

"You're exaggerating."

Alexandra wished she possessed Victoria Fontaine's self-confident bravado. "I am not. Everyone thinks I'm a husband-stealing strumpet. And at least half of those who think I dallied with Lord Welkins think I killed him, as well."

"Lex," Vixen protested. "Don't even say that!"

"You know it's true. Even if they don't blame me for his death, they certainly delight in talking about it."

"I hope you realize your new employment certainly won't stop anyone from talking about you."

Alexandra opened the bedchamber door and motioned to Lord Kilcairn's two liveried footmen, standing practically at attention in the hallway. With polite, blank-faced nods they hefted her trunk and carried it downstairs. Nothing remained besides her hatbox and a small valise of odds and ends. She sighed as she snapped the valise closed. That was everything she owned. "Odds and ends" seemed a fair description of her life these days.

"Lex, I know you heard me." Victoria gazed at her, violet eyes concerned. "Does Kilcairn have any idea about your last position?"

"Yes, he does. He didn't seem bothered in the least."

"Well, I suppose he wouldn't be. His own reputation is far worse than yours. He probably *likes* the rumors."

Alexandra forced a smile, trying to push away another

rush of nervousness. "Perhaps that makes me lucky. He seems determined that his cousin marry well; if she does him credit, she'll do me credit, as well."

Victoria stood, her expression still skeptical. "At least keep your bedchamber door locked at night."

Somehow she didn't think a locked door would stop Lucien Balfour if he was intent on entering a room. Her pulse jumped at the thought, and she scowled. *What was wrong with her?* "I shall."

"And if something isn't to your liking, please say you'll come back here right away. You don't have to be independent all the time."

"I promise, Vixen. Really. Don't worry."

Impulsively Victoria flung her arms around Alexandra and hugged her. With a belated smile, Lex returned the embrace.

"I'll see you soon," she said, gathering her hatbox and her dog and turning for the door.

"Be careful."

Alexandra marched into Balfour House behind the footmen, her speech practiced and ready on her lips. Just inside the foyer, though, she slowed and stopped. Except for the butler and a housemaid, the hallway stood empty.

"Where is Lord Kilcairn?" she asked, even as she realized how ridiculous the question sounded. The lord of the manor did not appear to welcome every employee. Still, the earl had given a forceful impression that he took a personal interest in hiring her, and part of her was disappointed that he wasn't there awaiting her arrival.

"Lord Kilcairn has gone out for the evening," the butler said in the same toneless voice he'd used that morning. He gestured her toward the stairs, where the laden footmen had already reached the landing. "This way, Miss Gallant."

"Are . . ." She realized she didn't know the names of her charges, except that Kilcairn's cousin was Rose. A governess couldn't very well inquire after the household's family by their familiar names—not without even having been introduced. And neither did she wish to begin her acquaintance with Kilcairn's staff by admitting to complete ignorance.

"Is there something else, Miss Gallant?"

Alexandra cleared her throat. "No. Thank you."

Scowling, she lifted Shakespeare and trailed the footmen and her trunk upstairs. The whole situation was so odd. Since she'd left Miss Grenville's Academy, she'd been careful about the positions she took—pleasant households with well-behaved children or kind, elderly women in genuine need of a companion. Taking the post offered by Lady Welkins and her awful husband had been her first real mistake. Working for Lord Kilcairn might be another.

"This is your bedchamber, Miss Gallant," the butler said from behind her. "Mrs. Delacroix has taken the green room in the corner, and Miss Delacroix is in the blue room adjoining yours. Lord Kilcairn's quarters are at the other end of the hallway."

The footmen emerged from her room and, bowing, returned downstairs. Alexandra nodded at her guide, grateful he'd supplied her with the names of her charges. "Thank you. Are Mrs. Delacroix and Miss Delacroix in this evening?"

"You are to be introduced to them in the morning, Miss Gallant. Dinner will be served in your bedchamber, and breakfast is set downstairs promptly at eight. I am Wimbole, should you require anything further."

"Thank you, Wimbole."

The butler gave a stiff nod and turned on his heel. Alexandra watched him disappear down the stairs, back into the bowels of the huge house. Squaring her shoulders, she entered her bedchamber.

"My goodness."

The room was splendid. All of her previous postings had been in affluent households, but nothing she'd seen before could rival this. The bedchamber was larger than some sitting rooms she'd seen, and no doubt Lord Kilcairn's private rooms were even larger.

Though Wimbole hadn't named her quarters, she felt certain the butler had shown her into the gold room. No other name fit. The bed's canopy drapings were gold, as was the heavy, elegant coverlet. The curtains hung green and gold in the three windows, while the two sitting chairs placed before the roaring fire were a darker bronze with gold thread running through the intricate, Oriental pattern.

Shakespeare sat on her foot to get her attention, and with a start Alexandra knelt to remove his leash. The terrier bounded off to wander every nook and cranny of his latest home, tail wagging at each newly discovered scent.

While her dog pranced about and growled happily to himself, Alexandra unfastened the trunk and began unpacking. Coming into a situation blind was not the way she worked. She had *never* accepted a position without first meeting her charges. In the morning she fully intended to lay out her conditions for accepting employment in Kilcairn's household. If he didn't like any of them, or if she didn't like the Delacroix ladies, she would . . .

Her hands slowed as she set out her toilette items. If

she left this post, it would probably be another six months before she could find another household willing to hire her. Resolutely she went back to her task. That, she would worry about tomorrow.

Tomorrow arrived earlier than she expected. When Alexandra first opened her eyes into complete darkness, she couldn't decide what had awakened her, much less where she was. Then Shakespeare *wumph*ed, and blinking sleepily, she remembered both.

Fumbling for the candle on the bed stand, she sat up. As dim golden light flickered in the room, Alexandra spied her dog by the door, looking from her to the exit and wagging his tail pitifully.

"Oh, goodness, Shakes," she whispered, swinging her feet out from the warm bed and onto the cold floor. "I'm so sorry. Just a moment."

She couldn't recall where she'd put her slippers, if she'd even brought them. But her dressing robe lay across the foot of the bed, looking shabby against the magnificence of the quilted golden coverlet.

"Get your leash," she instructed, shrugging into the robe.

The terrier dashed to the dressing-table chair, leaped onto it, and reared onto the table to pull the coiled leash down. That done, he dragged the braided leather line over to her.

She hooked the leash to his collar, picked up the candle, and hurried to the door. The bolt and the hinges were both thankfully silent. With Shakespeare tugging her forward, they stepped into the silent, moonlit hallway. "Shh," she reminded him as she padded down the stairs in her bare feet.

As they reached the foyer, the grandfather clock

standing there chimed. Alexandra glanced at it as they passed—fifteen minutes before three. The front door opened easily. A night breeze lifted the hem of her gown and robe, and she suppressed a shiver as cold air traveled up her bare legs. Leading the terrier around the side of the house to the small garden, she said, "Hurry, Shakes. It's cold."

"Trying to escape already?"

Alexandra whipped around, a shriek stuck in her throat. Lord Kilcairn stood at the border of the garden, looking at her. "My lord!"

If not for the candlelight, he would have been invisible, for he was clothed in black from his boots to his greatcoat to his beaver hat. The veriest edge of snow-white cravat glinted at her as he shifted. "Good evening, Miss Gallant. Or rather, good morning."

"My apologies," she said with a shiver, induced more by his imposing presence than by the cold. "I neglected to take Shakespeare outside before I retired for the evening."

"You'll catch your death out here."

"Oh, no. It's quite pleasant this evening."

The earl stepped forward, shedding his caped greatcoat as he approached. "If you die of pneumonia, Miss Gallant, I'll have to hire someone else for the devil spawn," he said, lifting the coat and placing it over her shoulders. "And I don't want to go through that horror again."

The coat was heavy and warm from the heat of his body, and smelled faintly of cigar smoke and brandy. She abruptly remembered his deep voice talking of hot, slow kisses, and swallowed. "Thank you, my lord."

"In the future, Miss Gallant, I would prefer that Shakespeare not relieve himself in my garden. And under no circumstances are you to go wandering outside in your bare feet and nightclothes." He paused. "Though I believe a competent teacher of etiquette would know that already, wouldn't she?"

Alexandra narrowed her eyes, a flush creeping up her cheeks. "I am afraid I have made a bad impression, my lord. No doubt you will wish to dismiss me now."

He shook his head. "As I told you, I don't relish having another flock of prissy hens in my house looking for employment," he said, a drawl of humor touching his deep voice.

So she was a prissy hen, was she? "I am pleased you think so highly of my services, my lord."

"At the moment I think more highly of your bare feet," he murmured, then gestured at Shakespeare. "Your dog has completed his task."

Reconciling the two statements took a moment. Alexandra blinked. "Yes. Thank you," she muttered. "Come along, Shakes."

Lord Kilcairn kept pace beside her as she returned to the house, his bootheels clicking in rhythm with the padding of her feet. In the foyer he slid his hands along her shoulders and gently lifted his coat free. As he hung it in the alcove, Alexandra shivered again, though by now she felt decidedly warm. Men did not touch her in such a familiar manner; she wasn't used to it, and she didn't like it—which didn't explain why she had the sudden strong urge to lean back against his broad chest and feel his arms around her.

"Shall I continue removing garments?" his low voice came from behind her. " 'Twould be my pleasure." She felt him move still closer, his breath touching the nape of her neck. "And yours, I think."

Wondering where her sense of propriety had vanished

to, Alexandra started for the stairs, not daring to turn around and acknowledge his scandalous words. "Good night, my lord."

He made no move to follow her. "Good night, Miss Gallant."

When she reached her room, she closed her door and stood there, listening. The stair landing creaked with the weight of his approach, and Alexandra slipped the bolt shut on her door, locking it. His quiet tread passed without pause down the hallway, and a moment later a door shut softly.

In taking the position at Balfour House, she'd obviously made a very large mistake. After the intolerable annoyance of being pursued by fat, smelly Lord Welkins, she'd meant never to enter a household again containing any male between twelve and seventy.

Lord Kilcairn was in prime condition and astoundingly compelling and attractive, and he'd made his interest quite clear. Apparently she'd gone completely mad.

Alexandra bent down and freed Shakespeare from his leash. However much she needed employment, and no matter how intriguing he might be, she was not going to become anyone's mistress. Ever.

Lucien finished wiping shaving soap from his chin, tossed the cloth at Bartlett, and exited his private chambers—and nearly ran into Alexandra Gallant. Her presence surprised him and started that damned rush of blood in his veins, but he only checked his forward progress enough to nod at her. "Good morning. Where's Shakespeare?"

"One of your grooms came to collect him this morning," she said stoutly, "as you well know, I'm sure. And

I am perfectly capable of caring for my own dog."

"You have a more pressing task at hand," he returned, starting down the stairs. "One which will be considerably more difficult than taking your dog for his constitutional."

"I enjoy an early morning stroll myself, my lord."

He heard her descend the stairs after him. "I doubt you'll have time for one."

"If I might ask, is there some pressing reason you wish Miss Delacroix's education to be completed so swiftly?"

"Yes, there is. I will be marrying soon myself, and I want her taken off my hands prior to that."

"I . . . see."

She paused, but he resisted the temptation to turn around and view her expression. Miss Gallant, he'd immediately discovered, tended to let him know precisely what she might be thinking.

"Lord Kilcairn," she began.

That had taken all of five seconds. "Yes, Miss Gallant?"

"I do not wish—"

"Good morning, cousin Lucien."

Lucien turned his attention to the petite figure waiting outside the breakfast room. "Oh, good God," he muttered, his good humor flagging. "Today she's a damned peacock."

Rose Delacroix straightened from her curtsy, the curled ends of three blue-dyed ostrich feathers forming a canopy over her blond head. With her dress of a lighter blue covered by a green pelisse, she lacked only a beak to complete the image. He opened his mouth to tell her so.

"Good morning," Alexandra said warmly from behind

him. "You must be Miss Delacroix. I am Miss Gallant."

"Your new governess," Lucien explained, moving to one side so Alexandra could pass him. "Behave this time."

His cousin's pert, hopeful expression collapsed. "But—"

Miss Gallant spun to face him. "My lord, chastising someone for an imagined future ill deed that may never even come to pass is hardly correct. Or fair."

He met the martial light in her turquoise eyes. "That," he said flatly, pointing at his cousin, "is your charge. I am not."

"I have found that the more positive examples there are present, the easier a behavior is to learn," she said firmly.

Obviously the woman didn't have a fearful bone in her body. "Do not presume to include me in this nonsense."

She lifted her chin. "If you don't agree with my methods of instruction, perhaps I should leave."

"Oh, not again," Rose whimpered, a tear running down one cheek.

Ignoring his cousin, Lucien descended the remainder of the steps. "You are not escaping that easily, Miss Gallant. Come in to breakfast. You can start by teaching her to use utensils." He stopped and faced her again. "Unless you're afraid of failure."

"I am not afraid of anything, my lord," she said, squaring her shoulders and stalking past him, Rose in tow.

"Good."

Chapter 3

So he intended to marry soon. Alexandra glanced at his broad back as he spoke to one of his footmen. Unless his temperament and manners improved in his wife-to-be's presence, she pitied the poor girl. It would take Attila the Hun's daughter to stand up to Lucien Balfour. And if he was marrying, why was he promising—threatening—to kiss females with whom he was barely acquainted?

Alexandra made a point of sitting next to Rose Delacroix at the breakfast table. She couldn't abandon the poor girl to Kilcairn's tyranny—though preying on her sympathy might very well have been the earl's plan. Ignoring the freshly ironed edition of the *London Times* at his elbow, Kilcairn buttered his bread and then sat back, eyeing her with the same expectant expression Rose wore.

Wishing that the aggravating master of the house had made himself scarce for this critical first meeting between student and governess, Alexandra turned her attention to her new charge. Though her face was lovely, her garish gown drew one's gaze the way a carriage accident would. And from Kilcairn's reaction, this was not Rose's first dress disaster. Her wardrobe would have to be seen to immediately.

Alexandra smiled encouragingly. "Tell me, Miss Delacroix, what you like best about yourself."

"Oh, my," the young lady said, blushing. "Well, Mama says my looks are my finest asset."

"She might have been more specific," Kilcairn countered, lifting a fine eyebrow. "Your looks are your onl—"

"And you are just seventeen?" Alexandra cut in, wishing the earl would devote his mouth to eating.

He glanced sideways at her, then lifted the newspaper and snapped it open. She took it as a sign that he would attempt to behave himself, and a thrill of success ran through her as he conceded the point.

"I will be eighteen in five weeks." With a nervous glance at the flimsy newspaper shield protecting her from Kilcairn, Rose returned to her breakfast. Lifting a pinkie delicately in the air, she crunched into her toasted bread and yanked the remaining piece free from her teeth.

It reminded Alexandra of Shakespeare attacking a shoe during his puppy days, and she flinched. "Where is Mrs. Delacroix this morning?" Making a show of taking up her own toast, she pulled a small piece free with her fingers and placed it into her mouth.

Rose attacked her meal with renewed vigor, giving no sign at all that she'd noticed her tutor's subtle coaching. "Oh, she doesn't usually have breakfast," she said through a mouthful of food. "Rising early is too hard on her nerves. She hasn't adjusted to London yet, I'm afraid."

Alexandra waited a moment, but Lord Kilcairn declined to return to the conversation from behind his newspaper. "How long have you been in London?" she urged.

"We arrived from Dorsetshire ten days ago. Cousin Lucien is looking after us."

"That's very good of h—"

"*Miss Gallant* is looking after you," the earl interrupted, still behind his paper. "I am tolerating you."

The girl's pretty blue eyes filled with tears. "Mama said you would be glad to have us here, since you have no one else."

The *London Times* smacked onto the table. Alexandra jumped, ready to come to her pupil's defense, but at the angry expression on the earl's face, she stifled her censure. There was clearly something going on beyond what had been said, and before she jumped into the middle she wanted to know what it was.

"A new situation is never easy on anyone," she said in her mildest voice, and sipped her tea.

Kilcairn looked at her in silence for several long seconds, obviously weighing what he wanted to say against what politeness dictated he should say. "Quite right, Miss Gallant," he finally muttered, and stood. "Excuse me, Miss Gallant, Cousin Rose." With the butler on his heels, he slammed back out into the hallway.

"Oh, thank goodness. I'm so glad he's gone," Rose breathed when the door had closed.

"He does have rather . . . strong opinions," Alexandra agreed absently, wondering what had set him off. Surely it hadn't been Rose's offhand comment about his being alone. Not after the rumors she'd heard about his endless evenings of drunken debauchery with friends and women of questionable morals.

"He's awful. I thought for certain you would leave, too."

Alexandra forced her attention back to her student. "Too?"

"As soon as we arrived he dismissed my Miss Brookhollow, and she'd been with me for nearly a year. And the governesses he hired after we arrived were just dreadful."

"How were they dreadful?"

"They were all old, wrinkly, and mean. But then they would say something Lucien didn't like, and he would swear at them and they'd run off—so I suppose it doesn't matter if I didn't like them, anyway."

Alexandra sat for a moment, absorbing that convoluted bit of information. The incarnation of hell on earth seemed to have a much milder temper than her cousin. "It has been trying for you, no doubt. But that is over with, and things will get better from here."

"Does that mean you intend to stay?"

That was a very good question. "I shall stay as long as I'm needed," she said carefully, hoping the earl wasn't eavesdropping. She had the feeling she might need the leverage of being able to quit.

Rose's slender shoulders slumped in a sigh. "Thank goodness."

"Well, then." Alexandra swept her gaze along the frills of Rose's hideous peacock gown again. "I'd like to meet your mother. And perhaps after breakfast we'd best get to work."

Lucien pulled the rapier free from the ebony walking cane that concealed it. Flexing the long, thin blade between his fingers, he eyed the weapon's new owner.

"This wouldn't do much more than cause a few scratches, Daubner."

"Come, come, Kilcairn, it's a work of art."

Stout, chubby fingers reached for the blade, but Lucien flicked it out of his companion's reach. He might not be able to take his annoyance out on his houseguests, but his friends weren't going to be so lucky. "Artworks have on occasion nearly bored me to death, but I don't think they're truly lethal," he said dryly. "Get yourself something stouter."

"A man needs a stout staff for emergencies," a third voice said from the shop's entry.

Lucien looked up. "Robert," he acknowledged, hoping the rest of his cronies weren't going to appear, as well. He was too damned distracted this morning for the wolf pack—the main reason he'd settled for conversing with slow-witted William Jeffries, Lord Daubner. "Some of us are naturally equipped with stout staffs."

With a jaunty grin, Robert Ellis, the Viscount of Belton, descended the steps and joined them in the blade shop. "So why are you purchasing such a flimsy one?"

"It's not for me," Kilcairn returned, and flicked the blade in Daubner's direction. "Our count feels the need to enhance his apparatus."

Lord Daubner chuckled uneasily, his slightly protruding eyes on the rapier. "As Belton said, it's just for emergencies. And Wallace gave me a good price, didn't you, Wallace?"

"Aye, my lord."

From the corner of his eye Lucien noted the shopkeeper backing into the storeroom to avoid being drawn further into the conversation. Lucien stifled a dark smile. Wallace could give Miss Gallant a lesson in avoiding trouble. "You might as well walk down the street clutching a spoon as this sad thing."

"It's not the weapon, Lucien." Robert lifted another rapier down from the wall. "It's how you wield it."

"Oh, goodness gracious," Wallace muttered from the storeroom doorway.

"Gadzooks," Daubner blustered, waddling at full speed for the corner.

Robert lifted his blade and swung it across at Lucien. Shifting his weight, the earl blocked the move and in the same fluid motion flattened the viscount's rapier against the display table. "So it is. Point taken."

With a frown, Robert released his grip on the weapon, leaving it on the counter. "Don't want to play today, eh? You might have said so." He rubbed his knuckles where they'd collided with the hard wood.

Lucien returned the rapier to its ebony scabbard and tossed it to Daubner. "You didn't ask."

The viscount eyed him for a moment, then swiped a lock of wheat-colored hair back from his forehead. "Lost another governess, did you?"

Immediately an image of the turquoise-eyed goddess who kept the devil spawn company in his breakfast room banished everything else from Lucien's mind. "Found another one," he said brusquely. "Accompany me to Boodle's for luncheon."

Daubner cleared his throat.

"You, too, Daubner."

"Ah. Splendid."

Belton fell into step beside him as they left Wallace's shop, while Daubner brought up the rear. Pall Mall was still fairly uncrowded, as were the clubs lining the way, but none of Mayfair would remain that way for much longer. Once the Season began in earnest, getting a good table and competent service would become a contest of wealth and skill. It was a contest he generally won.

"Are you still going to Calvert's tonight?"

"I haven't decided."

Robert looked at him, brown eyes quizzical. "What happened to 'anything to escape that damned harpies' nest'?"

Miss Gallant had happened—though Lucien wasn't about to reveal that. Certainly he lusted after her; spending an evening away would hardly affect that one way or the other. But at the moment she held more interest for him than Calvert's overexplored debaucheries. "Afraid they won't let a pup like you in without me?"

"You are my calling card to the dregs of London," the viscount agreed with a faint smile. "Are you going, Daubner?"

"Lady Daubner would have my head if I made an appearance at Calvert's," the stout man said grimly.

"*If* she found out," Lucien supplied. "Don't tell her."

Daubner jabbed a finger into Lucien's shoulder blade. "Easy to tell you ain't married, Kilcairn. You don't need to tell the ladies; they just know."

The earl shrugged, annoyed at the abuse to his shoulder and to his dark blue morning coat. "What does that matter?"

"What does what—"

"When are you going to unveil them?" Belton interrupted, as Lucien narrowed his eyes.

"Unveil whom?" he asked, lengthening his stride. Let Daubner work for his meal; it would do the sot good, anyway. The day he let a female dictate how he lived his life would be the last day he took a breath, because he'd throw himself off the Tower Bridge if it ever happened.

"Unveil Mrs. and Miss Delacroix. Not that you've spoken of them beyond hurling a few curses, but over the past few days you've seemed even more annoyed than previously."

"When I'm annoyed," Lucien said, looking sideways at his companion, "you'll know it."

"You can't deny, though, that everyone's going to want to set eyes on Kilcairn's cousin. Lucifer's only living relation and all that."

Before Rose Delacroix saw the light of Mayfair's chandeliers, Miss Gallant would instill manners, grace, and style in her. He had no intention of displaying his pink-flamingo cousin to the peerage now. After he did, though, and once the brat was married off, he could go about his own search—and hopefully produce an heir of his own before he expired from the hellish strain of marriage.

Lucien suppressed a shudder. "Learn to live with disappointment," he suggested, starting up the shallow steps to Boodles. "I'll unveil her when I'm ready to do so."

"Selfish bastard," the viscount muttered.

"Compliments will get you nowhere."

Alexandra sat straight-backed in one of Lord Kilcairn's comfortable morning room chairs and wondered whether the smile pasted on her face looked as stiff as it had begun to feel. Draped on the chaise longue across from her, a froth of blankets and pillows practically smothering her and making her look like a huge orange-haired ball of fluff, Mrs. Fiona Delacroix launched into the second half hour of her diatribe on the state of modern society.

"The nobility in particular has failed to live up to expectations," Fiona sighed. "Even in my own family, I'm forced to confess."

"Surely not," Alexandra offered, sipping tea to give her cheek muscles a moment to relax.

"Oh, yes indeed. When Lucien's cousin James died in the war last year, we sent our condolences to Lucien, and I even offered to sit as matron of Balfour House during high mourning."

"How generous." She tried to imagine Fiona Delacroix managing a huge, ancient London household draped in formal, deep mourning. After less than an hour's acquaintance, she couldn't conjure anything more than yards and yards of black bombazine covering everything. Overdressing seemed to be a defining Delacroix trait.

"Yes, it was exceedingly generous of me to offer, with the way I hate to travel. But do you know Lucien's response? He sent me a letter. I have it memorized. In fact, I don't think I shall ever be able to forget his cruelty." Mrs. Delacroix fluffed a pillow to bring herself more upright. "It said, 'Madame, I would sooner join James in hell than have you join me here.' Can you imagine? And when dear Oscar died, he waited nearly seven months before bringing us to London."

"And that was only because dear Oscar's—and my father's—wills demanded it." Lord Kilcairn stepped into the morning room doorway.

"You see? He doesn't even deny it!"

The earl leaned against the door, his gaze on Alexandra. It was a full moment before she realized he held Shakespeare's leash in one hand, and that her dog sat beside one gleaming Hessian boot.

"It's the truth, Aunt Fiona. I see no reason to deny it."

"Bah!"

"The same to you, Aunt. You and Rose will have to excuse Miss Gallant for a short time. No doubt she needs a moment to reconsider the terms of her employment."

"Oh, please stay!" Rose cried. She'd been silent since her mother's recital began, and Alexandra had nearly forgotten her presence.

Alexandra sipped her tea again. "You jest, my lord," she said easily. "Mrs. Delacroix was just catching me up on some Balfour family history."

He glanced from her to his aunt, and she abruptly sensed that he wasn't pleased. "How pleasant. I require a word with you, Miss Gallant. Now."

"Of course, my lord." Clenching her jaw at the order, she set aside her teacup and stood. "Mrs. Delacroix, Miss Delacroix, if you'll excuse me."

"I like her, Lucien," Fiona barked. "Don't you even think about running her off like the others."

"Wouldn't dream of it," he drawled, stepping back to allow Alexandra to pass.

"I should hope not! Your firing Miss Brookhollow has left me completely without suitable company. And I—"

Kilcairn shut the door on her complaint. "Ah. Much better."

Alexandra drew herself upright. "My lord, I am—"

"Not accustomed to being ordered about like a footman," he finished, turning on his heel.

Shakespeare trailed along behind him down the hallway, tail wagging and claws clicking on the polished wood floor. Alexandra hurried to catch up to the pair of them. "No, I am not," she agreed. "Nor do I—"

"Appreciate being forced to spend any length of time with that batty old—"

"That is *not* what I was going to say. Stop interrupting me, if you please."

The earl halted so quickly she nearly ran into him. Alexandra looked up into his eyes, startled by what she saw there for a fleeting moment. She had surprised him.

"What was it you were about to say, then?" His gaze continued to hold hers.

"I . . . May I be forthright?"

"You have been to this point."

"Why did you hire me?"

With a scowl the earl turned to the staircase. "We have been through this already, Miss Gallant."

"Yes." Alexandra took a deep breath and followed him. "You made it very clear that you wanted to see me naked and kiss me. And that you want to see Miss Delacroix married well. I will assume that in your mind these two things are somehow related, though I fail to see how. Anyway, you are making the second—and only realistic—part of my reason for being here impossible."

He leaned against the railing, an arrested expression on his face. "We did say you should be blunt, didn't we?" he mused.

She shook her head. "Forthright, my lord. But if I have offended—"

The earl lifted a hand. "If you henceforth speak to me in any manner other than bluntly—or forthrightly—I will be deeply offended."

Alexandra started to make a reply, then closed her mouth again. "Very well."

"How am I making the second part of your task impossible, then?"

"In order for Miss Delacroix to marry well, she needs

to learn the subtle nuances of society: politeness, reserve, poise, sensi—"

"I see your meaning. Continue."

"You, my lord, exhibit none of these characteristics, and further, by your intolerant, cynical manner, you discourage both Miss Delacroix and Mrs. Delacroix from adopting any of them, themselves."

He smiled, a slow, delicious curving of his lips. "I am a poor example of propriety and manners."

Alexandra nodded. "Yes, my lord."

"But you're not otherwise discouraged by what you've encountered so far?"

She glanced back toward the upper floor and the closed drawing room door. "If I am to be blunt, perhaps we might speak in your office?"

He followed her gaze and then turned back down the stairs. "Your little dog and I are going for a walk. Join us."

"Very well; so long as we are chaperoned."

She thought she heard him sigh. "Very well."

Since he continued downstairs without waiting to see if she would follow, Alexandra gathered her skirt and trailed after him. He was so peculiar, arrogant and charming at the same time, and she still really had no idea why he had hired her—other than his much-stated physical attraction. And though she could see why he wouldn't want Fiona Delacroix supervising the staff at Balfour House under any circumstances, she didn't understand why he would exclude his relations—apparently his only living relations—from mourning rituals and from his life. That, she didn't like. Not one bit.

Lucien found himself surprised and off balance once again that day. While he had nothing against surprise, it had been some time since he had felt its effects in such rapid succession.

He knew who had caused these unusual circumstances, of course. Miss Alexandra Beatrice Gallant strolled beside him beneath the scattered trees of Hyde Park. A green parasol of inferior craftsmanship shaded her pretty face from the mottled sunlight, but it did little to hide her mood from his curious gaze. She was annoyed—at him, apparently, because she'd seemed perfectly content to sit in the drawing room and listen to his relations' mindless babbling until doomsday.

"Your groom is falling back," she noted, glancing over her shoulder. "Please request that he not lag more than twenty steps behind us."

"Twenty steps. Is that in a book somewhere?"

"I'm sure it must be. Please inform him, my lord, or we will have to turn back at once."

Lucien studied her profile, torn between amusement and horror. She *would* turn back, and he wasn't finished speaking with her. "Vincent," he barked, not turning around.

"Yes, my lord?"

"Keep up, damn it all."

"But . . . Of course, my lord. Apologies, my lord."

"What was it you wished to discuss with me, Miss Gallant?" he asked, watching her watch the vehicles rumbling along the carriage path in their afternoon ritual.

"Miss Delacroix's previous instruction was not quite as awful as you led me to believe, my lord."

"So you feel your presence is unnecessary? I have to disagree. She couldn't snag a shepherd in this condition."

Her lips twitched with a fleeting smile. "She is your cousin. She could snag anyone."

"Anyone with pretensions of gaining nobility, wealth, or rank," he corrected, guiding her little dog back onto the walking path when the terrier tried to flush a pigeon. "Not anyone who is already possessed of them."

Several of the carriages had begun to slow and then swing in their direction. Lucien cursed under his breath and turned them onto a path more sheltered by trees. "So you feel my cousin is trainable. Something else concerns you, though, unless I am mistaken."

She hesitated. "Your aunt concerns me."

For the first time since he'd let the harpies into his home, Lucien grinned. "Welcome to my world, Miss Gallant."

"That's awful."

"I'm an awful person."

"Mrs. Delacroix concerns me only because your peers will see her in association with Miss Delacroix," the governess resumed. "While I'm certain she is a . . . fine lady, she appears to be very outspoken. I fear this may have a detrimental effect on her daughter's public presentation."

"She'll destroy all hope of matrimony."

"I didn't say—"

"Yes, you did."

Miss Gallant stopped. "My lord, if I am to help Miss Delacroix, I must be able to do so unchallenged. Please stop interrupting me."

He smiled at her, noting the color in her cheeks. Proper or not, annoyed at him or not, she was not unmoved by him. "I asked you to be blunt."

"You hired me for my manners."

"I hired you because I want to peel you out of your clothes and make love to you."

She gaped at him again, blushing furiously. "That is—

you are—you have gone too far! I am leaving," she stammered, and turned around.

Lucien reversed course and caught up to her. "You will be chaperoning Rose to any and all outings I see fit for her to attend," he said, wondering if he'd truly pushed her too far, or if she was only making an expected show of propriety. He was definitely unused to exercising decorum. "We will exclude Aunt Fiona from as many of them as possible. For the ones she must attend, I will make certain she behaves as much as she is capable. Is that acceptable?"

"*You* are not acceptable, my lord! I have tried to overlook your lack of manners, because for all I knew, your reputation may have been rumored rather than earned. But you have proven to me that this is not the case. I must give my—"

"Could I snag a proper wife under the present circumstances?" he interrupted.

She cleared her throat. "How do you mean proper?"

"Of good family and good breeding stock, virginal, and hopefully attractive."

Alexandra scowled. "Are you looking for a wife or a brood mare?"

"It's the same thing, really."

"No, it's not. What about love?"

Lucien grabbed up a stick and tossed it out of their path. "*Love* is a word we give for the desire to fornicate so we seem more refined than farm animals."

For a long moment Miss Gallant was silent. "I think, my lord," she said finally, "that since you don't intend to offer love, you must at least offer good manners. Ladies almost universally expect that."

"And so to return to my original question, could I snag a—"

"No." She flushed. "No, my lord. I don't believe you could."

Lucien gazed across the park, torn between amusement and annoyance. She'd only said what he expected, but it wasn't precisely flattering to hear it. "Then I shall have to enlist your services, as well."

"Beg par—"

"Lord Kilcairn? How splendid to see you this afternoon."

Lucien looked over as the nearest carriage pulled even with them. "Lady Howard," he acknowledged, "Lady Alice. Good afternoon. Have you met my cousin's companion, Miss Gallant? Miss Gallant, Lady Howard and Lady Alice Howard." From their expressions he was being more pleasant than usual, but their interruption had given him a moment to consider whether his new plan was brilliant or merely insane. Brilliant, he hoped.

Alexandra curtsied prettily. "Pleased to make your acquaintance, Lady Howard, Lady Alice."

"Miss Gallant." Lady Howard eyed her, then returned her attention to Lucien. "Lord Howard and I will be holding a small dinner party at our home on Thursday. I would be delighted if you and your aunt and cousin—and your cousin's companion, of course—could attend."

It was too soon to spring Rose on the unsuspecting *ton;* but on the other hand, the Howards were fairly low in their social circle, with no prospective mates likely to be in attendance to see his cousin's bumbling. "We would be pleased to attend. Thank you for the invitation, my lady."

As the carriage drove off, Lucien began walking faster. "We'd best make our escape before we get invited anywhere else," he muttered.

"Miss Delacroix is not ready," Alexandra stated stiffly, obviously still angry with him.

"I know that. But the Howards and their circle are fairly forgiving. Instruct her in specific dinner-party etiquette."

"I will not continue to work for you under these circumstances."

He slowed again. "Under what circumstances?"

She blushed again. "You must stop saying such things to me."

"What things?"

"You know very well. Improper and ungentlemanly things."

Lucien smiled. "That's why you'll be instructing me—and Fiona, while you're at it—in propriety, as well. I'll require a great deal of your time and personal tutoring, I'm certain."

"I will do no such thing!"

"Yes, you will. I've just increased your salary to twenty-five quid a month as compensation for your added duties. In addition, I am giving you a generous clothing allowance."

Miss Gallant uttered a very unladylike curse. Lucien grinned, turning his head to hide it. *Ah, victory.*

"I will not be responsible for your success or failure."

"Fair enough." For the moment, anyway. "Anything else?"

She glanced up at him, her expression the odd, distant one he had noticed when he'd rescued her from Aunt Fiona. Immediately his curiosity rose another notch, but she said nothing.

"I will take your silence to mean you are utterly ecstatic in regards to all other aspects of your employment," he prompted as they neared his home.

"You should be nicer to your aunt and your cousin," she said in a quiet voice. "They've lost a husband and a father."

"My first lesson?"

"If you wish to call it that."

"Don't feel too sorry for them," he replied, unable to keep well-honed cynicism from touching his voice. "As my sole relations, their family line is likely to become extremely well off in the future."

"Do you think a promise of future wealth makes up for losing a loved one?"

"Do you speak from personal experience?" he asked, rather disturbed to realize that her mood affected him.

Alexandra looked up. "Of course not, my lord. I have no prospects at all."

That hadn't quite answered his question, but it was an intriguing beginning to a number of new ones.

As they strolled up the drive, he noted that Vincent had fallen far behind them again, as he'd been instructed to do in the first place. Though Lucien hadn't been able to spend as much time with Miss Gallant as he wanted, he felt quite satisfied. He'd learned a little more about her, though not nearly enough to quell his curiosity or his desires. And he'd begun to advertise to the *ton* that he was willing to spend a proper afternoon in the company of a proper young lady. That should make things easier when he began his own spousal hunt in earnest.

In addition, he now had a legitimate excuse to spend more time with Miss Gallant. And if she could improve his manners and demeanor, he would gladly proclaim her a damned miracle worker.

Chapter 4

Alexandra lay on her bed and pulled a knotted rag back and forth across the coverlet for Shakespeare.

Twenty-five pounds a month was a small fortune. At her first position, that had been her income for the entire year. And even if she could have afforded to fling the bribe back in her employer's face, she didn't think she would have done it.

Alexandra suspected that had a great deal to do with the way he kept throwing challenges at her. Making Lucien Balfour marriageable could very well qualify her for sainthood. She smiled. Alexandra, patron saint of impossible, egotistical, arrogant men. Of course, the shivers he sent down her spine might have had a little to do with it, as well. Lord Kilcairn was a curiosity, an enigma, and she hadn't yet begun to figure him out.

Shakespeare flipped upright, ears perked toward the door. A moment later, someone knocked hesitantly.

"Miss Gallant?" a female voice called.

Alexandra stood to slide the bolt back and opened the

door. "Miss Delacroix," she said, surprised. "Come in."

"Actually, could you come to my bedchamber for a moment?"

"It's nearly time to dress for dinner."

"Yes, I know." The girl glanced over her shoulder. "That's what I wanted to ask you about."

Curious, Alexandra nodded and stepped into the hallway. "Of course."

"You see," Rose continued in a hushed voice, leading the way down the hall, "Mama said I should wear my yellow taffeta to dinner as it complements my eyes, but I really don't think cousin Lucien likes taffeta very much."

As they entered her bedchamber, Alexandra noted the maid standing by the huge wardrobe, the two full-length mirrors flanking the dressing table, and the second standing wardrobe on the far side of the bed. "You brought all this with you from Dorsetshire?"

"All of the clothes. Cousin Lucien provided the second wardrobe, and the white room for the rest of Mama's and my things. All of my formal gowns are in there."

Alexandra lifted both eyebrows, then pasted on a smile as the girl faced her again. "My goodness."

Rose indicated the bright yellow gown laid across the end of the bed. "What do you think? Mama says yellow is my best color, but Miss Brookhollow always recommended blue over yellow because it's more reserved."

"Well, let's see the blue one," Alexandra suggested, hoping it was more suitable for London society than the rest of the garish apparel she'd seen on her pupil.

The maid disappeared into the voluminous wardrobe, and reappeared a moment later clutching an even more vivid version of the blue peacock gown.

"Ah." Alexandra cleared her throat. "May I have a look at your things?"

"Oh, I knew it wouldn't do," Rose said mournfully, her familiar pout beginning and her blue eyes swimming with tears.

Alexandra looked at the maid. "Will you excuse us for a few moments?"

"Of course, ma'am." With a curtsy she vanished, closing the bedchamber door behind her.

With their audience dismissed, Alexandra returned her attention to her charge. "Miss Delacroix, as you know, Lord Kilcairn hired me primarily for the purpose of polishing your deportment. He has requested this in order to enable you to secure a husband of sufficient means to support you and your mother."

Rose nodded, though her tentative expression indicated she hadn't deciphered exactly what they might be discussing.

"Are you crying because this is not what you want for yourself, or because it's not going as smoothly as you'd like?"

Her charge blinked a few times, and then her expression cleared. "Cousin Lucien doesn't like anything I've done, and I did so want to please him. And Mama."

Alexandra felt a slight headache beginning. "Do you wish to marry a nobleman, then?"

"Oh, yes."

"And will you work with me to do whatever is necessary to see that this happens?"

"Oh, yes, Miss Gallant!" The girl clasped Alexandra's hands. "So you think there's hope for me?"

Alexandra smiled. "Yes, I do. And please call me Alexandra, or Lex. All my friends call me Lex."

Her charge smiled prettily, her eyes lighting. "Thank you, Lex. And you must call me Rose."

"Well, then. Let's have a look through your wardrobe, and tomorrow we shall make an appointment to see a dressmaker."

In a sense, Alexandra envied Rose. The young lady wanted to marry a nobleman; apparently it didn't matter whom, as long as he qualified on that one count. Her wardrobe was all wrong, but that could be fixed. Once she had cousin Lucien's approval and thereby presumably his backing, the wedding would take place. All that remained to be determined was the date and the name of the groom.

They finally resorted to using one of Alexandra's gowns, a pale yellow and blue sprig muslin that had always been her favorite. Resolutely she pinned the hem for the shorter girl. First things first: she needed to make Lord Kilcairn see that his cousin was more than a pretty peacock; if they couldn't convince him that Rose could improve, he would never consent to her even being seen in public, much less her going hunting for her titled husband.

At half past six they made their way to the dining room. Behind the half-open doors Fiona Delacroix's sharp voice spoke, followed a moment later by Lord Kilcairn's low, drawling answer.

Alexandra adjusted one sleeve of Rose's gown, ignoring her own flutter of nerves. He had stayed at home to dine, when as far as she knew, he almost never did so. And she wondered what he would have to say about *her* favorite gown, just a little large across the bosom for young Rose.

"Head high," she murmured from behind Rose, "as though you don't care what anyone thinks."

With a nervous nod, Rose stepped forward. Wimbole, waiting in the entry, threw the double doors wide to admit them. The earl stood; he did have manners, whether he chose to display them for his female houseguests or not. Gray eyes swept across Rose, and then found Alexandra, waiting in the doorway.

"Cousin Lucien." Rose curtsied and took the seat Wimbole held out for her.

"What are you wearing?" Fiona barked. "I've never seen—"

"Yes," Lucien echoed, and Alexandra drew breath for a rebuttal. "You look remarkably human this evening."

Slowly Alexandra let her breath out.

Rose smiled. "I borrowed it from Lex."

Lord Kilcairn took Wimbole's place behind Alexandra's chair. "Lex?" he murmured, leaning over her shoulder to scoot the chair forward as she sat. "It doesn't suit you. Not enough curves or secrets. I prefer Alexandra."

She closed her eyes as her name rolled softly from his lips. Before she could conjure an appropriate response, he straightened and returned to his own chair. It was probably just as well, because she had no idea what to say. The sound of her name had never caused her to break into delicious shivers before.

"You cannot wear your governess's gowns. It's not seemly."

Alexandra started and opened her eyes. The Delacroix ladies looked at one another, one belligerent and one near tears again, while the earl sliced off a bite of pheasant.

"Miss Gallant has taste," he said. "Given that fortunate circumstance, she will accompany Rose to Madame Charbonne's tomorrow. I have it on good authority that

Charbonne is the most accomplished dressmaker in London." Glancing at his aunt, he took a swallow of port. "Perhaps you'd best see her, too."

"Lucien, I will not—"

"Or you may remain indoors. I don't care either way."

"How dare you—"

"Mrs. Delacroix," Alexandra interrupted, before sharp objects began flying across the table, "you seem to have a much better grasp of color than I do. I would greatly appreciate your assistance tomorrow."

The older woman blustered for a moment. "Going about London is so hard on my nerves," she finally said in a milder tone, "but I cannot abandon my daughter to the whims of some unknown dressmaker."

Madame Charbonne was hardly unknown, but Alexandra refrained from pointing that out. She hoped Kilcairn would do the same, and relaxed a little when he only lifted an eyebrow and continued eating. Having him about with the volatile Fiona Delacroix was definitely not helping her cause any—but on the other hand, she could become very used to the way he said her name.

She wondered if seduction was truly his aim, or if he was just amusing himself. Why he saw fit to bother with either when the quarry was a mere ruined governess, she had no idea. Perhaps he was bored this early in the Season. A more worrisome, disturbing thought was that he wasn't bored at all.

The dress Miss Gallant lent Rose had to be the finest thing she owned. From the moment Lucien had first set eyes on his new employee, he'd noted that she dressed well, if conservatively. He didn't mind that—in fact, he rather liked guessing about the parts of her left to his imagination. But the muslin gown was lovely, even on

Rose's slighter frame. He would have liked to see Alexandra in it.

"My lord," the turquoise-eyed goddess said, pulling him out of his reverie, "do you possess a pianoforte?"

"I own several. Why?"

As her gaze met his, a still-unexpected jolt of desire went through him. Lucien took a long swallow of port, draining his glass. *Damnation.* He wasn't used to showing this much restraint with a woman he wanted. If she'd been anyone else, he would have made an offer by now, and she would have either accepted or been sent on her way.

The problem was, he didn't know what approach would work, and a refusal was unacceptable. She certainly didn't look or act like any governess he'd ever encountered, and she didn't react to his flirting like any blasted woman he'd ever encountered. She intrigued him, and he loved a good puzzle.

"I would like to assess Miss Delacroix's skill at playing."

Lucien scowled. "I don't want to hear it."

"You need not be present, my lord. But if she is to attend a dinner party, we will need to know where to place her if and when the hostess calls for music."

"In the back of the room," he answered promptly.

A familiar sniffle began off to his right, and he stifled a further comment. The blasted chit was a watering pot.

"Indeed. One makes the greatest show emerging from the back of the room." Brief amusement twinkling in her eyes, Alexandra patted his cousin's hand. "But before we place her there, we must know her skill."

"When is this dinner party?" Aunt Fiona asked. "And who is holding it? Why wasn't I informed?"

"Thursday, the Howards, and because I didn't choose to tell you."

Rose gasped. "Thursday?"

"That's more than enough time for us to prepare you, Miss Delacroix."

Lucien stopped his own answer, as Miss Gallant again beat him to it. He wasn't used to that. And obviously she hadn't yet realized how futile deterring him was when he chose to show his temper. Fortunately, he happened to be in a very good mood this evening.

"But cousin Lucien, you said you'd never let any of your cronies set eyes on me."

"I have no—"

"No doubt Lord Kilcairn is merely jealous," Miss Gallant interrupted smoothly. "You are, after all, very attractive."

Lucien turned a baleful gaze on the governess. Apparently she had taken his request for blunt honesty between them to mean she could be insolent whenever and wherever she chose.

Aunt Fiona cackled in her impression of laughter. "No doubt you've hit on it, Miss Gallant."

That was too damned much. Lucien stood, swearing. "Wimbole will show you the music room and the pianoforte. Don't break anything."

"Where might you be going, Lucien?" Fiona asked, still chuckling.

"Jezebel's Harem," he snapped, and turned to Alexandra. "Ever heard of it?"

Her expression stiffened, the humor leaving her eyes. "Yes, I have, my lord," she answered. "I presume that we shouldn't wait up for you?"

"Don't."

* * *

The most notorious gambling den and brothel in the west of London generally had enough diversions to satisfy even him. Lucien was as surprised as anyone when he didn't avail himself of anything more distracting than a game of piquet. In a little over two hours he'd won a hundred quid off the Marquis of Cooksey, and he barely cared enough to add up the amount.

It was his own fault. He didn't distract easily, and his thoughts remained securely anchored to his cousin's governess. His mood lightened only when he decided that she would have to pay for her insolence—in a manner of his devising. It would certainly involve nudity, whatever it was.

"Lucien?"

He started and looked up from his cards. "Robert. I didn't expect to see you here tonight."

Cooksey pushed back from the table. "Might as well take my seat, lad," he grumbled. "Thanks to Kilcairn, I'm completely to let this evening."

The viscount slumped into the vacated chair as the marquis left to find other entertainment. "Vauxhall fireworks were completely fogged in, so I came looking for you."

"Bad luck you didn't get here an hour ago. I might have split Cooksey with you." Lucien shuffled the cards between his long fingers.

"Or you might have taken me out, as well," Robert returned, signaling for a glass of port.

Lucien eyed him. "What were you doing in Vauxhall Gardens, anyway?"

The viscount ran a hand through his sandy hair. "My mother will be in London next week."

"And?"

The viscount opened his mouth to reply, then hesitated and took a drink instead. "And everyone knows your opinion on this particular subject. I will not discuss it with you."

Lucien frowned. "What subject?"

Robert shook his head. "No."

This was becoming interesting. "I'll wager you for it. We'll cut the deck. If I have the high card, you tell me your little secret."

"And if I win?"

"You can have Cooksey's hundred quid."

Lucien would never have taken the wager himself, but then he was a good six years older than young Robert, and carried a great many more secrets he had no wish for the *ton* to know. He barely had time to count to five before the viscount snatched the deck of cards from him and slammed it onto the table.

"I'll go first," Belton stated, and cut deeply into the deck. He looked at the card, then let out a breath and turned his wrist so Lucien could view it. "Nine of clubs."

Robert replaced the cards onto the deck. Lifting an eyebrow, Lucien leaned forward and took the top card. Without looking, he flipped it onto the table.

"Jack of spades." The viscount glared at him, then sat back and crossed his arms over his chest. "I should've saved myself the trouble and just given in."

"You shouldn't have taken the wager. Out with it."

"Damn blast it," Belton snarled. "All right. I'm thinking of marrying."

For a long moment Lucien looked at him. "Why?"

"I am twenty-six. And . . . I've just been thinking about it. All right?"

"Familial obligation and all that," Lucien supplied. No wonder Robert had been reluctant to discuss the subject with him. He, and the *ton*, had long ago declared himself completely unmarriageable. Only the direst of circumstances had conspired to change that, and he had no intention of discussing his own musings about marriage with Robert Ellis. Not this evening, and not until he'd netted a female.

"Yes, familial obligation." Robert eyed him like a cat sizing up a very large and very ferocious dog. "So? Don't you have anything devastatingly insulting to say about it?"

Lucien sipped his port. "What are you looking for in a female?"

"Nothing you've been seen with. Don't worry, Kilcairn, I can find someone without your assistance."

"You mistake me. I'm merely curious as to what sort of female, in your opinion, would make an acceptable Viscountess of Belton."

"You're merely curious."

"Yes." Alexandra hadn't appreciated the specifications he'd named to her, and she seemed fairly sensible for a female. Perhaps Robert had some better ones in mind.

"Well, I'm . . . I'm not really sure. I'll know when I see her."

"Don't you have some general requirements?"

"General requirements," Robert grumbled, glaring at him. "Of course I do. I want her to be attractive, and of good background and wealthy family, and reasonably intelligent."

"Why intelligent?"

"You're impossible!" the viscount burst out, startling the nearest patrons. "Marriage is a lifelong commitment."

Another softheaded idealist. "Marriage is a business commitment."

"Good God. Whether it is or not, wouldn't you at least like to be able to converse with your chosen partner?"

"One doesn't marry to gain a partner," Lucien argued. "One marries to gain an appropriately well-bred vessel on which to get an heir. And, if circumstances require it, one also marries to gain enough wealth to continue maintaining one's estate."

Robert narrowed his eyes. "Look. Just because your father—"

"My father was a whoremonger who married to beget a legitimate heir. Other than those few necessary moments of marital coitus, he didn't allow it to interfere with his life."

The viscount stood. "I pity any woman who might end up with you."

"So do I." Lucien made a show of yawning. "Sit down and play piquet with me, Robert. And talk of something more pleasant, will you?"

Belton obviously had nowhere else to go this evening, because after a show of reluctance, he seated himself again. "Deal the damned cards, then."

Lucien obliged. "How was Calvert's affair?"

"Deathly boring. You're practically the only bad *ton* in London now. Once the Season begins and the rest of the nefarious nobility arrives, though, I'm certain I'll hardly miss your presence at all."

The earl stifled a grin. "Once the Season begins, I'll join you in the debauchery."

"Are you certain of that? King of diamonds."

"King of hearts, seventeen pips. What are you talking about now?"

"Your point. I heard that you're going to attend the Howards' dinner party on Thursday."

Damnation. "Ill news travels fast. Yes, I am. What of it?"

"If Calvert's is too boring for you, an hour in Lord Howard's company will kill you, Lucien."

"If I'm to marry off the devil spawn, I can't very well do it at Calvert's." Lucien gave Robert a speculative look. "Why don't you join us at the Howards'?"

"What?"

"You want to get married, and so does my adorable cousin. What could be better?"

"Your adorable cousin, 'the incarnation of hell on earth'? I thought we were friends, Kilcairn."

"Even sight unseen, you have to admit she meets most of your requirements."

"Other than being of good family, which requirements were those, precisely?"

"You'll have to join us at the Howards' to find out."

Robert regarded him speculatively. "All right, Kilcairn. I'll attempt to get myself invited. But you'd best not disappoint me."

Feeling that he'd boxed himself into a corner, Lucien nevertheless managed a dark smile. "I never disappoint."

"How did you find the park this morning, Miss Gallant?"

"Lovely. Thank you, Wimbole." Alexandra tried to hide her subtle glance down the hallway past the butler, and her resulting disappointment, as she handed him her shawl. The earl hadn't returned home by the time she went to bed last evening, and she had hoped to see him this morning.

She didn't miss him, of course—neither his arrogance nor his inappropriate conversation nor his knowing gray eyes—but she needed clarification on several instructional points for Rose. That was the only reason she wanted to see him. Alexandra turned to her walking companion. "Marie, thank you for venturing out with me."

The maid curtsied. "My pleasure. His lordship said Sally or I should go with you whenever you wanted to go walking."

"That was thoughtful of him, but I'm sure you must have more pressing duties elsewhere."

"Not when you wish to go walking, miss."

From Rose's description, Lord Kilcairn hadn't been nearly as accommodating toward the household's previous governesses. Alexandra glanced at Wimbole. "Has the earl risen yet this morning?"

"Yes, Miss Gallant. He rode out just after you left. I don't expect him back until this evening."

Blast it. "I see. Thank you."

"He did leave you a note, Miss Gallant." The butler produced a silver tray from the hall table, the missive lying neatly across it.

With effort she refrained from snatching it off the salver. "Thank you, Wimbole."

Opening the note as she and Shakespeare climbed the stairs, Alexandra noted that Kilcairn's handwriting reflected her view of him to perfection: dark, elegant, and scrawling. She could hear his deep, cynical voice as she read the words. " 'My line of credit is open with Madame Charbonne. She is expecting you. Be certain she knows the first set of gowns is to be ready by Thursday. I expect you to be adequately attired, as well. Kilcairn.' "

"Hm," Alexandra said. "It just drips with warmth, don't you think, Shakes?"

The terrier *wumph*ed. She took that as agreement, and with a chuckle hurried to change into suitable shopping attire. Both of the Delacroix ladies were waiting in the foyer as she returned downstairs.

"I will not tolerate it!" Fiona snapped at Wimbole.

Unless Alexandra was mistaken, the butler looked relieved to see her approach. "Miss Gallant, the coach is waiting to take you to Bond Street."

"Do you hear that? He means for us to take the closed-up coach, when the day is perfectly fine. It's just cruel. Cruel and heartless."

"I'm certain Lord Kilcairn has his reasons, Mrs. Delacroix," Alexandra said in a soothing voice, gesturing Rose toward the front door.

"Yes, he's a tyrant. His father's entire side of the family—nothing but tyrants. Thank God most of them are dead!"

"Mama, I want a new gown," Rose said plaintively. "Please let's go, before cousin Lucien returns and changes his mind."

"By all means," Alexandra seconded, and led the way out to the coach.

Closed up or not, it was magnificent, and she settled inside with a small sigh. The last time she'd used Kilcairn's transportation, she'd been too nervous to notice anything but the uneasy fluttering of her stomach. She noticed more now, though. Not even the finest transport she'd ever ridden in could compare with this. Mrs. Delacroix climbed in opposite her, still complaining about being a helpless prisoner never meant to see the light of day. Rose took the seat beside Alexandra and clasped her hand.

"Do you know of this Madame Charbonne?" Rose asked, her eyes bright with excitement.

"I have heard of her, yes. She's rumored to be the finest dressmaker in all England. I don't even know how

Lord Kilcairn was able to make an appointment for you to see her."

"Because he's a tyrant," Mrs. Delacroix cut in, peering out through the open crack of one curtained window. "Oh, such finery. And to think I'll never be allowed out to see it up close."

"I'm certain that's not true," Alexandra countered. "Lord Kilcairn is only waiting for the right moment, so that you and Miss Delacroix will make the most favorable impression on his peers."

Fiona sniffed at that, and turned to fanning her face with a handkerchief. She was going to be a problem, and Alexandra doubted that the earl's threats would have much effect on his aunt when he wasn't present to enforce them. Rose could shine as the brightest diamond of the Season, but as soon as anyone set eyes—or ears—on her mother, they would run away, aghast.

In her various employments she'd come across jealous siblings, but never a parent who actively, if unconsciously, worked to sabotage her daughter's debut into society. Rose, practically vibrating with excitement and nervousness, looked out her own window. Alexandra hid a scowl. She would do what she could, but Lord Kilcairn could only expect so much.

The coach rumbled to a halt, and then rocked as the footman hopped down from his perch at the back of the vehicle. A moment later he pulled the door open and flipped down the steps to hand them out. Bond Street spread out on either side of them, crowded with shops dedicated to satisfying the whims of the rich. The sidewalks weren't as busy as she expected, but the Season wouldn't officially begin for another few days.

She turned to the shop beside them. A beautiful green silk gown stood draped over a headless mannequin in the window, and a large sign on the door proclaimed that the shop was closed. Alexandra paused, surprised. "Oh, dear. There must be some mistake."

"No mistake, ma'am," the footman said, and knocked on the door. "Lord Kilcairn has it all arranged."

The door opened to the accompanying tinkling of a little bell on the inner knob. "You are Lord Kilcairn's party?" a young woman asked.

"Yes, we are," Alexandra answered, surprised.

"Please, come in." The woman curtsied and backed away from the entry.

Alexandra trailed into the shop behind the Delacroix ladies. It was small, neat, and very efficient looking. The same description fit the petite woman who approached them from the back room. "Good morning," she said, in a heavy French accent. "I am Madame Charbonne." She continued forward, stopping before Alexandra. "You are Miss Gallant, yes?"

"Yes."

"*Bonne*. Lord Kilcairn said you would guide me in the ordering of gowns for Miss Delacroix and Mrs. Delacroix."

Now, *that* was something Alexandra had never expected to hear—that she was to be instructing the country's premier dressmaker. She smiled. "I'm certain your eye is more skilled than mine, *madame*."

The dressmaker smiled back at her, then gestured at a short row of chairs set against a side wall, next to stacks and stacks of material. "Let us begin, then."

With her assistants taking notes, Madame Charbonne painstakingly measured Rose and Fiona. Alexandra had the feeling that the dressmaker rarely took so personal an interest in the initial stages of gown creation, but nothing about this fitting was remotely similar to anything she'd ever experienced. Evidently the Delacroix ladies were a bit overwhelmed as well, because neither Rose nor Fiona—to Alexandra's relief—had spoken more than two words since their arrival.

"And now you, Miss Gallant, *s'il vous plaît*?" the woman said, straightening.

"Me? Oh, no, I don't think so," Alexandra protested, flushing. If there was one thing she knew for certain, it was that Madame Charbonne did not make gowns for governesses.

"Lord Kilcairn said specifically that you were to be fitted, as well."

She frowned. "Specifically?"

"Oui, mademoiselle."

It was still ridiculous, but the very thought of wearing a Madame Charbonne gown made her want to grin in giddy delight. "Well, I suppose we should get on with it, then. I wouldn't want to delay you any further today."

The dressmaker unwound her measuring tape and smiled. "Do not worry about that. I am being well compensated for my time this morning."

"I'm not surprised," Alexandra said.

"What on earth are you two babbling about?" Fiona demanded, turning from her perusal of a bright yellow satin.

Belatedly Alexandra realized she and Madame Charbonne had been conversing in French. "I beg your pardon, Mrs. Delacroix. Your nephew apparently wants me to have a new gown, as well."

"Of course he does," the older woman stated. "We can't have you being seen with us in *those* shabby clothes."

Madame Charbonne leaned closer to measure Alexandra's shoulders. "If I thought she, rather than Lord

Kilcairn, would be paying for my services, I would charge quite a bit more money," she murmured, though her discretion wasn't necessary. Obviously neither of the Delacroix ladies spoke French.

Alexandra stifled a chuckle. "The best revenge would be to make her a gown to her own specifications," she returned in the same low tone.

"Naughty, naughty," a deep voice said in perfect French from behind her.

Rose shrieked, clutching a borrowed dressing gown tightly across her bosom. "Cousin Lucien!"

Alexandra whipped around, nearly strangling herself on the measuring tape. "My lord! You weren't spying on us, were you? That would be . . . quite . . . inappropriate!"

Arms folded, he leaned against the wall beside the room's back entry, his eyes twinkling and a slight, sensuous smile on his lips. She had no idea how long he'd been there, but he'd obviously overheard her conversation. "Very composed of you, Miss Gallant," the earl drawled. "But you're blushing." Thankfully, he continued to speak French.

"Of course I'm blushing! I am not accustomed to being fitted for gowns in the presence of men!"

"A ridiculous oversight I mean to address at the earliest opportunity. Women dress to please men. Why shouldn't men then be in on the process from the beginning?"

"Looking attractive pleases oneself," she replied in English. "It is a man's good fortune if the result pleases him, as well."

"Spoken like a true bluestocking."

Now he was going too far. "I am *not* a bluestocking. I am well educated."

"My lord?" Madame Charbonne put in, and Alexandra jumped.

"Madame?"

"Do you wish me to continue, my lord?"

Out of the corner of her eye, Alexandra saw Fiona elbow Rose in the back. The girl chirped in surprise as she stumbled forward. "Cousin Lucien, I would be delighted if you would help me choose a gown," she blurted, blushing furiously.

Looking annoyed at the interruption, the earl glanced away from Alexandra. "No, you wouldn't."

Alexandra gritted her teeth. "Your cousin has requested your opinion, my lord. And very prettily, too, I might add."

He arched an eyebrow. "Very well. I shall stay." With another lazy look at Alexandra, he crossed the room and dropped into one of the waiting chairs.

All right, that settled it. Lord Kilcairn was being deliberately difficult. And in his arrogant, cynical way, he found the whole thing amusing. Alexandra turned her back on him and allowed Madame Charbonne to continue her measuring. Ignoring the earl was like ignoring chocolate, but he didn't need to know the effect he had on her.

He'd been correct in expanding her teaching duties to include himself. No doubt he considered the challenge a joke, but she didn't. This was her area of expertise, and Lord Kilcairn was about to go back to school.

Lucien put up with the tittering and complaining and preening for nearly an hour. Deciding he'd thereby qualified for sainthood, he stood and stretched. "Excuse me a moment, ladies."

He stopped just outside the shop's front door and

pulled a cigar from his coat pocket. When the door opened behind him, he knew who it was without having to turn around.

"You look better in that burgundy than cousin Rose does," he said.

"I am not looking to find a titled husband. And that is a filthy habit."

Lucien turned around, amusement tugging the corners of his lips upward. "You need to be more specific where filthy habits and myself are concerned. Did you follow me only to stop me from smoking cigars?"

"I'm afraid you need a great deal more work than that."

Immediately intrigued, Lucien returned the unlit cheroot to his pocket. "Let me guess. You want another wage increase before you'll take on such a horrific task as reforming me."

"No, I do not."

"Pray tell me what concerns you, then."

Alexandra cleared her throat. "I am a governess. I shouldn't be wearing a gown made by Madame Charbonne."

Lucien eyed her. "If you hadn't wanted one, you wouldn't have let her measure you for one."

She blushed. "Perhaps not. But the point is not what I want, but rather, what is proper. It is not proper for—"

"No, it's not proper," he interrupted, stepping closer. "But you'll wear it anyway, won't you?"

She took a step backward, which he immediately pursued. "My lord, I—"

"Won't you?"

Again she hesitated. "Of course I will. I have no doubt it will be the finest gown I'll ever own."

He had his doubts about that. She was only trying to

make him feel like a blackguard, though, and at the same time giving him the opportunity to say something honorable or noble. He was, however, a full-blooded blackguard. Achieving that title had taken years of hard work at debauchery. And a few cleverly worded sentences would not even begin to convert him. "Then thank me, instead of lecturing me about my bad habits."

Alexandra lifted her chin in the way he found so damned appealing. "I will not thank you. You've made a poor decision, which I think you'll regret as soon as one of your peers realizes what your governess is wearing. And who she is."

"Alexandra," he murmured, wishing they were somewhere other than the middle of Bond Street so he could kiss her, and wondering why that stopped him this time. "I have long since ceased caring what my peers think. I wish to see you in that gown, and so I will."

"It is not a great victory, my lord."

He nodded. "But I consider it the first of many. Actually the second, when we take into consideration that you are, after all, working for me."

She met his gaze squarely, only the color in her cheeks belying her perfect calm. "One of many mistakes I've made, my lord," she answered.

"And one of many more to come, I hope." Letting her read into that whatever she chose, Lucien glanced back toward the shop. "Give my excuses to the incarnation of hell on earth and her mother."

"She's not so bad, you know."

Wanting to touch her, he settled for stroking one finger across her soft, smooth cheek. "Tell me that again on Friday morning. You have three days, Miss Gallant."

Lucien watched her go back into the shop. He wanted to bury himself in her, and he hadn't even managed a kiss. She knew what he wanted, too. She had to know it, because he'd told her to her face. Lucien scowled as he climbed into his phaeton and headed east toward his boxing club.

With half a dozen mistresses scattered about town, and that many more due to arrive in London over the next few weeks, satisfying himself wouldn't be a problem. But he didn't want them and their idle chatter and ready bodies. He wanted Alexandra Gallant.

And he wanted her to want him. While he clearly interested her, she'd shown herself to be more than capable of resisting any improper urges. She certainly felt comfortable enough with him to insult him at leisure. Of course, he liked that, too.

Blast it all, he needed to find a wife—as quickly and as painlessly as possible. Lucien eyed a trio of young ladies emerging from a hat shop. Petite, pretty, and giggly—he dismissed them without a second glance. Marrying didn't preclude having Alexandra as his mistress once he'd convinced her of his charms, but lusting after the blasted governess was distracting him to an absurd degree.

Lucien sighed. He'd simply have to take his frustration out on his sparring partner. It was either that or lie in wait for Miss Gallant in some dark hallway; or in his garden; or in the library; or in his office; or . . . Lucien shook himself. Perhaps he'd best find a wife first. He was certainly acquiring enough pent-up desire to have sexual intercourse with just about anyone. If it weren't so painful, it would be amusing.

Chapter 5

"Remember, Rose," Alexandra chided, "there are five courses yet to go."

"But I'm only eating a little, just as you said." Rose plunked her fork down on her empty plate and began pouting again. "This is so stupid."

Reminding herself that Kilcairn was paying her twenty-five pounds a month, and that she had dealt with stubborn seventeen-year-olds before, Alexandra smiled and shook her head. "It's not stupid. And your rate of food consumption is fine. But that's the thirty-second time you've sipped your wine. I'm afraid you're completely sluiced over the ivories."

Thankfully Rose relaxed her tensed shoulders and giggled. "It's only pretend wine."

Alexandra settled herself more comfortably in the dining chair she'd taken opposite her student. She was glad both the wine and the meal were imaginary; otherwise, both she and her charge would have to order Madame Charbonne to let out their new dresses before the dinner party.

She'd chosen this method of instruction to make Rose more conscious of what her hands were doing, rather than what her mouth was tasting. The problem, though, was more basic than that.

"The difficulty is that you seem to be using your wineglass as a delay. Every time I ask you a question, you take a sip of wine before you answer," Alexandra pointed out.

"That's so I have time to think up an appropriate response. Miss Brookhollow taught me that."

She'd thought as much. "Yes, it's a good trick. But you need more than one, my dear, or everyone will know what you're doing—and by the end of the meal you will be so drunk that no response could possibly be appropriate."

"More than one?" Rose asked, looking dismal. "I can barely remember that one."

"Oh, it's simple," Alexandra answered casually, though she was concerned. This should have been the easy part. They had barely touched on dinner conversation, and not at all on after-dinner proceedings. She was keenly aware that the Howard dinner would be a test of both Rose's skills and her own. And there was one man in particular to whom she intended to prove herself—and Rose, of course. "Pick five things and do them in sequence, over and over again."

"What? I don't understand."

"Allow me to demonstrate." She sat forward again and sipped her wine, just as Rose had done. "Oh, yes, Lord Watley. I know exactly what you mean." Alexandra then lifted her napkin and wiped the corner of her mouth. "Fascinating indeed." Placing her napkin back on her lap, she readjusted it. "How brave of you." Next she took an imaginary bite of her imaginary dinner, chewed, and swallowed. "Oh, I am simply overcome." Lastly, she scooted a few imaginary potato slices into a pile on her plate. "Thank you so much."

Rose giggled again. "I'm completely lost, I'm afraid."

"That's all there is to it. Drink, napkin, napkin, bite, fiddle. Each time you need a moment to think, go through your list and use the next one. You can vary it, of course. If you need a long moment, take a bite. If only a quick, easy reply is necessary, do nothing, or adjust your napkin. But other than that, just go through your list."

Her student gaped at her. "That's brilliant, Lex!"

Alexandra grinned. "Thank you, but I can hardly take credit. I had good teachers."

"You went to school to learn that?"

"I went to school to learn a great many things. That was one of them. Miss Grenville's Academy deserves the credit."

"Drink, napkin, napkin, bite, fiddle." Nodding with each word, Rose repeated the sequence. "I can remember that, I think."

"Very well. Let's go over it, and your dinner conversation, once more."

Rose sighed. "Who are you going to be this time?"

"I haven't been Lady Pembroke yet. We'll try her."

"But I can't marry her," the girl complained, making a face.

At least her student kept focused without any difficulty, Alexandra reflected. "You can marry one of her sons, though. Including the Marquis of Tarrenton."

"He's boring."

"But he's wealthy."

"Oh, that's better, then. All right."

Alexandra stood and removed her things to another

location, this time sitting at Rose's left. "Besides," she continued, "never assume that the person you are speaking to is the only one listening. You will be overheard, and whatever you say—or do—may be repeated."

They were halfway through the exercise, and Rose was becoming more assured in her strategic delays, when someone scratched at the dining room door.

"Come in," Alexandra called, hoping it wouldn't be Kilcairn. All she needed was to have the acerbic earl destroy Rose's new-forming confidence.

Rose's maid, Penny, stepped into the room and bobbed her head in a curtsy. "Excuse me, but Mrs. Delacroix says it's time for bed, Miss Rose. She says you need your sleep."

Alexandra glanced at the porcelain clock sitting on one of the sideboards. "Oh, my. I hadn't realized it was so late. We'll continue in the morning, Rose."

When the ladies had departed, Alexandra sighed and sat back in her chair. In reality she disliked the little tricks for delaying one's replies, looking on them only as a necessity for covering a slow wit. Until Rose matured a little, however, she would need them. Alexandra couldn't recall ever being as insecure as Miss Delacroix, but she'd been on her own since halfway through her seventeenth year. She hadn't had time to hesitate. In fact, until the last six months, she had barely taken time to breathe.

Male voices exchanged greetings down in the foyer, and then Kilcairn's familiar, assured boot-steps climbed the stairs. With a curse Alexandra straightened, wishing she'd held her reflections until after she'd returned safely to her bedchamber. She kept silent, hoping he would pass by, and knowing he wouldn't.

"You gave up on her, did you?" the earl's deep voice asked as he stopped in the doorway.

"I did not. She went to bed, just a few moments ago. And she is progressing quite well, thank you."

He was wearing his evening attire, all black and gray and magnificent, and even while her mind registered him as dangerous and arrogant and his propositions as unacceptable, her pulse skidded and jumped, and her breath caught. Lord Kilcairn strolled forward to take the vacated seat beside her.

"Well enough to attend the party on Thursday?" he asked, looking with some curiosity at the empty plates and glasses and the littering of silverware on the table.

For a moment Alexandra wished she had an actual glass of wine or better yet, whiskey—to sip. "Yes, I believe so. It would help, though, if you would be a bit kinder to her."

"Trying to govern me, as well, are you, Alexandra?"

"It is the task you gave me, my lord." She'd never realized her own name on someone else's lips could have such . . . strength. But Kilcairn knew exactly what sort of effect it had on her. She could see it in his amused gray eyes, damn him. "Your cousin has very little self-confidence."

"She's so loud, no one would think it."

"Her mother is loud. Rose barely says a word." Alexandra sneaked a sideways look at his lean, dark profile as he sank back in the chair.

"They both yammer more than your dog."

She refrained from pointing out that Shakespeare didn't yammer. "Might I ask you a question?" she said instead.

He faced her, placing his elbow on the table and his chin in his hand. "Ask."

Oh, my, he was beautiful. "Why do you dislike them so much?"

The earl lifted an eyebrow. "The harpies?"

"Yes."

"That's none of your affair." Despite the words, his voice was quiet, a silky drawl that twined its leisurely way down Alexandra's spine. "Suffice it to say that I do."

"Rather *Richard the Third* of you, don't you think?" Alexandra asked, keeping her outward self as calm as he appeared to be. He wouldn't beat her in a battle of words; she wouldn't allow it.

Kilcairn smiled, that sensuous, dark smile that made her breath stop. " 'Since I cannot prove a lover / To entertain these fair well-spoken days, / I am determined to prove a villain / And hate the idle pleasure of these days.' "

She shook her head, impressed once again. "No. More like the big bad king imprisoning his young, defenseless nephews in the Tower and then having them murdered."

"A bully, you mean."

"You must know that's how it appears."

"I know it appears that way to them. Does it to you also, Miss Gallant?"

At first glance it had. She had the distinct feeling, though, that bullies didn't quote self-deprecating lines from *Richard III* with quite so much ease. "I don't feel it is my place to say, my lord. I am an employee."

The earl reached out and stroked her cheek with the back of one finger. She froze, trying to memorize the sensation. When she didn't move, he straightened again and tucked a stray strand of her light hair behind one ear. The entire time his gaze held hers, as though he was watching, studying her reaction. She didn't know what he saw; she felt like a moth drawn helplessly to a flame. Moving, speaking, breathing—everything became impossible. And then, cupping her cheeks in both hands, slowly he leaned forward and touched her lips with his.

Alexandra's eyes closed. His soft, firm mouth skimmed and caressed and teased hers until she simply wanted to sink to the floor. For the first time since she had decided on spinsterhood, she didn't feel like a spinster. She felt molten, on fire. She leaned into him, and with a quiet, low sound, he deepened the embrace of their mouths.

Even knowing she was in the presence of an expert lover didn't change the heart-stopping thrill of being kissed. And she'd *never* been kissed like this. She'd never dreamed such a kiss existed in anything but fairy tales. Unable to help herself, Alexandra kissed him back, awkwardly and inexpertly. Her lack of expertise didn't seem to bother Kilcairn, though, as his hands slid down her shoulders to her waist and hips. Without any seeming effort at all, he lifted her onto his lap, never lessening his attentions to her mouth and lips.

Finally, when she felt ready to burst into flames, he pulled away. Dazed, Alexandra lifted her head. "Oh, my," she breathed, her hands loose around his shoulders.

His eyes held hers, something seductive and secret in their depths. "That is something, I fear," he whispered, "that Rose will never learn."

"What?"

"How to make men desire her as I desire you." He lowered his gaze to her lips, and then captured her mouth again in a rough, demanding kiss. She squirmed closer on his lap and tightened her embrace, not wanting to miss the least little breath of his attentions.

He couldn't be as cynical as he claimed. Not if he

could kiss like that. But Alexandra wasn't foolish enough to believe that a lack of cynicism would keep him from rendering her naked and placing warm, slow kisses on her bare skin. The thought made her tremble with a deep, yearning ache that was more heated than fire. That was when she realized she'd best put a stop to this, right now.

"My lord," she managed shakily, turning her face from his.

His lips traveled along the line of her jaw. "Yes?"

"You must stop!"

"What in God's name for?"

The tip of his tongue caressed the base of her throat, and she gasped, her fingers digging helplessly into his shoulders. "I am attempting to teach propriety. This is certainly not the way to do it!"

"My cousin isn't here."

"But you are." With effort she pushed away from him and stood. Slowly, reluctantly, his hands slipped away from her hips and her waist. She knew if he'd wanted to, he could have kept her imprisoned on his lap, clinging to him helplessly, and it seemed significant that he'd let her escape. She would sort out exactly what it meant later, when her mind regained the ability to function again. "I am a governess," she stated, lifting a hand to fix her hair. "Not a mistress. And you, according to your own request, are one of my students."

His jaw clenched, the earl looked at her for a long, dark moment. He gestured toward the door. "Go, then."

Kilcairn's voice sounded tight and strained, and Alexandra paused. "Are you well?"

"Absolutely not. Good night."

"No? May I help?"

He scowled at her. "Yes, but you won't."

"I . . ." She'd learned enough interesting new things during that kiss to be able to deduce what he was talking about. "Oh."

"Leave, Miss Gallant. Now."

She hesitated, then nodded and pulled open the door. "Good night, Lord Kilcairn."

"Perhaps you'll dream of me, Alexandra. I'll be dreaming of you, I think."

Closing the door softly behind her, Alexandra hurried to her bedchamber. Once inside, though, she spent a good five minutes trying to decide whether to lock the door. Finally good sense got the better of her, and she slid the bolt home.

As she changed into her nightclothes, she kept finding herself immobile before the roaring fireplace, her fingers tracing her lips. He had wanted her, and it would have been frightfully easy to give in if only he would promise to keep kissing her like that. Dream of him indeed. She'd be lucky if she closed her eyes at all.

Lucien strode around the dining room table, running estate accounting figures through his head. Bales of hay, number of cattle, the price of barley—the amount of coal necessary to keep Kilcairn Abbey warm through the winter. Nothing worked.

"Damnation," he swore, and followed that curse with several even more colorful ones.

This was too much. A man of his experience and reputation did not, under any circumstances, moon after an overaged virgin—and certainly not when he employed her as a governess. When he'd kissed her, he'd hoped that would serve to ease the tumult she caused in him. Now, though, aside from being painfully aroused, he had felt her hesitant, then eager, response. And then she'd trotted off to bed, safe and sound and still virginal, and he'd let her go.

He did one more circuit of the room, then halted before the door. What he needed was a distraction from his distraction. Throwing open the door, he headed down the stairs and into the back hallway where a dozen small, practical bedchambers stood tucked beneath the upstairs ballroom. Stopping before the first door, he rapped on the hard wood.

The muffled answer he received didn't sound very polite. Unruffled, he knocked again, louder.

"All right, damn it all," a voice grunted. "The house had better be on fire."

The knob turned and the door opened. Rubbing one eye, Mr. Mullins gazed blearily at his employer. Immediately he straightened, blanching. "My lord! I had no idea—"

"Mr. Mullins," Lucien interrupted, "I have a task for you."

"Now, my lord?"

"Yes, now. I want a list. A list of twelve—no, make that fifteen—single females, of noble family, good character, pleasant appearance, and aged somewhere between seventeen and twenty-two."

He intentionally cut off the age at two years younger than Miss Gallant. If a female hadn't found a husband by twenty-two, she was obviously possessed of some deficiency, mental or otherwise. He hadn't discovered Miss Gallant's fault, yet, but he was sure to do so posthaste.

"Females. Yes, my lord. But . . . for what purpose?"

"For the purpose of marriage, Mr. Mullins. Have the list ready for me first thing in the morning, so we may begin eliminating prospects."

As the solicitor stared at him, Lucien turned on his heel and headed back upstairs. Wimbole had retired for the evening, and the hallways were dark and quiet. Lucien entered his private quarters, dismissed his valet, and stripped out of most of his clothes. Pouring himself a brandy and downing the majority of it at one go, he sat in the dark looking out at the moonlight, and seeing a pair of turquoise-colored eyes.

He spent most of the night there. When in the morning Bartlett scratched at the door and then entered the master bedchamber, unbidden, Lucien had just managed his first consecutive twenty minutes of sleep all night.

"Damnation. What time is it?" he grumbled, reaching over the side of the chair and throwing a boot at his valet.

Bartlett caught it and made his way over to the east window, cloaked by heavy blue curtains. "Seven in the morning, my lord. Mr. Mullins has gone out, but he wished me to inform you that he will be back by eight, in time for your meeting." He pushed the curtains open, and bright yellow daylight flooded the room.

Lucien groaned and threw an arm across his eyes.

"Do you wish Wimbole to make up something for your head this morning?" the valet asked, picking up his scattered clothing.

"No. I'm not drunk. Just tired. Have the harpies or Miss Gallant risen?"

"Miss Gallant and Sally left for Hyde Park some fifteen minutes ago. Penny and Marie were summoned to Mrs. Delacroix's bedchamber as I left the kitchen."

Bartlett's cool efficiency was often irritating, but the valet kept his mouth shut, and he had impeccable timing and taste, which compensated for his occasional stodginess. "Bring me some coffee," Lucien ordered.

"Yes, my lord."

Lucien rose and pulled on the shirt and breeches Bartlett had laid out for him the night before. Thank God he and Robert had already planned to attend the boat races on the Thames today. Otherwise, he had a very good idea that he would spend the entire day mooning after his blasted cousin's blasted governess.

He'd been turned down before, albeit rarely, and it hadn't bothered him. He knew from experience there were a multitude of ladies he could seek to ease his frustration. And he knew just as surely that he would not be visiting any of them today—or until he'd resolved this damned annoying little standoff with Miss Gallant.

Being the proper, etiquette-minded lady that she was, she would spend breakfast lecturing Rose on how one conquered one's baser emotions in favor of propriety, and he would be forced to listen to every word and know she meant it to apply to him. He didn't want to hear it, and he didn't want to give her the satisfaction of saying it in his presence. Therefore, he finished his coffee upstairs and then went to find Mr. Mullins.

"This is what you came up with?" he asked, tossing the list back onto his desk.

"You did give me rather short notice, my lord," the solicitor said, looking hurt. "And there are fifteen names, and they all fit the requirements you stated to me last night."

"Fine. At least two of them can be counted on to attend the Howards' party tomorrow evening."

"My lord, is it truly your intention to marry—"

"Eliminate Charlotte Bradshaw immediately, though," he interrupted. "Her brother is addicted to making poor wagers, and if I become his relation-in-law, he'll expect me to make good on them. In fact, review the entire list. The fewer familial connections any of them have, the better."

"But you wanted them to be of good family."

"Good, *dead* family would be preferable."

"My lord, this is not an easy task you've—"

"I want a list of fifteen *acceptable* females by Friday morning. Is that clear?"

Mr. Mullins sighed and crumpled his piece of paper. "Yes, my lord. Very clear. I shall see to it at once."

Alexandra barely set eyes on Lord Kilcairn over the next day and a half. She would have said that he was avoiding her, except that he didn't seem the type. It was more likely that he was avoiding his cousin and his aunt. As she was almost constantly in Rose's company, his absence made more sense when explained that way. She told herself she was thankful, because preparing for the dinner party was going to be difficult enough without his sharp-edged commentary.

Even so, she couldn't help feeling a bit . . . disturbed. Whenever she closed her eyes, she could feel his lips on hers, his hands running down her back, and the tall, solid strength of him. His absence gave her time to think and consider what drew her to him.

What it didn't do, though, was give her a chance to tell him exactly what she thought of his forward behavior—as if she knew what to say, anyway. The proper thing would be to inform him of her displeasure, and to let him know that from this point on she expected him to behave like a gentleman. That, however, would preclude him from ever kissing her again—a thought that didn't please her one bit.

The door connecting her room and Rose's rattled and opened. "Lex? May I come in?"

"Of course, Rose. Let me take a look at you."

The girl hesitated in the doorway, then stepped into Alexandra's bedchamber. Madame Charbonne had selected a light blue silk gown for Rose's first public outing tonight. Seeing her charge, her blond hair piled atop her head and a thin strand of pearls kissing her throat, Alexandra could only agree. "You look splendid."

Rose blushed. "Oh, thank you. I'm so nervous."

"Just don't let it show." Alexandra finished tying her own hair back in a green ribbon that matched the scattering of flowers across her gown. The creation looked decidedly ungovernesslike, but it was the most lovely thing she'd ever owned.

"You look so pretty," Rose said, sitting on the edge of the bed. "Thank goodness cousin Lucien let you stay up here, instead of putting you down in the servants' quarters. If he'd done that, we'd never have been able to chat like this."

Alexandra paused. "Your previous governesses didn't stay in this bedchamber?"

"Oh, no. Lucien said he didn't want them cluttering up the place. They stayed downstairs where Wimbole and Mr. Mullins and the other servants have their quarters. They're very good rooms, but too small to keep a decent wardrobe in. And Shakespeare wouldn't have liked it at all, either." She petted the terrier napping on Alexandra's pillow.

"No, I imagine not."

At the Welkins' estate she'd had servants' quarters, though at other country manors she'd been given larger or smaller accommodations, depending on the houses' size. For some reason it hadn't occurred to her that her quarters here were unusual, though now she couldn't believe she'd been so naive. She wondered what Lord Kilcairn's other employees must think of her, and what they said to their fellows at other houses.

"Are you feeling well?" Rose asked into the silence.

She started. "Yes, quite."

"Good. Because I think I should faint dead away if I had to go to the Howards' without you to help me."

Alexandra went over to sit beside the girl. "Don't worry, Rose. It's going to be a small party, as Lord Kilcairn said. And everyone will expect you to be a little nervous. If you get confused about something, just look at me. I'll be close by, and we'll manage splendidly."

She didn't voice her concern over one very significant item: Mrs. Fiona Delacroix. The earl had promised to see to her, but his comments tended to aggravate rather than quiet his aunt. Rose didn't need an additional cause to fret, though, so Alexandra kept her silence and hoped that Lord Kilcairn would keep his word.

He was down in the foyer when she and Rose descended the stairs, and abruptly she realized how nervous *she* was at spending any length of time in his company. She still had no idea what to say to him about their kiss, and he was sure to bring it up at the first opportunity.

She sent up a quick prayer that he wouldn't mention her folly in front of his relations—or in front of anyone else. She couldn't bear it if the rumors were to start again. She hadn't precisely encouraged Lord Kilcairn, though she hadn't resisted him as strenuously as she had Lord Welkins, either. She hadn't resisted Lucien at all, really.

The earl watched her approach, his eyes hooded in

the half darkness of the foyer. "Good evening ladies," he said in his low drawl, coming forward.

"My lord."

"Mama will be down any moment now," Rose said, curtsying and still looking extremely nervous. "I'm afraid she . . . wasn't very happy with Madame Charbonne's gown."

Alexandra didn't blame the girl's hesitation in speaking, given her cousin's typical reaction to her. She readied a soothing comment in case he answered in his usual caustic fashion.

"The more fashionably late we are, the better," was all he said, though, and Alexandra relaxed a little. Perhaps the devil meant to behave himself this evening, after all. If that was the case, it would be the first time he'd done so, but after that kiss she was certainly willing to give him the benefit of her wavering doubt.

Chapter 6

Lucien considered riding his horse to the Howard soiree and leaving the females to follow in the coach. Not having to listen to the Delacroix ladies prattle for half an hour was tempting. Even more appealing, though, was the notion of Miss Gallant cooped in the small passengers' compartment with him—two additional relations present or not.

And so he sat beside Aunt Fiona as the coach rumbled toward Clifford Street and Howard House. With Mrs. Delacroix's orange hair hidden beneath a beige hat and her rotund figure disguised inside a stylish rust and beige evening gown, she could almost pass for an aristocratic matriarch—as long as she didn't open her mouth.

Once he'd dumped Rose and Fiona into the care of Miss Gallant and their hosts, Lucien intended to busy himself elsewhere. Not gaming, drinking, or slipping away for a smoke, though—he'd save those pleasures for later in the Season, after he'd secured a bride.

At an event this deathly boring, several respectable females were likely to be present, and Lady Howard had invited at least two of the prospective brides from Mr. Mullins's list. A little tête-à-tête with a proper female should prove—to him and to Miss Gallant—that once a woman scented money and a title, she would happily marry a crooked old fence post, much less him.

Across from him, Rose and Alexandra talked in low voices, no doubt going through one last rehearsal before they arrived. He didn't envy Alexandra her task, though she seemed to have more than enough fortitude to see it through. Thank Lucifer they weren't trying to marry Aunt Fiona off again. He doubted he had enough money to convince the governess to see to that job.

Though he hated to admit it, Miss Gallant had been correct on at least one count—he should never have encouraged her to wear a Madame Charbonne gown. It had nothing to do with her complaint that she didn't look like a governess, though she didn't. It was simply that he couldn't keep his eyes, or his overheated imagination, off her.

"Is there anyone in particular to whom you wish to present Rose this evening?" Alexandra asked, meeting his gaze.

"My friend Robert Ellis, the Viscount of Belton, will likely be attending. He's been curious to meet cousin Rose."

Alexandra's gaze sharpened. "And why is he so curious?"

From her expression, she had guessed the answer to that, or at least she thought she had. "Why should he not be?" he returned coolly, daring her to accuse him of something improper. "Wouldn't you be curious to meet the Earl of Kilcairn Abbey's only living relations?"

"Yes, I suppose so," she answered grudgingly.

"Though you don't seem to encourage discussion of that topic."

Lucien narrowed his eyes. "Don't I?"

"No, you d—"

"Why shouldn't this Lord Belton be curious about my daughter?" Fiona cut in. "She's an angel. You should be happy to show her off to your friends."

"Is the Viscount of Belton unmarried?" Rose asked, chewing her lower lip.

At least she seemed to want to be married and out of his care as much as he wanted her to be. "Unmarried and looking for just the right female to change that circumstance," he answered.

"Of course, that is not the purpose of this evening, is it, Lord Kilcairn?" Alexandra said stoutly.

"Do we have another purpose?" he asked, giving her a skeptical glance. "I know this isn't for my health."

"Yes, we do have another purpose. Rose," Miss Gallant said, turning to his cousin, "please remember that tonight is just to get you comfortable with gatherings of the *ton*. One thing at a time. It will be a small, informal party, as Lord Kilcairn has told us. You will have time for chatting, but you mustn't let any one person—male or female—monopolize your attention."

Lucien hid a slight grin. "Do I get to monopolize any one's attention?"

"I'm sure you may do as you please, my lord."

"I'll remember you said that."

Alexandra blushed. "I didn't mean—"

"Oh, I'm so nervous I doubt I'll be able to say a word," Rose put in.

"We can only hope the occasion will equally affect your mother." He slouched, annoyed. He should have had Rose and Fiona ride horses, so he and Alexandra could converse undisturbed.

"My Rose will show herself very well," Fiona stated, "and everyone will know how proud we are of her." She adjusted her elbow-length gloves. "Though I do wish that Charbonne woman had thought to add feathers to her ensemble. Feathers in the hair add such a touch of elegance, you know."

"Perhaps on a more formal occasion," Alexandra soothed.

"Or a trip to the London zoo." Lucien brushed aside the window curtains and glanced out at the growing darkness. "No doubt the headgear would impress the baboons. You might want to stay clear of the ostrich pen, though. Bad form, to stare at an animal when you may be wearing one of its relations."

The familiar pout appeared again. "Mama!"

Aunt Fiona gasped. "You are an awful, awful man, Lucien," she sputtered. "If you weren't my relation, I would positively hate you."

"I assure you, the feeling is—"

"You shall be the prettiest young lady at dinner, Rose," Alexandra interrupted. "Feathers, or not. You have nothing to worry about."

"Is that so?" Lucien countered, annoyed at having several promising insults stifled.

Miss Gallant glared at him, looking every inch the offended governess despite her becoming gown. "Yes, it is. First impressions are lasting impressions, my lord, as you well know. All Rose needs to do is make a positive first impression."

Her comment reminded him of his first impression of her, and returned him to the contemplation of how much he would like to slip her out of her gloves and her dainty pearled shoes and her exquisite gown and run his hands along her soft, warm skin. A slow smile curved his lips.

The coach rocked to a halt, jarring Lucien out of his reverie. Bringing his lust back under control, he helped his aunt and his cousin to the ground. Miss Gallant came last, and he noted her hesitation before she accepted his hand and descended the steep carriage steps to the ground. He leaned closer, curling his fingers around hers. "You mesmerize me," he murmured.

"You like to make trouble," she returned, freeing her fingers—but not before he felt their trembling. Alexandra caught up to Rose at the front entry, wrapping her arm around the younger woman's.

Her reaction to his touch distracted him from replying. Sweet Lucifer, he wanted her in his bed. As he had no intention of escorting his aunt, he followed the ladies inside. Again his gaze found Alexandra, straying to her green and white skirt as it swayed from side to side with the movement of her slender, rounded hips.

The butler, polite and hardly shocked at all to see the Earl of Kilcairn Abbey on his doorstep, led their group upstairs to the drawing room. They paused in the doorway, and Lucien stifled a curse.

Miss Gallant stirred at his elbow. "You said this was to be a *small* gathering," she whispered.

"It is, by London standards," he lied, and stepped forward to greet Lord and Lady Howard.

He didn't like being outmaneuvered, but tonight that had obviously happened. Half a hundred guests, nearly twice what he'd anticipated, milled about in the Howard drawing room and spilled over into the adjoining music room and library. He hadn't known so many of them were even in town this early in the Season. And he certainly wasn't naive enough to pretend that he had no idea about the cause of the sudden hush and then the excited chattering that filled the room as his party entered.

"Lord Howard, Lady Howard," he said in a mild tone, though he would have been perfectly happy to strangle either or both of them, "I'd like to present Mrs. Delacroix, Miss Delacroix, and my cousin's companion, Miss Gallant."

"We are so pleased to meet you," Lady Howard gushed, taking Rose's hands and all but ignoring Aunt Fiona. "You must know, Miss Delacroix, everyone has been dying to set eyes on you."

Rose curtsied, blushing, and with a heavy sigh Lucien waited for the stammering and the tears to begin. The lack of mortified embarrassment had been enjoyable for the short time it lasted.

"You have a lovely home," his cousin said in an unsteady voice. "Thank you for having us here."

Lucien stepped back beside Alexandra. "By God, she *can* be taught."

"Hush. You might have warned me you were going to make a spectacle out of her presentation. Directly after dinner Mrs. Delacroix will have to claim a headache. Rose will never make it through twenty women chattering at her."

The glance she sent him made it quite clear that she expected him to see to Aunt Fiona's poor health. No one—and no woman, certainly—had ever ordered him to do anything. Nevertheless, he gave her a slight nod. "I have no wish to suffer through this, either. For God's sake, I could be at White's getting drunk right now."

"Then this evening is a nice change for you, as well."

"It's a change," he admitted darkly, wondering if she was a teetotaler as well as the most damnably proper female he'd ever met. "I wouldn't call it nice."

Fortunately he'd timed their arrival late enough that it coincided with the beginning of dinner, and they were spared most of the introductions. Lady Howard had seated him between Lady DuPont and Lady Halverston. It was a wise decision on his hostess's part, considering his reputation and the advanced age of the two matrons. When he spied Daubner moving to his designated place at a secondary table, though, a more practical arrangement occurred to him.

"But . . . " Daubner stammered, as Lucien strolled over and switched place cards with him.

"No need to thank me. I know how you dislike these drafty windows."

"But . . ."

Lucien heroically took the seat beside Aunt Fiona. Cousin Rose and Miss Gallant took their own places at the first table, luckily side by side. The view was better than he would have had from his original seat, and he caught Alexandra's eye as she sat.

"Comfortable?" he mouthed, just loud enough for her to hear.

"Most assuredly, my lord," she responded, and returned her attention to Rose.

Lucien glanced at his aunt. "Your daughter looks passable," he admitted grudgingly.

"Of course she does. Half the young men about Birling have been calling on her, with her not even out yet. But I know what's proper, and just who she should be saving herself for."

"I hadn't realized you'd left Dorsetshire so bereft. We should never have removed her from her natural element."

"Rose will *not* be marrying a farmer, or a vicar, or a squire."

When Miss Georgina Croft arrived at her place on his other side, Lucien decided perhaps the evening wouldn't be a complete waste of time, after all. She had placed number six on Mullins's preliminary list.

"Good evening," he said, standing and holding her chair out for her.

She blushed to the roots of her dark brunette hair and looked vainly about for her place card to be other than where it was. The small placard remained exactly where he had discovered it, though, between himself and half-deaf Lord Blakely. "Good evening, my lord," she finally said, curtsying.

"Good evening," he repeated, sitting after her. Belatedly he realized he had no notion how to speak to a virginal debutante without frightening her to death. Hmmm. Having Alexandra tutor him didn't seem quite so absurd now.

Miss Croft swallowed. "It's quite cool tonight, isn't it?"

Ah, standard innocuous conversation. Disappointing, but at least he wouldn't be overtaxed this evening—not unless Miss Gallant joined in. "Not surprisingly so, considering how early in the Season it is."

"Indeed. We have been blessed with a mild winter."

At that same moment, the nearly identical bit of conversation echoed a table away. Lucien glanced up as Rose finished commenting on the mildness of the winter to her table mate. Alexandra met his gaze, and he lifted an eyebrow. Her lips curved in the beginnings of an amused smile before she looked away.

Abruptly he wondered if she found this mindless silliness as absurd as he did. That would be extremely intriguing, considering that she taught the nonsense for a living. With renewed enthusiasm he turned back to Miss Croft. "What brings you into London so early?"

She glanced at her mother, seated at the far end of the table. "My father had some business affairs to attend to. What brings you here, my lord?"

"Familial obligations."

" 'Familial obligations?' You've never even bothered to notice us before."

Lucien flinched as Aunt Fiona's grating voice rose above the chattering. Damnation, he'd forgotten about her. "What was that, my dear?" he asked, favoring her with a brief, unamused smile.

She apparently realized from his expression that he wouldn't allow the conversation to continue in that vein, because she blanched. "Oh, you know," she tittered, and reached for her glass of Madeira.

By the time the ladies rose to excuse themselves at the end of the meal, Lucien had the headache that Fiona was about to claim. With Georgina Croft taking a swig of wine every time he asked her a question, she was at least two sheets to the wind—which served to relax her conversation, but not to improve her wits.

He stood as Aunt Fiona withdrew from the table to join the other ladies regrouping in the drawing room. Before he could take more than a step to head her off, Miss Gallant materialized beside him. Lucien read her glare, and with stifled amusement took his aunt by the arm.

"Miss Gallant," he announced, "I'm afraid my aunt is feeling unwell."

Aunt Fiona stared up at him. "I am n—"

"Oh, poor dear, she had a headache this morning," Alexandra cut in with masterful timing, swooping in to take Fiona's other plump arm. "She did so want to come tonight, though."

"What in the—"

"Come, Aunt," he commanded. "We'll get you home and to bed at once. I'm sure Lord and Lady Howard will understand."

"Yes, a good night's rest is all you need, Mrs. Delacroix. It will be just the thing."

Miss Gallant took Rose in tow as well, and they swept through the crowd for the door. With a few swift goodbyes and apologies, they made it outside and plunked Aunt Fiona into the waiting coach.

"You'd make a fine major general, Miss Gallant," Lucien said, taking his seat as the coach rocked out of the drive.

"Thank you, my l—"

"What is the meaning of this?" Fiona squawked. "I feel as though I'm being kidnapped!"

"We should be so lucky."

"My lord," Alexandra chastised, but completely unrepentant, he only grinned at her.

"I'm just glad to escape." Rose fanned at her face. "So many people, all looking at me!"

Lucien looked at her, wondering if he'd ever been so callow and naive. It didn't seem likely. With his father's reputation paving his way, either flaw could easily have proved ruinous. "You are the *ton*'s newest oddity. They'll look at you until they find new game to ogle."

"Mama!"

Before he could explain himself, Alexandra cleared her throat. "In a sense, Lord Kilcairn is correct."

"He is?"

"Well, yes. I would have worded it a bit differently, but—"

"Coward," he interrupted.

"—but that is precisely what I meant by first impressions. In a month, some of those gentlemen and ladies will have only a vague recollection of whether they wish to be seen in your company or not." She smiled in the dim light, and something odd thumped and skittered in Lucien's chest.

"And?" he prompted.

"And after tonight, with perhaps an additional evening of the same quality, I should think none of them would mind engaging in a conversation with you, Miss Delacroix."

"Oh, thank you, Lex."

"Splendid." Aunt Fiona chuckled. "But I didn't see your friend, Lucien. Lord Belton, wasn't it?"

He kept his gaze on Miss Gallant, trying to decide what, precisely, had just happened, and whether he was pleased or annoyed by it. "Robert has good sense. He didn't attend, obviously."

He spoke more sharply than he'd intended, but Fiona's softheaded gloating irritated him no end. For God's sake, the woman would have ruined the evening for all of them—and for the other Howard guests—in another two minutes. When Alexandra sent him another glare, he smirked at her. At least his comment had shut up his relations; he'd put up with more than enough prattling for one evening.

By the time he disembarked from the coach and strolled into the house, all three ladies had already vanished up the stairs. "Wimbole, cognac," he ordered, heading into his study.

With a sigh he undid his cravat and sank into the armchair nearest the fireplace. The butler appeared at his elbow a moment later, and Lucien lifted the amber-filled glass off its silver tray. He took a swallow, letting the warm liquid burn down his throat to his gullet. "Find Mr. Mullins."

"Yes, my lord."

The solicitor must have been hovering nearby, because the door opened immediately after the butler left. Lucien continued watching the crackling fire through half-closed eyes.

"Mr. Mullins, scratch Georgina Croft off the list. I asked her to name her favorite author, and she said, 'I rather like the original one.' Thinking she meant the Bible, I then asked her which passage she preferred. Her answer was something along the lines of 'the passage where he goes looking for Guinevere.' "

"She thought you asked her to name her favorite Arthur. I would have picked the same one."

At the sound of Alexandra's soft voice, it took every bit of willpower Lucien possessed to remain seated and look calmly back at her, standing in the doorway with her arms crossed over her chest. "All of which makes her either deaf or dim."

"So you only carry on affairs with intelligent females?" she asked, stepping into the room and closing the door behind her.

"Are you asking out of general or personal interest?" he returned, watching her approach. This looked like a seduction, but considering she'd been annoyed with him five minutes earlier, he thought it more likely that she planned an ambush. She would find that he didn't succumb easily.

"I've never heard of anyone making a list of potential spouses and then eliminating candidates when they don't pass literary snuff."

"Actually, it seems a rather sound method."

"And yet, didn't you tell me you preferred more mature females? Miss Croft looked barely eighteen."

"I don't believe in setting limits." He sipped his cognac, grateful that his headache had departed—by supreme coincidence at the same time his relations had retired for the evening.

"But you have your solicitor keep your list of women for you."

Slowly he smiled, and noted with satisfaction that her gaze lowered to his lips. "Did you have a reason for coming in here? Other than to express your jealousy, of course."

"You—"

The door opened again. "You wanted to see—"

"In a moment, Mr. Mullins," Lucien growled.

"Apologies, my lord." The door shut again.

"You were saying, Alexandra?" he prompted, taking another swallow of cognac.

"It would be impossible for me to express jealousy, because I feel none." She stalked over to his desk and back again, the firelight catching the beading of her dress and making the length of her shimmer.

"Then why are you here?" he murmured, his pulse stirring. That dress hadn't been a mistake, after all.

"To ask why you continue to censure your cousin and your aunt for their behavior when yours is ten times worse!"

His grin deepened. "Ten times? It's a wonder anyone tolerates me at all."

"Yes, it is."

"Please, tell me what you find lacking about my character."

She turned to face the fire. "I will not."

"Why not?"

"You know very well that you aggravate people. You do it on purpose. I am not about to humor you by listing your carefully cultivated faults."

"I'm positively diabolical."

"You're mean," she corrected. "Giving the description extra syllables doesn't alter the fact."

Lucien eyed her, the veriest twinge of a headache resuming. Alexandra had probably spent the entire ride home deciding exactly what she wanted to say to him and how he might attempt to parry each thrust.

"How am I *mean*, then?" he asked, setting aside the cognac, and more curious about her answer than he cared to admit.

"You constantly insult and belittle your relations, to begin with."

He lifted an eyebrow. "There's more?"

"There is." Alexandra squared her shoulders, pinning him with her direct, angry gaze. "And I say this only because you indicated that you wanted my assistance in perfecting your manners."

"So I did. Continue."

"The Delacroix ladies have just lost their closest male relation, and you flatly refuse to show even the least bit of compassion for their bereavement, much less for their plight. That is hideously insensitive."

"They're here, aren't they?" he growled, becoming less amused.

"Because of a piece of paper—not because of any feelings on your part. You made that quite clear. Did you even send them your condolences?"

Lucien clenched his jaw. She knew how to argue, for damned certain, but he had no intention of letting her goad him into revealing anything he wished to keep private. "I paid for the funeral."

"That is *not* the same thing."

Something in this wasn't about the Delacroix harpies, or even about him. She was too angry for anything less than a personal pain. "Whom did you bury?" he asked quietly.

Alexandra opened her mouth, then snapped it shut again. "As if you would care, when you can't even be moved to mourn your own family," she finally snarled, and turned on her heel.

Lucien surged to his feet. As he grabbed her wrist she spun to face him, her face flushed and her bosom heaving with her fast, angry breathing. His electrified reaction to her wildly flying pulse immediately altered what he had been about to say. "I do mourn," he said. "But not for public display."

Alexandra stared up at his face, the anger leaving her expressive countenance. "It's your cousin James you mourn, isn't it?"

He wasn't that transparent; he knew it. Yet more than half the time, she seemed to know exactly what he was thinking. "Why did you let me kiss you?" he countered.

She flushed. "Don't change the subject."

Still gripping her wrist, he drew her nearer. "My subject is more interesting."

"N-not to me, my lord."

Lucien smiled, then leaned forward and softly touched his lips to hers. "Is that more interesting?" he murmured.

"I do not think—"

He kissed her again, more deeply. "Or this, perhaps?"

Her head tilted up and her eyes closed. Completely lacking the will to resist his beckoning goddess, he kissed her once more. "I'm very interested myself."

Slowly Alexandra opened her turquoise eyes to look at him. "You can stop the argument," she said in a low, soft voice that sent tremors skimming along his muscles, "but not the reason behind it."

The words sounded cool and courageous, but he knew her moods well enough to sense how unsettled she was. He wasn't about to give in now. "That's right; we were discussing my ill manners. A proper gentleman wouldn't have kissed you. Therefore, in this instance, behaving makes no sense."

"*You* make no sense," she countered, pulling her arm free of his grip. "You can't mourn one relation and pretend to care nothing about another."

"But I can choose whether I discuss it or not—and I choose to discuss a more interesting topic. Your lips, to begin with."

"That subject is closed."

Lucien couldn't resist grinning at that. "Good night, then, Miss Gallant."

Before he could move away, she gripped his sleeve in her fingers. The gentle tug brought him up short. "Why won't you talk about it—about my subject?" she asked. "I would listen."

Lucien looked down at her face, only inches away. "I don't require anyone else to listen to my expressions of grief," he murmured. "What I'm interested in is having you in my bed. Does *that* subject interest you, Alexandra?"

She released him and backed away. "N-no."

"Are you certain? I know you enjoyed kissing me. This would be much better."

"Good night, my lord," she stammered, and fled.

After a moment Lucien called in Mr. Mullins and resumed his seat. She hadn't said no, that last time. And that was more interesting than anything he and his solicitor could discuss.

Chapter 7

Evidently Lord Kilcairn thought Rose had passed her first test. By the end of the week he had accepted invitations on his cousin's behalf to two more dinner parties, an evening at the opera, a fireworks festival at Vauxhall Gardens, and the first grand ball of the Season. As his acceptances went out, more invitations began to pour in.

Apparently everyone wanted to be a part of the phenomenon of Lucien Balfour's venture into proper society—though Alexandra knew he was using the ploy only to gain more attention for Rose.

However, he had scheduled Rose's various appearances without consulting Alexandra, which annoyed her no end. There were steps to be followed, ways to smooth someone's way into society's highest circles, and he was ignoring all of them—if he had even considered them in the first place.

That was the reason she'd been avoiding him for the past three days: she simply didn't want to speak to him. It had nothing to do with the way he'd suggested they become lovers, or the way she'd fled the room instead of telling him *no* in no uncertain terms. Or the way she'd been dreaming about his intoxicating kisses for the past few days. For heaven's sake, she didn't even like him. Besides, she was supposed to be teaching him propriety; he was not supposed to be instructing her on behaving like a shameless strumpet.

Shakespeare at her side, Alexandra left her bedchamber. Kilcairn had been correct about the scarcity of her free time—her early morning walks were now so early they were verging on becoming late evening walks.

Halfway to the stairs, she paused at the black-banded portrait of James Balfour. His complexion and his hair were both lighter than his cousin's, and his half-smiling expression made Alexandra want to smile back at him. His face was so open, and she wondered what had made Lucien so mysterious and enigmatic, and why she found that to be so much more compelling.

"What are you puzzling out now?"

Alexandra jumped as Kilcairn materialized out of the dark hallway behind her. "My goodness!" she whispered when her heart resumed beating. "You frightened me half to death!"

"If you hadn't been concentrating so intently, you might have heard me stomping up behind you."

She couldn't imagine him stomping anywhere. "You are supposed to simply apologize."

"For your lack of attention?"

Alexandra sighed. "You're up and about early," she amended.

"So are you."

"Shakespeare and I are taking a walk."

The earl moved a step closer. "With Sally or Marie."

"Of course."

He reached out and touched her cheek. "A pity."

She sternly stopped herself from leaning into his gentle caress. "Lord Kilcairn, there is something I need to make clear to you."

His fingers dropped. "First, let me make something clear to you, Alexandra. I want you. I desire you. But I am not some mindless beast, nor am I an idiot. You are in my employ. I will *ask* you—a few more times. I won't order you. After that, *you* will have to ask *me*." He leaned still closer, favoring her with the sensual smile that was so different from his cousin's open, affable expression. "But I will say yes."

"And what about the kissing, my lord?" she whispered, hoping the Delacroix ladies were still abed, and that he wouldn't realize—or at least he wouldn't admit that he knew—that she was asking for his embrace.

"The kissing," he repeated, his gaze lowering to her mouth. "Yes, that, too." Leaning down, he brushed her lips in a featherlight kiss that immediately left her aching for more.

He straightened, and she nearly toppled over as his mouth left hers. Hurriedly she righted herself. "My lord," she said shakily.

"Just ask me if you want another," he said, grinning.

"You are very arrogant," she snapped.

"Yes." Lucien stepped around her, bending down to pet Shakespeare as he passed.

For a moment Alexandra had to close her eyes and concentrate on breathing. Lucien probably thought he had shocked her, but she appreciated his blunt words. The problem was that his lessons were so much more interesting than hers.

Since she was headed the same way, not following him down the stairs seemed foolish. "Where are you going so early this morning, my lord?" she asked, as they reached the foyer and Wimbole appeared with the earl's caped greatcoat. "Surely you don't rise this early to ride."

He accepted his coat and hat from the butler. "Unfortunately, I won't be riding this morning. I'm going on a picnic." Kilcairn flashed her his devastating smile again. "Jealous?"

Alexandra flushed, very conscious of the apparently deaf Wimbole. "I am only curious about which duties and attentions to your cousin you mean to neglect today."

His expression immediately darkened. "All of them, if possible," he snapped.

Wimbole hurriedly pulled open the front door, and the earl strode out to his phaeton and a waiting groom. A moment later the horse and carriage left the drive at a fast trot.

"A picnic?" she repeated skeptically, trying to decide whether she was more frustrated or annoyed with the earl. "At six o'clock in the morning? Whom does he think he's fooling?"

"Mrs. Halloway the cook packed the basket herself," the butler unexpectedly contributed, as he closed the door again. "Sally will be present to accompany you in just a moment."

"That's fine." Alexandra donned her own heavy cloak. Her attention on the front door and the departed earl, she fastened the wrap's single clasp at her neck. "It seems awfully early for luncheon, don't you think?"

"His lordship said I shouldn't expect him back until evening. I would surmise that wherever he's going is some distance away, or that he had other business to see to first."

"He didn't inform you of his destination?"

The butler smiled briefly. "Lord Kilcairn keeps his own counsel, Miss Gallant."

"Yes, I've noticed that."

A moment later Sally joined them, and they headed out for a brisk walk in Hyde Park. It didn't do anything to clear her head, but she suspected it would be the quietest hour of her day. And by the time she returned and changed for breakfast, the chaos had indeed begun.

Leaving Shakespeare on her bed for his morning nap, Alexandra closed her bedchamber door. She scarcely had time to register Rose's presence before the girl pounced on her.

"Lex, Mama says I must wear my new green gown to Vauxhall Gardens!" she wailed.

"Good morning, Rose," Alexandra returned pointedly, curtsying.

"Oh, good morning," the girl said, bobbing, and wiped a tear from one cheek.

"Well, as long as you bring a shawl, your green gown should be fine. Join me for breakfast, and don't fret. You look splendid in gree—"

"But then I shall have to wear my pink silk to Lady Pembroke's ball, and cousin Lucien will never dance with me!"

Feeling distinctly as though she'd missed a step somewhere, Alexandra guided the younger girl toward the stairs. "And why wouldn't your cousin dance with you, pray tell?"

"He hates pink! The last time I wore pink, he said I looked like a flamingo." Rose stamped her foot and began crying in earnest. "I don't even know what a flamingo is!"

That didn't bode well. Lord Kilcairn had made it

clear, though, that Alexandra was only to educate his cousin socially; anything academic, other than music and conversational French, would only take time from her primary task. "It's a bird," she explained, leading the way into the breakfast room. "Don't cry, dear. It makes your skin blotchy."

Rose wiped at her cheeks. "It does?"

"Yes. And you have such a lovely complexion."

"Thank you, Lex."

Alexandra had half hoped that the transparent distraction wouldn't work, but Rose immediately became more concerned with studying her reflection in the mantel mirror than with whatever had caused her tears in the first place. Alexandra had hoped for a bit more substance. They sat to breakfast, the student in far better humor than the teacher.

"What do you wish to do today?" Alexandra asked. "I believe your cousin will be absent until evening and your mother has a luncheon, so we have the house practically to ourselves."

"I want to practice dancing again. Waltzing, especially."

"Your waltz is incomparable already, Rose," Alexandra countered, hiding another frown behind her morning cup of tea. "And you can't waltz in public until you've been presented at Almack's, which won't happen until you're presented at court, which—"

"Which won't happen for another two weeks, when I turn eighteen. This is so silly. I'm the cousin of the Earl of Kilcairn Abbey. Can't I just be presented a little early? It's not as though my birthday won't happen."

"No one is presented early," Alexandra said firmly, a bit surprised at her charge's sudden self-confidence.

"Well, Mama says I should be."

That explained it. "I might have known."

"Beg pardon?" Rose looked up from the peach she was dissecting.

Alexandra hadn't realized she'd spoken aloud. "Since we're alone," she amended in a louder voice, "I thought we might try a bit of drawing room French."

"Oh, Lex, yesterday was drawing room etiquette, and the day before that was stupid country dances and quadrilles. Can't we at least do something fun?"

"And tomorrow night is the Hargrove dinner, and the night after that is Vauxhall Gardens. I leave it up to you, Rose. *You're* the one who wants to marry a title."

"Do you really think you can teach me French in one day? Miss Brookhollow tried for six months, and we hardly got beyond *je m'apelle Rose*."

Trying not to flinch at the girl's accent, Alexandra pasted on a smile instead. "I can teach you drawing room French in a day. That will suffice for now."

Rose slumped in her chair and sighed. "I'm already getting a headache."

Alexandra felt a headache coming on, as well. "Nonsense," she said brightly. "We'll begin at once."

"Oh, all right." The girl nodded. "What sort of bird is a flamingo, anyway?"

Ah, academic curiosity, after all. "A . . . tall, long-legged, pink one. It gets its unique coloring from eating shrimp found—"

"Does it look anything like a swan?"

She sighed. "Somewhat. With a slightly larger beak. They are known to—"

"A larger *beak*?" Rose shrieked, and began crying again.

"Damnation," Alexandra muttered, and scooted her

chair closer to pat the girl on the back. "There, there, don't fret now."

"Where is my nephew?" Fiona demanded, sweeping into the breakfast room. Her orange hair, tied into ribbons to promote curling, stood out in every direction, eclipsing the faint sunlight peeking in through the window.

"Good morning, Mrs. Dela—"

"It is *not* a good morning. Where is Lucien?"

"He left nearly an hour ago, I believe," Alexandra answered when Wimbole vanished out the door. "Is something amiss?"

"Of course something is amiss. My maid has informed me that he's gone off to have a picnic today, with some marquis's daughter!"

"Yes?"

"Yes! He leaves my poor Rose here all alone so he can go spend time with complete strangers! I am shocked. Shocked and aghast!"

"Well," Alexandra began slowly, "I'm certain he—"

"No! Do not try to comfort me! Rose, you must work harder if we are to soften Lucien's heart."

"Yes, Mama."

With that, Lucien's aunt fled back upstairs, calling for muffins and chocolate to settle her nerves in time for her luncheon. Alexandra was ready for a stiff brandy herself.

Despite what the earl had told Wimbole, he showed no sign of returning home in time for dinner. Alexandra spent another two hours after the evening's meal with Mrs. Delacroix, listening to her new-gathered gossip and an accompanying diatribe on scandalous Paris trends and the shameful new fashion of dampening one's chemise to make the dress fabric cling to one's curves.

Finally she escaped into the library with a glass of warm milk and an edition of Byron's poetry. She could just as easily have retreated to her bedchamber, but she knew very well why she didn't.

Just why she felt the need to wait up for the earl required a much more complicated answer, one she wasn't quite ready to think through. All day she'd caught herself staring off into space, remembering the caress of his mouth on hers. His shocking propositions didn't seem quite so outrageous when she thought of how very well he kissed. She would never do anything about it, of course. Nevertheless, she couldn't help but feel warm and even flattered. Lord Kilcairn knew much more of the world than she did, and still he claimed to desire her.

"I wasn't aware that young, single ladies were supposed to read Byron," his low voice mused from the doorway.

She jumped. "Most gentlemen don't seem to be aware that women should read at all." Alexandra took in his impeccable dress and the intelligent gray eyes that seemed to study every gesture she made, and felt herself growing warm and fluttery all over again. "How was your picnic?"

He scowled. "Hellish. How was your day with the harpies?"

"I assume you refer to Mrs. Delacroix and Miss Delacroix? Very productive, thank you. And Mrs. Delacroix has become acquainted with Lady Halverston, who shares her negative views on the trend of dampening chemises."

"It's the best damned trend since bare breasts on Amazons." He sat in the chair opposite her. "Is Rose ready for dinner tomorrow?"

"You might have asked me that before you accepted

the invitation," she said, closing the book and setting it aside.

"I don't intend to design my social schedule to accommodate my cousin's governess," he said without heat. "If it matters, I have been selective in my choices for my dear cousin. And for my aunt, though you might not believe it."

"Yes, I had noticed," she answered, annoyed at his arrogance and knowing he was deliberately behaving that way. Kilcairn apparently *liked* being insulted by her, so not obliging him would simply be rude. "I wouldn't have expected someone of your reputation to know so many staid peers."

The earl made a face. "How else am I supposed to avoid them?" He leaned his head back, watching her through half-closed eyes. "Have you thought about my little speech this morning?"

A shivering rush ran clear down to her toes. She'd barely been able to think of anything else. "You want an answer?"

"That depends on what it is. Come, Alexandra, while you're preparing all these lovely young ladies for marriage, don't you ever wonder about it for yourself?"

Alexandra's nervous excitement began to slide toward annoyance. "That was not marriage you were proposing this morning, my lord."

"No, it wasn't. Call me Lucien tonight."

"Why?"

"Because I want to hear you say it."

She sat back, assuming the same relaxed position he had taken, though she felt as though she were marching straight into battle. "You think you can get whatever you want, don't you?"

His slight, cynical smile appeared. "That's hardly a

revelation. Tell me something about myself that I don't know."

She would have preferred more time to concentrate on that very difficult question, but he looked like he might pounce on her again if she couldn't distract him with conversation. "All right. You're not as cynical as you think you are."

One gray eye opened. "Explain."

"In the matter of marriage, a true cynic wouldn't be so fastidious."

"You find me fastidious," he repeated.

"Terribly."

The eye closed again. "I'm stunned."

"How many potential wives have you interviewed?" she continued, eager to prove her point.

"Three, including today's selection. So by speaking to them I'm being fastidious?"

Apparently he couldn't fathom being called fastidious. Alexandra let a small smile escape her lips. "Yes. Why did you speak with them?"

"Because I don't want my child and heir born to a complete twit."

"A true cynic would assume everyone, including his own child, would be a complete twit, regardless of the circumstances."

He straightened. "Your argument is faulty. I'm searching for an appropriate bride because it is in my best interest to do so."

"The point being, you think an appropriate bride exists."

A muscle in his lean cheek twitched. "Ah. But appropriate for what? You neglected to clarify that point."

"For being your wife, of course. Your companion, the mother of your children, the—"

"Child," he corrected. "One's enough. And I don't need or want a companion. That assumes I'm incapable or incomplete by myself."

"But you are."

"Only in the area of child-begetting, my dear."

Alexandra looked at him for a moment. "You're just baiting me. If you say any old outlandish thing to distract me, then it's not a fair argument."

"I assure you, I am perfectly serious. The only distraction in here is you."

"But according to you, I'm good for nothing but . . . begetting."

He shook his dark head. "No, that's what a wife is for."

"Good Lord!" she burst out, shooting to her feet. "Who raised you—gorillas?"

"An endless selection of governesses and tutors," he said quietly.

"I'd heard your father was somewhat indiscreet in his affairs, but even so, I can't believe someone as intelligent as you would actually hold to that view of wom—"

"I barely knew my father, love. I had set eyes on him a total of five times by my eighteenth birthday."

"I . . . Oh. I'm sorry," she fumbled, sitting again as she thought of her own amusing, affectionate father.

"So you think you have the key to my soul now, eh?" he continued, smiling a little. "You don't—but that is another tale." He stretched, the movement doing wonderful things to the muscles of his thighs. "Good night then, Miss Gallant." The earl braced his hands on either arm of his chair and rose.

She blinked, ready for practically anything—except the end of the match. "So you concede?"

"I concede nothing. You were the one who called me fastidious."

"I still say you are," she countered, "and you know it's true. That's why you're fleeing."

"Don't tempt the devil, Alexandra," he murmured, stepping closer, "unless you want to get burned."

She caught her breath. "I thought the phrase was 'don't play with fire,' " she corrected unsteadily.

Instantly Kilcairn strode forward, grabbed her hands, and yanked her upright. Before she could utter a word, his lips clamped over hers in a hard, hot kiss.

Her mind splintered into a thousand little pieces, so all she could do was feel. As his mouth molded with hers, he bent her backward. The only thing keeping her from collapsing back into her chair was his arms around her waist. With a low groan he tightened his grip, pulling her close against him as he deepened the embrace of their mouths.

If being kissed by Lucien Balfour was to be burned, she welcomed the fire. *Passion*, her mind kept saying as her heart thudded and her arms swept around his shoulders in a fervent embrace, *this is passion.*

As he shifted to nuzzle her throat and jaw, Alexandra became aware of his growing arousal, and of the warmth between her own legs. Tangling her fingers into his black, wavy hair, she gasped and tugged his head back. "Stop!"

He lifted his head and looked down at her with glinting gray eyes. "Then let go," he murmured in a voice that shook just a little.

Realizing she still had one hand grasping the back of his coat and the other twined into his hair, Alexandra reluctantly released him. They stood immobile for a long moment, with him towering over her and still holding her close in his arms, and then he slowly lifted her upright.

"You are a very unusual woman, Alexandra Beatrice Gallant," he whispered, and then turned and left the room.

Alexandra collapsed into her chair, every bone and muscle turning to pudding. She knew what he'd meant by his last comment—undoubtedly every other woman he'd ever kissed like that had become his lover without protest or delay. She'd been so tempted to let him continue; to make him continue. More than anything she wanted to feel his warm, strong hands on her naked skin.

With a deep, unsteady breath she pushed to her feet again and crept out of the library to her bedchamber. That was what she needed—privacy and a chance to sort things out in her head. After ten minutes of restless pacing before the fireplace, Shakespeare uneasily following in her wake, she realized that she'd learned three very important things about Lucien Balfour. Firstly, he was much more of a gentleman than he claimed, or perhaps even realized, because he'd stopped when she'd asked, when she hadn't even been all that certain she meant it. Secondly, when he claimed to be attracted to her and to want her, he wasn't just teasing. And third, she had been close to figuring out an important part of him—which she intended to discover.

Lucien sat with his chin in his hand and stared out his office window. Across from him Mr. Mullins read the list of monthly expenses aloud for his approval. Usually, out of contrariness and because he had taken a reluctant liking to his solicitor's determined and unflagging mildness, he demanded detailed explanations for at least half the items. Today, though, Mullins might have been speaking Mandarin Chinese for all the attention Lucien paid.

He was getting soft; that was the only explanation. At thirty-two years of age he'd become a doddering old fool, softheaded and with the wit and will of a gnat. The other Lucien Balfour—the sane one—wouldn't have stopped when she asked; he would have cajoled and persuaded her until she willingly changed her mind. Yet for some absurd reason he'd desisted and spent yet another frustrated night stomping about his bedchamber.

If there was something he wanted, he obtained it. That was the law, as far as he was concerned. Alexandra Beatrice Gallant seemed to have made up an entirely new set of rules, though, and he seemed utterly unable to ignore or bypass them, just as he couldn't forget or ignore the woman herself. Sweet Lucifer, maybe she was right—he was becoming fastidious.

"Is that acceptable, my lord?"

Lucien blinked. "Yes. Thank you, Mr. Mullins."

"You're . . . entirely welcome, my lord."

He resumed staring out at the garden as Mr. Mullins departed the room. Before he could sink into another Alexandra-scented daydream, a small, white ball of fluff pranced into the room through the half-open door and sat on his foot.

"Good morning, Shakespeare," he said, leaning down to scratch the terrier behind the ears.

"Shakespeare!" A tall, slender form dashed into the room behind the dog, then stopped short.

"Good morning, Miss Gallant," Lucien continued, considerably more heartened by the arrival of the second intruder.

She curtsied. "Good morning, my lord. I must apologize. Shakespeare escaped when I opened my door. It won't happen again."

"No doubt he dislikes being closed in all day. He's better behaved than my relations; let him have the run of the house."

Alexandra stepped closer. "Thank you for the generous offer, but I don't believe Mrs. Delacroix likes him very much."

"All the more reason to have him about."

She smiled. "I should censure you for saying such a thing, but as this concerns Shakespeare's happiness, I shall let it go."

Lucien gazed at her. "You should smile more often, Alexandra."

"You should give me cause to smile more often."

"Are you saying your happiness depends on me?"

"I'm saying your cooperation makes my happiness easier to obtain."

"Your cooperation would make *my* happiness easier to obtain, as well," he returned, sweeping his gaze along her length.

Blushing, she turned for the door. "I don't believe you will ever be happy then, my lord."

"I was happy for a moment last night."

She stopped. "A pity, then, that you've vowed never to be so with your wife. Whoever she may be."

Back to throwing that in his face again, was she? "My marriage ideals offend you."

"Yes, they do. If you happen to settle on a woman with even a modicum of intelligence, I suggest you not enlighten her as to your feelings—or the lack thereof."

Somehow when she said it, it made him sound like a complete ass. "Yes, my goddess. But shouldn't you be concentrating on making my cousin acceptable to a marriage-minded gentleman?"

"Yes, my lord."

The look she gave him told Lucien she considered him a cheat for pulling rank, but any conversation with Miss Gallant seemed to turn his brain to mush. He'd take any advantage he could get—that was another of his rules. As Alexandra stalked out of the room, the little dog at her heels, he wondered how long it would be before that rule crumbled into dust, as well.

Since Miss Gallant would no doubt avoid him for the remainder of the day, Lucien went out for luncheon at Boodle's. The Viscount of Belton had just taken a seat by the window, and with a slight smile Lucien went to join him.

"You've made yourself scarce these last few days," Robert said, as he inspected a bottle of Madeira.

"Not that you've been around to notice."

"Too true." Robert glanced up at the footman hovering beside him. "This will do. Thank you."

"Very good, my lord." The man hurried off to greet another patron.

"My mother arrived early," the viscount explained. "I've been practically housebound for four days, listening to all the gossip west Lincolnshire has to offer."

"Anything interesting?"

"Not a jot." Robert poured them each a glass of wine. "Much more interesting things going on here."

"Name one," Lucien said, raising the fine crystal goblet and studying it. Any distraction would be welcome.

"Well, it seems that a certain bachelor has apparently hired a notorious adulteress and murderess as a companion for his female relations."

Lucien stopped breathing. "Really?" he said, sitting back.

Robert nodded. "That's the rumor. Also that both the young ladies in his household are stunning, and that said companion must be extraordinary if said bachelor is willing to risk life and limb—notice the singular, *limb*—to have her in his possession."

Lucien's first instinct was to defend Miss Gallant, which surprised him. He knew what his peers were about—turning her into some sort of praying mantis who mated and then bit her partner's head, or nether regions, off for sport—all so they could bring some amusement to the dull beginning of the Season. His second instinct was to laugh at the idea of any man possessing her.

"I hired her," he said, "because she was the most qualified woman to apply for the position. Don't waste time fluttering about me with rumors, Robert. I don't give a damn about them."

"Humph. I thought you should at least be aware of them. And my own interpretation of your motivation varies a little from yours, but say whatever you like."

"You're in fine form this morning," Lucien noted with some annoyance. Generally when he indicated he wanted a subject dropped, the person dropped it. Immediately.

"I'm well rested," Robert reminded him, "and quite capable of keeping up with you for another three minutes. Perhaps four."

"Favor me with your interpretation then, Robert."

"As I see it, your cousin, though pleasant looking, is such a harpy that you needed someone even more notorious with whom the *ton* could compare her. That being the case, you found Miss Gallant. And you being you, she's stunning in addition to being notorious."

Lucien shrugged. "I'm brilliant."

"You're devious."

"It's the same thing."

Actually, Lucien preferred the viscount's version to the truth. Ruthlessness and deviousness were much easier to accept than whatever it was that threatened to turn him into a blithering idiot around Alexandra. Miss Gallant would no doubt scoff at anything but Robert's version herself. He hadn't exactly acted like a dashing romantic last night.

"In retrospect," Robert continued, "if I'd known who all the players were, I would not have missed the Howards' dinner. No one will miss the next gathering you attend. I'd wager you a thousand quid on that, Lucien."

"I'm disappointed," Lucien drawled, watching as their luncheon approached on silver platters. "I thought the draw would be my cousin—not her damned governess."

"You knew you would draw a crowd. And I really wish that in the future you would let your friends in on your little secrets."

"I don't have any."

"Friends, or secrets?"

He smiled. "Exactly."

Chapter 8

Alexandra wondered whether Lord Kilcairn had heard the gossip. If he was aware of it, he'd made no effort to inform her. She didn't know why she expected that he would, but it would have been a nice gesture.

She stood uneasily behind him in line as the butler announced the guests arriving at the Hargrove dinner. Even Rose knew by now not to show nervousness or embarrassment under any circumstances; Alexandra had to hold hard to her own precepts.

"Are you all right, Lex?" Rose whispered.

Obviously she needed to work on her composed expression, if even a self-absorbed seventeen-year-old girl had noticed her discomfiture. "I'm fine, Rose. Are you ready?"

"Mais oui," her pupil chirped.

"They might think to open a window," Mrs. Delacroix grumbled from the girl's other side, waving her ivory fan wildly. "A person could suffocate in here."

"One can only hope," the earl murmured, stepping

forward to hand over his invitation. "You might conserve air by not speaking as much, Aunt Fiona."

"How dare you!"

Alexandra was thankful he seemed content to spar with his aunt; she didn't quite feel up to it herself. With the exception of a few pointed questions, Lucien had left her alone since yesterday morning, but it didn't help. She didn't need to see him looking at her to know he was paying attention. Very close attention.

By playing the governess and hanging back out of Kilcairn's line of sight, she managed to avoid a direct introduction to Lord and Lady Hargrove, and she breathed a small sigh of relief. As their party passed into the drawing room, though, that same breath caught in her throat.

"Ooh, it's magnificent," Rose exclaimed, grabbing her hand. "Look, they've opened the ballroom, and engaged an orchestra! I didn't know there was to be dancing!"

While the girl jabbered excitedly about the balloons and streamers and the orchestra in the corner, Alexandra turned her attention to the crowd. Lucien had been right about the Howard dinner last week; the guests had been mostly from the *ton*'s lower circles, nobility who looked upon the Earl of Kilcairn Abbey with unreserved trepidation and awe.

Tonight was different. If she had been the fainting sort, the sight of the Duke of Wellington chatting with Prince George over by the refreshment table would have sent her to the floor. She didn't recognize many of the other faces, but she knew she would recognize their names.

"Goodness," she said under her breath, taking a step closer to Lord Kilcairn.

He looked as unperturbed as ever. "Impressive, aren't

they?" he murmured. "Don't worry—in a word-tangle with you, none of them would come out alive."

Alexandra looked up at him, surprised. "Was that a word of comfort, Lord Kilcairn?"

His sensuous lips twitched. "You caught me at a weak moment."

"I hadn't realized such a thing existed."

He *had* heard the rumors, or he wouldn't have bothered with any kind words. Of course, he was practically the only noble in London with a reputation worse than her own.

"Yes, I surprised myself."

"Be careful, my lord," she continued. "I'll think you're getting soft."

A devilish light touched his eyes. "Not where you're concerned."

Before she could reply to that, a tall, blond gentleman approached from one of the side rooms. He offered his hand to Kilcairn, but his gaze danced between her and Rose, as though he couldn't decide upon which to concentrate his attentions.

"Robert," the earl drawled, shaking his hand, "you dragged yourself away from your mother for the evening."

"Actually, I brought her with me," the younger man returned. "As I mentioned previously, she finds life much more exciting here than in Lincolnshire."

Kilcairn's eyes narrowed, and he gestured at the females surrounding him. "Robert, my aunt Fiona Delacroix, her daughter Rose, and their companion, Miss Gallant. Ladies, Robert, Lord Belton."

"My lord," Alexandra said, curtsying. Rose and Fiona followed suit.

So this was Kilcairn's friend—the only one she'd

heard him claim since her arrival. The viscount looked to be in his mid-twenties, five or six years younger than the earl, and a notch or two shorter. Though his brown eyes and smiling mouth were less compelling and fascinating than the lean planes of Kilcairn's face, she concocted that he was quite handsome.

From the looks the two men garnered from the other ladies present tonight, she wasn't the only one to view them with admiring eyes. For a moment she wondered how many of them would have refused if Lucien had offered them what he'd offered her. And then she had to wonder how many of them had already accepted and been discarded.

"Ladies," the viscount returned amiably, nodding. "I've been looking forward to meeting you. Lucien often speaks of his fondness for his cousin and aunt."

"Indeed, Lord Kilcairn has never been one to conceal his true feelings," Alexandra said softly. She'd probably hit on his one positive trait—he didn't lie. Kilcairn's gaze lingered on her, but she pretended not to notice.

"I'm so pleased to meet you," Rose gushed, blushing prettily. "With so many important, daunting personages in attendance tonight, it is quite a relief to meet a friendly one."

"Thank you, Miss Delacroix. Might I return the compliment?"

"Thank you, my lord."

Lucien leaned closer to Alexandra. "Did you teach her that?"

"All except the 'personages' part," she whispered back. "That was a nice addition. She sounded quite good, don't you think?"

"I'll reserve judgment until she's spoken more than a paragraph," the earl murmured back, his low voice in her ear making her shiver. "And even then, my compliments go to you."

"Will you be dancing this evening?" Lord Belton continued.

"*Mais oui*, all but the waltz."

Ah, success. Alexandra smiled as drawing room French proved its usefulness once again.

"Of course. Will you stand up for the first dance with me?"

Rose, her blush deepening, curtsied again. "I would be pleased, my lord."

The viscount took her hand and placed it on his arm. "With your cousin's permission, I should like to introduce you to some of my acquaintances."

Rose looked up at her relation hopefully. "Cousin Lucien?"

Lord Kilcairn, his gaze on Belton, lifted an eyebrow.

"For God's sake, Kilcairn, I'll be good," the younger man said, grinning.

"By all means, then. Take your time."

Alexandra watched the two of them stroll into the crowd. So far, so good. When Rose put her mind to it, she was a fairly quick study.

"That's one out of earshot," Kilcairn said. "Now to find someone for Aunt Fiona to chat with." He gazed about the room for a moment. "Ah, there we are. This way, ladies."

"Oh, there's Lady Halverston." Fiona smiled, waving across the crowd. "I should go see her."

"No," Lucien said flatly. "You've gathered your quota of gossip for the week."

The peculiar warm, fluttery feeling began in Alexandra's stomach again. It seemed Lord Kilcairn's chivalrous streak remained intact—undoubtedly by now Lady

Halverston would know all about her and Lord Welkins.

"Don't you think we should be chaperoning my dear Rose, then?" Fiona asked, picking at the fingers of her gloves. "She's all alone, poor thing."

"I'm more concerned about someone acceptable chaperoning you."

"Lucien, you are an awf—"

The earl stopped before an elderly, elegantly dressed couple seated at one side of the room. "Lord and Lady Merrick, may I present my aunt, Fiona Delacroix? Aunt Fiona, the Marquis and Marchioness of Merrick."

Immediately in good spirits again at the sound of titles, Fiona curtsied. "I am so pleased to meet you," she tittered.

"Ah, thank you, my dear. Do sit with us."

Fiona gracefully sank down onto the chair beside them. Alexandra stepped forward to take the seat on Mrs. Delacroix's other side, but stopped when Kilcairn's warm, gloved hand slid down her bare arm.

"No, you don't," he murmured, leading her toward the salon. "I'm not that cruel."

Alexandra shrugged out of his loose grip, hoping no one else had seen it. "I cannot go about with you," she hissed. "I am an employee."

"Then we'll find Rose for you," he said, as they made their way through the connected series of rooms.

"I can find her myself."

"But then I'll have nothing to do."

"I don't require your gallantry."

"I'm not offering any. I'm trying to avoid boredom."

She made an annoyed sound. "Who are Lord and Lady Merrick?"

"A pleasant old couple from Surrey. Deaf as stones,

both of them. And I imagine they'll never be more grateful for the affliction than tonight."

Alexandra repressed the sudden desire to laugh. "You knew the Merricks would be here tonight, didn't you?"

"Of course."

"Ah. You can't expect to find deaf people on whom you can foist your aunt at every soiree, though. She has acquaintances now."

"Her acquaintances should be grateful for the reprieve."

He gestured her into a salon. Still more of the glittering nobility stood about chatting in the small room, with Rose and the viscount and a half dozen other young people at the far end.

"She hasn't been killed by an angry mob yet, anyway," he said cheerfully.

"I'll go tend to her now." Alexandra turned away.

"Save a waltz for me."

Her pulse fluttering, she faced him again. The time had obviously come for another lesson in propriety. "Rose doesn't waltz."

He looked at her, annoyed. "Did I say I wanted to waltz with cousin Rose?"

From the corners of the room, the murmurings had already begun. The small thrill of nervous anticipation his words started in her was no match for the dread over what everyone must be saying. "I have no business being seen with you."

"I pay your salary," he returned, undaunted, and gestured a footman for a glass of whiskey.

Alexandra wished that pummeling thickheaded, arrogant earls were within her realm of expertise. "Governesses don't dance when the Prince Regent is in attendance, for heaven's sake. And no mama would wish her daughter to marry a man who would dance in public with a . . . with me."

"Call me Lucien, then, and you may go hover about Rose."

"I will not," she declared.

"You're blushing."

"You're embarrassing me. Even if you have nothing to lose by shocking people, I do."

He didn't look a bit repentant, though she supposed that would have been too much to hope for. "You're the one prolonging your own agony," he said, his gray eyes dancing.

She took a deep breath. He'd likely been planning something like this from the moment she'd refused to utter his given name the other night. "Very well, *Lucien*, might I go now?" she enunciated.

Lucien delayed a moment before answering. "Yes, you may, Alexandra," he returned with a slight, superior smile.

He seemed entirely too self-satisfied, when all he'd done was bully her. "If that is the way to please you, my lord, perhaps you should have all of the young, single ladies present line up and say your name. That way you could immediately eliminate the ones whose accent displeases you."

Kilcairn narrowed his eyes. "Go see to Rose."

She escaped before he could come up with a more scathing response. When she reached Rose's side and glanced back, he had vanished. He'd already warned her about playing with fire, and yet she continued to bait him, full knowing what the consequences might be. The only explanation that made sense was that for the first time in her life, she was beginning to enjoy being burned.

* * *

He hadn't considered that he wouldn't be able to dance with her. Despite her cynical commentary, she was right; his purpose at the soiree tonight was as matrimonial as his cousin's. Waltzing with a ruined governess wouldn't gain him any points with husband-seeking young ladies, or their mothers.

Even so, he was disappointed—he wanted something this evening that he couldn't have, and as Alexandra had pointed out, he wasn't used to that. In addition, her continual teasing over his conjugal efforts left him damned annoyed. It would serve her right if he dragged her out onto the dance floor, slid his arms around her slender waist, and waltzed with her all evening long.

With a last glance at the salon doorway, he strolled back through the maze of guests toward the main ballroom. To one side of the refreshment table stood a tall redheaded woman, surrounded by male admirers. Eliza Duggan had been the subject of an interesting contest last Season. He'd won with less effort than he'd anticipated, and tonight he wasn't in the mood for her inane tittering. As she caught his eye he nodded and moved on, looking for more virginal game.

Finally he spied what he sought. The debutantes stood bunched together like a flock of chickens waiting for a fox, all fluffed feathers and nervous chattering. Thank God that Alexandra had talked Rose out of blasted feathers. With another glance behind him to make sure a certain caustic governess wasn't in view, he approached. "Good evening, ladies."

They curtsied like an undulating ocean wave. "My lord."

Though only about half of them were on his finalists' list, all but one at least had some potential. "I have frightfully few partners for this evening," he said in his most congenial tone, "and I was wondering if any of you have a space on your dance card for me."

At the looks of shock and horror they exchanged, Lucien realized he'd made a mistake: he'd given them the option of turning him down. It was a foolish blunder, and he blamed it on Alexandra Gallant. She'd made him so self-conscious about being polite to the delicate little things that he'd strayed into foppishness.

He broke into their stammering before they could flee. "Miss Perkins, surely you have a quadrille left for me. And, Miss Carlton, a waltz would be lovely."

"But . . . Yes, my lord," Miss Carlton squeaked, bobbing another curtsy.

"Excellent. Miss Perkins?"

"I . . . would be pleased, my lord."

With a smile he allowed the rest of them to escape. A prolonged conversation with more than one or two of them at once would kill him. As a reward for his efforts and patience so far, he went looking for another glass of whiskey. Matrimony—what a damned annoying thing to have to spend one's time doing.

"What are you doing, terrorizing the virgins?"

Lucien downed half his fresh glass. "Where's my cousin?"

Robert accepted a glass of Madeira from the footman. "She and Miss Gallant went to check on your aunt. Delightful girl. What were you so horrified of?"

The earl looked at his friend. "You liked my cousin?"

"Yes, I did. She's very charming."

"You're insane."

The viscount chuckled. "I am not. You simply have no tolerance for women."

"I have great tolerance for women under certain circumstances," Lucien corrected. "Though I have to admit, this isn't one of them."

"Which doesn't answer my question. Why the debutantes?"

Lucien glared at him. Finding a proper wife wasn't exactly something he could do without being noticed by the *ton*; and reluctant as he was to discuss anything personal, Robert was bound to find out eventually. Better he do so from the source than from wagging tongues. "Robert, I'm nearly thirty-three, with no male relations to speak of. I'll leave you to do the arithmetic."

He strolled away, angling for the corner where he'd deposited Aunt Fiona. Luckily she hadn't wandered off, and a few feet beyond her, Alexandra and Rose conversed with a striking dark-haired girl a year or two older than Rose.

"Ladies," he said, stopping at Miss Gallant's elbow.

She jumped, the warm smile she had for her companion heating his veins as she looked up at him. "My lord, may I present Lady Victoria Fontaine? Vix, Lord Kilcairn."

No wonder Alexandra looked so pleased. She'd found a friendly face—one that wasn't his. Lucien sketched a shallow bow. "Lady Victoria. A pleasure."

"My lord." She offered a mischievous smile that was obviously used to capture young men's hearts on a regular basis. "I've heard so much about you."

"Really?" He reached down and took her hand, bringing it slowly to his lips. "Perhaps you would favor me with a waltz, and we might discuss the bounds of your knowledge?"

Beside him Alexandra uttered a strangled sound, which he ignored. He hoped she was jealous, but it was far more likely that she didn't want him anywhere near her friends. For someone with a poor reputation, she certainly seemed haughty about his.

"I would be pleased, my lord."

He smiled at the petite woman, relieved at finding another female with something sturdier than feathers for a backbone. "Not as pleased as I am."

"You mean to marry?"

Lucien stifled a strangled sound of his own.

Despite the escalating scale, Robert had at least kept the volume down. Even so, enough of the guests around them had heard that by morning the entire *ton* would know of his search. The viscount deserved to lose a few teeth, but that would only make the gossip more interesting. "Yes, Robert. Didn't I make that clear?"

Lord Belton stared at him. "But you . . . your father . . . you hate—"

"Spit it out," Lucien urged, noting that Alexandra had suddenly become very interested in the viscount's stammering.

"Well, it's just that everyone knows you mean never to marry," Robert finally managed.

"I've changed my mind."

"But—"

"Of course my nephew will marry," Fiona broke in, brushing past Alexandra. "Why should he not?"

Lucien scowled. If there was one thing he didn't need, it was assistance from Aunt Fiona. He opened his mouth to tell her that when a commotion at the nearby refreshment table caught his attention. With an audible gasp, a young lady teetered and collapsed onto the floor. Instantly a herd of older females gathered to hurry her out of the drawing room.

"Poor thing must have gotten too warm," Aunt Fiona

clucked. "I've already complained about how hot it is in here."

"Miss Perkins," Robert announced, craning his head to get a glimpse. "You've lost a dance partner, Lucien."

"Hm. What a coincidence," Alexandra murmured from beside him, "for her to lose consciousness just as we all learned you were looking for a bride."

"All the better for me," he returned in the same tone. "I've eliminated her without having to engage in an actual conversation first."

The music for a quadrille began, and Robert stepped forward to take Rose's hand. "I believe this dance is ours," he said, and led her away.

Lady Victoria's partner likewise claimed her, leaving Lucien in the company of his aunt and Miss Gallant. He hadn't claimed anyone's first dance himself, preferring to observe his options. As Alexandra leaned closer, he was doubly grateful to be without a partner.

"I'm confused, my lord," she said.

"I doubt that."

"I was under the impression that you had no great expectations of your future spouse."

"I don't," he said flatly, fortifying himself for another attack on his matrimonial search methods.

"And yet she must have enough courage to stand up to you, she must be able to converse in an intelligent manner, and she must have at least some knowledge of literature and the arts."

"You think my standards are too high, then."

"I think you have more standards than you're admitting to."

"Well, once I've eliminated every eligible female, I shall simply have to lower my standards until some chit or other matches up to them."

"So perhaps you shouldn't be so quick to eliminate Miss Perkins, after all," she pressed, obviously undaunted by his warning glare. "You may find that no 'chit' can refrain from losing consciousness at the idea of marrying the Earl of Kilcairn Abbey."

"You're right," he said, granting her a smile when he truly wanted to wring her slender neck. "I shall ask her and her parents to accompany me to the races on Saturday. That should give her the opportunity to make a better showing, don't you think?"

"Y-yes, my lord."

If he had to guess, he would say Miss Gallant was wishing she hadn't pursued the conversation. In better humor, he folded his arms and went back to watching the dancers. Aunt Fiona stood closer than he realized, but when he glared at her she hesitated, then trundled off. Alexandra uttered a disgusted sound and followed his aunt back to her deaf friends. Lucien smiled. That would teach her.

Chapter 9

To Alexandra's surprise, Mrs. Delacroix joined her and Rose at the breakfast table in the morning. Even more unexpected, considering that they hadn't returned to Balfour House until well after midnight, Fiona was in good spirits.

"Rose, Miss Gallant, good morning," she said as she swept into the room. "Don't tell me dear Lucien hasn't yet risen? Tea, Wimbole. And honey."

"Actually, I believe Lord Kilcairn went riding this morning, Mrs. Delacroix," Alexandra said as the butler and a footman hurried to provide Fiona with utensils and a cup of tea. "It's delightful to see you up and about so early, though."

"Yes, well, we have things to do today, girls."

Rose swallowed a mouthful of biscuit. "We do?"

"Indeed. Today we will visit the British Museum."

Alexandra nearly choked on her coffee. "We will?"

"And tomorrow I will have the coach take us to Stratford-on-Avon. That Shakespeare lived there, didn't he?"

"Well, yes, but—"

"And, Miss Gallant, you've read his works, haven't you?"

"Yes, I have. What—"

"You must select one of his better-known plays to read to us this afternoon. Rose will take one of the parts, naturally."

Wondering if she'd somehow awakened in the wrong household, Alexandra set down her cup. "I had intended on another lesson in ballroom etiquette today," she said. "The Bentley ball is tomorrow night, as you know."

"You can do your etiquette lessons on the way to the Museum," Fiona said dismissively, "not that I've seen any change in my Rose's good manners. Do you think dear Lucien will wish to accompany us?"

Wondering when Lucien had become "dear" and trying not to frown at the insult to her teaching skills, Alexandra shook her head. "I . . . doubt it, Mrs. Delacroix. He mentioned attending the horse auctions today."

"Mama," Rose finally broke in, her expression as confused as Alexandra knew hers must be, "why are we going to a smelly old museum? Lex was going to take me shopping for gloves and hair ribbons this morning."

Fiona laughed, reaching across the table to pinch her daughter's cheek. "Nonsense. You know we've been wanting to see the sights of London."

"No, we—"

"And the weather is so pleasant, what could be more fun?"

Alexandra could think of several things that would be more fun than accompanying Mrs. Delacroix anywhere in public. Since Kilcairn failed to appear in time to put a stop to the nonsense, though, she reluctantly acquiesced.

Before she'd left the Fontaine household, the British Museum had been on her list of places she wanted to explore in town. The educational foray would undoubtedly be beneficial to Rose, if the girl paid any attention—though it wouldn't help her find a husband.

Still, as Alexandra stood in the Grecian wing two hours later, she was glad they'd come. The drawings she'd seen of the Elgin Marbles were flat, pitiful renderings compared with the works themselves. While Fiona and Rose read aloud every information placard in the room and tittered at the scantily clad statues, Alexandra stood and gazed, her fingers curling with the desire to touch the cool marble forms.

"You are the reason men build monuments," a deep, familiar male voice said from behind her.

"And why is that?" she asked, her gaze still on the sculptures and friezes.

"To see that look of reverence and awe on your face." Lord Kilcairn drew even with her, close enough to touch but not doing so.

Without looking, she knew his eyes were not on the artworks. "I must urge caution, my lord, or you'll further damage your reputation as a cynic."

"I imagine my secret is safe with you."

She turned and looked at him. He had the look of a dark-haired Greek god, and Alexandra wondered if beneath his fashionable clothes the smooth contours of muscle and bone matched the splendor of the statues. As she met his gaze, she blushed. "I thought you were going to the horse auctions today," she said, dismayed that her voice shook a little.

"I was. What do mummies and marble friezes have to do with preparing for a grand ball?"

"Lucien!" Fiona scurried over to join them, Rose in tow. "I knew you would wish to join us."

"I didn't wish to join you," he countered. "I wish to know what in damnation you're doing here."

His aunt's expression became offended. "Dancing and balls aren't everything, you know. My Rose has a particular fondness for history and the arts."

Lucien glanced at his cousin, skepticism in every line of his lean, powerful body. "She does?"

"Indeed. If you ever bothered conversing with her in a civil manner, you might realize that."

If Fiona didn't recognize the hostile look in Lucien's eyes, Alexandra did. She stepped forward, blocking his view of his aunt and cousin. "Well, since we're all here and we're all so fond of history, perhaps we should continue. We were about to head into the African area, my lord."

"You were about to return to the carriage and Balfour House," he stated, folding his arms.

Fiona's chin lifted, and Alexandra steeled herself for a fracas in the middle of the staid British Museum. Enough people had noticed Lord Kilcairn's entrance that keeping a family riff quiet would be impossible once Fiona let loose, but Alexandra glanced about for the nearest escape route for Rose and herself, anyway.

"As you wish, Lucien," his aunt said, and flounced toward the entrance.

With a look between her mother and her cousin, Rose hurried after Fiona. Stunned at the quiet resolution, Alexandra blinked and turned to leave, taking one last look at the Marbles as she passed. The air stirred beside her, and her pulse fluttered in response.

"The next time you feel the urge to look at naked men, do let me know," Lucien murmured.

She blushed furiously. He *had* known what she was thinking earlier, and she didn't know why that should surprise her. Almost from the moment they'd met, he'd seemed able to read her thoughts. Still, she couldn't allow him to think he'd bested her so easily, or she would never have another moment's peace.

"No doubt you would be pleased to indulge me," she returned with as much cynicism as she could muster.

As they stepped around the corner, he grabbed her wrist and yanked her into a curtained alcove where broken plasters and a ladder leaned against one wall. Then his mouth met hers in a hard, hungry kiss. He pressed her back against the wall with the length of his lean body, and his hands swept up her hips to brush breathlessly across her breasts.

Alexandra gasped, sweeping her arms around his shoulders and pulling herself closer against him. Her heart thudded so hard she thought he must be able to feel it in his own chest. Oh, God, she wanted what he kept offering her—to be the focus of his attention, his desire, to be touched and held and loved. It would be so easy to give in. Everyone thought she'd already done it anyway. Everyone but her—and Lucien Balfour.

Slowly he lifted his head. "You want me, don't you?" he whispered, his gray eyes dark and deceptively lazy.

With every bit of remaining willpower, she shook her head. "No. I don't."

He kissed her again, his tongue teasing at her teeth. "Liar."

Alexandra clung to him, trying to regain her breath and her sanity, and at the same time wanting him to continue kissing her. "I am not anyone's mistress," she gasped, reluctantly letting her hands slide from his shoulders.

"Those are only words, Alexandra," he murmured, but released her.

"So are 'food' and 'clothing,' " she said, feeling cold as he backed off to allow her to pass. "They're also real things that I need to survive. I won't rely on your continuing desire for me to keep me fed. I stand on my own."

Lucien looked at her for a long moment. "I will find out who has made you so determined to survive with no help from anyone, " he said quietly.

Shakily she straightened her hair. "You might ask yourself the same question, while you're at it." She left the alcove.

"No, cross her off, too, damn it."

Mr. Mullins looked up from the list spread across the office desk. "As you wish, my lord. Might I ask why, though? Her family is quite wealthy, and there are no siblings, and—"

Lucien plunked his chin into his hand. "She squints."

"Ah. Perhaps you might suggest . . . eyeglasses?"

"If she had any intelligence, she would have taken care of that herself." The murmur of female voices drifted to him from the sitting room, and he caught his breath, listening. They'd bloody well better not be talking about him.

"Well, with the elimination of Miss Barrett, who you say is . . ." He flipped through several pages of notes.

"A mouth breather," Lucien finished, rising. Now the chits down the hall seemed to be laughing. Ballroom etiquette lessons did not involve laughter, as far as he knew.

"Yes, that's right. With her elimination, then, only five prospects remain for your perusal."

"What?" Lucien shook himself. "Yes. Five. That hardly seems enough from which to choose. Find me some more."

The solicitor made a choking sound. "More?"

"More. Do you have some difficulty with that?"

"No, my lord. It's just that . . . well, I thought the idea was to eliminate all prospects but one—that one being the lady you would then—"

"Excuse me," Lucien said, and left the room.

"Marry," Mr. Mullins finished, sighing.

As Lucien strode down the hallway toward the sitting room, the muted voices of his houseguests became clearer. He slowed, listening to the unlikely sound of Rose reading Rosalind's part in *As You Like It,* her voice halting and slow, and pausing in all the wrong places. " 'But are you so much in love as your rhymes speak?' "

Alexandra's voice, much more confident with the words of the hero, Orlando, followed. " 'Neither rhyme nor reason can express how much.' "

Her musical tone stirred his pulse, and he stopped outside the half-open door to listen. How long he might have stood there mesmerized, he didn't know, because just then Aunt Fiona's grating voice broke in. Lucien shook himself and pushed open the door the rest of the way.

"Perhaps I didn't make myself clear earlier," he said darkly, taking in the three of them as they sat on his couch, Alexandra and an open book in the middle. "This afternoon cousin Rose is to be tutored in preparation for the grand ball tomorrow evening."

"But Rose adores Shakespeare," Aunt Fiona protested, pulling the book onto her lap with far less care than it deserved. "I see no harm in indulging the dear child for one afternoon."

"You see no harm in pink taffeta, either. Miss Gallant, a word with you?"

Alexandra rose so quickly that he thought she must have been anxious to escape the harpies' clutches. Keeping in mind her dislike of being overheard, he led her a short distance down the hallway, then turned to face her.

"I don't recall that reading *As You Like It* was to be a part of my cousin's studies," he said, noting that a lock of her burnished hair had fallen across her temple. He wanted to brush it back from her face, and sternly restrained himself.

"Her request surprised me as well, my lord," she returned in a low voice. "I don't feel it is my place, though, to deny anyone the opportunity to indulge in scholarly pursuits."

"She's never read Shakespeare before in her life. I could hear that, even if you couldn't. Rose was not the one whose interests were being indulged."

Alexandra narrowed her eyes. "I am perfectly capable of reading Shakespeare on my own time. Speaking of which, I haven't taken a day off from my duties since I arrived. I would like to have Monday off."

"Why?"

He could practically hear her teeth grinding, her jaw was clenched so tightly. Lucien stifled a grin.

"Since you have requested that I instruct you in propriety, it is my duty to inform you that that is a rude, importunate question, and one which I have no intention of answering."

Damned stubborn, proper chit. "For your information, I am looking out for my own interests. Naturally I don't want you going about looking for other employment opportunities."

"For *your* information, everything you do is for your own interests."

"And?"

"And no, I am not looking for other employment. No one would hire me, anyway." She paused, but he kept silent. "May I be excused on Monday?" she finally asked.

He held her gaze. "No."

Alexandra's eyes flashed. "Then, my lord," she began, her voice tight and angry, "I must resign my post, imm—"

"Yes," he interrupted with a growl. "Yes, damn it."

"Thank you, my lord." She sank down in a curtsy more elegant than his cousin would ever manage. "I'll go see to Rose, as you wish."

Scowling mightily, Lucien watched her vanish back inside the sitting room. It didn't bother him that she had called his bluff; he'd expected that she would. What bothered him was the sudden panic that hit him when she'd mentioned quitting. He'd spoken before he could stop himself, given in before he could come up with a way of saving face.

He'd lost ground in their little battle, and they both knew it. Lucien swore. He needed something to gain him more leverage with her, and he needed it fast.

Obviously word had spread that both the Earl of Kilcairn Abbey and his cousin were looking for spouses. Alexandra sat to one side in Lucien's rented box at Vauxhall Gardens and simply watched.

From the moment they'd arrived, a steady stream of young men and women had stopped by to talk about Paris, the weather, the upcoming hunting season, and the fireworks exploding overhead—anything but matrimony. She'd thought the situation at Balfour House had become as absurd as it could get. Obviously that wasn't the case, and now that the *ton* was involved, the insanity would only intensify.

All of the visitors stared at her, as well, but so far no one had said anything—which she was sure had more to do with Kilcairn's formidable presence than any kindness on their part. She had to admit she was grateful for the unexpected reprieve; a powerful personage had definite uses.

"Did you see that?" Rose said, prancing over from her vantage point at the front of the box. "That was the Marquis of Tewksbury! My dance card for the ball tomorrow night is practically filled already. Oh, I wish I could waltz!"

"It's wonderful," Alexandra agreed. "Remember not to show too much excitement, though. They are the ones who should be pleased at being allowed to spend time with you."

"Good God," Lucien enunciated in an exasperated tone, resuming his seat a few feet away. "I should shoot Robert for wagging his damned tongue. They're like a damned roving pack of hounds, scenting blood."

"Surely you realized that news of a wealthy earl's willingness to marry would spark all sorts of interest," Alexandra said, tucking her wrap closer around her shoulders.

"No, not really. I'm not a pleasant person."

At least he seemed to have gotten over his anger of the afternoon. She wasn't certain why she'd been so insistent, except that she wanted him to know his intoxicating kisses hadn't swayed her from her decision, or her duties. Now she had to think of somewhere to spend the entire day on Monday.

"They don't know you, Lucien," Fiona said.

He lifted an eyebrow. "Meaning they'll eventually realize my unpleasant nature?"

"Of course not."

"A pity. For a moment I thought you'd made a point, Aunt."

Fiona glared at him, then took her daughter's note card and examined it. "You have a quadrille left, dear one. Perhaps your cousin might wish it?"

"Why would I wish that?"

Rose's eyes filled with tears, and Alexandra grimaced. They'd gone for three days without crying, and she'd hoped to extend that dry spell at least through the weekend.

"Dancing with your cousin will indicate that you support and approve her willingness to marry," she pointed out.

The earl eyed her, his expression disdainful. Finally he snatched the card from his aunt's fingers, scrawled his name on it, and returned it and the pencil to his cousin.

"Oh, how splendid," Fiona gushed, clapping.

Alexandra felt like applauding as well, and turned to view the fireworks so she could hide her smile. Whether he had done it to help his own cause or Rose's, the earl had finally made a positive step toward his cousin.

"Well, well, well," a male voice said from the shadows beside the box. "Alexandra Beatrice Gallant, in London."

The blood drained from her face. For a moment she allowed herself to indulge in the absurd fantasy that if she didn't look, he wouldn't be there.

"And who might you be?" Kilcairn's low voice demanded.

He almost sounded jealous, but that was ridiculous—for both of them. Lucien had no reason to be jealous, and she had no right to think anyone would protect her but herself.

"Lord Virgil Retting," the voice replied, while Alexandra stared, sightless, at the dark and flashes of exploding light and tried to regain her wits. "Aren't you going to introduce me, Alexandra?"

She lifted her chin and faced him. "I'm not inclined to, no."

He'd gained weight since she'd last seen him. His square face had rounded, and his neck pushed out against his high, starched collar. The only place he'd lost anything was the top of his head; his brown hair had thinned across the top, and he'd let it grow longer to try to hide his shiny pate.

Lucien was watching her, his muscles tense despite his relaxed pose. A leopard, ready to defend his next meal, except Virgil Retting wasn't interested in the kill—just in mauling her a bit, and leaving her for the buzzards.

"Terribly rude, for an etiquette governess," Lord Virgil chided. "That is how you're earning money these days, isn't it?"

"To repeat myself, Lord Virgil," Kilcairn broke in, "who are you?"

Virgil shrugged. "Guess I'll have to do it myself, then. I'm just in town from Shropshire. My father's the Duke of Monmouth." He smiled, teeth gleaming in the dim lamplight. "Alexandra here is my cousin."

"Not by choice," she said, wishing she could turn and escape.

Lucien touched her shoulder, forcing her to look at him. "You are niece to the Duke of Monmouth?"

She couldn't tell whether his tone was more accusatory, shocked, or curious. "Again, not by choice."

"Ha," Lord Virgil broke in, "how do you think *we* feel? A governess in the family? And now she's tramping about London as if she thought she belonged, trying to embarrass those of us who actually have homes here."

Tittering came out of the darkness, and Alexandra realized the box was still surrounded by members of the *ton* trying to catch Kilcairn's attention and favor.

Slowly Lucien stood, leaning his hands on the outside of the box. "Lord Virgil Retting, you're a buffoon."

For a moment Alexandra had forgotten that catching Kilcairn's attention could be a two-edged sword. She looked from him to Virgil, startled.

"I beg your pardon?" her cousin sputtered.

"That's not necessary," the earl replied, his voice dripping with kindness. "Most buffoons simply can't help themselves. Clearly you're one of those."

"You're . . . Kilcairn, aren't you?" Virgil said, his voice tight.

"Good for you, Lord Virgil. Anything else?"

The tittering had begun again, but this time Alexandra found it gratifying. So many times she'd wanted to slay her cousin in just such a way, and she hadn't dared.

"I insist that you not insult me again in that way, sir. It is completely inappropriate."

Lucien leaned down on one elbow, to bring himself eye to eye with Virgil. "All right. How about if I just say you're fat and stupid, then?"

"I . . . I will not tolerate this abuse!" Alexandra's cousin spat.

"What's wrong? You came here for the purpose of insulting us, and you didn't expect that we might return the favor? Good evening, sir. Go away before I let you drown in your muddy puddle of wits."

Virgil turned to glare at Alexandra, his eyes full of humiliated anger. "My father will hear of this," he snarled.

"And so will the rest of London," Lucien said calmly. "Good-bye."

Alexandra's cousin opened his mouth to reply, thought better of it, and stalked off into the night.

With a yawn, Lucien seated himself again. "Fetch us some Madeira," he ordered one of his footmen, standing just outside the box.

"Yes, my lord."

With a shudder, Alexandra began breathing again. "I'd really like to leave," she muttered, her voice shaking.

"Thompkinson!" Lucien called.

The disappearing servant stopped in his tracks. "My lord?"

"Fetch the carriage."

"Yes, my lord."

"Thank you," Alexandra said, yanking her wrap as closely around her shoulders as she could manage.

"No. Thank you," he returned. "I don't think I can stand this bootlicking and toadeating for another minute."

Fiona patted her arm. "Yes, dear. What a horrid man. Are you really the Duke of Monmouth's niece?"

"Mama," Rose chastised with uncharacteristic sensitivity. "She'll tell us later. Come along. I'm cold, too."

Kilcairn didn't say another word until they arrived back at Balfour House and disembarked from the coach. As his aunt and Rose made their way upstairs, he clamped warm fingers around Alexandra's arm. "Wimbole, Miss Gallant and I will be in the garden for a moment."

"Yes, my lord." The butler returned Alexandra's wrap to her shoulders. The earl hadn't shed his greatcoat, and the heavy cloth rustled against his legs as he followed her outside and down the front steps.

"You want to know why I didn't mention my relations when you hired me," Alexandra said, walking down the rose-lined path. "I have nothing to do with them, and they have nothing to do with me."

"So all the while you were browbeating me about being kind to my relations, you were busily detesting yours. A bit hypocritical, don't you think?"

"No. It's not the same at all. Now, please, I'm very tired, and I don't wish to discuss it any further."

"But I do."

She hadn't thought he would give in. And after he'd insulted Virgil so splendidly, he did deserve some kind of explanation. Her breath fogged in the night air as she sighed. "What do you want to know, then?"

"Your Lord Virgil Retting is obviously a pompous ass," he said flatly, "but there is an older brother, is there not? What of him and your uncle?"

"Thomas, the Marquis of Croyden, is my other cousin. He spends most of his time in Scotland, and I don't know him very well. My . . . uncle, I have nothing to do with, and we're both perfectly happy that way."

"So I see. Why this animosity?"

"Why your animosity toward your relations?"

He sat on the stone bench that stood to one side of the path. "Are we playing tit for tat now? Sit."

Hesitantly she joined him on the bench. Heat radiated from him, and she couldn't help edging a little closer to his dark, solid form. "If you're just being kind, I really have no need to unburden myself to you."

"You think I'm being kind? How unusual for both of us."

She glanced up at him. In the near darkness his gray eyes twinkled, like distant starlight. "You drove my cousin away. That was exceedingly kind."

"That reminds me of another question I have for you. Your tongue is as sharp edged as mine; I've felt its effects. Why didn't you flay Virgil Retting with it? He made a damned easy target."

Alexandra stood and paced a circle around him. "These are *my* troubles. I've dealt with them on my own to this point, and I am perfectly capable of continuing to do so."

The dark form on the bench remained immobile. "I didn't say I meant to do anything about them; I just want to know what they are."

Growling with frustration and knowing he wouldn't let up until she surrendered, Alexandra planted herself directly in front of him. "You first, then."

"Impertinent chit. You know once you begin bargaining with me, you will lose."

She shivered again as a tingling warmth ran down her spine. "I'm not saying anything until you do so."

For a long moment he kept silent, the clouding of his breath the only sign that he wasn't some dark garden sculpture. "I don't want to marry," he finally said, his voice low and subdued.

"What a surprise," she said dryly, shivering again.

He opened his coat, exposing his cravat and lighter jacket beneath. "Sit down before you freeze standing there."

She was becoming frightfully chilled, but she wasn't a fool. Alexandra sat on the bench again, as far from him as she could, then gasped as he reached across her thighs, scooped a hand under her bottom, and dragged her close up against him. With a warm rustle, his arm and one side of his greatcoat enfolded her.

"Do you know anything about my father?" he asked, tucking her up against his broad, solid shoulder.

"Only that he had . . . several mistresses, and that he died nearly fifteen years ago."

"My father had more than several mistresses. Lecherous behavior and gambling were his favorite pastimes, I believe. He and my mother lived under the same roof for three months, until I was conceived. He then retired her to Lowdham, a small Balfour estate in Nottingham. There she gave birth to me, and then spent the next eleven years complaining about how much she missed London and her friends and her life, though she made no noticeable attempt to reclaim any of them. I saw my father a total of six times, including the viewing at his funeral services."

"Oh, my," Alexandra said softly.

"I've been informed on numerous occasions, usually by commitment-minded females, that the combination of viewing my mother's abject helplessness and misery and the state of my parents' marriage left me with a distaste for the whole bloody procedure. I'm inclined to agree."

"But now you do intend to marry, despite your distaste."

He paused again. "I'd drawn up papers to have my cousin James and his offspring inherit the Balfour lands and titles. He died in Belgium last year when a wagon carrying gunpowder exploded in the middle of his encampment. I'm not actually certain it was his body I buried. There wasn't much of him left."

He spoke calmly, but Alexandra felt the tension in the

muscles of his arm and thigh. Almost without thinking, she laid her head against his shoulder, and he relaxed a little. "You miss him," she said.

"I miss him. Anyway, dear Uncle Oscar became the only other living male in my family tree. He went next, which means—"

"Which means if you produce no heirs, Rose's children will inherit your fortune and your title."

"And she's nearly of age, so here we are, in our own little pit of hell and horror."

"You might let her family inherit."

Lucien snorted. "I don't dislike my ancestors that much. Besides, it would deny me the opportunity to turn out like my father. I seem to have followed him in nearly every other aspect of my life."

"I doubt that." Though she'd heard wild, scandalous stories, she couldn't imagine him being intentionally cruel—not to someone who didn't somehow deserve it.

"Any other commentary?" he asked, shifting on the cold stone. "You've read my book, then. Now open yours for me, Alexandra."

She'd hoped he had forgotten her side of the bargain. "Compared with yours, it's fairly simple."

"Enlighten me."

"I don't expect it to soften your heart toward me or my so-called plight."

"I don't have a heart. Speak."

Alexandra tried to edge away from him, but she might as well have been attempting to move iron. His grip wasn't tight, but it was firm and infinitely sure of itself. "Very well. My mother, Margaret Retting, fell in love with and married a painter. His grandfather was an earl, but he had no pretensions of living among the peerage or of being able to afford that life. My uncle had already inherited the dukedom, and as far as he was concerned, Christopher Gallant was a nonperson. He disowned my mother on the spot."

Lucien stroked his finger along the back of her hand. "Continue."

"Both of my parents insisted that I be well educated, as my birthright obviously wasn't going to keep me fed. Two years after they enrolled me in Miss Grenville's Academy, they both died of influenza. It . . . cost me everything I had to bury them and settle their few debts." Her throat tightened, as it did whenever she remembered selling off her mother's jewelry and her father's beautiful paintings for a fraction of their worth.

"And your uncle was unwilling to assist you financially."

It wasn't a question, but Alexandra shook her head anyway. "I wrote him. I didn't even have enough money to finish out the school year. He wrote me back, and the letter wasn't even franked. I had to pay for it when it arrived. His Grace said he had warned my mother against her folly before she married, and he had no intention of paying for her mistakes after her death. I inferred that I was counted as one of her mistakes."

"It's always nice to know there's someone in the world who's more of a bastard than I am," Lucien mused. His fingers stroked hers again, and she wanted to curl her hand into his. "It's comforting, in a way. Tell me the rest of your tale."

"There isn't much else. Miss Grenville arranged for me to tutor students until I finished school, and then I hired myself out as a finishing governess or companion. And here I am, chatting with the Earl of Kilcairn Abbey in his very enjoyable rose garden."

"What of Lord and Lady Welkins?"

With a shove she freed herself from his coat and stood. "That is another tale entirely, and one which has nothing to do with my feelings toward my relations." That wasn't quite true, but she'd given him enough ammunition to use against her tonight. And no one would hear that tale—ever.

He held her gaze. "So you won't tell me anything about it?"

"No, I won't."

He stood, tall and solid as a statue, but much more alive. "Yes, you will. Eventually. When you trust me."

"I will never trust you. You said yourself that if not for your father's will, you would never have taken Rose and Fiona under your care—which, as far as I'm concerned, makes you very like my uncle."

His eyes narrowed in the darkness. "You have a nasty streak yourself, Miss Gallant. And don't put your private hatreds on my shoulders. Some of the facts are admittedly similar, but the circumstances are entirely different." With a swirl of his greatcoat, he turned for the front door. "Good night."

She stood looking after him. "Good night."

Chapter 10

Virgil Retting yawned over a strong cup of tea and tried to keep his eyes focused. He hated rising this early in London. None of his cronies would be up and about for another five hours, and he still felt half fogged from last night's attempts to drown out his encounter with the odious Earl of Kilcairn Abbey.

"If you were so anxious for my company that you had to barge in during my breakfast, you might at least say something. You look like a bloody intoxicated pigeon."

"You told me not to speak to you." Virgil eyed the imposing figure seated several yards away at the head of the huge oak table. "You make it very difficult, Father."

The Duke of Monmouth finished off a honey-slathered biscuit. "I told you not to ask me for money," he corrected, jabbing a table knife in his son's direction. "If you have nothing else to speak about, then remain silent."

Coal-black eyes viewed Virgil for a moment, making him feel like he was five years old and wetting his bed again. Finally the cold gaze returned to the morning's newspaper. The duke had no doubt been awake since before dawn, calling in his London staff of solicitors, agents, and accountants, and settling into Retting House for the Season. The man never seemed to sleep, and had the blasted habit of knowing everything that transpired even during the rare occasions he did close his eyes.

That phenomenon had made Virgil's early arrival at Retting House imperative—if someone else brought Monmouth the news, someone else would get credit for it. "I'm not here about money, Father. Must you always say such shabby things about me?"

"You continue to present me with nothing pleasant to discuss."

"Well then, you should thank—"

The butler appeared in the doorway. "Your Grace, Lord Liverpool and Lord Haster are here for your morning meeting."

"Splendid. Two minutes, Jenkins."

The butler nodded. "Yes, Your Grace."

"But, Father—"

"Virgil, spit it out or wait until tomorrow morning. I'll be free between ten and eleven."

"I saw cousin Alexandra last night."

The duke paused, his tea halfway to his thin, unsmiling mouth. "That is the news that got you out of bed before noon? Of course she's in London. The Fontaines arrived here four days ago."

Virgil shook his head, a rush of pure glee warming his veins. Surprising His Grace was rare enough to warrant marking the occasion with a national holiday. Especially when the surprise meant someone else would be the focus of Monmouth's ire for a change. "She wasn't with the Fontaines."

"She's found employment, then." Monmouth pushed away from the table. "That should keep her out of trouble. Excuse me. It's bad form to keep Haster and the prime minister waiting."

If Virgil knew anything, it was not to let such a moment slip through his fingers, even if he did have to rush it a bit. "She's living at Balfour House," he said to his father's retreating back.

The duke swung around again. "She's living where?"

"At Balfour House. I saw her in a box at Vauxhall Gardens, sitting right beside Kilcairn. He nearly bit my head off when I approached to inquire after her."

"Kilcairn has his cousin in town, I heard. She's of age or something."

"Yes, I saw her, too. She's a pretty little dab. Nearly as pretty as cousin Alexandra."

Monmouth strode to the dining room door, shut it, and resumed his seat. "You're certain it was she, and that she was with Kilcairn? You weren't intoxicated, were you, boy?"

"No, Father." Thank goodness he hadn't begun drinking—heavily, anyway—until after he'd left the Gardens. "It was definitely her, and him. I told you, he was so irritated at my approach, I had to give him a setdown to shut him up. Very hostile, and with a crowd standing about, too."

"Damnation!" the duke exploded. "She should know better, even with her father's poor lineage. After that idiocy we had to suffer through with that nobody Welkins, I've bloody well had enough. If something foul happens again with her after a peer like Kilcairn, the Retting name and reputation would never escape unscathed."

"I could scarcely believe it myself," Virgil said solemnly, nodding. "Right under our noses, as though she didn't care a hang about the standing of her relations. She knows we spend the Season in town."

"She might have gone to Yorkshire if she intended to continue carrying on like a strumpet." Monmouth slammed his fist on the table, rattling the china. "I have a tariff bill to present in Parliament, for God's sake." With another growl he stood again. "I shall make some discreet inquiries about the *ton*'s opinion in this," he announced. "I may have to denounce her publicly if this display continues."

The duke yanked open the door and stomped down the hall toward his private office. Virgil helped himself to the substantial remains of breakfast. Now Kilcairn and Alexandra would see which of them was the stupid buffoon. Their happy little rut-fest was about to come to a very unclimactic conclusion.

"This was a stupid idea," Alexandra said, nibbling on a biscuit and scanning the narrow, quiet street.

"It was your stupid idea," Vixen returned. "Just remember that. And quit looking about like that. I feel like we're about to be ambushed by Bonaparte or something."

"I can't help it." Alexandra nodded her thanks as a waiter brought them another plate of sandwiches. Taking luncheon at the quaint outdoor café had seemed a grand idea for her Monday off, but that had been before Vauxhall Gardens, and before she'd realized her cousin knew she was in London.

"I'm sure Lord Virgil won't even be awake yet. And the clubs are blocks from here, even if he is."

"You're right, of course. It's silly of me. Please, have a cucumber sandwich." It wasn't just Virgil who concerned her, though. It was everyone who might have heard what he said, and everyone those everyones might have talked to about it. She forced a smile. "So. Tell me about your latest conquest."

"No one seems to believe me when I say I'm simply not interested in marriage," Lady Victoria bemoaned, then flashed a quick grin. "If I actually married someone, I wouldn't be able to have those very interesting little conversations like the one I had with your Lord Kilcairn the other night."

Alexandra choked on her tea. "I know you two chatted," she croaked, "but what was so interesting?"

Her friend rose and circled the table to smack Alexandra between the shoulder blades. "For goodness' sake, you're jealous, aren't you?"

She cleared her throat, wishing she'd had a moment's warning before Victoria sprang such a thing on her. "I am not jealous! I don't even like him all that much. And he's not *my* Lord Kilcairn."

"Well," Victoria said, as she took her seat again, "neither are you my companion, governess, or tutor any longer. I don't *have* to tell you anything Kilcairn and I might have discussed."

Alexandra was ready to throttle Vixen if she didn't confess what she and Kilcairn had chatted about. She was not jealous, though; at least she'd made that clear. "I don't care if you tell me anything or not," she said haughtily. "From my experience, Kilcairn rarely says a repeatable word, anyway."

The younger woman chuckled. "You have become positively transparent."

Alexandra frowned. "I have not."

"Oh, all right. I'll take pity on you. He asked me all sorts of questions about you—were you always so annoying, had you ever actually admitted to losing an argument—things like that."

"He did not!"

At that Vixen succumbed to an attack of out-and-out laughter. "He did! I swear it, Lex."

Her frown deepening, Alexandra stood and collected her purse and her parasol. "Well, Kilcairn and I are going to have a little chat, then."

"Before you do that, perhaps you should try to remember just how sweet he was last night."

Alexandra blushed. He'd been sweet indeed, but she hadn't told Vixen about that—only about Vauxhall. Belatedly she realized that that must have been what her young friend was referring to. "Yes, I suppose you're right."

Lady Victoria looked at her quizzically for a moment, then began chuckling again. "I suppose I am. And I suppose there are some tales you don't tell me."

Finally Alexandra gave in to a reluctant grin, then laughed. "You suppose correctly, my dear. Now, let's go somewhere else before my very short streak of luck runs out."

"You really had no clue that your governess was Monmouth's niece?" Robert asked over half a roasted chicken and a tankard of ale.

"None at all. I'm too damned busy creating my own scandals to keep up with everyone else's." Lucien sat back, letting cigar smoke curl up past his teeth.

A third luncheon companion leaned forward to refill his own tankard. "Don't see what it signifies, anyway. A mistress is a mistress."

Taking another puff of his cigar, Lucien glanced across the table at Francis Henning, wondering just who had invited that mutton head to luncheon. Half a dozen wags and gossips had appeared throughout the morning, evidently having forgotten how much he disliked wags and gossips.

" 'Governess,' Henning," he corrected. "Not 'mistress.' One extra syllable."

"What's one syllable among friends?" Robert asked with a faint grin.

"I'll let you know if I run across any to ask."

"Now, Kilcairn," Lord Daubner said thickly, his mouth full of chicken, "if you hadn't looked so damned surprised when Lord Virgil approached, no one would have latched on to it. It's the first time most of us have ever seen you nonplussed, what?"

Robert lifted an eyebrow at him, and Lucien cursed under his breath. William was correct, and so was Henning. He had no regrets over his handling of Virgil Retting, but if he'd had forewarning, he might have waited for a more private arena before reacting.

The gossip didn't bother him much, but it would bother Alexandra—and that concerned him. Her candor last night—and her genuinely dismayed look when her cousin appeared—had made it very clear that she literally had nowhere else to go. He wasn't used to being anyone's last bastion of security, and he certainly hadn't helped anything by displaying his slack-jawed amazement at her lineage.

He really hadn't considered her position at all until the gossips had pounced on him this morning. He'd been more concerned with Alexandra classifying him as another bastard of the same color as her uncle. She'd obviously been upset and angry, but the comparison rang more true than he cared to acknowledge.

Blinking, Lucien brought himself back to the present.

He'd missed a large portion of the luncheon conversation, but from Robert's tense expression, that was probably a good thing. Putting out his cigar, he stood. "If you'll excuse me, gentlemen."

Robert rose at the same time, and Lucien heard his friend's sigh of relief as they exited the club. "I was beginning to worry about bloodshed in there. My compliments to you on your unprecedented restraint."

"I think my ears began bleeding when Henning arrived," Lucien returned. "I didn't hear much after that."

The viscount strolled beside him in silence for half a block. Lucien recognized the preoccupied expression on his friend's face, since he'd worn the same one himself for most of the night. He waited. Finally Robert cleared his throat.

"Not to pry," he began, "but what are you going to do?"

"About what?"

"Well, about your cousin finding a respectable husband, and you finding . . . whatever sort of wife it is you're looking for, with a prime subject of scandal residing in your house. Not the most discreet affair you've ever embarked on."

Lucien ignored that. "She's been residing in my house for more than three weeks now."

"Yes, but now she's a mistress who's concealed her identity from you."

"She is not my mis—"

"And despite your wealth and rank, some of your more promising matrimonial candidates won't want you calling when you have a highborn mistress—governess—under your roof. Especially one who's rumored to have murdered her last lover. That might be exciting for you, but it's dangerous territory for a proper young lady to step into."

"You should be pleased. That would leave more matrimonial candidates for you and your mother to sift through."

"Lucien, don't change—"

Lucien stopped, his breath catching as he abruptly realized what he'd been missing all morning. "What was that you said?"

"I said it was dangerous terri—"

"No. Before that."

Robert looked puzzled. "I said a lot. My pearls of wisdom are for you to commit to memory, not me. What—"

"You said 'highborn mistress.' "

"I said 'highborn governess,' " the viscount amended uneasily. "It was just a general point of information. I didn't mean—"

"Robert, I forgot. I have an errand," Lucien interrupted, stepping out into the street to hail a hack. "I'll see you tonight."

"Yes . . . well, all right," Lord Belton said from behind him as Lucien ordered the driver to Grosvenor Street.

Alexandra *was* highborn. Terribly scandalized—ruined, actually—but highborn. And he needed to think, which was not his strongest suit where Miss Gallant was concerned.

"I'm not going." Alexandra unfastened her necklace and set it back on the dressing table.

Shakespeare looked up at her and wagged his tail.

"Thank you, Shakes. I'm glad you agree."

The door connecting her bedchamber to Rose's rattled. "Lex?"

"Come in," she called, frowning at herself in the mirror. *She wasn't going.*

"Is it too pink?" Miss Delacroix glided into the room, trying to see Alexandra's reaction and the dressing mirror at the same time as she spun about the floor. "I think it's too pink."

"It's perfection. You look lovely."

The girl leaned over and kissed her on the cheek. "Oh, I know. Isn't it wonderful?" She twirled again, all curls and pink silk and lace. "Cousin Lucien can't possibly say I look like a flamingo tonight."

"I'm certain he'll say no such thing." If none of her other lessons had sunk in, at least he knew better than to give Rose even the remotest cause to cry.

"Why aren't you ready to go?" Rose stopped long enough to notice that Alexandra hadn't put on her shoes or her necklace, and that her hair still hung loose down her back. "Cousin Lucien will be angry if we keep him waiting."

"I'm not going." Trying to make light of the news, Alexandra smiled at Rose's surprised expression. "You scarcely need me tonight, and your mother can chaperone you."

"Why aren't you going? What happens if I forget what I'm supposed to say, or if I start conversing with an unacceptable person?"

Pointing out that her own governess was probably the most unacceptable person she would encounter didn't seem helpful. "I just have a bit of a headache," she lied. "Don't worry. You'll be fine."

"Oh, I hope so."

Rose hurried downstairs, and Alexandra sat back in

her dressing chair. She wasn't precisely abandoning her charge; while the gossip was still fresh, she'd be doing more for Rose by her absence than by her presence. And it had nothing to do with her own misgivings about mingling with the *haute ton* after the other evening.

Every time she'd been outside over the past few days, she'd looked for Virgil, and whispers, and people laughing behind her back. She'd only been able to stand luncheon with Vixen for an hour. To deliberately attend a gathering of the *ton*, knowing that they all knew what the Retting side of the family thought of her, was too painful to contemplate.

Her door suddenly opened. "Get dressed," Lord Kilcairn said, stopping just inside the room.

She jumped, remembering Vixen's warning about locked doors, and knowing at the same time why she hadn't heeded it for the past week. "I have a headache."

His expression curious rather than angry, he took in her scanty additions to the lavish room. "And I will have a larger headache with no one to herd the harpies. Get dressed."

He was all in black, tall and strong and magnificent. The sight forcefully reminded Alexandra of the Greek statues in the museum. A sculptor couldn't begin to do justice to Lucien Balfour, though; no piece of stone could possibly capture the glint in his eyes, or the arrogant, confident tilt of his head. She'd always thought that in strength there would be safety, but she knew that being in Lucien's arms would be dangerous—dangerous to the remains of her reputation, to her hard-won independence, and to her heart.

"You're staring."

She blushed furiously. "My apologies. You look very nice this evening."

Immediately he closed the distance between them. " 'Nice'? Define 'nice.' "

Damnation. Alexandra stood, so he wouldn't look so formidable looming over her like that. "I believe your education would have been sufficient to provide you with numerous definitions for the word, my lord."

He pursed his lips, his gaze taking in every inch of her. "I like your hair loose like that," he said, and slowly reached out to run his fingers along the strand that hung down her shoulder.

She shivered. "You'll be late," she reminded him. "And you shouldn't be in here."

"Don't be missish." His arm lowered, but his gaze never left her face. "I gave you Monday off," he said, his soft voice taking the censure from the words. "Not tonight. Attend to your duties, Miss Gallant."

"I would be serving Rose better if I stayed behind."

He frowned. "Show a little backbone, Alexandra."

She blinked. "Beg pardon?"

"Not blunt enough?" He lifted an eyebrow. "Don't be a coward."

"I am *not* a coward."

"Prove it."

"This is not for me; it's for Ro—"

"Now you're just stalling. *I* am Rose's guardian. And *you* are accompanying us, either in your stockings and over my shoulder, or in your shoes and on your feet." He tilted her chin up with his long fingertips. "Is that clear?"

Short of stomping about and throwing things, neither of which was likely to do any good, she seemed to have little choice. "Give me a moment, then."

He folded his arms across his broad chest. "I'll wait here."

Kilcairn was clearly in a bullying mood, and though she would have liked to put him in his place, she seated herself and began putting up her hair. Small shivers ran up and down her spine and made her fingers shake every time she looked in the mirror and saw him standing there, watching her. He continued to observe her as she returned the necklace to her throat and fastened her shoes, as if the Earl of Kilcairn Abbey had nothing better to do than pay absolute, utter, and complete attention to her.

"I should hire a maid for you," he said, leaning forward to lift a last hair clip off the dressing table and hand it to her.

"You don't think my toilette is adequate?"

He shook his head. "You should have someone to brush your hair for you."

"I've brushed my own hair since I was seventeen," she said, trying to cover the tremor in her voice. She almost preferred his direct assaults; they were easier to defend against. "Shall we go?"

Lucien nodded. "After you."

She preceded him down the hallway, still trying to calm the uneasy quavering of her insides. The looks and mutterings didn't bother her; she had encountered them before, she told herself. It was nothing new, nothing different, and nothing to worry about. Just who she was trying to convince, she had no idea, since she wasn't listening to any of it.

"No one will give you any trouble tonight," Lucien's low voice murmured as they reached the foyer. "I won't allow it."

Alexandra stopped. She was almost grateful for the offer of support, because it reminded her that she couldn't rely on anyone else's whims to keep her head above water. She'd learned to swim all by herself. "Thank you, my lord, but I can look after my own interests. I am not some shivering peagoose."

"You're shivering now," he said in the same soft voice.

"I am n—"

"Thank goodness you're coming!" Rose pranced forward and grasped her hand. "Now I shan't worry about anything."

"The rest of us will shoulder your load, then, cousin," Lucien said, intercepting Shakespeare and handing the terrier to the butler. "Don't wait up for us, Wimbole," he instructed.

The butler nodded. "Very good, my lord."

They climbed into the coach, the earl seating himself opposite Alexandra as he usually did. She hurriedly looked away, busying herself with last-minute instructions and reminders for Rose. His mere presence was enough to put her on edge with nervous excitement. A little less nervousness tonight would have been quite all right.

"Do you think Prince George will be there?" Rose asked. "What if he asks me to dance?" Her blue eyes widened. "What if he asks me to waltz?"

"Step on his foot," the earl suggested. "That'll make him leave you alone."

"Lucien!" Fiona chastised. "Oh, I'm so nervous. Smile as much as you can, my dear."

Alexandra cleared her throat. "If His Majesty asks you to waltz, curtsy and thank him, and then inform him that you are not yet out. If he persists, waltz with him. He is the Regent, after all."

"Will Lord Belton be there, do you think?"

"Yes, he'll be there." Lucien glanced at his pocket watch.

"Don't forget, my dear, your dance card is already full."

"Oh, no! What shall I do if he wants—"

"He may have my dance," Kilcairn offered as he faced the window, looking like nothing so much as a black panther desperately wanting out of his cage.

"No, he may not!" Fiona burst out. "You must dance with your cousin!"

"I'll dance with whomever I please, Aunt."

Mrs. Delacroix began picking at the delicate lace on her sleeve. "Oh, no," she fretted. "Miss Gallant said you must dance with Rose, or she'll never make a good match. You promised, Lu—"

He threw his hands up. "All right! Just stop cackling for a moment."

By the time the coach jockeyed into the crowd of vehicles aiming for the drive at Bentley House and pulled them up to the door, Alexandra's imagined headache had become real. She was more than happy to disembark from the coach and take a deep breath of cool night air.

"Lex, stay close by me," Rose whispered, wrapping her arm around her companion's. "There are so many people, I don't even know who to look at first."

"First, look at your host and hostess," Alexandra suggested. "After that, look at whomever you want. All of the young gentlemen will be looking at you."

"Or at the liquor table," Lucien put in from over her shoulder.

He was relentless. "Oh, look," Alexandra said, gesturing toward the packed entry to the ballroom, "it's Julia Harrison. Isn't she on your list of finalists, my lord?"

To her surprise, he gave the young woman only a disinterested glance. "Time for that torture later." He handed their invitation to a waiting footman and ushered them into the ballroom.

"The whole world is here," Rose breathed, holding Alexandra's arm tightly.

"The best part of it is," Mrs. Delacroix agreed happily. "Everyone's simply glittering."

Alexandra was more interested in Kilcairn's conversation. "You've given up looking for a bride, then?" A small, very well hidden part of her fluttered into excited life.

"Not a bit." He gestured for a glass of port.

The delicate, fluttering thing flopped over and died. "Ah. Just not tonight, then."

His sensuous lips curled into a smile. "Not exactly. My search has narrowed to the point that I can conclude the interviewing. I'm nearly ready to enter into negotiations."

The headache began pounding at her skull with renewed enthusiasm. "Well, congratulations. I never thought you would find one, much less several. How will you make your final decision?"

Lucien shook his head, his gaze unreadable. "I haven't determined that yet, though I have a few ideas."

"Who are the lucky finalists?"

"I'm not about to tell you, Miss Gallant. I don't want you making fun of the poor things."

Whoever they were, Alexandra abruptly didn't like them. She pasted a cynical smile on her face. "Well, might I suggest you hold a poetry contest for your finalists? You could marry the winner—or the loser, depending on your final determination as to the importance of literary acumen."

"Hm," he mused, though she couldn't tell whether he was angry. "I'll take your suggestion under consideration."

Lucien wondered what Alexandra would have said if she'd known how strongly he was considering placing her on his list—at the top of his list. As he saw it, he had no choice in the matter, anyway. None of the other so-called contestants he'd encountered could match even her shadow.

Rose was surrounded by gentlemen vying to renew their positions on the evening's official dance card. He supposed it was shoddy that he didn't really give a damn who married her, so long as it got her and Fiona out of his life. Lucien glanced at Alexandra again, a goddess in yellow and sapphire—which, despite Madame Charbonne's best efforts, didn't begin to do justice to her turquoise eyes.

Lord Belton appeared, and Lucien grabbed him by the elbow before he could join Rose's contingent. "Dance with Miss Gallant," he ordered.

Robert shrugged free of his grip. "Good evening, Kilcairn."

"Dance with—"

"I heard you," the viscount interrupted. "Why should I dance with your cousin's governess?"

"Better the governess than the student."

A thin line appeared between Robert's brows as he frowned. "I delight in dancing with Miss Delacroix."

"I'm not amused, Robert. You've had your fun at my expense."

"I'm not joking. Rose's company is quite refreshing, compared with the eager misses my mother's been throwing at me."

He seemed serious, but Lucien wasn't in the mood to debate over how refreshing his cousin's company was. "I concede to your rampant insanity," he said.

"It's not—"

"I will owe you a favor if you dance with Miss Gallant."

Robert paused in midresponse. "A favor."

"Yes."

"Hm. Very well. A favor. This should be amusing."

Lucien trailed behind the viscount as he returned to the thinning crowd around Rose. Alexandra stood to one side, her expression easy, unless he looked into her eyes. He probably shouldn't have made her accompany them, but the idea of an evening alone with the Delacroix ladies—and without her—horrified him.

"Lord Belton!" Rose exclaimed, curtsying.

"Miss Delacroix. You look lovely this evening."

"Thank you, my lord."

Robert cleared his throat, glancing sideways at Lucien. "I was just asking your cousin if I might call on you tomorrow afternoon for a carriage ride and picnic in Hyde Park. He graciously agreed."

Her blue eyes widening, Rose clapped her hands together. "Really, cousin Lucien?"

Lucien kept the scowl from his face as he nodded. "Of course." He elbowed the viscount in the back.

"And now," Robert continued, jumping, "I see they are about to commence the first quadrille of the evening. Might you—"

"Oh, my dance card is full," Rose said mournfully, shooting a glare at her mother. "I wanted to save one for you, but—"

"No matter. We'll have more time to chat tomorrow."

The viscount turned to Alexandra. "Would you do me the honor then, Miss Gallant?"

She blanched, her gaze darting from Lucien to Robert and back again. "My lord, I don't think—"

"Why, yes!" Aunt Fiona exclaimed, making Lucien wonder briefly if she'd completely lost her mind, as well. "You are the Duke of Monmouth's niece. Surely you're allowed to dance."

"But I don't want to d—"

"Allow me to insist," the viscount pressed.

Lucien stood back and watched, feeling like a master puppeteer as everything fell into place without his having to say a word. If Robert's idea of a favor was to be able to converse with and feed Rose, he was welcome to do so—though that seemed like a very large waste of time.

Alexandra agreed to dance the quadrille with Robert. For a moment Lucien considered taking the floor as well. That, though, was not what he wanted—to touch her fingers in passing and relinquish her immediately to some overweight peer. When he danced with her tonight—and he would—it would be a waltz.

Chapter 11

Alexandra watched Rose turn, dip, turn again, and take her partner's hand. If the girl did one thing truly well, it was dance. Of course, watching her from the side of the room instead of the middle of the dance floor would have made the view even more satisfactory.

"You've taught her well." Lord Belton uttered his compliment in the same smooth tone Lord Kilcairn used when he wished to be charming. The viscount's efforts, though, weren't nearly as effective as the earl's lures. In response to Robert Ellis's compliments, nothing the least bit shivery happened to her. Instead, she felt rather annoyed that he would try such a tactic on her.

She waited until the dance brought him back to her side. "Her skill is natural, my lord. I take no credit."

"Ah." He stepped away and then around and back again. "You've a fine talent yourself."

"Thank you, my lord." At the moment, dancing was a talent for which she was exceedingly grateful. She couldn't have turned down the viscount's request without causing a scene, and just standing still beneath the eyes of the *ton* was difficult enough without worrying about tripping or missing a step.

"My pleasure."

She glanced at her partner in time to catch him looking across the wide, mirrored ballroom at Kilcairn. The earl leaned against the wall, oblivious to the young ladies nearby trying to catch his attention. With everyone watching, she didn't dare glare at him, but he seemed to know her feelings. Giving a slight, sensuous smile, he lifted an eyebrow.

Obviously he was up to something; he wasn't even attempting to look innocent. And she had a good idea what that something must be. "Lord Belton," she asked as she and her partner met again, "did Lord Kilcairn put you up to dancing with me?"

The viscount blinked. Alexandra reflected that young ladies didn't ask such direct questions, particularly of their social superiors. But she was not trying to snare a husband, nor to impress anyone with anything other than her success with Rose. If she was being too blunt, she blamed it on Kilcairn's influence and aggravating manner, anyway.

"I . . . generally don't require another man to convince me to dance with a beautiful woman, Miss Gallant."

She met his gaze. "Not generally," she repeated. "Well, though I thank you for the gesture, your gallantry isn't necessary. I don't require dancing with a handsome gentleman to convince me to do my duty by Miss Delacroix."

He looked surprised again. "You speak your mind, don't you?"

"I have found it pointless to do otherwise. Fortunately, I am in a position where I have very few people to impress. Everyone else knows exactly what they think of me without us ever having had occasion to meet."

"Good God," the viscount muttered, but in the flash and swirl of dancers she couldn't tell whether her response amused or appalled him.

Whichever it was, at least he was a gentleman. Lord Belton finished the quadrille with her and guided her back to Mrs. Delacroix before excusing himself from their group—in something of a hurry, Alexandra thought, though that might simply have been her interpretation. Rose, out of breath and flushed with excitement, joined them a moment later.

"Oh, did you see? The Marchioness of Pembroke was right in front of me! And I think I saw the Duke of M—"

"Not too excited, Miss Delacroix," Alexandra reminded her with a smile. "Calm, and quiet. Remember, they—"

"They should be as thrilled to meet me as I am to meet them," Rose finished, giggling.

"I would be thrilled to be introduced to any of them," Fiona stated with a scowl. "Everyone just ignores me, like I'm not even here."

"If only that were true," Kilcairn agreed as he joined them.

Alexandra stepped up to his broad shoulder. "Don't do that again," she murmured at his back.

"Do what?" he said to the air.

"If I want to humiliate myself, I can go dance naked on the refreshment table. I don't need you or your cronies to embarrass me."

Lucien turned around and met her gaze. "I think watching you dance naked would be a very uplifting experience. I hope you'll indulge me one day."

Flushing, she moved away again. "Don't expect me to participate in your amusements."

"I'm trying to encourage you to participate in your own."

There he went again, acting as though he knew everything. "I am not some deprived—"

"Excuse me, Miss Gallant?"

She jumped and whirled around. "Yes . . . sir?"

The large, heavyset gentleman shot a glare at Lucien. "For God's sake, Kilcairn, introduce me."

The earl scowled, but complied. "Daubner, Miss Gallant. Miss Gallant, William Jeffries, Lord Daubner."

"Pleased, Miss Gallant," the big man said, taking her hand. "Belton wagered me ten quid I wouldn't dare waltz with you. Said you'd put him in his place, and you'd do the same to me in a Yorkshire minute."

Alexandra felt her temperature rising. "I am *not* going to be the object of anyone's wagering."

Lord Daubner smiled, revealing a row of slightly crooked teeth. "You *are* spectacular. I'll split the winnings with you."

"I am not—" Alexandra stopped as she caught the expression on Lucien's face before he wiped it away. He didn't want her dancing again—which was odd, considering he'd started the mess. "I am not going to split your winnings," she amended, smiling, "but I would be happy to waltz with you, my lord."

"What would your wife say, Daubner?" the earl asked without a trace of his usual cynical humor. "I thought she didn't approve of you socializing with other females."

"Lady Daubner's in Kent with a sick aunt. Besides, Kilcairn, like you said—no need to tell her everything, what?"

Alexandra watched Lucien choke down his reply and manage a half-civilized nod. To her eyes, he looked jealous—again—and a small thrill spun down her spine. As Lord Daubner escorted her onto the dance floor, though, she told herself it was more likely that Lord Kilcairn didn't want his friends playing with his latest toy. But she was one toy with a mind of her own.

"Lucien, be a dear and fetch us some punch," Aunt Fiona cajoled.

He kept his gaze and his attention on the departing governess. "No."

Alexandra might have thought she was teaching him a lesson by leaving him stranded with the harpies while she went and enjoyed herself, but it was a lesson he had no particular desire to learn. He gestured at a footman.

"Fetch the ladies some punch," he ordered.

"Yes, my lord."

"Thank you, cousin Lucien."

He nodded. "Excuse me."

Alexandra was waltzing, which annoyed him in the extreme. She was supposed to be waltzing with *him*. Lucien scowled, then spied Loretta Beckett, one of the remaining females on his rapidly shrinking list.

"Miss Beckett," he said, "would you do me the honor?" He gestured at the other dancers.

Miss Beckett curtsied. "With pleasure, my lord."

She waltzed adequately, thank Lucifer, and whoever had dressed her had enough sense to put her in dark colors to contrast with her pale skin and complement her brunette hair. Lucien maneuvered them toward Alexandra and Daubner. Realizing he'd been silent since they'd stepped onto the floor, he glanced down at his partner's upturned face. *What did one begin with? Ah, that was it.*

"How are you enjoying the weather this Season?"

Miss Beckett smiled. "In truth, my lord, I've hardly had time to spend two minutes together out-of-doors. I've received reliable reports from those luckier than I that it's pleasant."

"Yes, I agree," he said absently. Daubner danced the way he thought, meandering about the room in a completely random fashion. Lucien cursed, wishing the idiot would pick a path so he could move in and establish a position within earshot. "And what do you think of the fashions from Paris?"

"I think that as everyone else seems enamored of them, I had best like them, too."

Damn Daubner. Alexandra might as well have been dancing with a bull in a china shop. Unless Lucien began mowing couples down, he'd never catch up. "What's next? Ah. Your favorite author."

"I suppose everyone says Shakespeare, for how could one not, but aside from the Bard, I have become quite fond of Jane Austen. Have you read any of her works?"

Belatedly Lucien turned his attention to his dance partner. "Yes, I have. Her views of the nobility seem somewhat harsh, but I suppose it's a matter of perspective." He glanced from her to his fast-moving governess, sensing a basic similarity in literary acumen. "Might I ask who is responsible for your education, Miss Beckett?"

"I attended Miss Grenville's Academy in Hampshire. Have you heard of it?"

That answered that question, though Miss Beckett's responses seemed more . . . rehearsed than Alexandra's witty, spontaneous ones. It was the difference, he supposed, between an apt student and an apt person.

Lucien paused, nearly missed a step, and rushed the next one to catch up. Alexandra Gallant was not just a bright, lovely female; she was an intelligent, attractive person. He couldn't recall if he'd ever considered a woman to be an actual, sensible human being before.

"My lord? Have you heard of Miss Grenville's Academy?"

Lucien took a breath, trying to pull his scattered thoughts back into cohesion. "I have. The Academy has an impeccable reputation." At least it did as far as he was concerned. "My cousin's companion attended there."

"Yes, I know. Begging your pardon, my lord, but on the Academy's behalf I must say that most graduates are not as . . . wild as Miss Gallant."

"I know. It's a damned pity."

"Beg . . . beg pardon?"

He smiled, not the least bit amused. "So you think I might have made a better choice on my cousin's behalf?"

"Now that you mention it, Lord Kilcairn, it surprised me to hear that Miss Gallant had found employment in London."

He wondered if Miss Beckett had any idea how thin the ice was beneath her feet. Whatever his private plans for Alexandra Gallant, she resided beneath his roof and was therefore under his protection. At the same time, he knew Alexandra wouldn't appreciate his making a scene, and he could practically hear her voice telling him not to frighten the debutantes.

Lucien continued to gaze at his waltz partner levelly. It had been a very long time since he'd felt compelled to do what someone else told him to do, even if that someone happened to be Alexandra Gallant. "Miss Beckett, I realize it's early in the Season, but do you have anyone in particular paying his attentions to you?"

Her dark eyes positively sparkled. "I have a few beaux," she admitted. "No one I've lost my heart to, though."

"You can't lose a thing you don't possess," he returned in the same easy tone. "I suggest you marry quickly, my dear, before your looks alter to match your character. I doubt even the ugliest lord in England would care to be leg-shackled to a saggy-breasted witch with foul breath and warts."

Miss Beckett made a small, gasping sound. Her fair skin paled even further, and her pretty brown eyes took on a glazed look. And then she fainted.

The proper, gentlemanly thing to do would have been to catch her against his chest and carry her to one of the chaise longues scattered about the edges of the room. Lucien stepped back and let her fall, noting that she recovered enough to collapse gracefully and without hitting her head against the polished floor.

A herd of females rushed in to control and minimize the damage, while Lucien didn't bother wiping the annoyed expression from his face. As the women transported Miss Beckett to safety, he turned on his heel and strolled out to the balcony for a cigar.

"What did you do to that poor girl?"

Lucien finished lighting his cigar on one of the balcony lanterns. "Aren't you breaking your own rules, Miss Gallant? Rushing out to the balcony to see a single gentleman?"

"I brought an escort."

He turned around. Daubner, looking equal parts amused and terribly put out, hovered in the doorway just beyond Alexandra. "Go away, Daubner," Lucien ordered.

"You stay right there, my lord," Alexandra returned,

before the baron could take a step. "What did you say to that girl, Lord Kilcairn?"

"I will not be interrogated by a governess." *And certainly not in front of company.* "Daubner, go away."

"He is not going—"

"Daubner, out!"

"Apologies, Miss Gallant," the baron mumbled, and fled.

"Damnation," she snapped.

Lucien closed the distance between them. "Cursing now? How improper."

Narrowing her eyes, Alexandra backed toward the curtained door. "I'm sure you think that chasing your friend away is the height of hilarity, or that since I'm ruined, you might as well have your amusement." She lifted her chin. "Or perhaps you don't care."

"Do you have a point?"

"Yes, I do. After you see Rose married, I will have to go to one of your peers out there in the ballroom for employment. I'd hoped to prove myself a competent governess, despite the rumors. I will not have you destroying my chances of making a decent living." With a flounce of her skirts, she turned her back on him. "Good evening, my lord."

His own anger deflated as she strode back toward the ballroom. "What do you mean, 'good evening'?" he asked, following her.

"It's a common expression, my lord, denoting a departure. I'm sure you're familiar with—"

Alexandra stopped in the doorway, just as Lucien clamped a hand down on her shoulder. His long fingers had the strength of a steel vise, but she was actually grateful for his steadying grip as she caught sight of the figure standing just inside the ballroom.

"Cousin Alexandra."

Not again, she thought, as Virgil Retting sketched her a shallow, overwrought bow. *Not now*. She shrugged her shoulder, and Lucien released her. "Virgil. I was just leaving. Good night."

"What a pity."

He'd brought friends this time, she realized. A half dozen young men stood ranged behind him, ready to laugh at every witticism he managed to utter at her expense. "Yes, I'm sure you're heartbroken. Excuse me."

"But I wanted to dance this next waltz with you, cousin. We so rarely frequent the same establishments. For example, I hardly expected to see you here tonight. I see, though, that you're still on Kilcairn's tether."

She felt Lucien stir behind her. Whatever he said this time would probably mortally wound Virgil; apparently he had already whetted his appetite for mayhem on Miss Beckett this evening. "I would be happy to dance with you, cousin," she said quickly, before her volcanic-tempered employer could erupt. "I hadn't realized you wished to socialize with me."

Her cousin chuckled, glancing back to be certain that he still had an audience. "Well, it's not socializing, precisely. I try to perform a certain number of charitable deeds each month, and I was one short. Dancing with you will catch me up."

The gallery laughed, and Alexandra felt her cheeks turn scarlet. She knew exactly what she wanted to say in response; the words had formed almost simultaneously with his vacuous commentary. She clamped her jaw shut and smiled. "As it pleases you, Lord Virgil."

"I was wondering something, Lord Virgil," Kilcairn said in a carrying voice from behind her.

"Please don't," Alexandra whispered.

Virgil's smile faltered for a moment. "Wondering what, Kilcairn?"

She felt the earl hesitate. Finally he took her arm, wrapping it over his. "I must decline. Miss Gallant has urged me to be polite."

"Is that all she's urged you—"

"And it is obviously impolite to engage in a battle of wits with an unarmed man."

Alexandra breathed a shaky sigh of relief. Lucien did care about how far he went, and what it might cost her. And whether he realized it or not, he had quite possibly just saved her life.

Virgil's face turned a blustering red. "Kilcairn, you—"

Lucien lifted his free hand. "Take a moment to consider your next words, Lord Virgil. I have *very* limited patience."

Before Virgil could venture a reply, if he intended to do so, Lord Kilcairn guided her past the gauntlet, which seemed to last the length of the ballroom. She knew she should thank him, or run away, or something, but all she could do was keep her feet moving and grip Lucien's arm so she wouldn't stumble.

"Do we have to go home?" Rose asked plaintively, as they rejoined her and Mrs. Delacroix. Alexandra gathered her wits enough to notice that Lord Belton had reappeared beside the girl.

"Yes, we do," Lucien answered.

"That will never do. Please stay," Alexandra managed, dropping her hand from his arm and hoping she hadn't left a bruise. "This is your evening, Miss Delacroix. It was never intended to be mine, for heaven's sake."

"Yes, Miss Gallant is right," Fiona agreed. "Rose's

dance card is full. It would be horribly rude if we had to leave early."

"You should stay, Lex," Lady Victoria Fontaine said, as she appeared beside them. She curtsied. "My lords, Mrs. and Miss Delacroix."

"Lady Victoria," Lucien acknowledged, his expression easing a little.

Alexandra didn't like that, or the way everyone was trying to bully her. "Vixen, go away," she grumbled. "We're starting to look like an armed encampment."

"Don't let that idiot Virgil send you running off again, Lex."

"Again?" Kilcairn murmured.

Oh, no. "My lord, please don't—"

"You're staying, Miss Gallant."

She knew instinctively that no one argued with that tone, but she had little choice. "If I stay, I'll have to dance the next waltz with him." With impeccable timing, the orchestra chose that moment to strike up the waltz. "I promised."

Lucien took her hand. "You're waltzing with me."

The strength of his grip made any further argument impossible. She was glad for that; it saved her the disgrace of conceding. And she supposed it was disgraceful that she did want to dance with him. Despite Virgil, and despite the further opportunity for scandal, she wanted to dance in Lucien Balfour's arms.

"No arguments?" he asked, sliding his hand around her waist and pulling her close.

"None. Except that six inches of light should show between us the entire time we're waltzing."

Unexpectedly he laughed, a wicked, merry sound that made her smile back at him.

"What's so amusing, my lord?"

"Six inches isn't nearly enough, Alexandra. Not where you and I are concerned."

She met his gaze as they swayed into the dance, color rising in her cheeks. Even though she didn't know precisely what he was referring to, she felt assured that it was scandalous—and from her experience kissing him the last time, she had a good idea that he was discussing something anatomical.

"Hm," he murmured. "Still no arguments?"

"You're only trying to distract me so I won't remember that I was leaving even before Virgil appeared."

Light gray eyes looked steadily back at her. "I wasn't trying to hurt you, you know."

"Don't be nice." Good lord, he was graceful. She'd never danced with anyone as self-assured and skilled as he was.

"You're contradicting your own lessons now—wasn't I supposed to work on being nice?"

"I don't want to talk about it," she snapped. "Just please don't antagonize Virgil any further."

For a moment they danced in silence, and for that time she could almost forget the hostile looks and her hostile relation in the shadows at the edges of the room. Here, with the Earl of Kilcairn Abbey, they didn't dare approach, and didn't dare say anything cutting or unkind. Alexandra looked up into his eyes again and found him watching her closely, as he always did. "Now, my lord. What did you say to Miss Beckett?"

"Did you know her at Miss Grenville's Academy?"

"No. I knew she attended, but that would have been well after I left."

"I told her she had foul breath and warts. And saggy breasts."

Some of his distractions were definitely more effective

than others. "Foul . . . Why in the world would you say such a thing?"

"If you won't discuss Lord Virgil Retting and what kind of hold he has over you, then I have no intention of explaining Miss Beckett's shortcomings."

"You don't need to know everything."

"I need to know everything about you."

Her pulse fluttered unsteadily. "Why?"

His lips curved in his slow, sensuous smile. "I don't know."

That answer unsettled her more than all of his charming comments and insinuating lures. It mirrored how she felt about him: she had no idea why he so intrigued her, but she felt almost powerless to resist even his most aggravating, obvious enticements. "Can I trust you?" she whispered.

"You have to decide the answer to that, Alexandra," he said after a moment. "But we won't discuss your idiot relation any further until we've returned to Balfour House and my idiot relations are safely locked away for the night."

The music stopped. Lucien remained in front of her, one hand still warmly around her waist, as the other dancers drifted toward the refreshment tables.

"Let go," she murmured, less embarrassed than she expected. "Go find another female for the next dance. I believe it's a quadrille."

"If I'm prancing about with some other female," he said, releasing her, "I won't be able to make certain you haven't fled into the night."

Thank goodness he was being arrogant and bossy again. Her legs had been beginning to feel rather wobbly, no doubt a reaction to his unexpected empathy. "You'll just have to trust me," she said, and returned to Mrs. Delacroix's side.

Chapter 12

Being the subject of further gossip might prevent Alexandra from ever finding another decent position, but it certainly didn't discourage the men present at the Bentley ball—or the less stodgy ones, anyway—from asking her to dance.

She had decided to sit quietly in a corner with Mrs. Delacroix and think; she had a great deal to contemplate. Immediately, though, she realized that quiet reflection would be an impossible task. Fiona had apparently acquired gossip about every guest in attendance, and she insisted on sharing it. In addition, some gentleman or other approached to claim Alexandra's hand for every remaining dance that evening.

Alexandra wasn't naive enough to pretend that their interest baffled her, but since they considered her to be Kilcairn's property—and she frowned as she realized that—at least their innuendos remained fairly restrained. And their continuous attentions served both to keep Virgil Retting at a distance, and to keep Fiona's wagging tongue from deafening her.

"I'm exhausted!" Rose said as she slumped against the coach's soft cushions at the end of the evening. "I'm so glad we stayed."

Fiona patted her daughter's knee. "You were so well liked, child! Did you see, Lucien, how many young men—and ladies—wanted to converse with our Rose?"

The earl had settled back into one corner, his eyes closed in the half dark. "Miss Gallant has succeeded beyond my wildest expectations."

"That is because Rose is a superb pupil," his aunt argued.

Alexandra flexed her aching toes in their thin slippers. "She is more than superb."

"You know what I've been thinking?" Mrs. Delacroix sat forward, her green eyes gleaming.

"I couldn't begin to imagine," Lucien said dryly.

"Rose's birthday is scarcely ten days away. You should throw her a grand party, Lucien. Invite only the best of London. I will help arrange for the decorations and entertainment. It will be so festive!"

Finally the earl opened one eye. "What horror," he said, and resumed his supposed nap.

Rose sniffled.

"My lord," Alexandra said hurriedly, trying to stop the flood before it could begin, "the decision whether to host a party should never be made at two o'clock in the morning—and certainly not after such an exhausting evening."

"Very well," he muttered. "I'll decline in the morning."

Rose's eyes began to fill with tears, but Alexandra motioned at her to be calm and indicated that she would take care of matters. They rode the rest of the way in silence, and she almost thought Kilcairn had fallen asleep—though the more likely explanation was that he simply didn't want to talk to his relations any longer. Alexandra didn't, either. She was too worried over whether he would renew his questions about Virgil Retting once they returned, and what she would tell him if he did.

She knew what she *wanted* to tell him—everything. Just to be able to speak to someone else about her private woes would be such a relief. After tonight, and the way he'd come to her rescue at least twice . . . No one had ever attempted to rescue her before. Alexandra smiled a little into the near darkness. How odd to think that her one and only champion had a reputation at least as shoddy as her own.

The coach rocked to a halt. Lucien stirred, opening his eyes with no sign at all that he'd been napping, and followed the three women into the house. Alexandra shed her wrap and her bonnet and started up the stairs behind the Delacroix ladies.

A warm, strong hand slid around her waist and pulled her backward a step, holding her firmly against a tall, strong chest and torso. "Tell them good night," he whispered into her hair.

"Good night, Rose, Mrs. Delacroix," she said, trying to keep her voice steady.

Rose stopped and turned around, peering down into the shadowy foyer. "Aren't you coming to bed, Lex?"

"I'll be along in a moment. I need a new selection from the library."

"I couldn't keep my eyes open to read," Fiona declared as she reached the top of the stairs. "I'm going to sleep until noon. Good night, Lucien."

"Aunt Fiona. Rose."

"Cousin Lucien."

Alexandra waited until she heard two doors close. "Let go."

"No."

"Fine. We can stand in the foyer all night, then."

The muscles across his hard, flat stomach tightened, as though he was suppressing a laugh—or a curse. His grip loosened and slid away. "Have you ever lost an argument?"

She put several steps between them and then turned around. "No."

"Hm. Neither have I."

Relieved to find him still in good humor, she couldn't resist another dig. "By the way, you lost points during your argument with Lord Virgil."

Lucien took a step closer. "And how did I manage that?"

"You used a cliché. To be precise, 'a battle of wits with an unarmed man.' "

A slight frown furrowed his brow. "That is not a cliché. And I wanted to be certain he understood the insult, anyway. I hate wasting my finest material on the unworthy."

She nodded. "Of course. Well, good evening."

The earl took another step toward her. "Not so fast, Alexandra. Explain. And don't pretend you're baffled by the request."

"The demand, you mean."

"Whatever."

Alexandra looked at him for a long time. Tonight her shoulders felt almost stooped from her load. If anyone else could manage the weight, even just for a few moments, it would be Lucien Balfour. "I need to tread carefully where my relations are concerned."

He took her hand and guided her toward the dark library doorway. "Why?"

"If they—if my uncle, especially—were to publicly distance themselves from me, I would be left completely . . . unprotected."

She couldn't see a thing, but Lucien led her unerringly to the library's overstuffed couch. He nudged her backward onto the cushions and lit the nearby lamp. Then he sank down close enough beside her that their thighs touched.

"And it is necessary for you to be protected because . . . ?"

"Because their support, unwitting or not, is all that keeps the gossip and rumors at a civilized level."

Lucien slowly reached up and pulled the clips from her hair. She trembled as the golden waves tumbled down around her shoulders, and again as he curled his fingers through the wavy mass.

"You're leaving something out," he murmured, leaning closer to rub his cheek along her hair.

"I . . . My goodness."

"Continue."

With a ragged breath, she complied. "Lady Welkins hates me."

Long fingers continued twisting and whispering through her hair. "You did nothing wrong."

Leaning back against his shoulder, Alexandra closed her eyes. "I pushed Lord Welkins down the stairs."

The fingers stilled. "Why?"

"It was an accident," she said, her voice quavering. "Mostly an accident."

"He had several mistresses, as I recall," Lucien said in a quiet, low voice, and shifted his fingers to her wrist, where he began unfastening her glove.

She kept her eyes closed, hardly daring to breathe lest she disturb the odd, electric sensation within her. "Yes, I know. He wanted another one."

"You refused."

"I told him that was not the reason I took the position in his household."

"I've heard that speech, I believe." He gently tugged the left glove from her hand, and slowly circled her palm with the tip of one finger.

"Unlike you, he was unwilling to wait for a change of heart on my part."

The finger paused, then resumed its trail. "You've had a change of heart?"

Alexandra opened her eyes. "My lord, I—"

"Close your eyes," he ordered in the same soft voice. "Relax. I didn't mean to change the subject."

She felt nothing close to relaxed, but strangely enough, she did feel safe—and completely befuddled, which was no doubt his intention. "I was climbing the stairs, on my way back to Lady Welkins's bedchamber with a book for her. He was waiting at the top of the stairs, and met me at the landing. He . . . pushed me against the railing."

The fastenings of her right glove opened one by one. "Did he hurt you?"

"No. He kissed me. I was . . . I was actually quite surprised. Then he grabbed my skirt and tried to yank it over my head. His hands . . ." She stopped. Lucien would know what she couldn't say. "I pushed him away, as hard as I could."

Lucien slipped her remaining glove off. "So why did you say it was 'mostly' an accident?"

"I knew we were at the edge of the landing."

"But you didn't know he'd fall down half a flight of stairs and have an apoplexy."

"No. I hoped he would fall down half a flight of stairs."

"Naturally. Otherwise you wouldn't have been able to get away from him."

Alexandra closed her hands, trapping his fingers between her palms. "You aren't surprised."

"I would have been surprised if you'd done nothing. But you weren't arrested then. Why do the rumors bother you now?"

Freeing his captured fingers, he lifted her hands to his lips. Featherlight kisses along the insides of her wrists made her breath catch and her pulse race. "I ran back downstairs to . . . see to him, but he died while I was kneeling there."

"Good." His voice sounded cold and matter-of-fact, and she had the distinct feeling that she never wanted to be on his bad side when he was truly angry.

Alexandra wanted to kiss him, touch him, bury herself in him, deep down where she'd be safe. "I ran back into the library and pretended to read until one of the footmen found him and sounded the alarm. Lady Welkins was very jealous and she knew Lord Welkins . . . had been pursuing me, and she wanted to have me arrested. The Bow Street runners would have taken me off to jail in chains then and there, except I told them my uncle was the Duke of Monmouth, and he would be *very* displeased at the uproar."

"And then no work for six months."

She shook her head.

For a moment he was silent. "I have one more question, Alexandra."

"Only one?"

"For now. Do my attentions displease you?" He tilted her chin up with his fingertips.

They should. But her reasons for accepting the position had had more to do with Lucien Balfour than Rose, though she hadn't been able to articulate how, or why. Until now. "I like your attentions very much," she said, looking into his eyes, "though I'm not quite sure why I'm receiving them."

Lucien smiled. "I told you why. I want to cover your naked skin with slow, hot kisses." He lifted her backward, across his legs. "I want to make love to you." His fingers gently traced her cheekbones as he leaned in to touch his lips to hers.

Alexandra forgot how to breathe, and then remembered again in a ragged rush as she felt the tie around her waist come loose. "Lucien," she managed, and then couldn't speak as his mouth found hers again.

Unable to resist, she swept her arms up around his shoulders and pulled herself closer against him. The warmth running just under her skin turned to fire, so hot she could scarcely think of anything except how it felt to touch him, and to be touched by him. He was smooth and steel, all at the same time.

"I don't want you to dance with anyone but me, ever again," he said, his own voice unsteady. The buttons running down the back of her gown unfastened, one by one.

The possessiveness in his tone thrilled her. "You told Lord Belton to dance with me."

"That was so I could." Her gown slipped from her shoulders. "My attempt at propriety. Stand up."

"I'm not certain I can," she said shakily, still clinging to his shoulders.

With a low growl deep in his chest, he kissed her

again, his tongue and lips teasing at her mouth until she opened to him. She could feel him, feel his growing arousal against her thigh. When his hand slipped around to the front and dipped down to cup her breast, she gasped. His fingers touched and caressed and teased, until she had to lean into him, wanting more of the flame that centered wherever he touched her, and in the secret, yearning place between her thighs

She protested when he stood her on her feet, but he only chuckled. With a whisper of silk he slid her dress up past her knees, past her thighs, above her waist, and then over her head and onto the floor. Alexandra stood there in nothing but her shift, watching his face as his gaze traveled slowly up the length of her body, pausing at her hips and her breasts and then returning to her face.

"Take off your shift," he said.

Her breathing fast and unsteady, she watched his hungry gaze lower to her chest again. She looked down to see her nipples erect and straining against the flimsy material of the shift. Her first instinct was to cover herself, until she realized the effect her near-nakedness was having on Lucien.

"Take off your coat," she countered, lifting her hands to open the buttons of his waistcoat. When he complied without argument, it amazed her to realize how much power she had over him—at least tonight. Lucien shrugged out of his dark coat and then let her slide the waistcoat down his shoulders. As she did so, he ran his fingers up her arms and pulled her against him. With a yearning moan she raised on her tiptoes to receive his kiss.

"You could have gone home with any of the ladies at the ball tonight," she said, pulling his shirt from his breeches. She needed to feel his warm skin against hers.

"Why me? Why an overaged, ruined governess?"

"I want you." He helped her lift his shirt over his head. "All of those idiots you danced with—they wanted you, too. Why me, Alexandra?"

She ran her hands along his bare, smooth chest, fascinated by the hard muscles beneath her fingers, so much more alive than the statues standing cold and silent in the museum. *I don't love them*, she almost said, and stopped herself just in time. "I don't trust them," she said instead.

"You trust me?" he repeated huskily, pausing in his exploration of her shoulders and throat.

Alexandra half closed her eyes as touch overloaded her senses. "I don't want to, but I do."

"That's right. Miss Gallant makes her way in the world alone, doesn't she?"

She tried to read his expression, but only intense curiosity and heat and desire looked back at her. "Miss Gallant has found that to be the wisest way to proceed."

Very slowly Lucien slipped the thin straps of her shift down her arms. "But not tonight," he murmured.

She shook her head. "Not tonight."

The shift rustled to the floor, leaving her naked except for her stockings and her shoes. She expected him to enfold her again, but instead he knelt in front of her. He removed her shoes one by one. Then he slid his palms up her right leg to the top of her stockings. Apparently he removed clothing from women all the time, because he was very good at it. Every tug and every slide of her stockings became another caress.

Her knees felt weak, and she dug her fingers into his bare shoulder for balance and for strength as he removed her other stocking. She could easily have swooned into his arms, but if she did that, she might miss something—

and she had no intention of missing anything tonight.

"What did Lady Victoria mean when she said you shouldn't flee again because of Virgil Retting?"

Alexandra frowned. "I don't want to talk," she stated.

He chuckled. "This is the only moment I can be assured of getting an answer out of you." Lucien stood again and kissed her. "Tell me."

She felt ready to growl with frustration at the delay. "About two years ago, before my employment with Lady Welkins, I came across him in Bath. I was so angry at seeing him, alive and healthy and wealthy, that I gave notice and left just so I wouldn't have to look at him again."

"He is fairly stomach churning," Lucien agreed. He walked a slow circle around her, his hands running across her shoulders, her back, her buttocks, and her stomach. She should have felt embarrassed, or shocked, but everywhere he touched her seemed to come alive, leaving her craving more. And there was more; she knew it. Her body knew it. "Kiss me again," she demanded.

He grinned and bent his head to comply. Gentle fingers trailed down from her shoulders to caress and tease her breasts, a delicious torment she could never have imagined before tonight. Lucien lowered his head further, and his lips and his tongue on her nipples brought her to moaning arousal.

"Lucien," she shuddered, twining her fingers into his hair.

At her cry he swept her up into his arms and laid her down on the couch. Kneeling beside her, he suckled first one breast and then the other until she could breathe only in short, panting gasps.

"Tell me how you feel," he whispered, trailing his mouth with agonizing slowness down her belly, up again to her breasts, along her collarbone and up her throat before capturing her mouth again.

"On fire. Please, Lucien."

"Please what?"

The only term she knew for it was the one he'd used earlier. "Make love to me."

He smiled. "As you wish."

Turning to sit on the floor, he pulled off his boots. Alexandra kissed his shoulder blades and ran her palms around his waist and his flat, well-muscled stomach. Shifting up on one elbow, she kissed and nibbled his ear. He groaned again. Encouraged, she slipped her hands down to assist him with unfastening his breeches, using the opportunity to explore the hard, straining bulge there.

"Wanton," he rasped, setting her hands away from himself as he shrugged the breeches down to his thighs and then kicked out of them.

"It's your fault," she retorted, fascinated and hot and terrified at the sight of his full, hard erection. With a slight grin he let her look, and then lay down along the deep couch beside her.

She reached for him again, and this time he endured her heated, fumbling exploration for several moments, his jaw clenched, before he pushed her hands away.

"Good God," he moaned, and shifted atop her.

Again her body seemed to know what to do, even if her mind had lost the ability to produce any kind of rational thought. She bent her knees, welcoming his hardness pressing at her thighs. "Now," she said, pulling at his hips.

He kissed her again, deeply and roughly, and shook his head. "Now we go slowly," he countered, every muscle tense.

She knew instinctively how tightly he was holding himself, how difficult this would be for someone as used to bedding women as he was. "Now," she repeated, and lifted her hips.

Pain shot through her as his length filled her. She would have pulled back, but he clasped her hips to his. "Wait," he commanded in a hissing breath.

He held her there for a long moment as the pain faded away. She could feel all of him inside her, as though he were touching her and holding her everywhere at once. "Lucien," she whispered again.

With another deep kiss he began to move his hips slowly, and then harder and faster as she found and matched his rhythm. Her body tightened and clenched and shattered inside, and she cried out in pure ecstasy. A moment later he buried his face in her hair and groaned, holding himself tightly against her before he collapsed.

Trying to regain her breath and her senses, Alexandra ran her hands along his back, welcoming his warmth and his weight. "So that's what Byron was writing about," she said, more intensely satisfied than she could ever remember being in her life.

He chuckled, the sound resonating in her own chest, and raised on one elbow to kiss her again. "Now you see why young, virginal females aren't supposed to read him."

"I'm nearly twenty-four," she replied, kissing him back, "and I don't believe I'm virginal any longer."

"I should say not, thank God."

Having his skills at sex compared to Byron's poetry was not a bad way to conclude the evening, Lucien decided—though he had no intention of ending the evening yet. Alexandra Gallant had an extraordinary wit, beauty, courage, and passion. She'd befuddled him from the moment he had first seen her in his study, and he wasn't through with befuddling her.

As his breathing returned to normal, he sat up. Alexandra looked three-quarters asleep, for which he could hardly blame her. Given that tonight had been her first experience with sexual intimacy, she'd been spectacular.

"Do you think Lord Belton will offer for Rose?" she asked, sitting up beside him to pull on her shift.

No hysterical tears and cries of regret from his Alexandra. She took what the world gave her and dealt with it. Lucien smiled. *His Alexandra.* Now, what would she think of that? "Robert's got more sense than that. He's just trying to ruffle my feathers."

"In that case, you definitely need to hold a birthday celebration for your cousin. Mrs. Delacroix was right."

Lucien sat back on the couch and looked at her, noting that she seemed to have retained her fascination with his nether regions. "Back to business as usual? Parties and dinners and what to wear to luncheon on Thursday?"

She made a face at him and knelt on the floor to find her stockings. "Beg pardon, my lord. You are the expert at . . . what comes after making love. What are we supposed to discuss?"

He took a quick breath, wondering how much he should tell her of what he'd decided that evening, and about his belated realization that he'd already found and interviewed the woman he wanted to marry. "How about your future?"

Alexandra paused in the middle of gathering up her dress. "Are you telling me to leave?"

He shot to his feet. "For God's sake, no! What in hell made you think that?"

She looked up at him, her cheeks and lips still flushed

and her hair a disheveled golden halo. "I told you, I'm not used to—"

"Neither am I," he interrupted. "Generally, there doesn't seem to be much to say afterward." Or nothing he wished to say, anyway.

"Oh."

"But I meant your future here," he continued. "With me."

She straightened, holding her crumpled gown before her like a shield. "I am not your mistress."

Lucien lifted an eyebrow. "Whatever you wish to call it, I have some feeling of responsibility toward you."

"Well, don't. You didn't do anything to me I didn't want done. My reason for being here hasn't changed, has it? You still want me to help Rose snare a husband, don't you?"

He looked at her. "I'd be an idiot to say no. So yes, of course I do." Lucien grabbed his breeches and stepped into them. She was infinitely easier to deal with when she was naked. "Now, may I escort you to your bedchamber?"

Apparently she didn't want to argue tonight any more than he did, because she nodded. "Very well. Any decisions can be made in the morning."

Biting his tongue at her damned no-nonsense practicality, Lucien gathered up the rest of their things and opened the library door. They walked up the stairs and down the dark hallway in silence, and he briefly wondered what kind of attack Aunt Fiona would have if she saw them creeping about half naked in the middle of the night. It would almost be worth the bother of having her discover them.

Outside her door she stopped. "Good night," she whispered, taking her slippers out of his hand.

"Alexandra, I—"

She put her free hand over his lips. "Good night," she repeated. "If I let you in, I'm . . . not sure I'll be able to let you leave."

He leaned down and kissed her, thrilling at her eager, heated response. "I wouldn't want to leave," he murmured against her mouth. "And don't think this is over, Miss Gallant."

Somewhat to his relief, she smiled and kissed him again. "I'm beginning to believe I might enjoy some more lessons from you, Lucien."

He stepped back and let her slip into the dark bedchamber. For several minutes after she closed her door he stood there, listening and hoping she might change her mind and invite him in. Finally he headed down the hallway to his own rooms.

Whatever ideas Alexandra had about her independence, he had no intention of letting her go. Not until he'd figured her out, and not until he'd figured out what she'd done to him—and why he'd begun enjoying it so much.

Chapter 13

With only four hours of sleep, Alexandra didn't even try to talk herself into going on her morning walk. Lying curled up beneath the warm covers felt too pleasant, and her dreams had been even better. She smiled and stretched, stiff and tender in places she hadn't even realized she had muscles. Dreams hadn't been the best part of the evening.

She lay there for another few minutes, until she heard Rose heading downstairs. Uttering a reluctant groan that woke Shakespeare, she climbed out of bed and got dressed. Rose's education wasn't going to progress with her sleeping the day away, and she needed to convince Lucien to hold the birthday celebration. His support would do more for his cousin's chances at a good match than any amount of skill the young lady acquired at conversational French.

She paused as she put up her hair. That was the way to proceed: business as usual, as though nothing had happened and nothing would happen again. And if either she or Lucien had any sense, that was the truth. She had absolutely no regrets about last night. Being the focus of his attentions and passion had been every bit as intoxicating and fulfilling and satisfying as she had imagined.

This morning, though, she wasn't certain she was up to facing him. As he had said, "mistress" was only a word, but she didn't like what it implied—that she belonged to him, and that she existed only in relation to how well she satisfied him. She had worked too hard to allow that. And if Kilcairn didn't agree, she wouldn't hesitate for a moment to set him straight.

"Oh, bother," she muttered, and glanced down at Shakespeare. "He may just want to forget the entire evening, you know."

The terrier wagged his tail and scratched at the door.

"All right, all right."

None of the servants looked at her oddly as she and Shakes made their way downstairs, so at least no one had seen her and the earl. She had a small bit of luck remaining, anyway.

Spying their approach, Wimbole left his post by the foyer to take charge of Shakespeare. "Are there any special instructions for Vincent this morning, Miss Gallant?"

She handed the end of the leash to the butler. "I would appreciate if Vincent gave him a good walk. I think it may rain this afternoon, and I don't want anyone getting soggy on our account."

Wimbole actually smiled. "Very good, then." He tugged on the leash. "Come along, Shakespeare."

Next the butler would be hiding dog treats in his pockets. Chuckling, Alexandra strolled into the breakfast room—and stopped dead, her jaw dropping. Rose sat at the table, a fashion magazine open before her and her breakfast plate pushed to one side. Leaning over her shoulder and gesturing at a sketch on one of the pages was Kilcairn.

"Good morning, Miss Gallant," he said, straightening.

Alexandra wondered if the responding rush of blood through her veins showed on her face. She hadn't expected the sudden lust that hit her as their eyes met. So much for business as usual. "Good morning," she said breathlessly.

"Oh, Lex, come see what cousin Lucien found!"

Straightening her shoulders, she joined them at the table. Lucien watched every step of her approach, and if Rose and two footmen hadn't been present, Alexandra thought he would have pounced on her. At least she hoped so, because she very much wanted to be pounced upon.

"What have you found?"

"A gown for the opera next week! Isn't it exquisite? Do you think Madame Charbonne could complete it in time?"

"No doubt she can be persuaded," the earl said dryly. "Have some breakfast, Miss Gallant. You must be hungry after your exertions last night."

If she hadn't been blushing before, she was now.

Rose nodded happily and closed her magazine, returning to her ham and biscuits. "I'm starving. I don't think I sat down for five hours straight."

Lucien pulled a chair away from the table, and with a quick glance at him, Alexandra sat. "Thank you, my lord."

"My pleasure." His fingers brushed her cheek as he straightened and returned to his own seat.

This was absolute torture. She could barely look away from him long enough to butter her toast. His own expression of canary-eating satisfaction didn't help matters in the least. Alexandra wasn't sure whether she wanted to whack him or kiss him. She took a deep breath. Mooning over the Earl of Kilcairn Abbey was not on her agenda for the morning.

"My lord, have you given any further consideration to a birthday party for Miss Delacroix?"

"I have."

"And?" she prompted after a moment of silence.

"And I'm awaiting a response to a note I dispatched this morning," he said calmly. "Soiree planning will have to wait until then."

"A note to whom?" she persisted, frowning at him.

Lucien looked up at her from beneath his long lashes, a smile touching his mouth, and then turned his attention to his morning paper. "Cousin Rose, what do you have planned for today?"

"Lex and I are going shopping for hats, and then we need to work some more on my drawing room French."

Amazed at the sight of the black panther playing with the mouse and keeping his claws sheathed, Alexandra looked from Lucien to Rose and back again. Not one barbed comment so far. Not even a look of suspicion or boredom from either party. *Something* was going on.

"I meant to ask you before," the earl said. "What, precisely, is 'drawing room' French?"

Rose finished her mouthful of toast. "It's much better than real French. When a gentleman says something to you that doesn't require an answer, but only an acknowledgment, you respond in French, thereby giving the impression that you speak the language."

Alexandra added a good memory to Rose's list of natural talents. The explanation was almost word for word the one she had given her pupil last week. She waited for Kilcairn to spring, hiding behind her cup of coffee. The morning's peace had been pleasant while it lasted.

"I see," the panther purred. "What sort of expressions do you utilize?"

For the first time even Rose looked surprised, but when nothing caustic followed, she smiled again. "*Mais oui, mais non, d'accord, á bien sur,* and . . . " She glanced at her companion.

"And *absolument*," Alexandra finished.

Lord Kilcairn sat back in his chair. "Amazing. When I think how much time I wasted with my tutor on actual French when I was young . . . ah, *quel dommage*!"

"Ooh, I like that one, too. *Quel dommage*."

Finally some sarcasm. Alexandra recognized *that* Lucien Balfour, though he was still behaving in an extremely mild fashion. Perhaps last night had sated him, though she knew that before her arrival at Balfour House he certainly hadn't been celibate. She studied her coffee cup for a moment. Though she couldn't be entirely certain, she thought he had been celibate since her arrival—except for last night. Except for her.

Wimbole entered the room, a letter perched on his silver tray. "My lord, the reply you instructed me to wait for has arr—"

"Splendid."

Lucien wiped his fingers on a napkin and took the missive. Flipping it open, he glanced at it, then up at Rose with a smile. For the first time, Alexandra was conscious of a distinct feeling of jealousy running down her spine. She took a deep breath. Next, she'd be baring her claws at poor Rose. For heaven's sake, Kilcairn kept a list of prospective brides—a list upon which neither she nor Rose appeared. A few weeks ago she'd thought those ladies deserved her pity. Now she wasn't certain what she thought they deserved.

"Well, my dear," Lord Kilcairn said, "how about a week from Friday for your party?"

"Oh, Lucien, really?"

"I believe so."

Rose sprang to her feet and hurried over to kiss him on one cheek. She continued around the table and hugged Alexandra. "I have to go tell Mama!" The girl skipped for the door.

Alexandra would have called her back, but she wasn't all that displeased to see her go. Besides, the two footmen remained. Hopefully their presence would be enough to encourage Kilcairn to continue behaving. "Someone sent you permission to hold a party?" she asked, gesturing at the letter. "How unusual."

"No. But before the harpies fly off to spread the news, we all have an appointment."

"An appointment with whom, pray tell?"

"Prince George. Rose is to be presented this afternoon."

For a long moment she stared at him. "You're bamming me."

Lucien lifted an eyebrow. "Wealth has its privileges."

"I would say so. But doesn't Rose have a luncheon invitation for this afternoon? A picnic in Hyde Park with Lord Belton?"

He finished off his coffee. "I've already sent over a note to cancel. Robert can thank me for saving him later."

His affability had apparently fled with Rose, which didn't leaven Alexandra's suspicion over his behavior in the least. "Lord Belton might actually like her, you know. You didn't force him into making the invitation, did you? The way you forced him to dance with me?"

His fine brow furrowed. "Did he tell you that?"

"I am not without deductive abilities, my lord."

For a moment he gazed at her, then glanced at the two footmen. "Thompkinson, Harold, excuse us for a moment."

"Lu—" Alexandra began, then stopped her protest as the servants vanished.

"What are you deducing right now?" he asked, rising to close the door behind them.

She sighed to cover her sudden delighted trembling. "That you're making yet another error in judgment."

"Come here."

"I most certainly will not. Open that door before your servants confirm the *ton*'s rumors about me—about us."

"My servants don't gossip. Come here, Alexandra."

"It's not proper, whether anyone gossips or not."

Lucien left the door, circling the table and stopping behind her chair. "I'm allowing Rose's birthday extravaganza," he said. "How much exemplary behavior do you expect me to exhibit?"

She wanted to lean back toward him, like a bee unable to resist a flower. "You can never overdo exemplary behavior."

Lucien tilted her chair back and looked down at her with glinting gray eyes. "I beg to differ," he murmured, and leaned down to kiss her.

If anything, her body's reaction was more electric now than last night. She wanted to mold herself to him, to wrap herself around him and never let him go. Slipping her hands up to either side of his face, she tangled her fingers through his dark hair.

He came around in front of her, and leaned more deeply into their kiss. Fleetingly Alexandra wondered if he'd locked the door, because if his body was reacting anything like hers, they weren't going anywhere for a while.

"Lucien, you wonderful boy!"

"*Damn*," he hissed, yanking her chair upright, and dropped into the seat beside her just as the door opened and Mrs. Delacroix swept into the room, Rose on her heels. "Beg pardon, Aunt?"

Alexandra was hard-pressed not to stare at him. He sounded so cool and collected that she couldn't believe he'd been involved with her less than a heartbeat ago. She took a swallow of coffee, wishing it were something stronger.

"I said you were wonderful!" Fiona repeated. "Why didn't you tell us last night? You might have saved me a great deal of anxiety!"

"I had a few arrangements to make first. Miss Gallant and I were just discussing one of them."

Alexandra couldn't resist a glance in his direction, and abruptly realized why he'd seated himself at the ladies' arrival. She stifled a very inappropriate chuckle. Obviously he hadn't been unmoved by their kiss, after all. "Yes, we were," she seconded brightly. If Aunt Fiona only knew. "Might I relay the news, my lord?"

"Of course."

"Well, Miss Delacroix, it seems you will be able to waltz at your birthday party."

Rose's eyes widened. "What?"

Alexandra nodded. "Your cousin has arranged for you to be presented to Prince George this afternoon. With the Almack's assembly tonight and thereby your permission to waltz nearly assured, you—"

Rose squealed and dashed around the table to hug Lucien. "Oh, thank you, thank you, thank you!"

He had the good grace to look uncomfortable. "Just following your governess's recommendations," he muttered.

"Thank you, too, Lex!"

"Oh, my!" Fiona exclaimed, sinking into a chair. "What does one wear to meet Prince George?"

"Something very conservative," Lucien said, before Alexandra could. "He detests idle chatter, too, so unless you wish Rose to be banished from society, you will refrain from talking, Aunt. Is that clear?"

Alexandra waited for the explosion, but Fiona only lifted a painted eyebrow. "Of course. Come, Rose, we must start dressing you at once. Thank goodness I had the foresight to have Madame Charbonne make a presentation gown for you!"

"Yes, Mama." At the doorway, though, Rose stopped, a dismayed look crossing her pretty features. "But what about Lord Belton? I already said I would accompany him for luncheon. He'll be so disappointed."

Realizing she'd best make her escape as well, before she lost the chance or the desire to do so, Alexandra stood. "Lord Kilcairn has already informed him. They will reschedule at the first opportunity."

"Miss Gallant," Lucien said, making a surreptitious grab for the trailing edge of her skirt, "we still have something to discuss."

She flicked the muslin out of his reach, feeling giddier than she ever had as a schoolgirl. "I believe your cousin and I should review court etiquette again before her presentation, my lord."

He shoved the chair beside him backward, trapping her. In a second he had the edge of her gown twined in his long fingers. "After we finish our discussion," he stated, his gaze daring her to make another attempt to flee.

Seemly or not, she already felt warm with excitement and anticipation. "Miss Delacroix, I believe your mother is correct," she said, turning to her pupil. "Your lessons will be more effective once you are in the proper attire."

Rose nodded and pranced out the door with her mother. "Oh, I can hardly contain myself," she giggled, as they vanished back down the hallway.

"Neither can I," Lucien said dryly, hauling on Alexandra's skirt to bring her in closer.

She leaned away from him. "The door is open, my lord," she murmured through clenched teeth. She might be insane, but she wasn't stupid.

From his expression he didn't care if they were in the middle of Pall Mall. Lucien stood, moving his grip from her skirt to her hand. "Let's close it, then."

"This is decidedly unwise, my l—"

Pulling her around the table with him, he slammed the door, locked it, backed her up against it, and captured her lips in a rough, openmouthed kiss that left her no doubt of his intentions.

Last night he'd been gentle and cautious in his seduction; this morning he had no concerns over her virginity or her desire. Alexandra gasped as he lifted her in his arms and set her down on the edge of the table.

"Lucien, someone will realize what we're doing," she protested, her voice and her breathing unsteady.

He grinned, the heat and lust in his eyes making her glad she was sitting down. "Then we'll have to make it quick," he said in his low drawl.

"But—Oh, my," she breathed, as his hands slipped up her ankles, knees, and then past her thighs, lifting her gown with them. "All right, but hurry."

Lucien chuckled. "As you wish."

Swiftly he freed himself, shoving his breeches down to his thighs, and pulled her closer to kiss her again. At the same time he entered her. Alexandra threw her arms around his shoulders for balance, reveling in the feel of him moving deep inside her. She was still a bit sore, but nothing remained of the initial sharp pain of last night. She smiled at him.

"You like this, don't you?" he asked huskily, watching her face with his usual intensity.

"Yes," she panted. "I hadn't . . . realized we could . . . be together this way. Upright, I mean."

"Your second lesson," he returned. "With several more to follow."

"More?" she asked, and then could do nothing but throw her head back and gasp as she tightened and then exploded inside.

Lucien clutched her to him and groaned from deep inside his chest. "Definitely more."

Lucien paused outside the open drawing room door. Inside Rose banged happily away on his antique pianoforte. The instrument would never recover, but at least his cousin wasn't weeping over something or other. In fact, he hadn't heard a sniffle in three days, since he'd given in about the party. The concession had been a fair trade for the relative quiet. With a half smile at his own pun, Lucien started downstairs for his office.

"Lex, who do you think will offer for me first?"

Lucien paused, straining to make out the conversation over the mangled Beethoven.

"Who do you hope offers for you?"

Alexandra had managed to keep away from him for three days, or at least to have a chaperone present. While her success solidified her position as the most skilled etiquette governess of all time, it had become damned frustrating. He knew she wanted him again; he could see it in her eyes. And he certainly enjoyed giving her lessons.

"Oh, I don't know. Lord Belton is very nice, but I don't think Mama's set on him."

"Rose, I know you have an obligation to your family, but don't you think your own choice is at least as important as your mother's?"

The music stopped, and Lucien leaned against the near wall. He had the distinct feeling that this was a conversation he didn't want to miss.

"I think Mama's too busy complaining about cousin Lucien even to notice if I've made a choice."

"Still, at least you've noticed someone in all of this London chaos. And Lord Belton *is* nice. That is an important first point. You wouldn't want to marry anyone who was mean."

Lucien frowned. It was damned insulting that a woman of Alexandra's intelligence and learning had to resort to using words of no more than two syllables to make a point. Aside from that, he had more than a suspicion that he qualified as one of the "mean" gentlemen she was discussing.

"Cousin Lucien's been nicer, the past few days," Rose said thoughtfully. "Mama's even remarked on it."

Lucien silently applauded her surprising insight. Perhaps his cousin wasn't quite as empty-headed as he'd thought.

"Yes, he has been. Has he mentioned whether Lord Belton has rescheduled your picnic?"

Damn. He'd forgotten about it completely. Desperate as he was to be rid of Rose and Fiona, though, as long as they were at Balfour House, Alexandra would remain there, as well. That fact had occupied him for the past three days, and had seriously lessened his appreciation for irony.

"Ah, Lucien, there you are. I've been looking everywhere for you."

Aunt Fiona reached the top of the stairs behind him, and he cursed his inattention. "I was inspecting the ballroom," he improvised.

"Good. I'm glad you're taking such an interest in Rose's party."

"Yes, well—"

"But I fear your staff doesn't share your enthusiasm. Wimbole has just informed me that he will not send anyone to a printer's shop for invitation samples, whether the festivities are only a week away or not."

"That's correct." He started around her for the stairs.

"And he also says that you haven't approved my purchase of decorations."

Wimbole was becoming entirely too chatty. "It's *my* purchase of decorations, and I am not going to approve two hundred yards of pink bombazine."

Rose appeared in the doorway. "Mama, you said you would decorate in yellow."

"Perhaps a combination of the two would be more to everyone's liking," Alexandra said, strolling into view behind her charge.

Lucien gazed at her. He had no choice; she drew every part of him. So much for a night—and an all-too-brief morning—together curing his obsession for her. That previous torment had been heaven compared with this torture. Now he knew what he was missing.

"Lucien must decide," Fiona declared.

He shook himself. "Decide what?"

"Pink or yellow?"

"Why would you think I gave a damn?"

"Then why won't you purchase the bomba—"

"Because I will not have any room in my house looking like a whore's boudoir unless you intend to supply the whore," he snapped.

"Lucien!" Fiona gasped.

Alexandra made a sound that might have been either a cluck of disapproval or a stifled laugh. "Please, my lord. Your language."

Rose sniffled. "Now I'll never have a party."

He had already opened his mouth to tell his cousin what a relief that would be, when Alexandra's put-upon expression stopped him. Skittish as she'd been, he had no intention of allowing her to use his "meanness" as an excuse to continue avoiding him.

"Of course you're having a party," he grumbled. "Miss Gallant is in charge of your presentation into society, so she will also decide your color scheme and decorations." He glanced at his aunt. "And she will approve your invitation list."

Aunt Fiona's face reddened. "I will not have a governess dictating who will attend my parties!"

He took a step closer. "Yes, you will, unless you wish *me* to dictate who will attend."

"I am only here to advise," Alexandra said hurriedly. "We all want Rose's birthday to be spectacular." She glanced at Lucien. "I must earn my keep somehow."

He knew exactly where that came from, and ignored it. Governess, lover, or mistress, he would call her whatever she wished. "Excellent. We're all agreed, then."

"Oh, very well." Fiona smoothed the frown from her round face. "But, Lucien, I must insist that you go over the guest list with us, anyway."

"I'll be happy to throw as many bachelors in Rose's direction as will fit in the house. Other than that, only my purse intends to be involved."

To his surprise, Rose put a hand on his sleeve. "You've been to so many more elegant soirees than I have," she said. "I want my party to be the grandest one ever. I would like if you would help us plan it."

Good God, now they wanted him hanging about. If not for the turquoise-eyed goddess standing in the doorway, he would have made certain his cousin knew just what he thought of her party plans thus far, and then he would have fled to one of his clubs. That, though, would have left him with two major problems: First, Robert would no doubt find him if he went out, and he would have to reschedule Rose's picnic, and then Robert would offer for Rose just to annoy him. Rose would marry, and Alexandra would leave.

The second problem would be nearly as unpleasant, because it would involve apologizing to Alexandra for being mean again, at which point she would insist that he make amends to Rose—and he would do it, because the blasted governess had him wrapped around her little finger, and her smile was swiftly on its way to becoming his sunlight.

He cleared his throat. "If you insist, cousin, I would be . . . happy to help."

That sent Aunt Fiona into raptures, which annoyed him no end. He was willing to ignore it, though, because Alexandra sat beside him on the couch, and for the first time in three days he was able to spend over an hour in her company. It belatedly dawned on him that if he wanted to extend his time with her, all he needed to do was spend more time with Rose—and to a lesser degree, thank God, with Fiona. Abysmal as that was, it was better than having Alexandra evade him until the end of time.

After an hour in his relations' presence, he was beginning to wish the end of time were somewhat nearer. "No. Take him off the list," he said.

"But Lord Hannenfeld has been looking for a wife for two years," Alexandra countered, continuing to write.

"Hannenfeld supported peace negotiations with Bonaparte, and I won't have him in my house."

"Oh, that nasty Bonaparte!" Fiona exclaimed, accepting another biscuit from a footman. "If we'd made peace with him, perhaps your dear cousin James might still be alive."

The past hour's mild annoyance flared into anger. "What in damnation do you think you—"

"My lord," Alexandra interrupted.

He continued to glare at Fiona. "You have no right—"

Miss Gallant slipped her warm hand over his clenched fingers. "Lord Hannenfeld will not attend," she stated, and crossed the name off her list in a black, thick line of pencil. "If Lord Kilcairn says he is not welcome here, then he is not."

She was comforting him, easing his anger. No one that he could recall had ever made the effort before. He turned his hand to grip hers, then let go before she could pull away. Let her long for a more prolonged contact between them, as he did. "Good," he said, pulling his temper back in check. "We can't have Hannenfeld and Wellington at the same soiree, anyway."

Rose gasped. "Wellington? Do you think he'll attend?"

"I imagine so. He's particularly fond of my private stock of port. I'll send over a bottle with the invitation."

Alexandra looked at him sideways, the hint of a smile

touching her lips. "That's a bit devious, don't you think?"

"We want Rose's party to be unforgettable, don't we?"

"Ooh, write his name down, Lex," Rose urged, giggling.

"You're a good boy, Lucien."

He lifted an eyebrow. "I beg to differ, Aunt."

Alexandra cleared her throat. If she considered it her duty to distract him, he had no intention of discouraging her. In fact, he knew several ways he could stand to be distracted.

"I hesitate to mention this," she said, amusement touching her voice again, "but I notice a dearth of female guests. My lord, don't you have a list of ladies you'd care to invite?"

Fiona glared at the governess. "It's Rose's party."

Lucien had been about to answer in the same vein, but he had no intention of siding with his aunt. "I imagine I can name a few who are about Rose's age," he said reluctantly.

Alexandra looked at him. "I thought you preferred more mature ladies."

"I do." He smiled, watching the pretty blush rise in her cheeks in response. He liked knowing he affected her as much as she affected him.

"That reminds me," Aunt Fiona broke in, straightening Rose's sleeve. "Have you finished that *Paradise Lost* yet, my dear? I know how you were enjoying it."

Rose shook her head. "No, Mama. It's very difficult to rea—"

"Difficult to make time for, yes, I know, darling. That's how I know you've liked it so much." Fiona leaned forward to pat her nephew's knee. "She has no time for such frivolities. I tell her that all the time, 'Rose, you have no time for reading,' but she insists on it, anyway."

"You enjoy Milton?" Lucien asked, unable to keep the deep skepticism from his voice.

"Oh, yes . . . He's very . . . poetical."

"Yes, he would have to be," he agreed dryly.

"Now, now, you two, you can discuss your literature later. I have no patience for it myself."

Rose hadn't suddenly become a literature aficionado. Whatever nonsense his relations were up to, Lucien had run out of the patience to tolerate it. He pulled out his pocket watch and flipped it open. "Delightful as this has been, I have an appointment," he said, rising.

"Oh, Lord Kilcairn, I nearly forgot," Alexandra blurted, rushing to her feet. "I needed to ask you something."

"Yes?"

Blushing, she gestured toward the doorway. "It's a personal matter."

Lucien went hard. "Of course. After you."

He followed her out the door, down the hallway, and into the small corner sitting room. "What is it?"

Alexandra paused by the far window. "Close the door, please."

Curious, aroused, and a little worried at her odd behavior, Lucien complied. "Alexandra?" he said, facing her again.

She wrung her hands together for a moment, clearly agitated and not at all like the calm, collected female she'd been two minutes ago. Then, with what sounded like a combination of a growl and a curse, she strode back across the room, grabbed him by the lapels, lifted up on her toes, and kissed him.

The effect on him was astounding. In their previous encounters she'd been curious and eager, but never the aggressor. Sweeping his arms around her back and waist, he allowed her to push him backward against the door.

Alexandra continued to push and pull at him, molding herself to his body as though she wanted to be part of him. He wanted to drop to the floor and rip her clothes off, but she had started it, so he would let her dictate the terms—this time.

Finally she moved back a little in his arms to look at him, her lips rosy and swollen from the kiss.

"What was that for?" he asked.

"I almost like you today," she said, and kissed him again.

Being nice definitely had its benefits—at least, he assumed that was why she was being so friendly. "Wait until you see me tomorrow," he murmured against her mouth.

She backed away again, panting. "You're not behaving just because of me, are you?"

He didn't think he could have answered that if he wanted to. "Would it matter?"

Alexandra ran her fingers across his lips. "I don't know. I think it does."

"Regardless of either of our motivations," he said, running his palms down her hips to her firm, rounded buttocks, "I like the results. I'm beginning to think I should just marry you and get this nonsense—"

She ripped out of his grip. *"What?"*

"—over with." Despite her shocked expression, he was more interested in his own reaction. He was a bloody genius! He just needed to convince her their union would be in her best interest. "I can't believe I didn't think of this before. You need protection from your family, and I need a wife. It makes perfect s—"

"You need a mother for your heir, not a wife." She backed away farther, putting the couch between them as though she feared he'd gone mad. "You said so yourself, Lucien."

"What does that matter? You and I deal well together, and you're certainly of good family."

Alexandra jabbed a finger in his direction. "Stop that! I said I *almost* like you today. I don't need your protection; I can look after myself."

"I can do it better. Like you said, Alexandra, your next employment prospects look rather grim. This benefits both of us. Don't be a nodcock."

"I am not a nodcock, and *you* are the reason I'll have so much difficulty finding employment!" Her eyes narrowed, she stalked back to him and tried to shove him away from the door. "Move!" she demanded when he didn't budge. A tear ran down her cheek, followed by another.

"Why should I?"

"Because I changed my mind; I don't like you at all! And here's another lesson for you: you can't have everything you want, especially if it doesn't want you back!"

His jaw clenched, Lucien stepped aside. Alexandra bolted through the door and slammed it behind her.

"Damnation," he growled. It *had* been a perfect idea. They were perfect for one another. And besides, he loved her.

Lucien froze, letting that one, very large word tumble about in his mind. It didn't break anything there, and he rolled it around his chest a little more. *He loved her*—which didn't help things one blasted bit. "Damnation," he said again.

He had never expected his prospective bride to be

more reluctant to wed than he was. Nor had he expected to care for, to love, the woman he'd selected to marry. One of them was insane—and he didn't think it was Alexandra.

Chapter 14

"He said what?" Victoria set her tea down so abruptly that half of it sloshed out, overflowing the saucer.

Alexandra paced toward the fireplace again. "He said we should marry, because it would be convenient for him."

"Did he actually use the word 'convenient'?"

"Well, suffice it to say that he implied it very, *very* strongly."

"Lex, this is tremendous news! I wish you would sit down, you're making me dizzy."

With an annoyed look at her friend, Alexandra continued pacing. "I don't want to sit. Besides, your parents could return at any moment. I won't put them through the embarrassment of asking me to leave."

Vixen sat back amid a pile of pillows. "Fine. Pace, then. But have you considered that marriage to Kilcairn might be just as convenient for you? He's one of the wealthiest men in England, and no one dares cross him."

"But you should hear the way he talks about women,

and love, and marriage. It's awful. Sometimes I just want to whack him." The other half of the time she wanted to kiss him, and feel his strong, protecting arms around her, but she wasn't about to part with that information.

"He doesn't strike me as being a stupid man, Lex. Something must have given him the impression that you would agree to the match."

"His unmitigated arrogance gives him whatever impression he wants." She uttered an inarticulate curse. "Please, I don't want to discuss it any further. My parents married for love, and I will do no less, or I won't marry at all. For heaven's sake, we used to talk about that all the time."

"And now you're determined to become a spinster, without even having any fun first. Yuck."

"Vixen, he couldn't possibly want me and my problems added to his own. How long do you think it would be convenient for him to have Lord Virgil approach him and congratulate him on marrying a poor, ruined artist's daughter? And when he changes his mind about me, I'll be in a deeper hole than I am now."

Victoria looked at her for a moment. "What will you do, then?"

Alexandra shut her eyes. Telling Lucien exactly how she had felt about bowing to his convenience had been easy. Physically and emotionally removing herself from his presence, the next logical step, would be much more difficult. If only he hadn't said it that way, as though he'd simply fit a piece to a puzzle instead of proposing something as important and permanent as marriage. If only he'd said he cared for her and that he wanted to help her with her troubles, instead of offering to take them on his shoulders as a trade for her consent. If only he hadn't said he didn't believe in love, or even the sanctity of marriage.

"I have to leave, obviously," she said, her voice unsteady. "I've saved most of my salary; it will easily see me to Yorkshire or somewhere equally distant from the stupid gossips of London."

"Did he tell you to leave?"

She paused in her pacing. "No. But how could I st—"

"Look, Lex, he mentioned something unwelcome and you rebuffed him. He should be the one to feel guilty and to make amends. If Kilcairn is at all a gentleman, he won't send you away. At least not until you've helped him marry off his cousin and found another position."

"But he's not a gentleman." Alexandra plopped herself down in one of the morning room chairs. Obviously none of her lessons had made their way through his thick skull, if he'd thought for one minute that she would want to marry anyone as cynical and sarcastic . . . and warm and amusing and intelligent as he was. But she couldn't—she wouldn't—do it. She wouldn't rely on anyone besides herself. She couldn't trust anyone else not to let her down.

Vixen continued to gaze at her. "You like him, don't you?" she finally said.

Abruptly Alexandra needed to pace again. "What I feel toward him doesn't signify if he feels nothing toward me. And why in the world would I wish to have his poor reputation added to mine?" She shook her head, just the idea of seeing him again sending her into a near panic. "No. I need to leave. As soon as possible."

"Very well." With a sigh Victoria rose and walked to her writing desk. She lifted a letter, hesitated, then handed it to Alexandra. "This came yesterday. You seemed so determined to make a good showing here that

I wasn't going to mention most of its particulars to you. But if you've made up your mind to run . . . well, there you are."

"It's not running," Alexandra retorted, opening the letter. "It's relocating for the benefit of everyone concerned." She read the first few lines, then had to sit again. "You weren't going to tell me that Miss Grenville has died?" she faltered, tears filling her eyes.

Victoria swept up and sat beside her. "That part, I had planned to tell you at the first opportunity. Emma didn't know where to write to tell you about her aunt, but she knew how highly you regarded her."

"Patricia was like a second mother to me—and to Emma." She wiped at her cheeks. "How is Em?"

"She's grieving, but keeping busy. Miss Grenville willed the Academy to her. She wants to keep it running."

"Good for Emma. She'll be a wonderful headmistress. And the Academy may keep its name and its heritage."

"She's asked if you might be interested in a teaching position."

Alexandra let the letter drop into her lap. "*That's* what you weren't going to tell me."

"Not until you were ready to look for another position. But you are, and Emma Grenville has one available for you."

The butler scratched at the half-open door.

"Yes, Timms?"

He stepped into the doorway. "I beg your pardon, my lady, but Lord Kilcairn is in the library."

Alexandra's heart stopped.

"Lord Kilcairn?" Vixen repeated, glancing sideways at her companion. "I shall go see to him."

"Actually, my lady, he requested a word with Miss

Gallant. He said it was a matter of some urgency."

"Lex, do you—"

"I'd best go, then," Alexandra said unsteadily, rising to kiss Victoria on one cheek. "Thank you, and please don't say anything."

"Do you want me to go with you?"

"No. I can manage Lord Kilcairn on my own." Her poor attempt at self-confidence didn't even convince herself, but Vixen nodded.

"I'll be close by."

The image of petite Victoria defending her against tall, powerful Kilcairn almost made Alexandra smile, and she held firmly to that silly image as she followed the butler down the hallway. Lucien stood in the center of the library, facing the doorway. She took one look at his face and dismissed Timms.

"Lucien," she said, folding her hands behind her back.

His sensuous lips set in a thin, grim line and his tanned face pale and strained, the earl didn't budge as the Fontaines' butler softly closed the door. Gray eyes studied her face for a long moment. "I wanted to apologize," he said, his voice low and toneless.

"Ap—apologize?"

Lucien cleared his throat. "Yes. As you said, you are an employee, hired to tutor my cousin. We suffered a . . . temporary lack of restraint, but I had no right to involve you in my personal difficulties. I won't do so again."

Looking at his straight-backed, proud stance, Alexandra doubted he'd ever apologized to anyone before in his entire life. Even so, this was an aspect of Lucien Balfour she felt almost acquainted with. This was his honorable side, the part of himself he usually joked about—the side that had stood between her and Virgil

Retting and let her cousin escape virtually unscathed simply because she'd asked him to.

"How did you know I'd be here?" she asked, mostly to give herself time to decipher which game he was playing now—if any.

"Lady Victoria is the only acquaintance you've mentioned in London. Will you come back?"

That was it, she realized. He thought she'd left for good, or that she was about to. And he had come to find her, to stop her, to ask her to return. She, a ruined governess, had made Lucien Balfour bend. Trying to keep her breathing and her heartbeat steady, Alexandra nodded. "I said I would help Rose with her party, and I will do so."

Again he hesitated. "And after that?"

"I have been offered a teaching position at Miss Grenville's Academy. I will accept it."

A muscle in his lean cheek jumped, but otherwise he remained as still as a Grecian statue. "As you wish. My cousin was distressed at your . . . abrupt departure. I request that you return to see her as soon as you are able."

"I shall."

She expected him to offer to escort her back to Balfour House, but he walked past her and opened the door without another word. A moment later the front door shut. Alexandra stood there for several minutes. Finally he'd given her what she'd demanded when she first arrived: distance, respect, and propriety. She should have been relieved. She had her position, and no more temptations of physical or marital intimacy. Yet all she could think was that now he'd never want to kiss her again, much less make love to her. Instead of relief, she felt distinctly like crying.

* * *

Lucien made a point of not returning home until nearly midnight. He had dinner at White's with some friends, and then spent the next few hours losing at faro to several substandard players.

He wanted to return home, to make certain she was there, and that she hadn't packed up her things and her little dog and left. But if he rushed back, or worse yet, if he went home to wait for her, then she would know that every sentence he'd uttered at Fontaine House had been a lie.

His original plan of marrying Alexandra Gallant still seemed utterly brilliant. His execution of said plan, though, had been clumsy, stupid, and completely reprehensible. What he remained certain of was that he needed her to stay. Practical as she was, eventually she would see his point. Until then, he would consider himself in very unfriendly territory, with possible disaster behind each misstep or misspoken word.

After all, foul human that his father had been, even he had managed to marry the bride he'd chosen. Maybe Alexandra was right, and he couldn't have everything he wanted. But he would have her—or at least he'd make a damned good try at it.

To his surprise, his first obstacle wasn't Alexandra, but Robert Ellis, Lord Belton. With a good-morning only long enough to confirm in person that Alexandra had returned, he left the breakfast room and went out to the stable to view a new pair of carriage horses he'd purchased.

"Do you own any animals that aren't black?" Robert asked from the wide stable entry.

Damn. "It's a statement of style," he answered. "How'd you know I was here?"

"I didn't. Wimbole said you'd gone out, but I ran

across Miss Gallant in your garden. She told me where you were."

So she was keeping an eye on him—that was promising. "How fortunate."

"I thought so. She also mentioned that you'd been looking for me, to reschedule my picnic with Miss Delacroix."

"No, I haven't." Lucien handed his grooming brush over to one of the stableboys and headed outside—along the carriage path, so he could avoid the garden and its temptations.

Robert fell into step beside him. "Why not?"

"You can stop your charade, Belton. I know you're only attempting to drag my miserable existence a little further into the mud."

The viscount furrowed his brow. "Beg pardon?"

Lucien stopped. "Come now, Robert. Rose Delacroix? Leave be, so the rest of the rabble can have a go at her."

"Hmm. I won't contradict you, Lucien, because you won't listen to it, but I did promise your cousin a picnic. It would be both rude and improper of me to deny her one."

"My, my, aren't you polished this morning," Lucien said dryly. "Then have at it, boy. I'll even supply the luncheon."

Robert grinned. "And your phaeton and new pair, if you please."

"You mean for today?"

"Miss Gallant already informed me that Rose has no engagements this afternoon. She's gone to fetch her for me."

Miss Gallant's behavior was even more annoying than being outmaneuvered by a stripling like Robert. Alexandra suddenly seemed in a damned hurry to marry Rose off, and it didn't take much to determine why. When Rose found a husband, her governess would be free to find a new position, all strings tied off neatly.

"Go, then," he said, hiding his frustration with the ease provided by thirty-two years of practice. "I can only presume that an extended time spent with cousin Rose will cure you of the desire to repeat the experience."

"You've a black heart, Kilcairn."

Ha—little Robert comprehended. As of yesterday morning, he had become Miss Gallant's ideal gentleman. Lucien knew what she liked, what she wanted, and what she'd hoped to accomplish in teaching him her scattered lessons in propriety. What she didn't know was that she'd just succeeded beyond her wildest expectations.

He sent his footmen scurrying off with instructions, then led Robert inside. As they reached the foyer, Rose and Alexandra were descending the stairs, and he paused to wait for them.

"Are you certain you want to go anywhere with this scoundrel, cousin?" he asked, taking her shawl from Wimbole and placing it around her shoulders himself.

Rose blushed. "I'm certain Lord Belton is not a scoundrel." She giggled. "It will be fun, even if he is."

"I am a perfect gentleman." Robert took her arm. "And I'll have you know that your cousin here is providing us with both our meal and our transportation—and his new team."

"Really?" Rose gave him a surprised look. "Thank you, Lucien."

"My pleasure."

Alexandra looked at least as surprised, but she said nothing as Wimbole opened the front door. The phaeton waited outside, a picnic basket perched in the back, along with Vincent to tend the horses and serve as chaperone.

Lucien followed them out and handed Rose into the phaeton's high seat. Making certain Alexandra was near enough to see and hear, he kissed his cousin's knuckles before he released her hand. "You almost make me want to go on a picnic myself, Rose. I'll see you in a few hours."

He watched the carriage disappear down Grosvenor Street, then turned to head back inside. Alexandra stood watching him, suspicion in every contour of her lovely face. "After you," he said, gesturing.

"So you're a candle," she said, unmoving.

"I light up a room, you mean?"

"No. You're either fully aflame or out cold."

"That sounds more like your temperament than mine. I'm merely being polite."

Her eyes narrowed. "Yes, but why?"

"Someone told me it was the proper thing to do." He motioned her toward the door again. "If you don't mind. Parliament will be in session tomorrow, and I have a few papers to review."

Alexandra hesitated, then climbed the shallow steps. With her back turned, he allowed his gaze to longingly travel the curves of her slender body. This plan had best work, because keeping his hands and mouth and mind and body off her was already killing him.

Rose twirled in a circle while Shakespeare tried to catch the hem of her dress in his teeth. As the girl plopped onto the couch, Alexandra scooped up her dog and gave him an old knotted sock to play with instead.

"So you enjoyed yourself," she said with a smile, enduring her pupil's high spirits with a small twinge of jealousy. She hadn't felt like spinning since Lucien had last kissed her.

"We went out in a rowboat, and we fed bread to the ducks. By the time we left the lake there must have been fifty ducks quacking behind us. Robert said they looked like Admiral Nelson's fleet."

"Oh, Robert, is it now?" Fiona said from her nest by the tea cakes. "Did he give you permission to call him that?"

"He insisted. And I said he should call me Rose." She giggled, covering her mouth with both hands. "He said he might just as well call me Sunshine, but Rose would do."

"That's wonderful, my darling. Miss Gallant said that Lucien saw you off this morning."

"Yes, he did. He was quite nice, Mama."

Fiona dusted cake crumbs off her ample front. "Nice in what way?"

"He told me that seeing me almost made him want to go on a picnic himself."

Rose's mother beamed. "I knew having his family here would do him good. Don't you think so, Miss Gallant?"

Alexandra shook herself out of a daydream in which Lucien said nice things to her. Had it only been yesterday? "Yes. I would have to say I've seen a definite change in him."

"Why don't you go find him, Miss Gallant, and ask him to join us?"

"To join us?" she repeated dubiously.

"Yes. Rose will play for him."

"He said he had some papers to review."

"Miss Gallant, if you please," Fiona said, annoyance touching her already shrill voice.

"Of course." Tossing Shakespeare's sock into the corner to keep him occupied, Alexandra left the room. This had all been complicated enough to begin with. Now that she'd fallen in love with a man who looked to be quite possibly the world's worst husband after Henry VIII, it was impossible.

He had a compassionate side; she'd seen it. With the horrid example of his own parents and his own lifestyle, though, he didn't seem to have any idea of what made a marriage. If he did know, it didn't seem to be anything he wanted. She could not and would not be anyone's "convenience," whatever she felt for him in her heart.

His office door was closed, and she hesitated before she knocked. "My lord?"

"Come in."

Lucien sat at his desk, with what looked like several contracts and agreements open before him. He raised a hand at her, indicating that she should wait a moment, and finished scrawling something in the margin of one of the pages.

"Yes?" He lifted his head and looked at her.

From his expression, she might have been nothing more than a footman to him. "Mrs. Delacroix sent me to ask if you'd care to join us in the sitting room. Miss Delacroix wishes to play for you. I told her you were busy, but she insisted."

"So you've blown out your candle, as well?"

She wanted to respond to his cynicism, and sternly stopped herself. "Please, my lord. I don't wish to argue."

Lucien nodded, rising. "I'm glad you've decided to stay until after Rose's party."

"I'm thankful you didn't turn me away yesterday."

Something she couldn't decipher touched his face for

a fleeting moment, then was gone again. "You wanted to stay."

It wasn't a question. Alexandra stifled a curse and turned to lead the way back to the Delacroix ladies. She hadn't meant to let him know that. The next few days would have been so much easier if he'd thought she was merely fulfilling her obligation to Rose. "I dislike leaving a task unfinished," she improvised.

"So do I."

She spent the rest of the day making up underlying meanings to his response, and ending up with nothing but a splitting headache. For once, Rose played passingly well, and even Lucien was generous with his compliments. After that, every time Alexandra tried to turn the conversation to Lord Belton, it went right back to Kilcairn. By bedtime she knew that his favorite color was blue, his favorite composer was Mozart, and his favorite dessert was, surprisingly, chocolate cremes.

Even after the earl excused himself for the evening, the nonsense continued. If she hadn't known any better, she would have thought Rose and Fiona were pursuing Lucien's interest instead of Lord Belton's. Alexandra paused in her tickling of Shakespeare. It couldn't be. He detested them. Or he had, anyway.

"Oh, my," she said into the prattle. "I hadn't realized the time. I'd best get to bed."

"Yes, we all need our beauty sleep," Fiona agreed.

Alexandra excused herself and went to fetch Shakespeare's leash. Thankfully, Lucien—Kilcairn, now, for she hadn't any right to use his Christian name any longer—had become more lax about his "no piddling in the garden" rule, and she led the terrier downstairs and outside.

"I thought you'd end up out here."

She gasped. Seated on a stone bench in the shadows beneath the library window, Lucien puffed on a cigar.

"My goodness, you gave me a start," she whispered, wondering at how much had changed since their last midnight rendezvous by the roses.

The tip of his cigar glowed orange and faded as he inhaled. "I neglected something yesterday," he said in the low, intimate drawl that made her knees weak.

"What was that?"

"Are you going to stand all the way over there?"

She looked at the dark rose blooms surrounding her. "Yes, I think so."

"All right. I'll shout it if you wish."

"Fine." With an annoyed harrumph Alexandra tugged Shakespeare out of the shrubbery and stalked a few feet closer to the earl.

He looked at her for a long moment, then lowered his gaze. "When you . . . refused me yesterday, I—"

"I don't want to talk about that," she interrupted, more harshly than she intended. If she didn't work on keeping her anger, though, she would begin to cry.

"You may be pregnant, Alexandra," he murmured.

She froze, blood draining from her face. "I am not!"

"Shh. You can't know that yet. I wanted to assure you that if you are, I will take care of you."

"Hide me away at one of your country estates, you mean?" she snapped, tears filling her eyes. "The Balfour men seem to excel at that."

He whipped to his feet. "What would you have preferred that I tell you?" he growled. "That I would turn my back and leave you to the fates? I already asked you to marry me, and you refused. So you tell me, Alexandra. What do you want?"

With effort, Alexandra fought down her frightened,

angry panic. "I am not pregnant," she said as calmly as she could. "And I am leaving in one week. You don't need to concern yourself at all."

He ground his cigar out on the bench. "It's a bit late for that."

She pretended not to hear as she and Shakespeare returned to the house and her bedchamber. What he'd said had been correct, and noble, and in a way, exactly what she'd wanted to hear from him. And part of her—a very small part of her—wanted to be carrying his child. The decision of whether to stay or go would be removed, and she would never have to admit even to herself that she'd given in.

Alexandra sighed. That was how she knew she wasn't pregnant. It would have made everything too easy.

Fiona Delacroix moved away from the window and set down the book of French fashions she'd intended to take upstairs. Staying carefully quiet in the dim library, she listened until two sets of footsteps went up the stairs and faded away.

So that was it. She'd known something was afoot. The governess was after her nephew, and it sounded as though she'd gone a fair way toward catching him. Under the same roof—practically under her nose—Alexandra Gallant was a breath away from catching one of the wealthiest men in England.

Lifting her candle, she made her way over to the writing desk. She'd attempted it before, the little strumpet. She'd lifted her heels for Lord Welkins, and then no doubt did him in when he tired of her. Since Welkins had been married, she would only have been after his money. With Lord Kilcairn, though, no doubt she would want it all—his money, his land, and his title.

Well, not this time. Lucien Balfour was going to marry Rose, and that was that. She'd planned it for years; the moment was not going to slip away simply because her nephew had become temporarily infatuated with a woman who was practically a servant.

As for Miss Gallant, she knew where that miss belonged, too. Fiona sat and wrote out a note, folded it, and left it on the foyer table under some other correspondence to be delivered first thing in the morning. No doubt Lady Welkins had been lonely this Season. Lady Halverston had already mentioned knowing the unfortunate widow; Fiona would like to make her acquaintance, too. They apparently had something in common. Another widow to console Lady Welkins would be just what the baroness needed. And then Alexandra Gallant would go away.

Chapter 15

"Oh, nonsense." Alexandra gestured for Rose to precede her into the millinery. "I'm sure he's not pining over you."

"But it's true!" the girl insisted. "He's sent me a letter every day for the past week, and I know he's called on Lucien at least twice."

"They are friends, you know."

"Lex, you just aren't romantic."

Alexandra chuckled. Perhaps Rose had hit on her problem. If she had been romantic, though, she probably would have drowned herself in the nearest pond by now. "All right. I concede that you may very well be correct, and Lord Belton is indeed pining over you, but I don't want you to be disappointed if he's not."

Rose lifted a pretty blue hat off its stand to examine it. "I suppose you're right. Freddie Danvers at home, the squire's son, used to say he wanted to marry me all the time, but I never believed him. And Mama said it would take a dowry bigger than Dorsetshire to pay off his gambling debts, and he wasn't likely to find that with us, anyway."

Alexandra paused in her perusal of a practical brown schoolmistress's hat. Despite their lack of social skills, she'd assumed the Delacroix ladies to be wealthy. They'd seemed more concerned with netting a title than a mound of cash, though perhaps they'd been under the impression that the two went together, as they did with Lord Kilcairn.

"If your dowry wasn't a consideration, would you have wanted to marry this Freddie Danvers?"

Her student made a sour face. "Good heavens, no. He only has a six-room cottage, and no title at all. Even Blything Hall is bigger than that, and I wouldn't want to move somewhere smaller." She replaced the blue hat and moved on to a quaint green bonnet.

"Of course not. How silly of me."

"Now you're just teasing."

"I am not. Please, go on."

"About three years ago, when Lucien was in London, Mama and Papa and I went to Westchester and convinced his housekeeper to give us a tour of Kilcairn Abbey. You should have seen it, Lex. It has more than two hundred rooms, and six sitting rooms, and *two* ballrooms. Mama said she could imagine herself holding court there, while Lucien and I had all the neighboring nobility over for country balls."

"You and Lucien?" Alexandra asked slowly, her heart giving a distinct lurch. This was ridiculous. She had no reason to become so . . . irrational every time a female mentioned his name. Half the time she couldn't even decide whether she loved him or hated him.

Rose blanched, then with a nervous twitter put on the bonnet. "Oh, it's not me at all, is it?" she said, giggling, and flung it off again. "Do let's go somewhere else, Lex.

I don't like anything in here." With that she flitted off toward the door.

Alexandra looked after her for a moment. "Whatever you like, my dear."

That was odd. Exceedingly odd, unless her own recent suspicions were correct and Rose did have her cap set for Lord Kilcairn. She'd seemed so pleased by Lord Belton's attentions, though. Alexandra wondered if Lucien knew his cousin had developed a tendre for him. Given the way he'd been conducting his outrageous bridal search, he probably hadn't noticed.

"Lex? Come on."

"Right away." She hurried out the door in Rose's wake.

The first thing she needed to do was find out whether Rose preferred Robert or her Lucien. Alexandra frowned. He wasn't *her* anything, just as she wasn't his. She'd made that clear enough. And she was not jealous of a seventeen-year-old girl, whatever the circumstances. She wasn't.

The noontime crowd in front of the corner bakery finally forced Rose to slow, and Alexandra caught up and wrapped her arm around her student's. "Please slow down, my dear. I feel like a racehorse in the Derby." The girl still wore a tense expression, and Alexandra reminded herself that her primary duty was to see to her charge's well-being. "Shall we get a crumb cake?"

"Mama wouldn't approve."

"We won't tell her."

Rose gave a reluctant grin. "All right."

She stepped into line. Alexandra moved up behind her—and then froze at the sight of the woman walking toward them along the street. Small and wasted looking despite her straight back and elevated chin, her graying hair stuffed under a black widow's cap, she looked neither right nor left, but continued unerringly toward the bakery as though she knew Alexandra was standing there.

"Oh, no," she whispered, blanching, and grabbed Rose again.

"What—"

"Shh." Alexandra pulled her surprised charge backward, around the corner and into an alleyway. When they were well out of sight she stopped, putting her hand to her chest and trying to catch her breath.

"What is it? What's wrong?" Rose asked, her expression concerned.

Alexandra glanced back the way they had come. She'd best salvage what propriety she could. "I'm sorry, Rose," she said in a low voice. "That was inexcusably rude of me."

"Don't mind that. Are you all right?"

Slowly her breathing began to return to normal, though she'd probably be jumpy for the next week. "Yes, I'm fine. It's just . . . well . . . you see, I saw my former employer a moment ago. It . . . rather surprised me."

The girl's blue eyes grew round. "You mean Lady Welkins?"

She nodded. So even her pupil had heard the rumors. "I just didn't know she was in London. I should have realized."

"What are you going to do?"

"Nothing." Alexandra squared her shoulders. "I'll be leaving soon, anyway. I will simply stay out of her way as much as my duties allow."

"Well, I certainly won't make you talk to her," Rose said indignantly.

Alexandra smiled. "Thank you, Rose."

* * *

Fiona sipped her tea and half listened to the chatter around her. Mrs. Fox was lamenting the gout that kept her husband housebound all day, but didn't prevent him from venturing out to his clubs at night. Lady Howard had heard that Charlotte Tanner hadn't left her debut Season in London early because she was ill, but because she was with child—by a gentleman unknown. And right on schedule, Lady Vixen Fontaine had broken another poor boy's heart.

It was all very interesting, but it wasn't what she was waiting for. The butler opened the door to Lady Halverston's drawing room yet again, and Fiona looked up as she had every time someone had joined their tea over the past hour. This time she didn't recognize the woman being ushered into the room, and she straightened, setting aside her cup.

"Ah, Margaret," Lady Halverston said, rising to clasp the woman's hands, "I'm so glad you've come."

"Thank you, Lady Halverston. I was pleased to receive your invitation."

"Nonsense. We're happy to have you here." Lady Halverston urged her farther into the room. "My dears, please welcome Lady Welkins."

Fiona rose before anyone else could. "Oh, Lady Welkins, you have my deepest, deepest sympathies."

"Margaret, Mrs. Delacroix," Lady Halverston provided, and with a slight nod at Fiona, returned to her seat.

"You must call me Fiona, please. I already feel we have so much in common, and I couldn't wait to meet you. Do sit with me, won't you, my lady?"

"Thank you, Fiona." The thin woman, her dark hair turning to silver beneath her black widow's cap, sat on the couch and accepted a cup of tea from a waiting footman.

"I have only just put off my mourning cap myself," Fiona said. "My dear Oscar simply dropped dead one afternoon, leaving my poor daughter and myself all alone in the world."

"My husband was cruelly taken from me," the other woman responded, sipping her tea.

"My goodness."

Lady Welkins nodded. "I don't know if you've heard the rumors, but I firmly believe him to have been murdered."

Fiona put a hand to her bosom. "Oh, it can't be so!"

The other woman nodded. "By my own trusted companion, though I could never prove it, of course. Otherwise I would have seen her in prison, where she belongs."

The meeting was going to be even more productive than Fiona had expected. "You poor dear. It happened right in your own household, then?"

"Nearly under my very nose."

Fiona settled a look of dismay on her face, wishing Lady Welkins would hurry up and mention her blasted companion's name. She had enough woes of her own without listening to this drivel. "This is outrageous. And you say she was never arrested?"

"No. I dismissed her immediately, of course, but that seemed entirely too mild a punishment."

"Of course it does. I only ask, you know, because my nephew hired a new governess for my daughter, and oh, it would be so awful if we had to send the dear girl away."

"I'm sure you have nothing to worry about. That devious Miss Gallant would only choose a household with a wealthy man present for her to seduce."

Finally. "Did . . . did you say Miss Gallant?"

"Yes. Alexandra Gallant, that—"

"Oh, no. Miss Gallant is the name of my niece's companion."

Lady Welkins looked truly shocked. "Surely not!"

"It's true! She'd been living at Balfour House for the past month. And—Oh, no!" Fiona put her hands over her mouth as though holding in a shriek.

Her newfound bosom companion tugged at her arm. "What? What is it?"

"Just in passing, I thought Miss Gallant might have designs on my nephew. I didn't take it seriously, but now—Oh, my! Do you think she might do harm to dear Lucien?"

"Is your nephew wealthy?"

Fiona nodded. "He's the Earl of Kilcairn Abbey."

"The Earl . . . Surely he must have heard of Miss Gallant's reputation."

"My nephew is very stubborn. If he did know, he may have thought to reform her, or even that the rumors were unwarranted."

Lady Welkins stood. "They are very much warranted, I assure you. She pursued Lord Welkins relentlessly, and when he finally and definitively refused her advances, I know she pushed him down the stairs—and then I think she may have strangled him. The physician said it was his heart, but William was as large as a bull, and he was only just fifty."

"But no one saw her do it?"

The widow sank back onto the couch again. "No. You see how devious she is."

"I must go at once and inform Lucien!"

Grabbing her arm, Lady Welkins forced her to remain seated. "If you do that, she'll only escape again. You must observe her. Or better yet, let her catch sight of me. That might startle her into a confession."

"You would help me with this?"

"It would be my pleasure."

Fiona smiled just a little. "My daughter's birthday celebration is in just a few days. I will see that you receive an invitation."

Lady Welkins smiled back at her. "That would be wonderful."

Alexandra sat at the music room pianoforte and played her father's favorite dance tune. "Mad Robin" frolicked through the candlelit room, chasing away the near-silence of the huge house. Rose and Fiona had thankfully retired early, and Kilcairn had abandoned them for his office hours ago. Even rakes had paperwork, she supposed.

When she'd left Lady Welkins's employ, she'd thought—and hoped—never to see the woman again. Margaret Thewles, Lady Welkins, had every right to grieve for her dead husband; Alexandra felt bad enough about that herself. But to suddenly turn a man whose lecherous activities his wife had complained about daily into a saint was ridiculous. And to turn Alexandra into a murdering whore just to retain her own standing and avoid some mild embarrassment—that was unforgivable.

If Lady Welkins hadn't begun her tirade about Alexandra, no one in London would have had cause to give her—or her husband—a second thought. Perhaps that was why she'd made such a stink. At least people knew who Lady Welkins was now.

She tried to calm herself. Even though Lady Welkins had come to London, there was little reason for them to meet. With just over six months gone since her awful husband's passing, she wouldn't be able to dance, so she had little reason to accept any invitations to the same soirees Rose delighted in. That was some comfort, anyway. And with Rose's birthday only a few days away, the odds of Lady Welkins making trouble before Alexandra left for Miss Grenville's Academy were quite small. Or so she hoped.

"You play beautifully." Lucien's soft voice came from the doorway. "Something else for which I should thank Miss Grenville?"

Her fingers hit a few sour notes in response to his sudden appearance, but Alexandra continued to play. "My father taught me."

"Your father played?"

"Painting wasn't his only skill."

His quiet approach stirred the air around her. "Do you have any of his paintings?"

"I had to sell them to pay for my parents' burial, and to settle their outstanding accounts."

He seated himself on the other end of the bench, facing opposite her. "Do you have any family remaining on your paternal side?"

"I believe I have a few second cousins in the North, but I wouldn't know where to begin looking if I were inclined to do so."

"So here we sit, two orphans, all alone," he mused.

Alexandra glanced at his profile, quiet and sensuous as sin in the half dark. "You seem to be able to tolerate Rose."

He shrugged. "She's hardly anyone I could confide in."

"It's lucky you don't require a confidante, then."

For a moment he was silent, while the music danced in the shadowy corners of the room. "Yes, I suppose it's lucky neither of us needs anyone else."

She pretended not to hear his soft comment; with Lady Welkins in London, Lucien's company was rather comforting. Tonight she was content not to argue with him. The dance ended, but she began it again with barely a pause.

"Rose and I had a little chat this evening," he said in the same quiet tone.

"I'm glad you're becoming slightly more civilized." At the same time, a large, lonely portion of her heart wished he and his cousin hadn't begun to get along so well.

"She mentioned that you saw Lady Welkins today."

Her fingers faltered.

"Keep playing," he murmured. " 'Mad Robin,' isn't it? I haven't heard it for a long time. And never played so well."

He was only trying to flatter her, but she didn't mind all that much. "It was a family favorite."

"I didn't mean to upset you, Alexandra. I just wanted to make certain you were all right. Lady Welkins didn't see you, I assume?"

"No, she didn't."

"And you are all right?"

Alexandra closed her eyes, letting the music flow through her fingers. "I'll make do. After all, I'll only be in London another few days."

She expected a protest, but he remained silent for a minute. "I could have done without that being added into the conversation," he finally said.

"Then we won't speak of it."

"Alexandra, if I hadn't asked you to marry me, would you have stayed longer?"

"I don't know," she whispered. "Virgil and Lady Welkins would have been in London anyway, but . . . Lucien, it's not only because of you. I just shouldn't be here."

"I think here is exactly where you should be."

She didn't know what to say to that, and after another few minutes of silence he rose and moved to the door. "Good night, Alexandra."

"Good night, Lucien."

By the afternoon of Rose's birthday extravaganza, Lucien felt as though he were coming apart at the seams.

Keeping track of Lady Welkins and making certain the blasted woman and Alexandra didn't come within a mile of one another was taxing enough. Making the past few days even more difficult, he didn't want Alexandra to suspect that he might have anyone spying on her daily excursions, either.

In addition, he'd managed to evade Robert Ellis all three times the viscount had come to call. While he couldn't imagine that Robert actually meant to offer for Rose, neither could he come up with a better reason for the lad's persistence.

Keeping Rose single and Lady Welkins absent had kept Alexandra present, but after tonight he had no hold on her at all. At his request, Wimbole had begun checking on the stubborn chit's activities within the house, and this morning the butler reported that she'd begun to pack. With that news, the day seemed about as dismal as it could get.

And then he intercepted the letter.

He nearly missed it, and if he hadn't headed out the

front door for a breath of fresh air, it would have bypassed his notice completely. Thank God for the frilly decorating chaos that made him flee.

"Vincent, where are you off to?" he asked from his refuge on the front steps, as the steady stream of decorators, caterers, ice carts, and bakers went around to the back of the house.

The groom hesitated at the bottom of the steps. "Delivering a few messages, my lord."

"Doesn't Thompkinson do that?"

"Aye, my lord, but he's been put to the task of polishing a last coat of beeswax onto the ballroom floor."

"It wouldn't be a true party without someone slipping and breaking his head." Dimly he heard Aunt Fiona calling him from the depths of the house. "My missive to Lord Daubner can wait until tomorrow, if you have other duties."

"That's very kind of you, my lord. I've a last-minute invitation going to Henrietta Street, though, for Mrs. Delacroix, so Jeffries House is on my way."

Henrietta Street was on the fringes of Mayfair, where the newer and less illustrious *ton* dwelled. Considering that Aunt Fiona had only wanted the most glittering members of the nobility present at her daughter's party, Lucien's curiosity was immediately engaged. "Who's it for?"

Vincent held it out. "I only memorized the address, my lord. I don't read."

Lucien did read, but he still had to study the missive for several moments before he believed what it said. He glanced up at the groom. "Make your other deliveries, Vincent. I'll see to this one."

The lad doffed his hat and hurried off to saddle a mount. Anger curled up Lucien's spine, and the longer he tried to figure the whys and wheretores of the invitation's existence, the more furious he became. Deliberately he broke the wax seal bearing his house's initials and read it, then he crammed the damned thing into his pocket and made his way inside.

Aunt Fiona, Rose, and Alexandra stood in the middle of the ballroom watching the mad dash of activity around them. Lucien stopped in the doorway. "Everyone, out!" he roared.

Alexandra looked up at him, surprised, her turquoise gaze trying to read his infuriated expression. "What's wrong, my lord?"

Wimbole had appeared from another doorway, and immediately began ushering servants and workers out of the room. "Five minutes, Wimbole," he snapped, and the butler nodded.

Predictably his cousin's eyes filled with tears at the upset, and he gave her an annoyed glance. "Rose, excuse us for a moment."

A tear ran down one cheek. "But—"

"Now!"

She jumped and fled. A moment later, only Fiona and Alexandra remained. He had a fair idea how Alexandra would react to what he was about to say, and after a hesitation he gestured her toward the door, as well. "You, too, Miss Gallant."

"As you wish, my lord." With another curious, concerned look she left, closing the door behind her.

"What in the world is the matter, Lucien?" his aunt trilled. "We only have a few hours until the guests begin to arrive."

"How long have you been acquainted with Lady Welkins?" he asked, slamming the main double doors shut.

She paled, but kept her chin raised. "My acquaintances are my own affair."

He remained silent and angry, waiting for her to answer his question. She had done more than gone behind his back; she had tried to hurt Alexandra—and from her response, she had done it deliberately.

His aunt shifted. "I don't know what you're so annoyed at, anyway. We're just two widows, sharing our tales of misfortune."

"If you don't answer my question, you're going to have more misfortune than you'll know what to do with." He took the invitation from his pocket and threw it at her feet. "You will not see that woman again, and she is never—*never*—to be allowed into this house."

Green eyes glared at him. "You deny a lonely widow friendship, and yet you let that murdering female live under your roof, while your own cousin tries to make a proper debut in society?"

"That's right—it's *my* roof, Fiona. If I can stand having you living under it, I can stand anything. And Miss Gallant tries my patience far less than you do."

"What about her awful reputation?"

"What about mine?"

Fiona jabbed a finger in his direction. "Bah! Don't think you can fool me about what's going on. She's after your fortune, just like she was after Lord Welkins's. I know that she's sharing your bed. And you can't make me keep quiet about it, either."

Lucien's first thought was that Fiona had more intelligence than he'd given her credit for. His second was how much he'd like to throttle her. At the moment, though, considering how many people knew they were alone together in the ballroom, that might raise some sticky questions. "If I can't make you keep quiet here,

I can certainly send you back to Blything Hall, where no one cares what you prattle about."

"Don't threaten me!"

With effort he kept from growling. "Don't try to play this game with me. I'm better at it than you are."

"You—"

"What do you want?" he broke in.

"I want that woman gone from this house."

"She's leaving anyway."

"I don't want her coming back—ever. Together, Lady Welkins and I know enough about Alexandra Gallant to see that she never finds employment again. Anywhere. I want her gone."

The desire to throttle her was becoming stronger. "And after you've rid yourself of Miss Gallant? I presume you have something additional in mind."

"Yes, I do. I want you to marry Rose."

For a moment he could only stare at her. "What?" he finally choked.

"You marry Rose, and I'll leave Miss Gallant alone. I know you care for that whore—I heard you telling her you would take care of your bastard. So Rose is going to be Lady Kilcairn, and my grandchildren are going to inherit your titles, your land, and your wealth."

"By God, you're ambitious. Just how long have you been planning this?" he asked, almost admiring her audacity.

"Only since I saw what you inherited, and what dear Oscar didn't. Rose will have her party tonight, Lucien, and everyone will see how well the two of you suit. And then you will announce your engagement."

Fiona turned on her heel and left. Lucien stood there in the middle of the ballroom for several minutes. What his aunt proposed wasn't blackmail, precisely, because he wouldn't pay any consequences if she made her suppositions and allegations public. Alexandra would, though. He cursed. He'd been careless, and he'd left Alexandra vulnerable. He'd even allowed his damned aunt to have the last word, and so far only Miss Gallant had managed to do that to him.

Lucien narrowed his eyes. Fiona hadn't bested him yet. And she'd made a huge mistake: she'd given him time to make a plan.

Alexandra folded her new shawl and placed it with the other things in her trunk. The ivory-colored lace was too lovely and too delicate for travel. Most of her new things were too lavish for anywhere but London. As a teacher, she wouldn't have much use for them at all, but she couldn't bear to part with them. Not yet, anyway.

"Miss Gallant?" Lucien knocked at her door.

He sounded less angry than he had been in the ballroom, but something deadly serious remained in his voice. Whatever it was, today was difficult enough without the agony of spending time alone with him.

"Miss Gallant," the earl repeated, knocking again. "Alexandra, I know you're in there."

Shakespeare emerged from beneath the bed and trotted over to wag his tail at the door. Of course the terrier liked Lucien; in the earl's house he was allowed to do exactly as he pleased. Alexandra was, too, but unfortunately that freedom ended at the front door.

The latch rattled as something heavy hit the door, and the doorframe splintered. Lucien shouldered the door open the rest of the way and strode into the room. "You might have answered me," he said calmly, brushing splinters from his coat.

"My silence was my answer," she replied, and returned to packing.

Lucien squatted down and scooped Shakespeare into his arms. "We have a problem."

She set aside her old blue traveling hat for the morning. "I didn't think you'd begun roaring at everyone for no good reason."

"My aunt knows that you and I are lovers."

Alexandra flinched. "We *were* lovers. We aren't any longer. And I'm leaving tomorrow, so I don't care what she knows."

Absently he scratched Shakespeare's head. "She's struck up an acquaintance with Lady Welkins."

"She . . ." The room began spinning, and she sat down hard on the floor.

"Alexandra," Lucien said sharply, and knelt beside her. "You're not the fainting sort, remember?"

"I'm not fainting," she rasped, putting a hand to her forehead. "I'm going to be ill. Lady Welkins in London is . . . one thing. But Mrs. Delacroix knowing her . . . Oh, my goodness."

"It'll be all right. I have a solution."

Suddenly he was her white knight again, charging in to her rescue. Something, though, didn't make sense. She took Shakespeare out of his arms and tried to ignore the rush of her blood as their fingers brushed. "Why did you break down my door?"

He narrowed his eyes. "What?"

"I said, 'Why did you break down my door?' "

"Because you didn't answer me. And—"

"And why did you say 'we' have a problem? It seems to me that Lady Welkins is my worry."

"For God's sake, Alexandra." Lucien took a deep

breath, his gray eyes somber. "Fiona's threatened to cause trouble for you, unless . . ."

The last piece of the puzzle fell neatly into place. "Unless you agree to marry Rose."

He blinked. "How did you know that?"

"I have eyes and ears. And I've spent more time with your relations than you have."

Reaching out, he took hold of her fingers, his grip warm and sure. "Alexandra, my name can protect you. Even if Lady Welkins and Fiona both started spewing nonsense, if . . . if you were my wife, no one would dare come near you. Marry me, Alexandra. Please."

He was definitely getting better at proposing, and the part of her that longed for him wanted to sag into his arms and let him simply take care of her. But the other part of her, the cool, logical part that knew she couldn't rely on anyone but herself, couldn't ignore a very obvious chink in his plea—or a seventeen-year-old girl who regarded her cousin with some affection.

"And if you married me, you wouldn't have to marry Rose."

"I don't have to marry Rose anyway. Alexandra—"

"No." She climbed to her feet. "Fiona only wants me gone because she sees me as a rival to Rose. Thanks to Emma Grenville, I have somewhere else to go."

He looked up at her. "And the next time Fiona gets angry with me, she can spout enough nasty nonsense that even Miss Grenville's Academy won't employ you."

"Just to spite you?"

"Because she knows I care for you."

She set Shakespeare on the bed and went back to packing. "No. I am not going to be some chess piece for everyone to try to maneuver about the board. I'm leaving in the morning, and you can turn your antiquated ideas of chivalry toward helping Rose, who may be under the mistaken impression that she likes you."

Lucien climbed to his feet and grabbed her shift away from her. "You are not leaving. You are not leaving me."

He was much bigger and stronger than she was, but she'd never been afraid of him, and she wasn't now. Alexandra yanked her clothes back. "You've known for a week that today was to be my last day here. Don't pretend to be concerned over me now, when we both know it's yourself and the parentage of Kilcairn Abbey's descendants that troubles you."

"It is not—"

"And don't bellow at me. Volume is not going to change my mind." She flung the shift, uncaring of wrinkles, into the trunk. "Now, if you'll excuse me, I will say my good-byes now, so Rose will have her party to cheer her up."

Her voice wasn't at all steady, but he was so upset at having his brilliant little plan foiled that he probably didn't even notice. And after he stalked out of the room and left her to sit crying on her bed, he couldn't have known just how much she wanted him to say that he loved her, instead of coming up with some other reason that she needed to stay.

She'd run out of reasons that wouldn't end up breaking her heart. And whatever Rose's plans were, a fine governess and teacher she would be, stepping into the middle of someone else's opportunity. Rose certainly had more right to Lucien than she did. At least Fiona realized that, even if no one else did.

The good-byes went as she expected. Rose wept and threatened to lock herself in her room, until Alexandra reminded her that tears would make her cheeks puffy and that the entire gala that evening was in her honor. Mrs. Delacroix, outside her daughter's presence, didn't even pretend to be unhappy, though she did at least wish Alexandra well at Miss Grenville's Academy.

As for Lucien, he avoided her all evening as he went about being pleasant and charming to his guests. He did glare at her a few times, and then managed to vanish before she could demand an explanation as to why he thought this was all her fault. Fine. It would just make leaving him tomorrow that much easier.

Just as she was about to excuse herself for her third cry of the evening, though, he materialized at her elbow. "My lord," she said, and finished directing a footman to open one of the ballroom windows before people began fainting from the heat and stuffiness.

When the servant left, Lucien moved around in front of her. "I just wanted to suggest that after you finish packing tonight, you might sleep in the yellow room. I'm having it prepared for you, as your bedchamber door seems to have met with a slight accident."

"Thank you, my lord."

He stuck out his hand, the gesture abrupt and completely lacking his usual grace. "I will also say goodbye now; my coach will be waiting in the morning to take you wherever you wish to go. I suggest you leave before Rose rises, as I would like to keep her weeping to a minimum."

Alexandra nodded and shook his hand. For a moment she hoped he would pull her into his arms and carry her off, but it seemed he'd learned the lessons she'd taught him about propriety. He released her hand, bowed, and walked away. Alexandra watched him go, and wished she'd been a less proficient teacher.

* * *

Fiona watched the tense handshake and set, somber expressions of Lucien and Miss Gallant with glee. She would have preferred to have Lady Welkins present to serve as her exclamation point, but everything seemed to be going well without her. Lucien's affection for the girl gave him a much more effective inducement to marry Rose than anything else she might have come up with, anyway.

She returned her attention to the ballroom floor as the last waltz of the evening ended. Lord Belton had managed to secure it, no doubt with considerable assistance from Rose. The viscount escorted Rose back to the side of the room where her mother had been surrounded by her circle of new cronies, and she smiled at the young man.

"I wish my old feet were up to dancing. Lord Belton, you do make me envy these young ladies."

He laughed. "I would be pleased to escort you any time you wished."

"You are such a gentleman, my lord. If my mourning didn't prevent me from engaging in such frivolity, I might even dance a quadrille with you." Fiona straightened a lock of Rose's hair. The girl could never seem to keep from becoming disheveled. "My dear, will you fetch me a glass of punch?"

"I'd be happy to, Mrs. Delacroix," the viscount broke in, and started to turn away.

Fiona grabbed his sleeve. "Oh, I wouldn't have it, my lord. Rose is perfectly capable."

Rose gave her a sour look. "I'll be right back."

"You've put on a lovely party, Mrs. Delacroix. Several times Rose has commented to me how thrilled she is."

"Yes, anything for my darling."

The viscount glanced toward the crowd behind him. "Ah, there's Kilcairn. If you'll excuse me, I need to speak to your nephew for a moment."

She'd been right, and she'd caught him just in time, apparently. "My lord, are you intending to ask Lucien's permission for Rose's hand in marriage?"

Lord Belton looked surprised, but he smiled and nodded. "You've seen through me. Yes, I am. And I've had the devil of a time tracking him down this week."

Fiona sent a concerned glance in Lucien's direction, but he was well out of earshot. "In that case—my lord, he asked me not to say anything, but my sincere regard for you compels me to break my silence."

The viscount's brow furrowed. "About what?"

"You know how Lucien is about . . . well, about making fools of people."

By now he'd given her his full attention. "Yes, I do."

"Well—oh, dear, perhaps I shouldn't say."

"Please do, madame."

"Yes, yes, you're right. My lord, I'm afraid he's only been teasing you about Rose. It has been his intention to marry her himself, all along."

His handsome face paled. "You jest, madame."

She put her hand to her heart. "I could never be so cruel. It was my late husband's dearest wish, and after spending this time with her in London, Lucien several days ago informed me of his decision. He was going to announce the engagement tonight, with you in attendance, but he decided he wanted the evening to be Rose's alone."

She would have continued, but from the viscount's angry, distant expression, he'd stopped listening. A moment later he blinked and returned his gaze to her.

"You've been most kind, madame," he said tightly. "I must leave. Pray give my excuses to your daughter."

"Of course, Lord Belton. Again, please do not tell Lucien that I spoiled his joke. He'll be quite angry with me."

"Your secret is safe with me. And now, good evening."

Fiona watched the viscount make his way through the crowd, pointedly avoiding both Lucien and Rose. As he departed the room, she smiled. Dear Oscar would be so pleased.

Chapter 16

Alexandra put on her blue bonnet, fastened Shakespeare's leash, and followed the luggage-laden footmen downstairs. The sun was only a golden sliver above the rooftops as she shook Wimbole's hand and emerged into the brisk summer morning.

"We shall miss you," the butler said, and bent down to give Shakespeare a last doggie treat. "Good luck to you, Miss Gallant."

"Thank you, Wimbole." Just for a moment she hesitated on the front portico, blushing because she knew the butler must have guessed why. "Lord Kilcairn hasn't risen yet?" she asked anyway.

"He informed me that he would not be seeing you off this morning."

"Of course."

Well, that answered that. She'd refused to go along with his silly games and so now he was upstairs sulking, or worse yet, sleeping. If he'd truly cared about her instead of himself, he would have thought of something—done something—so she could stay.

Blinking another flood of tears away, she lifted the terrier into the coach and then climbed in after him. "Just take me to the nearest mail stage stop if you please, Vincent. You needn't drive me all the way to Hampshire."

The young groom doffed his hat. "As it pleases you, Miss Lex, though I'd be happy to drive you all the way." He shut the door and latched it, and the carriage rocked as he hopped up to the driver's perch. A moment later the vehicle rumbled into motion, and they were off.

Alexandra sat back in the black, cushioned seat and let the tears run down her face. Once she boarded the public mail stage, she wouldn't be able to indulge in weeping. She'd spent most of the night crying and feeling sorry for herself, but all it had done was give her a headache. Moping certainly didn't change anything. She'd fallen in love with a proud, aggravating man who didn't believe in such nonsense, and she wouldn't—she couldn't—be married to someone who only offered to wed her out of his own convenience and to spite his relations.

The coach turned another corner, and a moment later, another. She hoped Vincent wasn't lost, because he seemed to be taking a very roundabout route to the inn. She wasn't in any particular hurry, but the sooner she could begin teaching at the Academy, the sooner she could begin trying to put handsome, stubborn, impossible Lucien Balfour out of her mind.

Five or six minutes later, the coach rolled to a stop. "We're here, miss," Vincent called, and a moment later pulled the door open.

Shakespeare wagged his tail and hopped to the ground. Alexandra stood and looked out the door—to see the familiar back side of Balfour House.

"What—"

A dark, billowing cloth sailed over her head and enfolded her. Someone grabbed her around the waist, pinning her arms, and dragged her out of the coach. Before she could scream, a hand clamped over her mouth, nearly smothering her beneath the heavy material.

Shakespeare barked, and someone—it sounded like Vincent—shushed him. A moment later wood creaked, and she felt herself lifted bodily over someone's shoulder and carried down a flight of stairs. The stairs were narrow, because her feet bumped twice and her head once against the wall. That elicited a pained exclamation from her, and a low, barely audible curse from whoever carried her.

Finally he dropped her on something soft and comfortable and let her go. She lay still for a moment, listening, and then Shakespeare came wriggling up through the dark shroud to lick her face. Angry and breathing hard, Alexandra sat up and flung off the covering. She blinked and swiped her disheveled hair out of her face—and saw her abductor.

"Lucien!" she shrieked. "What in God's name are you—"

"I'm kidnapping you," he said calmly. "And your little dog, too."

She scrambled to her feet, and Lucien took a step backward. He wouldn't put it past her to aim a kick at his sensitive parts. And that would never do, because the two of them still needed to produce the Kilcairn heir.

"You are not kidnapping me!" she yelled, glaring at Vincent and Thompkinson and then returning her gaze to him.

"Yes, I am. And bellowing about it won't do you any good."

"This is ridiculous!" She stalked across the room toward the nearest doorway, but he moved over to block her path.

"Perhaps it is a bit odd," he conceded, wishing his practical miss would calm down a little so he could explain himself and his brilliant plan. "I am, however, completely serious about it."

"Where are we, anyway?"

"My wine cellar. My secondary wine cellar, actually."

"Your secondary wine cellar. Of course." She turned in a circle, then faced him again, surprise joining the anger in her eyes. "A four-poster bed? It's—"

"It's yours from the gold room. I knew you liked it."

"All right." She folded her arms across her lovely bosom. "I suppose I should ask why you've put me in the secondary wine cellar."

Finally, a reasonable question. Lucien gestured at the groom and footman. "Thompkinson, upstairs. Vincent, go drive the coach around a bit more. And make sure you lock the doors on your way out."

The groom doffed his hat and exited by the stairs leading into the garden, while the footman fled into the main wine cellar. Given Alexandra's sharp tongue, both were no doubt relieved to have escaped unscathed. Lucien steeled himself for the argument to come.

"Interesting," Alexandra said, her voice dripping with cynicism. "Now that you've had your servants help kidnap me, you send them away so they won't hear the explanation. Or do they know it already?"

"They know that I'm concerned for your safety, and that given your strong independent streak, holding you here even against your will is the only way to ensure it."

"And why are you concerned for my safety, pray tell?

Oh, it's not that Lady Welkins prattle again, is it? I'll be perfectly safe in Hampshire." She glanced around the dark cellar again. "Safer than here, apparently. No one has ever kidnapped me before."

"I'm glad to be your first—again."

Alexandra blushed. "You're drunk, aren't you?"

"Only a little. I've been up most of the night moving furniture and fixing locks and removing escape implements."

"Forgive me for not being flattered, my lord, but—"

"You called me Lucien a moment ago."

"You'd frightened me out of my skin. Now, do stop this nonsense and let me go."

"Not until you agree to listen to reason."

She put her hands on her hips. "About what?"

"About marrying me."

Alexandra actually laughed, though there was nothing resembling humor in the sound. "You kidnapped me in order to convince me that you're someone I can trust and rely on? Did someone hit you on the head, Lord Kilcairn?"

He frowned. "That is enough of that. You keep telling me what my motivations are for wanting to marry you. First I'm tired of looking for a wife, then I'm trying to protect you, and then I'm trying to thwart my family. Did I miss anything?"

"Now you'll want me to marry you to keep me from testifying against you for kidnapping."

Damn, she was clever. He moved closer to her, but she backed away. Apparently he wasn't going to win her over by making love to her—not today, anyway. "All of those might have had something to do with giving me the idea, but none of them are my reason for wanting you to be my wife."

"Please, enlighten me, then."

Thank God he hadn't sobered up from last night yet. Otherwise, he never would have been able to spit out the words. "I want you to marry me because I love you, Alexandra."

She stared at him for a long moment, suspicion and shock and anger warring with one another in her turquoise eyes. "You keep telling me words are just that: words, used to manipulate people into doing what you want. Coming from you, 'love' is just another word, Lucien. You don't believe in love. You told me so."

"I was an idiot."

"You're still an idiot. Open that door and let me go."

"No. You're safe here, and I'm going to convince you that I'm sincere. Fiona and Rose both think you're at Miss Grenville's Academy, as does your friend Lady Victoria."

Slowly she sat on the edge of the bed. "And how are you going to convince me?"

"I'm going to remove every damned obstacle you're using as a prop to disbelieve me. That's how."

Alexandra shrugged. "It sounds simple enough, I suppose. But you might consider that I don't need another reason to dislike the idea of marriage to an arrogant, cynical beast like you who has no qualms about destroying everyone else's life to prove a point only he cares about."

Her scathing tongue was in fine form. "I think you do care, Alexandra. In fact, I know you do. I've known it from the moment you walked into my house. I'll prove it to you."

"Don't bother."

Lucien headed through the doorway leading to the primary wine cellar and the stairs to the kitchen. "You'll be amazed," he said, and closed the door behind him. He locked it just as she reached it, and began rattling the handle and pounding on the heavy oak.

"Lucien! Lucien, you devil, let me out of here!"

"No!" he shouted back. "And don't hurt yourself in there."

He climbed the stairs up to the kitchen and locked that door as well, then left Thompkinson to hang about the kitchen and pretend not to be keeping guard. He'd hoped she would simply be so flattered at the effort he'd gone to that she would give in and save him the trouble of straightening everything else out first. Now, though, he'd have to make good on his word, and hope her keen sense of both the ridiculous and the logical would re deem him in her eyes.

Lucien paused on his way to his bedchamber. He did have quite a bit of redeeming to do. Before he'd met Miss Gallant, he really hadn't even considered the implications of some of the things he'd done.

James Balfour's portrait hung before him. He stepped forward and tugged the black ribbon off the corner. Today was the beginning of the new, improved Lucien Balfour: protector of the weak, defender of the innocent, worker of miracles, and hopefully, marrier of Alexandra Gallant—which would be the biggest miracle of all. "Well, Jamie," he said, straightening the frame, "wish me luck."

"This is ridiculous," Alexandra muttered, sinking back on the bed again. An hour of banging and rattling and shouting hadn't done anything but tire her out, and now the candles were nearly guttered.

The Lucien Balfour she knew until yesterday wouldn't have left her alone in a dark cellar, but this morning's version of the earl was obviously insane. He'd even removed all the wine from the one wall rack, so no doubt he planned on having her expire from thirst or hunger.

Someone scratched at the door, and she leapt to her feet and ran over to pound again on the heavy wood. "Yes? I'm here! Help me!"

"Sorry, Miss Gallant; it's me, Thompkinson. The earl said I should inquire and see if you needed anything."

"I need out of here!"

"Um, except for that, ma'am."

She let out an exasperated breath. "Fine. I need more candles, and something to do, for heaven's sake. And a mirror, so I can fix my hair. And something to eat, and drink."

"I'll see to it right away, miss."

When the door opened a short while later, two footmen entered carrying her dressing table and mirror, while another one brought in a very appetizing looking breakfast. "I just need a hand mirror," she said, eyeing the procession disbelievingly. Apparently half the household was involved in this insanity.

"The earl thought you'd like this better, ma'am."

Alexandra nodded, gathering Shakespeare into her arms. She hadn't thought they would make escaping so easy, but she certainly wasn't averse to taking advantage of their laxness. "Could you move it closer to the stairway there?" she asked.

Obligingly the servants lifted the table again. At the same moment, Alexandra bolted for the open door. She made it through the entry into the dim catacomb of the main wine cellar.

"Miss Gallant, wait!"

"Thompkinson, she's getting away!"

Stifling an exultant chuckle, she rounded the last wine rack before the stairs—and slammed into a broad, hard chest. "Damnation!" she grumbled, staggering backward.

Lucien grabbed her arm and pulled her back upright. "Not so fast, my little felon."

She glared up at him. "*I'm* not the felon. Let go."

"You didn't squash Shakespeare, I hope." His voice and expression were stern, but she thought she saw a twinkle of superior amusement in his gray eyes. It didn't improve her disposition in the least.

"If I did squash him, it would be your fault."

"Mm-hm. Back inside."

"No."

He bent and scooped her and Shakespeare into his arms. With no noticeable difficulty at all, he carried them back into her makeshift dungeon. As he set her down she realized she should have struggled, but the sensation of being in his arms had rather taken her breath away.

"I will keep someone posted outside the door from now on. If you require anything, it will be taken care of immediately."

"I require my freedom."

He actually grinned. "That is my ultimate goal, my dear one, but it will take a bit longer." With a wave of his hand he gestured the footmen to leave and followed them to the doorway, where he paused. "I almost forgot," he said, and produced a book from somewhere behind him. "To keep you entertained."

She made no move to collect it from him, and after a moment he set it on the empty wine rack. With a deep bow he backed out of the room and closed the door. A few seconds later the bolt slid shut, locking her in again.

Only when Alexandra couldn't hear any more movement from the other side of the door did she put Shakespeare back on the bed and retrieve the book. A small, pleased shiver ran down her spine. He'd given her the Byron.

"Cousin Lucien," Rose said, intercepting him just as he left the kitchen corridor. "Did Lex leave already?"

He nodded, continuing toward the front door. "Before I came downstairs."

"That's awful," her cousin quavered. "I hoped we could at least breakfast together, and then perhaps I might have convinced her to stay."

He glanced over his shoulder at her. "And how would you have accomplished that, pray tell?"

"I would have told her how much Mama and I like her, and how much fun she made everything."

Lucien paused. "Stop, cousin. You're practically moving me to tears."

An actual tear ran down Rose's cheek. "*You* should stop. I'm sure Lex left because you were so mean to her."

That was interesting. His cousin truly seemed to have no idea what her mother was up to. Though he didn't particularly want to debate who happened to be at fault for Alexandra's departure and despite her apparent ignorance of certain underhanded events, Rose was very much involved in the mess. Having her on his side might be beneficial.

Realizing he'd been staring at her and that her expression had become even more dubious, Lucien shook himself. He'd told Alexandra he would make things right. Rose was part of that—and very possibly an innocent party in the entire disaster. "Might I have a word with you?" he asked.

She paled. "Y-yes. I suppose so."

He gestured her into the morning room. When she entered, looking like a rabbit about to be roasted for supper, he followed her in and closed the door. "Take a seat, if you please."

"Am I in trouble?" she asked timidly, sitting in the overstuffed chair beneath the window. "I thought everything went very well last night, and I do want to thank you again for allowing me to have my party."

Lucien dropped into the seat opposite her. "You're welcome. And no, you're not in trouble. I am."

Immediately she reached out to touch his knee, then pulled back as though she'd been scalded. "Oh, my. What's wrong?"

Conversing with Alexandra was much easier—both because he could speak his mind and because he didn't have to ferret out the simplest turns of phrase before he uttered a sentence. "First, I think we need to set some rules."

"Rules?" Her brow furrowed.

"Yes. In this room, and with the door closed, you and I will be absolutely honest with one another. Do you agree?"

Rose hesitated, then nodded. "What else?"

"Whatever we say in this room goes no further than the two of us—unless we discuss it first."

"Yes. I agree."

So far, so good. In fact, he hadn't expected her to be able to make a decision at all. Perhaps Alexandra was right, and that given the right support, Rose could function as more than a pretty peacock. He was about to find out.

"Rose, did you come to London with the idea of marrying a specific titled noble?"

She flushed. "A specific—"

"Did you come to London with the idea of marrying me?"

"Did Mama tell you?"

"She mentioned it. Whose idea was it?"

"Mama and Papa both said I should be married to you. Ever since I can remember, I was going to marry you. When you visited us last, Mama even said I couldn't ride Daisy, my pony, because my dress might get soiled and you would think I wasn't a proper lady."

"I seem to remember something about that," he said dryly. "Do you want to marry me?"

She folded her hands neatly in her lap, a delicate gesture she'd obviously gotten from her governess. "You said we should be perfectly honest."

"I did."

"Well, I know you've been very nice to me the last few weeks, and that you might very well be falling in love with me, but I will tell you the truth, Lucien. Please don't be angry, but I really don't wish to be married to you."

Thank God. "Why not?"

"Um, well, you're very . . . fierce."

He smiled. "Am I?"

"Don't misunderstand me," she said hurriedly, sitting forward. "If you and Mama wish it to happen, I will marry you." Rose slumped a little. "In fact, I really don't see a way around it. Mama is very determined."

"How do you feel about Robert Ellis, Lord Belton?"

"Oh, I like him very much. But he's only a viscount. You're an earl, and much more wealthy."

"That's true. What if I were to tell you, though, that I—"

Someone scratched at the door.

He hoped his prisoner hadn't escaped again. "What is it?" he barked.

Thompkinson stuck his head in the door. "Begging your pardon, my lord, but . . . might I have a pen and ink and some paper for . . . for Wimbole, my lord?"

"Yes, of course. In my office." At least she wasn't asking for gunpowder—yet.

"Very good, my lord."

When the door closed again, Lucien returned his attention to Rose. "What if I were to tell you that I'm in love with someone else?"

Her blue eyes widened. "You are? With who?"

"Whom. Alexandra Gallant."

She stared at him, disbelief, horror, shock, and—to her credit—amusement, in turn, expressing themselves on her pretty face. "You're in love with my governess?" she finally gasped.

"Yes, I am."

Rose started giggling. "And I thought *I* was in trouble."

He scowled. "That's not why I'm in trouble." In his mind he could clearly hear Alexandra reminding him that he'd promised to be honest with Rose. Good God, now Miss Gallant was his conscience. Lucien paused and considered that for a moment. Perhaps she was. Perhaps that was why he needed her so much. "It's not entirely why I'm in trouble," he amended.

"Then what is it?"

"I . . . want to marry her, but she won't agree. She—"

"She turned you down?" Rose's chortling lengthened into full-out laughter. "Oh, my goodness."

This was not any damned fun. "She turned me down because she knew that you were supposed to marry me."

Slowly she sobered, and spent a long moment studying him while he chafed under her scrutiny. "You need me," she said finally.

Rose was definitely brighter than he'd given her credit for being. "Yes, I do."

"You need me to say it's all right for you to marry Lex."

Keeping a tight hold on his impatience, Lucien nodded.

"Well, it's not all right. Not if it leaves me with no one to marry."

"I see."

"You're not angry, are you?"

"Yes. But not at you." Lucien gazed at his hands. He knew what the next step was, but if she refused, it left him with nowhere to go. Nowhere that Alexandra would approve of, anyway. And that was the most important element of the damned plan. Alexandra had to be satisfied with the results. "What if you had someone else to marry?"

"He would have to be a nobleman. You mean Robert, I suppose?"

With a slight smile, Lucien let her take control of the conversation. "You said you liked him."

"I like him very much. He's . . . gentle, and he laughs when I say something silly, instead of just scowling at me."

"All right, Robert it is."

"But, Lucien, he left my party early last night. Mama said he looked upset at something."

He could guess why Fiona had been the one to notice Robert's departure. Blast it, the witch was still meddling. He'd have to put a stop to that. "Leave that to me. But I want your word, Rose: If Robert wants to marry you,

you'll agree to it. Even if Aunt Fiona would prefer that you marry me."

"Will you give me a good dowry?"

"A very good dowry. An exceptionally generous one."

"All right, then. I agree."

Lucien released a breath he hadn't even realized he'd been holding. "So do I. But remember, this is just between us for right now."

"Of course. I'd be an idiot to tell Mama."

"Thank you, Rose."

She stood and smoothed her skirt. "Don't thank me yet, cousin Lucien. First you have to get Robert to ask me to marry him."

"Oh, I will." Even if it killed all of them.

Chapter 17

"Oh, and a clock. I would like to know what time it is," Alexandra added.

His expression a little haggard, Thompkinson nodded and inched her prison door closed a bit farther. "Right away, Miss Gallant."

She had no sympathy for him at all, even if Lucien had bullied him into being her guard. The earl had apparently vanished somewhere, but she could still torture his servants. "Thank you. My correspondence should be ready by the time you return."

"Yes, Miss Gallant."

He pulled the door closed and slid the bolt. Alexandra leaned back against the empty wine rack and smiled. Much as she hated to admit it, this was becoming amusing. Heaven knew she'd never had her every whim catered to before.

"What shall we ask for next, Shakes?"

The terrier lifted his head, then went back to sleep in his fortress beneath her dressing table. He seemed perfectly content to remain in the wine cellar, now that

Thompkinson had supplied him with a nice, juicy mutton bone so big he could barely drag it about. Wherever the bone was, he would stay.

Alexandra signed her letter, folded it, and addressed the outside. As she finished, the door rattled and opened again. Thompkinson warily peered inside, no doubt fearing an ambush. When he spied her standing at the dressing table, he pushed the door open wider to allow Bingham to enter with the dining room mantel clock.

"Will this do, Miss Gallant?"

"Yes, thank you." She crossed the room and handed him the letter. "Please see that this is sent out at once."

The tic he'd apparently acquired over the last few hours made his cheek twitch. "Lord Kilcairn said nothing was to leave the house without him seeing it first."

She folded her arms, not the least bit surprised. The letter was more for him than for Emma Grenville, anyway. "I see. Please inform him, then, that Shakespeare has left him something to inspect in the corner." Alexandra pointed.

He bowed and dragged the awestruck Bingham out of the room. "I'll do that, Miss Gallant."

After the footmen left, she wandered the edges of the cellar, searching for another errand on which to send her guards. Eventually they were bound to leave the door unlocked by accident. Her bored gaze settled on her prison's single window. It was at the top of one wall, very small and obscured on the outside by garden vines, so that little light made it through to illuminate the cellar.

With another glance at the door, Alexandra dragged her dressing table's chair to stand beneath the dim opening. By climbing up on the delicate filigree seat and balancing on her tiptoes, she could just reach the bottom of the casing. The builders hadn't made it to open, blast it, but the wood frame gave a little when she jabbed it with her finger.

Climbing down again, she went looking for something with which to dig out the old wood. A table knife would have been perfect, but they'd already removed her luncheon tray. Lucien had been thorough in his search to collect and remove all possible weapons and escape implements.

With a grimace, she finished her circuit and sat in the chair. She could give in and let him do whatever he wished with her life, as he already did with everyone else around him. The years she'd worked to be independent and to be able to make her own way would be for nothing, though, if she allowed him to manage her life according to his own whims.

Alexandra stood and went to root in her trunk. Beneath the clothes and the shoes, she found what she was looking for—a decorative pin that had once been her mother's. Flower petals rounded the top, but the bottom consisted of several nicely pointed stems. Lucien Balfour needed to learn one more lesson: surprising her and locking her in a cellar was one thing—keeping her there was another.

Lucien shed his coat and dropped it onto the bench beside Francis Henning. "Do you mind?" he asked, confiscating Henning's rapier.

"No, of . . . of course not, Kilcairn. Have my mask, too."

"No need." Lucien flexed the blade, watching Robert Ellis's bout with Monsieur Fancheau, the establishment's owner and most-favored trainer.

"It's the rules, Kilcairn," Henning insisted. "Don't want an eye gouged out, you know."

"I am the goug*er*," he said absently, waiting for Robert to notice him. "Not the goug*ee*."

"Ah. Is that French?"

"I doubt it."

Lord Belton won the match and, breathing hard, removed his face mask. As his gaze met Lucien's, he stiffened. "Kilcairn."

"Care for a match?" Lucien asked.

"No."

"I'll let you win."

The viscount whipped his rapier up and down, the air humming with the speed of the motion. "No more of your damned games."

Murmurs began around the edges of the room. The more gossip he started, the more things he'd have to set right later. Lucien determinedly kept the smile on his face. "No games. I just need a word with you."

Robert dropped his mask to the floor. "I don't want to talk to you right now. I thought I was being fairly clear about that."

So much for being proper and polite. Lucien swung his rapier across Robert's path, stopping him. "Talk to me, anyway. And if you argue about it, I'll beat you senseless and then talk to you. Is that fairly clear?"

For a moment he wasn't certain which course the viscount would take, but with another hard glare Robert tossed down his weapon. "Outside."

Lucien recovered his coat and waited while Robert shed his padded chest guard and collected his own coat and waistcoat. He then followed the younger man out to the front steps. He wasn't certain exactly what had transpired last night, but obviously it truly troubled his friend. Though Robert's anger didn't affect him nearly as strongly as Alexandra's, it bothered him, anyway. He scowled as he started down the steps. Apparently once one began developing a conscience, the damned thing could arise at any time, no matter how inconvenient.

"All right, I'm listening. What's so bloody important, Kilcairn?"

"Rose was concerned that you left her soiree early last night, and that you appeared to be upset. Did she trounce on your toes during the waltz?"

Robert's face paled. "I warned you. No games. I am not in the mood."

"Don't threaten me, Robert. I already have enough rope coiled over my head to hang a regiment." He grimaced when the viscount's dour expression didn't change. "Look. I am not used to honey-coated sentimentality, so I'll ask you directly. What happened?"

"Ha! As if you didn't know!"

"If I did know, obviously I wouldn't be asking." Lucien paused, studying Robert's set features, and the circles beneath his eyes. He hadn't been the only one awake all night, apparently. Perhaps it was even for a similar reason. "You truly care for Rose, don't you?"

"That doesn't signify. And I won't provide you with any amusement by expressing my feelings in your presence. You did fool me; I'll admit that. But I won't sit at your knee waiting to be humiliated like your other toadeating friends."

Now things were beginning to make sense. "You spoke with my aunt last night, didn't you?"

"I will not betray a confidence."

Lucien lifted an eyebrow. "She lied, you know."

Robert stopped his retort and stared at him. "What? Who lied?"

"My aunt. She's turning into a little Iago, spreading venomous tales in every direction."

"Tales—like what?"

"That, I don't know. You'll have to volunteer some information first."

The viscount hesitated. "How do you know she lied, if you don't know what she said?"

"The odds are in my favor," Lucien said dryly.

"I feel as though you're setting me up for a good laugh."

"I'm not."

Robert sighed. "All right. She told me you were marrying Rose—that you had meant to all along and were only pretending otherwise in an attempt to make a fool of me."

"Hm. I would already have succeeded in making a fool of you, if any of that were true." He glanced away from his companion's suddenly hopeful expression. He wished Alexandra were so easy to please, but she had a much more suspicious nature than the viscount.

"You're not going to marry Rose," Robert said slowly.

Lucien frowned. "For God's sake, no! Why would I want to do that?"

"Because she's a delight."

"Well, I grant you that she's not as horrid as I originally thought," he conceded reluctantly, surprised that seeing Robert out of the doldrums actually made him feel . . . good. Sweet Lucifer—next he'd be drinking tea and gumming biscuits with the old wags at Almack's.

"So you've . . . you have no objection to my asking for her hand."

"You may have the rest of her, as well." Lucien couldn't help grinning at Robert's obvious elation. "Aren't you glad you didn't make me skewer you earlier?"

"I was tempted to try my luck." The viscount shook Lucien's hand vigorously, then sobered. "Why the elaborate deception, then?"

If Robert thought Fiona's deceptions were elaborate, he hadn't seen anything yet. "Join me at White's for luncheon. It's a long story, and will ultimately involve me owing you another favor."

"By all means, tell me, then."

This time Lucien hesitated. "It also requires your discretion."

The viscount put out his arm, stopping both of them. "Wait a moment. The Earl of Kilcairn Abbey is asking for my *discretion*?"

"And your patience."

Robert smiled, disgustingly happy at having his own problems vanish. "You have them both. But by God, they're going to cost you one hell of a favor."

With a last heave, Alexandra pushed the window out of the casing. It stuck for a moment in the tangle of vines outside, then thudded the few inches down to the flower bed.

She took a few seconds to admire her talent for larceny, then chipped away at the splinters remaining across the bottom of the opening. Her hands and arms were tired, but she'd already had to stop twice when Thompkinson entered her dungeon to check on her. He could reappear at any moment, and he was bound to notice that the window was missing.

When the wood was as smooth as she could make it with her flower pin, she climbed down from the chair and returned to her trunk. Unfortunately she'd never be able to get the blasted thing out the small opening. However, her main goal was to reach Vixen's home and then assess her situation from there.

Dropping the pin back inside, she pulled out her oldest shift and hurried over to drape it across the open casement. Shakespeare sat up on the bed and wagged at her, and for a moment she debated whether to take him along. She couldn't very well let him loose in the garden while she pulled herself through the window, because he was a notorious explorer and would instantly get lost. And she certainly couldn't pull him up after her without strangling him.

"Shakespeare, stay," she said as loudly as she dared.

Although the terrier continued to watch her curiously, he settled back down on her pillow. Lucien liked him, as did Wimbole, and one of them would look after him until she could rescue him.

With a last glance toward the door, she climbed up on the chair again. Grabbing on to the shift-covered casement with her fingers, she carefully stood on the chair's arms and pulled herself higher.

Thanking her father's side of the family for her height, Alexandra readjusted her grip and craned her head through the opening. She had to tilt her head sideways to accommodate her badly fraying bun, but at the moment her hair was the least of her worries.

She shifted her feet and stepped up onto the rounded back of the chair. It wobbled and skidded a little, then steadied again. Taking a deep breath and holding it, she pushed off with her feet and pulled upward with all her strength.

The chair went out from under her. With a gasp, she kicked upward and heaved herself into the opening. Her left elbow stuck in the corner of the casement. Flailing her legs sideways, she gave herself enough room to reach out into the garden. Now, though, she'd lost all forward momentum and hung there, half in and half out of the window, and completely out of breath.

"Damnation," she rasped, stretching for one of the firmly rooted vines. She wriggled and kicked, trying to scoot forward, but nothing happened. The shift beneath her slid just enough to prevent her from gaining any purchase on the windowsill.

Then a pair of black-clothed legs entered her line of vision. She froze, hoping the vines would keep her hidden. Blast it, she should have waited until evening, but the idea of running through any part of London alone in the dark made her nervous.

The legs stopped. "Ah, Miss Gallant?"

"Wimbole?" she gasped, the windowsill across her stomach beginning to cut off her air.

"Yes, ma'am."

"Wimbole, thank goodness. Pull me out of here, will you? Hurry, before someone sees."

"I'm afraid you'll have to get back inside the cellar, Miss Gallant."

She craned her head to look up at him, but couldn't view anything higher than his torso. "You mean you know about this, too?"

He squatted down. "I'm afraid so."

"A butler of your impeccable reputation? Surely you couldn't be party to keeping a woman captive against her will."

"Ordinarily, no. Of course not."

"But—"

"Please get back inside, Miss Gallant."

Even if she hadn't been stuck, she had no intention of retreating. "I will not! Now, assist me at once."

He shook his head. "If I let you escape, Lord Kilcairn will be quite unhappy."

"What about me? I'm the one hanging in the window!"

"Hush if you please, Miss Gallant. Mrs. Delacroix might hear you, and then we would all be in a frightful tangle."

That settled it. Absolutely everyone in the household had lost his mind. "You're in a frightful tangle now, Wimbole."

He frowned. "Perhaps I should explain myself."

"Oh, please do. I have nothing better to do." Her legs were beginning to grow numb, and she wriggled them again.

"I have been in Lord Kilcairn's employ for nine years. In that time I have witnessed various scandalous incidents, and I have kept my silence about them. During the same period, I have also watched the earl grow steadily more cynical and set in his ways." He leaned closer, glancing over his shoulder, and lowered his voice still further. "Whether you realize it or not, Miss Gallant, your presence here has had a profound influence on him—an influence that has been quite beneficial to his staff."

Alexandra stared at him. "What?"

He sighed. "To be blunt, the earl has been more pleasant to us—and to everyone else—since you arrived. It wasn't that he was cruel before, but more like he simply . . . didn't notice." The butler straightened. "Now, please get back inside."

She lowered her head to her arms. "I can't. I'm stuck."

"Ah. Then I'll fetch some assistance."

"N—"

As the butler's footsteps faded away, Alexandra reflected that despite the absurdity of the situation, she couldn't help but feel somewhat flattered. Ridiculous and aggravating as being held prisoner in someone's wine cellar was, no one had ever worked so hard to keep her safe anywhere.

Something grasped her ankles. Alexandra shrieked.

"Hush," Lucien said from behind and below her.

"Well, close the door down there," she hissed. "I don't want anyone else to see me like this."

"Already done, though you should have thought of that earlier." His warm, strong hands hesitated, then slowly slid up her legs beneath her skirt.

"Oh, my goodness," she said raggedly. "Stop that."

"Then stop wriggling your lovely bottom like that."

She wished she could see his face, to know whether he was teasing or if she was truly affecting him. Lucien tightened his grip and pulled on her legs. Alexandra began to slide backward, and instinctively flailed her arms to look for support before she could fall.

"Ouch. Damn it," he cursed, and thwacked her across the bottom.

It didn't hurt, but she felt vulnerable enough without him doing that. "Don't do that!"

"You kicked me in the jaw, chit."

"Oh. I'm sorry."

This time she distinctly heard him chuckle. "Let's give this another try, shall we? I won't let you fall."

He was taking most unfair advantage of her helplessness, for he was caressing her legs in a rather intimate manner—but it felt like forever since he had last touched her. Angry with him or not, she loved his touch—and the sound of his voice, and his lovely eyes . . .

She slid backward another inch or so, and then stuck.

Lucien tugged her legs again, and something tore. "Lucien, I'm caught."

This time she could have sworn it was his cheek running along her thigh. "Yes, you are."

Alexandra couldn't help the tremor that warmed her all the way to her toes. "My dress is caught," she amended. Hands caressed her thighs again, joined by a warm, slightly sucking contact that ran up the insides of her thighs with agonizing slowness. "Are you kissing me?" she gasped.

"Yes."

"Well, stop it. I can't breathe."

"Right. Hang on a moment. I'll get the chair."

He moved away and then returned, this time to slip his hands along her hips and waist. Alexandra was beginning to feel rather warm, and experimentally she wriggled again.

"Good God," he hissed, his voice much closer. "Where are you caught?"

"A little to the left, I think. Yes, right there."

His hand wedged between her body and the window casing. Pressing snugly against her left breast, he paused again. "Here?" he asked, and caressed her through the thin material of her gown. "Or here?"

She gasped, wiggling her bottom against his chest again. "Lucien! Don't . . . Oh, my goodness."

Her breathing did sound somewhat strained, and whether it was because of him or her predicament, he decided they'd best conclude this on the ground. He tugged the caught material sideways, and a moment later she slid backward into his arms. She flung her hands around his neck as her sudden weight overbalanced him and they half fell off the chair. Then his mouth found hers.

They thudded against the wall, but he scarcely noticed. He had been hard and ready since he walked into the cellar and saw her very attractive bottom wriggling in his window. And as volatile as she was, and as badly as he wanted her, he had no intention of giving her an opportunity to recover her senses.

"Lucien," she breathed, kissing him and curling her fingers into his hair to pull him closer.

At least she was using his first name again. He sank to the floor with her still cradled in his arms. And then a small, white, furry dog jumped into her lap and slathered his tongue across both their chins.

"Good God," Lucien bellowed, recoiling as the little monster reared up against his chest.

Alexandra, her arms still around his shoulders, began laughing. "Shakespeare, no!"

The cellar door rattled and opened. "My lord," Thompkinson said hesitantly, "I know you said not to—"

"Out!" Lucien roared.

The door closed again.

"Thank goodness we weren't *en déshabillé*," Alexandra managed, capturing Shakespeare in her arms and still laughing helplessly.

"We will be in just a moment."

"No, we won't."

Damnation. He knew giving her time to consider anything was a bad idea. Lucien shifted her on his lap. "Do you feel that?" he murmured, running his lips along her throat. "Do you feel me?"

She swallowed. "Yes."

"You want me, don't you?"

"Yes." This time she kissed him, openmouthed and hot and wanting.

That was enough for him. He stood, carried her to the bed, and set her down. Her dazed, lustful expression had him aching, but first he needed to get rid of a certain canine nuisance. Lucien scooped up Shakespeare and strode to the cellar door, opened it, and set him out. "Watch him," he ordered the startled Thompkinson, and shut the door again.

He expected another protest, but she raised up on her knees to meet him as he returned to the bed. She pulled his coat off his shoulders and tossed it aside, while he finished the work the window had begun on her burnt-sunlight hair and pulled the hanging clips free.

"This does not mean I've forgiven you," she whispered, pulling his shirt over his head and licking one flat nipple.

"It will," he returned, ripping the remaining fastenings of her torn dress open and yanking it off her. Her shift followed, and he lowered his head to her full, soft breasts.

She gasped in pleasure. "No, it won't." With shaking, anxious fingers she unfastened his belt and his breeches and shoved them down.

"We can argue later." Lucien nudged her backward, drew himself up over her body, and with a possessive growl, pushed inside her.

He relished her fierce, hungry response to his lovemaking. Alexandra's fingers dug into his back as he moved inside her, her hips moving in instinctive rhythm with his. They came together, and he muffled her exultant cry with a kiss.

As soon as he could breathe again, Lucien rolled off her and onto his back. A ragged piece of material still lay across the windowsill and fluttered in the slight breeze. She'd nearly gotten away from him, and he had no intention of letting it happen again. Not when he was so close to clearing the jumbled, rock-covered path between them.

Alexandra turned sideways and raised up on one elbow. "I have to admit, I'm glad it was you who rescued me, rather than Thompkinson or Wimbole."

"So am I. Don't do that again."

She lifted an eyebrow, beautiful and utterly arousing in her unashamed nakedness. "Or what—you'll make love to me again? It's not a very effective punishment, Kilcairn." She smiled, suddenly a sultry, if sated, kitten. "I like it too much."

He frowned, flattered and annoyed. "That is not—"

"It won't work, you know," she interrupted, shaking her head at him. "You're not convincing me of anything other than the fact that you're a charming rogue. I knew that before."

"Hm." Slowly he reached out and curled his fingers through her long hair. " 'Charming,' is it? I think I am succeeding. You've never called me charming before."

"You caught me at a generous moment."

"Obviously. And speaking of generous," he said, leaning over the edge of the bed to recover his coat, "as per my orders, Thompkinson handed me this." He pulled a letter from his pocket and dropped the garment again.

"So now you're stopping my correspondence?" She didn't sound the least bit surprised, but from the missive's contents, she hadn't expected it to leave the house, anyway.

With a sideways glance at her, he unfolded it. " 'Dearest Emma,'" he read aloud, " 'I'm afraid my arrival at the Academy will be delayed. I have been kidnapped by my arrogant, stubborn, pigheaded, interfering, insane former employer, the Earl of Kilcairn Abbey.'"

"I left out some adjectives, I think."

"You included quite enough of them, thank you."

"I need to let Emma know something," Alexandra insisted, her expression becoming more serious. "She has enough to worry about without me—or you—adding to it."

Lucien dropped the letter onto his crumpled coat. "I'll take care of it. A little more succinctly, I think." He pulled her back into his arms and kissed her again.

"Lucien, let me leave," she said, when he finally gave her a moment to breathe. "It's going to happen eventually. Don't make it any harder than it is already."

"Not yet. Not until there is nothing to push you in any direction but your own desire. Not until where you decide to go is completely up to you, Alexandra, and not dictated by circumstance or duty."

She held his gaze for a long moment. "Or convenience?"

"Or convenience." He sat up and looked around her makeshift room. "You need a rug. I'll send Thompkinson down with one. And I'll see to the damned window myself, if you can refrain from making another escape attempt for five minutes."

Alexandra stretched, this time obviously teasing him. "I'm a bit tired suddenly. I believe you're safe for five minutes."

"So are you. But only five minutes, chit." He leaned over and kissed her. "I do hope you realize I wouldn't bother to kidnap just anyone."

"And I do hope you realize I don't believe for one second that you're being altruistic."

"Of course I'm not. Not entirely, anyway. I want you in my life, Alexandra."

Turquoise eyes studied his. "Sometimes I almost believe you."

He smiled. "You see? I'm winning you over already."

Alexandra wished he would attempt to win her over more often. As a bonus, she got to watch him hammering the window back into place from inside the cellar. Thompkinson had made the mistake of suggesting they simply board up the opening, but Lucien insisted that she not be denied the limited sunlight the window provided.

He also insisted that she have a more comfortable chair in which to sit and read, and some more pillows for the bed. According to Thompkinson, the Delacroix ladies had gone out for luncheon, which was lucky, considering the amount of furniture being moved into the cellar.

Despite the bustle of activity, Alexandra noticed something different in the way the servants treated her. Whereas before they had always looked to Kilcairn for confirmation of any orders, now they did exactly as she said without hesitation on any subject—except, of course, for setting her free. She didn't know what Lucien might have told them, if anything, but suddenly she didn't feel like a fellow servant any longer.

And though no one commented about possible reasons she might have changed her gown in Lucien's presence, she knew they had noticed that, too. Their continued respectfulness, though, had to mean something. She continued to watch Lucien, content to sit in her comfortable new reading chair and gaze at his broad, strong shoulders as he refit the cellar window. Earls didn't do such things; earls didn't do a great many things that he did.

Alexandra blushed. They probably didn't do them nearly as well, either.

At half past two, Bingham hurried through the cellar door. "My lord, Wimbole says the ladies are returning."

Lucien hammered a last nail into the repaired window casing and hopped down from the chair. "Splendid," he said, handing the hammer to Thompkinson and retrieving his coat.

"So now you're happy to have them about?" Alexandra asked, setting aside the Byron, unread.

"Always happy to see my relations," he said offhandedly, and gestured the small troop of servants out the door. When the last one left, he strolled over to her chair. "I'll be back soon," he murmured, gray eyes glinting, and leaned down to kiss her.

She couldn't help her hungry response. "Perhaps I'll be here."

"You'd better be, Alexandra." He kissed her again, then slipped out the door, latching it behind him. "Behave," he said through the door, and then was gone.

Alexandra grimaced as she lifted her poetry book again. Now the rascal was telling *her* how to conduct herself. A smile curled her lips as she glanced about at the most splendidly furnished wine cellar in England. He was learning some lessons himself.

Chapter 18

The next step was simple. Lucien intercepted the Delacroix ladies in the hallway. "Aunt Fiona, might I have a word with my cousin?" he asked politely, despite the urge to spit in his aunt's face every time he set eyes on her. He was going to have to deal with her, but he had to time it just right or he could bring the rest of his carefully laid plan down around his ears.

"Of course, nephew. Don't be long, though, Rose. Don't forget—we are all going to the opera tonight, and you will need your rest first."

"Yes, Mama."

At his gesture, Rose preceded him into the morning room. He closed the door and paced to the window and back. The urge to skip steps and end the damned game so he could spend every moment with Alexandra was overwhelming, and he fought it sternly. Jumping ahead could cost him Miss Gallant.

"What is it, Lucien?"

He sat by the window. "I spoke with Robert."

She practically pounced on him, her blond curls bobbing as she knelt at his side. "And what happened? Is he angry with me? How—"

"He wants to marry you."

Rose threw her arms around him, and even kissed his cheek. "Oh, thank you, Lucien! I'm so happy. I don't have to marry you now!"

Lucien lifted an eyebrow. "Well, thank you very much."

"You don't want to be married to me, either. You told me so." She backed away, her expression suddenly suspicious. "You did give him your permission, didn't you?"

"Yes, I did. With bells on." He stood as she swooped at him again. "For God's sake, don't smother me."

Still smiling happily, she folded her hands in front of her. "What happens now? How will you get word to Lex? Will she come back to London?"

Lucien hesitated. He'd spent so long detesting his relations that the idea of trusting Rose even for a moment, much less including her in his plans, bothered him. But he needed an ally. More to the point, he needed *her*. "Actually," he said slowly, "Alexandra is still in London."

"She is? Where is she staying? Oh, I have to go tell her about Robert!"

"Remember, this is not a subject for the *London Times*." He grabbed her hand before she could go flailing and dancing about the room again. "This is important, Rose. We need to help one another."

Her smile faded, and she nodded. "What do we do, then?"

"First, we need to go tell your mother that we are engaged, and that we will announce it next Wednesday, at a dinner party."

"But—"

"And then, at the party, I will announce that it is you and Robert who are engaged."

Rose put her hands over her mouth. "Mama will be furious."

"Yes, I know." That, though, was where he would implement the second part of his plan. "I'll deal with her."

"Does Robert know about this?"

"He does. Do you agree?"

"Y-yes. It's very odd, but I think it's romantic. What about you and Lex, though?"

"Alexandra is . . ." He took a deep breath. "She's in the wine cellar."

"What? The wine—"

"Perhaps you might visit her. As long as you say *nothing* to Fiona."

"Oh, I won't. But why—"

"I have my reasons. They will be made clear soon enough. Just be sure you don't let her out. She's very stubborn."

Rose giggled. "I know. Because she won't marry you."

"Yet," he stated firmly.

Robert knew most of his reasons and plans already, but he didn't dare tell Rose any more. Alexandra would have the information out of her without the poor thing ever knowing it. The governess was so adept at addling his brain that he'd have to be careful around her himself.

"May I see her now?"

"First we should see your mother. She'll be suspicious if we delay before we prance in with news that I proposed to you."

"Yes. She said I was to tell her immediately."

Fiona was damned certain of herself. "Then let's not disappoint her."

"May I tell Lex that I'm not to marry you?"

"Certainly. Tell her all about how happy you and Robert will be. After we tell your mother how happy you and I will be."

Rose narrowed her eyes, suspicion entering her clear expression. "Are you certain you're not tricking me?"

Going through life lacking the appreciation that he—and Alexandra—seemed to have for its absurdities must be damned dull. "I'm certain I'm not tricking you into marrying me, Rose."

"Good. Because I really don't want to, you know."

"Yes, I had surmised that."

They mutually agreed that Lucien should be the one to tell Fiona the news. He led the way to the upstairs sitting room she occupied when she wasn't out gathering and spreading gossip, knocked, and opened the door without waiting for an answer.

"Fiona, Rose and I have news for you."

"Yes, my dears?"

Her look of calm superiority irked him no end, and he couldn't wait for the opportunity to wipe it permanently from her round face. "Rose and I have decided it would be to our mutual benefit to wed." *But not each other*, he added silently, just for luck.

"Splendid! Oh, this is the most splendid news! Come give your mama a kiss, Rose."

With a determined, nervous smile, Rose complied. She wasn't very adept at skullduggery, Lucien noted. Thank God the plan needed to unfold quickly—she wouldn't last long without blurting the whole bloody mess to Fiona.

"And you, Lucien, give me your hand."

He stifled his expression of absolute disgust and offered her his hand. *This is for Alexandra,* he reminded himself. He could wink at the Medusa to save his goddess.

"I'm so happy," Fiona chortled. "I shall tell absolutely everyone!"

"I have a better idea," he said. He'd known that threat was coming; she wanted to be certain he couldn't back out. Obviously she had no idea how little he cared about public opinion. "A dinner party on Wednesday."

"Ooh, we could make the reason for it a surprise!" Rose clapped. "Just think! We'll invite everyone! Do you think Prince George would come?"

"Prince George?" Fiona echoed, eyes widening.

"If I asked him, he would come." Lucien revised his opinion of his cousin upward once again. With the proper training, she could be a fine prevaricator.

"I still want to tell some of my friends," Fiona said stubbornly, though the suspicion in her eyes had lessened a little.

He shrugged. "I recommend against ruining the surprise, but inform whomever you like." The woman she could most hurt with her little tale was safely tucked away in his wine cellar. As for Fiona's own reputation, he didn't give a flying damn.

"I would like it to be a secret," Rose pressed. "You always try to ruin everything."

"I do not. Who do you think arranged for you to become Lady Kilcairn? It wasn't that flighty Miss Gallant. You may be assured of that."

"But, Mama—"

"Bah. Your viscount will find out eventually. He doesn't signify, Rose. The sooner you realize that, the better."

"Well, on that note," Lucien said, retreating to the door, "I'll leave you two to chat. I have some arrangements to make."

Predictably, Fiona didn't object, and he went downstairs to collect his hat and send for a mount. "I may be some time," he informed Wimbole.

The butler pulled open the front door for him. "Any special instructions in your absence, my lord?"

He nodded. "If—and only if—Fiona goes visiting, you may show Rose my selection of special wines."

"Yes, my lord. I will, of course, make certain the wines are kept in their protected environment."

"My thanks, Wimbole."

When Vincent appeared around the front leading his black gelding, Faust, Lucien swung up into the saddle and headed for Hanover Square. He didn't want anyone—much less any of his servants who might have contact with Alexandra—to know his destination.

As he arrived at one of the long line of elegant houses and dismounted, he was surprised to realize that he was nervous; not for himself, but for Alexandra. And because if he made a bad step now, she would never forgive him.

He swung the brass knocker against the solid oak door. When it opened, he caught the elderly butler's startled expression before it melded back into stuffy blandness. "Good afternoon, my lord."

Lucien handed over his calling card. "I need to speak to His Grace."

"If you'll wait in the morning room, I'll inquire."

"I suggest you inquire strongly."

"Y-yes, my lord."

It had only been an hour since he'd last seen Alexandra, and he was already chafing to be with her again. It was new to him, this need to have someone in his life, this yearning to hear her voice and feel her touch. Love had seemed cloying and suffocating—not a genuine emotion so much as a clinging neediness. But this was not like that. It was nothing like he'd expected, and it alternately amused, pleased, and horrified him.

He looked up as the morning room door opened. The Duke of Monmouth had the remains of what must have been an impressive demeanor: tall and big boned, he had lost the meat that would make him capable of intimidating by his physical presence alone. Evidently no one had informed him that without the gristle to back up his famous hostility, he only looked blustery. Lucien wondered how long it had been since Alexandra had actually seen him.

"I am not going to take her and whatever damned by-blow you've gotten on her into my house," the duke growled.

Lucien lifted an eyebrow. "Good afternoon, Your Grace." His gaze returned to the shorter figure following in the duke's shadow. "Didn't I specify that I wanted a private audience with you?"

"You're lucky to be allowed into this house, Kilcairn," Lord Virgil snapped, a lion now that he was in his father's formidable company.

"I beg your pardon. Should I be addressing myself to Lord Virgil?" Lucien barely stifled a smile. This politeness of Alexandra's did have its uses—it was blasted difficult to defend against, as he'd discovered firsthand.

"What do you want, Kilcairn? I won't allow you to blackmail me. I'm ready to disown her, you know. Wash my hands of her completely."

Lucien seated himself. "I don't recall that I've threatened anything, or that I've asked for anything but a few moments of your time."

"We know you, Kilcairn," the younger Retting snarled.

"Apparently you don't." Lucien kept his gaze on Monmouth. "Nor do I intend to enlighten you until we can speak in private."

Blustery black eyes met his cool gray ones. Monmouth should never have allowed Virgil into the room in the first place. It put the duke in the position of having to concede a point before the conversation had even begun.

"You've a head on your shoulders, Kilcairn," the duke said grudgingly. "Virgil, get out."

"But, Father—"

"Don't make me repeat myself."

With another glare the younger Retting stalked out of the room and slammed the door behind him.

Monmouth seated himself on the couch opposite Lucien. "I might as well have let him stay. You're not getting anything from me."

"I will."

"Damned sure of yourself, aren't you?"

"Frequently." Lucien sat back, assessing his opponent, and clicked open his watch. Alexandra was insatiably curious, and he was willing to wager that it was a family trait. He glanced down at the time. Half past three. He needed to get back soon, to see how the conversation between Alexandra and Rose had gone.

"What is it you think you'll get from me, then?"

Lucien snapped the watch shut again. "Since the unfortunate Welkins incident, your niece has felt somewhat unsure about her place in society."

"And so she should, the little strumpet. It took me weeks to quiet that down."

"I thought you hadn't been completely uninvolved. Sloppy, though. You left a mess."

The duke narrowed his eyes. "Not where *my* family is concerned. *You* stirred that mess up again, by having her here in London."

"The point being, a mess exists."

"The point being, all I do is snap my fingers and she's no longer connected to my family. Mess cleaned up. Permanently."

Alexandra claimed to have seen Monmouth in Lucien's own demeanor, in the way he treated his own family. Abruptly, he didn't like that very much. "Your mess, yes. Alexandra's, no."

She would kill him if she knew what he was about to tell her uncle. His only hope was that the end result would outweigh her fury over his methods. She'd left him little choice, anyway. She'd made Monmouth a barrier between them; he had to remove it.

"And this concerns me because . . . ?"

"Because Alexandra fears that without your nominal support, Lady Welkins might attempt to have her arrested, despite her innocence in the entire incident."

The duke harrumphed, while Lucien fought his impatience and let Monmouth take a moment to absorb the information. He knew what his own response would be, but then he was in love with the victim in question. If the dilemma had concerned Rose, the answer would have been stickier—though less so now than a few weeks ago.

"It's because she's in London," Monmouth finally grumbled. "She's got everyone's damned attention, especially because she's living under your roof." The old man leaned forward. "Or should I say, under your bed sheets?"

"You shouldn't be saying anything to make the situation more difficult for her than it is already."

"Ha! You're a fine one to talk about propriety. I was there the night King George found your father and Lady Heffington humping in the throne room—a week after he married your mother."

"On the throne itself," Lucien corrected coolly, flicking a speck of dust from his sleeve. "Or so I've been told."

The duke pushed to his feet and walked to the decanters of liquor on the side table. "I knew my sister's stupidity would send me to the poorhouse. Marrying a damned painter. Good God." He poured himself a brandy, not bothering to offer one to Lucien. "I can only imagine the stink if they dragged the chit off in chains, whether she deserved it or not. You tell her I'll give her a thousand pounds to go up-country. She has friends at that school where they took her in before. She'll get nothing more from me."

Lucien realized he'd broken the chain on his watch fob, and he tucked the blasted thing into his pocket. "I could give her a thousand quid to escape," he said sharply. "Or ten times that."

"I told you, she'll get nothing more fr—"

"Make an offer that doesn't involve her having to leave London," Lucien interrupted, standing.

"But I don't want her in London. I thought I made that clear."

Striding over to grab the duke's brandy from his surprised fingers, Lucien flung it against the wall. The fine glass shattered, showering the Persian carpet with flecks of refracted sunlight. "Let me make something clear, you pompous ass," he growled. "You are the only family Alexandra Gallant has. Unfortunate as that makes her, you will welcome her back into your arms, and you will make it very apparent that she is under your protection."

The door opened. "Father, I heard something break. Are you—"

"Out!" Monmouth roared. When the door slammed, he jabbed a finger at Lucien's chest. "How dare you threaten me!"

Lucien stood his ground. "I'm not threatening anything. I'm insulting you, the way you've insulted Alexandra."

"You bas—"

"You have a horde of solicitors and endless stacks of money ready to rush to your defense. She has nothing. That makes you a damned bully."

"Apparently she has you."

"There is that."

For a long moment the duke looked at him. "And just what is in this for you, Kilcairn?"

"I get to marry her."

The duke looked stunned. "Marry her," he repeated. "Why?"

"I have my reasons."

"But if you marry her, she doesn't need me to defend her against Lady Welkins's accusations. Your name provides as much a shield as mine does. Marry her, for God's sake, and leave the Retting name out of it."

Lucien shook his head. He was beginning to understand where Alexandra got her stubborn streak. "No. It has to be your name. And don't ask me to explain, because I won't." No one would believe him, anyway.

"Where is this tearful reunion supposed to take place?"

"I'm holding a dinner party on Wednesday." Now came the hard part, when he had to actually ask the question, and give Monmouth the chance to refuse. "Will you be there?"

The duke sighed heavily. "I'm not sure I would want you as an enemy, Kilcairn. I'll be there."

"Without Virgil."

"Without blasted Virgil."

When Lucien slipped into the cellar right at sunset, Alexandra's first thought was that he looked as though he could use a strong drink. "You've been busy," she said, picking a stitch out of her embroidery.

"Rose was here?"

"Yes, Thompkinson dragged her out about an hour ago. Apparently they spied your aunt approaching up the street."

Softly he shut the door behind him, and her heart fluttered a little. She was not going to succumb to his charms again, she told herself sternly. It was too difficult to kiss him and be angry with him at the same time, and she was determined to remain angry with him.

"That's the footstool from my bedchamber," he said after a moment, eyeing Shakespeare curled up on the plush burgundy beside her.

"Yes, the other ones weren't soft enough."

He turned his skeptical expression on her. "The other ones?"

"Yes. Shakespeare can be very particular."

"I see. Especially when his mistress is feeling particular, no doubt." He hesitated, then pulled her dressing chair over to sit opposite her. "What did you and Rose discuss?"

She wasn't used to seeing him hesitate about anything, and it unsettled her out of the speech she'd been ready to make about manipulating eighteen-year-old girls with his infamous charms. They'd nearly worked on her; Rose didn't stand a chance. If he was still being cautious, it had to be because of her—or because he was still plotting something. "We talked about how wonderful Robert is, and how wonderful her birthday was, and how pretty I look in my new green muslin, and—"

"And when do you get to the part where you discuss how wonderful I am?"

"Rose is easily impressed."

"Hm."

Alexandra couldn't help laughing at his put-upon expression. "I'm actually trying to recall whether we discussed you at all."

Lucien lifted an eyebrow and favored her with a sensual smile. "I find it difficult to believe that my name didn't arise once in the conversation."

Oh, my, she could just sit and look at him all day long. Alexandra shook herself. Gawking at Lucien Balfour wouldn't get her anything but flat on her back again.

"You're blushing," he murmured, his gray gaze touching hers.

"You don't need to point that out," she said, feeling her cheeks grow still warmer. "I am perfectly aware of it." She picked up her embroidery again. "At least all I do is blush. And someone might blush for any number of reasons. How do you ever control"—turning scarlet, she gestured in the general direction of his waist—"that?"

He chuckled. "It's gotten easier with age, though it's more difficult in some situations than others. So you wish to discuss degrees of arousal, then? I can surmise how that conversation will conclude."

The needle jabbed an untidy hole in her kerchief. "You are very aggravating."

"And you are very arousing." He grinned, obviously pleased with himself. "Tell me what you and Rose discussed, or make love with me."

Alexandra knew very well that his powers of persuasion exceeded hers, particularly when she was arguing against something she actually wanted—badly. "She's very grateful to you. What did you expect?"

"Don't try to turn me into a villain. Rose told me at least a dozen times that she didn't want to marry me. Reconciling her with Robert was in her best interest. It's just my good fortune that it happened to be in my best interest, as well."

He did make a fair argument. "What's your next step, then? Fiona obviously doesn't know what's going on."

"No, she doesn't. I'll deal with her when the time comes."

"And when will that be?"

Lucien shrugged. "Soon. I promised you, remember?"

"You cannot make everything right for me, Lucien. I don't expect you to."

His lips twitched. "I'm being gallant again, am I?"

"Except for the kidnapping and the lying to your aunt and all the other plotting you won't tell me about."

"I would dispense with all of it if you'd agree to marry me."

For a moment she wished he had the answers for all her arguments, so she could say yes and fall into his arms and never have to worry about anything ever again. It almost seemed foolish to turn him down—eventually he was bound to come to his senses and stop asking. That, though, was what stopped her. If that moment—the one when he realized winning her was only a clever game he was trying to figure out—came after she said yes and admitted to him how much she loved him, it would kill her.

Lucien stood. "The plotting continues, then." He leaned down and brushed his lips across her forehead. "I have to escort the harpies to the opera tonight. Wimbole plays whist, if you want company."

"Whist with your butler. A dream come true."

"The first of many." Shakespeare received a scratch on the head, which the terrier acknowledged with a wag of his tail. "Just make sure you're here when I return." He walked toward the door.

"You could keep me here for a year, my lord, and it still wouldn't change you. Or me."

Lucien faced her again. "Do you believe in redemption, Alexandra? Do you believe people can change?"

She searched his eyes, knowing he was asking her for something specific, and that her answer had to be right. "I don't believe a person can change to suit someone else," she said finally. "That only makes it an act."

"Yes—but do you believe one person can make another one *want* to change? For his own sake?"

For such a cynical, jaded, self-assured man, it seemed an almost childish question. "I'm willing to believe that," she whispered.

He smiled, the light touching his eyes. "Good. That's all I ask—for now."

Chapter 19

Redemption. How odd that such a word had come out of his mouth.

Lucien spent the next three days running about like a madman, sending out invitations to the second Balfour gathering of the month, conferring with Robert about the scheduling of the evening's events, and visiting Alexandra every spare moment. If Fiona found anything odd about his slipping down to the wine cellar every ten minutes, she most likely suspected that he had a drinking problem.

The entire time he worked at plotting Alexandra's reunion with her uncle, and while he pretended to have conceded victory to Aunt Fiona, he wondered about redemption. The Duke of Monmouth's story about Lionel Balfour had angered and disgusted him. So, too, did the recollection of much of his own behavior over the past few years.

It baffled him. Two months ago he wouldn't have spared either memory a second thought. Now he was obsessed with figuring out how closely his own deeds resembled his father's, and how he could have done some of the idiotic things that he had indulged in, and whether Alexandra was right to doubt his ability to love when there was no ulterior motive or game involved. They would both find out soon enough.

The task he'd thought would be the most difficult turned out to be the easiest. Between Mr. Mullins and himself, he tracked down and purchased half a dozen paintings by one Christopher Gallant. He knew Alexandra thought highly of her father's work. Upon viewing them, he was ready to share her opinion. Apparently so did several of the more renowned critics of British landscapes, and he arranged for a series of formal viewings over the next few months.

The prices for the works were considerable, and he was glad to pay them. Alexandra would be happy to hear of their increased value, as well. Of course, he had no intention of mentioning a word about any of his purchases until he had her securely in his arms—otherwise she would accuse him of bribing her. No, he would keep the paintings safe and sound at Kilcairn Abbey until she arrived there as his bride to see them lining the Great Hall with the family's other treasured works of art.

"Lucien, if you're having second thoughts about your grand party, please let me know so I can flee to China." Lord Belton leaned against his fireplace mantel.

"I'm barely having any thoughts at all," Lucien grumbled. "Though I do confess to being bloody annoyed at having to come to your house if I want to compose any private correspondence." He sat back, rereading his note, before he dusted it with sand and folded it. "You're not having second thoughts, are you, my boy?"

"About marrying Rose?"

"No, about swimming across the Channel."

"Very amusing." Robert strolled over to drop into the chair behind Lucien. "Rose will make a delightful viscountess, and I'm happy to have found her."

"But?" Lucien prompted.

"But our—your—treatment of your aunt bothers me. She's going to be furious, and she's also going to be my mother-in-law."

"Don't worry about your family valuables." Lucien chuckled. "She wants grandchildren so the lot of you can raise them to despise me."

"I just hope it's you she keeps despising. She'll be living under my roof at Belton Court, you know. Even if I keep my valuables, I could lose an ear or a toe."

Still chuckling, Lucien dripped wax onto the back of his correspondence to seal it and mashed his signet ring into the cooling globule. "Even if I could think of another way to resolve this mess, I don't think I'd do it. What kind of mother would force her only daughter—her only child—to marry me? Especially with you about as an alternative."

"Good God. Was that a compliment?"

He turned around, straddling the writing desk's chair. "What's not to compliment? You're a good man, Robert. A better one than I am."

"Hm. I'm less convoluted than you are. With certain benefits of family that you never had."

There it was again. He was damned both by nature and by upbringing. "Poor family's no excuse. My foul way of living is simply easier." Lucien rested his chin on the back of the chair. "I'm glad you found Rose, and that she found you. I hope one day to be as lucky."

"Balderdash. You are as lucky. The love of your life just happens to be locked in your cellar."

"That is for her own protection."

"All this has nothing to do with your being madly in love with her, then? Do you think I'm completely cork-brained? You practically swoon whenever you mention her name."

Lucien straightened. "I do *not* swoon."

Robert grinned. "I was speaking metaphorically."

"Well, I'm about ready to metaphorically bloody your nose," Lucien retorted, and stood. "Don't be late tomorrow."

"I won't be. When's the grand reunion to take place?"

"Right before I announce your engagement, and before Aunt Fiona can find a pistol with which to shoot me." And more important, before she could begin spouting any more rumors about Alexandra and Lord Welkins or himself.

"Good luck."

Lucien opened the door and handed his missive to Robert's butler for delivery. "It's a brilliantly composed plan. I don't need luck." He accepted his coat and his hat as Robert joined him in the foyer. "But thank you, anyway."

On his way back to Balfour House he had the coach stop at Madame Charbonne's, where he checked on the progress of one last item he needed for tomorrow evening's festivities. And then he went to get drunk. He was going to have to be sober for the festivities tomorrow.

Alexandra crouched just inside the cellar's garden entry and rattled the padlock. Atlas the Titan couldn't have opened the blasted thing.

The other cellar door opened. "Alexandra, I have . . ." Lucien's voice trailed off, and then he cursed. "Alexandra!" he called sharply. "Damnation!"

Gathering her skirts, she hurried back down the stairs and into the main part of the room. "Good afternoon," she said to his backside, which was all of him that she could see as he crouched to look under her bed. His backside looked exceedingly attractive.

He straightened sharply and whipped around to face her. "Where were you?" he demanded, closing the distance between them. The relief in his face surprised her. Did he really worry that much about misplacing her?

"I was exploring."

Lucien tilted her chin up with his fingertips and kissed her. "I like exploring."

She couldn't answer, because she was too occupied with kissing him back. It amazed her that a touch of lips and mouth could so affect every part of her, inside and out. "And where have you been?" she asked finally. "I haven't seen you since yesterday."

"Jealous?"

"No."

"I brought you something," he murmured finally, lifting his head.

"Hm. It wouldn't be a key, or a saw, would it?"

"You don't seem to have much need for those," he said dryly. "Take a look." Lucien gestured at a cloth-covered bundle draped across the bed. Shakespeare stalked about it, sniffing, obviously annoyed at having his territory invaded.

With a sideways glance, Alexandra pulled the covering off the mound. Rich burgundy and gray silk sparkling with beads and lace met her gaze. "It's a gown," she said slowly, taking it in.

"Do you like it?"

Alexandra held it up to the candlelight. "Of course I like it. You knew I would. It's beautiful."

"Will you wear it?"

"It's very formal. Are you going to bring Rose's party down to the cellar, or are you sending me out to the opera?"

The annoyed look he gave her almost made her smile. Let him be aggravated for once. She'd spent the last week in a cellar, for heaven's sake.

"Rose would like you to be present for the announcement." Slowly he reached out to brush a strand of her hair from her forehead. "So would I."

She trembled a little. "And how will you explain my reappearance to Mrs. Delacroix?"

He shrugged, still caressing her cheek with his fingertips, as though he didn't have a party and his guests and his relations and dinner and a hundred other things to worry about. "I'll think of something."

"Once you set me free, I won't let you lock me up again, you know," she whispered, trying to read the secrets in his eyes.

"I know. I hope I won't need to." Lucien bent his head and kissed her, so thoroughly she had to lean against his chest for balance.

He didn't seem to be implying that he was giving up, but neither could she imagine that he'd come up with something that would cause her to stay. She *wanted* to stay—with him forever, but she simply wasn't meant to reside in London. Too many people didn't want her there. If she could only remain because the Earl of Kilcairn Abbey deigned to lend her the protection of his name, then she couldn't remain. It wouldn't be right; it wouldn't be fair—either to her or to her proud, independent parents.

"A quid for your thoughts," Lucien said softly.

She smiled. "They aren't worth that much. Don't you have a dinner party to prepare for?"

With a slight frown he released her. "Yes, I do. And I'm doubling—tripling—your guard, my love. No surprises except for the ones I'm planning."

He looked so worried that she couldn't help chuckling. "I daresay I'll be here for my parole. And, Lucien, whatever else happens, you're doing a good thing tonight. Rose is very happy."

"She doesn't make much of a secret of that." With a last glance he turned for the door. "She says I'm her hero. Imagine that."

"The question is, do you like being a hero?"

Lucien paused. "Don't tell anyone, because it'll completely destroy my foul reputation but yes." He grinned almost sheepishly, looking like a schoolboy who had just pulled a prank. "I think I do. I'll be back for you in a few hours."

She plunked herself down on the bed. "I'll be here."

Though she had no idea when Kilcairn had scheduled the guests to begin arriving, Shakespeare started barking a few minutes after seven. She shushed him, willing to be kept prisoner for at least another hour or so, and went about donning her new, splendid gown and putting up her hair.

A nervous tremor made her fingers shake. Something beyond what Lucien had disclosed was going on tonight, and she disliked being left out of the planning. Mrs. Delacroix was the most likely reason for his secrecy, but short of giving Fiona and Lady Welkins her dungeon room in the cellar, she didn't know how Lucien thought he could fix anything, much less everything.

It really wouldn't matter after tonight, anyway. Lucien wouldn't have to worry about being forced to marry

Rose, or about prematurely losing Alexandra's help in dealing with his relations. Once he realized that, his silly insistence on keeping her captive and on marrying her would disappear. And so would she.

Hunger had started to make her stomach growl when someone finally slid back the bolt and opened her dungeon door. Thompkinson rushed in and scooped up Shakespeare with the ease of a week's constant practice, and then he stopped and stared at her.

"Are you all right?" she asked after a moment, torn between amusement and bewilderment.

"I . . . yes . . . aye, Miss—ah—Gallant. You . . . It's just that you look . . . very nice, miss."

Alexandra curtsied. "Thank you, Thompkinson. That's very kind of you." A moment later the hairs at the back of her neck began to tickle, and she looked toward the doorway.

Lucien stood there, devouring her with his eyes. She flushed, reading the hunger and the desire in his expression.

"I told you burgundy suited you," he murmured.

"It occurs to me that this is not the wisest choice of attire if I'm to make an inconspicuous entrance," she said, wondering why she didn't just sink into a puddle on the floor. Thank goodness for Thompkinson's presence.

"Just leave any worries to me." Lucien stepped forward and offered her his arm. "By the way, what are your reservations about marrying me, again?"

"Lucien, don't—"

"Ah, yes. Rose's happiness." He ushered her ahead of him to ascend the narrow stairs to the kitchen.

"That was only the first of them."

"Of course. We can't forget my abject laziness in finding a more suitable bride, or my chivalrous intentions of protecting you from the *ton*'s gossip."

It bothered her a little that he suddenly seemed easy enough about her reservations to joke about them. "And your lack of belief in love," she reminded him as they stepped into the kitchen.

To her surprise, he smiled. "At least my ill manners and ungentlemanly nature are only sad specters of the past." Lucien took her arm again as they headed upstairs to the drawing room. From the volume of chatter inside, he'd gathered quite a sizable group. "Let's see which other walls we can bring down tonight."

Wimbole flung open the double doors, and they strolled into the warm, noisy room. The first person Alexandra saw was Fiona Delacroix, literally glowing in yellow taffeta, her eyes ablaze with smug satisfaction. And then the woman caught sight of Alexandra.

She blanched, uttering an odd, furious screech audible all the way across the room. Alexandra started to pull free of Lucien's grip, intent on lessening the scene he'd no doubt counted on causing, when another figure emerged from the middle of the room and walked toward her with open arms.

"Alexandra, my dear niece! I was hoping you would make an appearance tonight!"

She stood frozen as the Duke of Monmouth embraced her and offered her a kiss on each cheek. This was the wall Lucien had meant to bring down, she realized. Rose and Lord Belton were only a distraction—a reason for him to bring in a crowd to witness this reunion.

And the crowd was definitely watching. Another scandal would destroy any chance of future employment for her anywhere in England and probably Europe, so Alexandra returned a kiss to the duke's angular cheek.

"Uncle Monmouth," she choked. "I hadn't realized you were in London."

Lucien stirred beside her, and belatedly she noticed how hard she was digging her nails into his forearm. As she met his gaze, she saw the calm, confident superiority in his gray eyes fade. The uncertain worry that took its place didn't appease her in the least.

"You arranged this, didn't you?" she said with a bright smile and a clenched jaw.

"Alexandra . . ." he began, then trailed off as she released his arm and took her uncle's in its stead.

"Let me introduce you to Rose Delacroix, Uncle," she said, wishing she could run screaming out into the night. How dare Lucien? How dare either of them? If they thought this tidy little public display would erase the past twenty-four years, and especially the last five, they had a large surprise coming.

Alexandra looked radiant as she introduced the Duke of Monmouth to Rose and then Fiona. She smiled and laughed, and easily breezed past Fiona's fury. And Lucien was worried.

"It's going better than you thought," Robert said, watching Alexandra chatting with Rose and her uncle.

"Yes, it seems to be." Perhaps he should have told her something, given her at least a moment to compose herself.

"Your aunt looks as though she's about to explode. When are you going to make your next announcement?"

Lucien shook himself, turning away from gazing at Alexandra. "Hm? Oh. In just a moment. Stay close by."

Alexandra was furious. He could see it, even if no one else seemed to notice. If he *had* told her about Monmouth's presence, though, he would never have gotten her up the stairs, much less into her uncle's arms. But Alexandra had more common sense than anyone he'd ever met. She would realize this reunion was in her best interest, even if she couldn't immediately be happy about it. He would give her the evening to let her calm intelligence win out over her surprise, and then he would ask her again to marry him.

He gestured to Wimbole for a glass of champagne, and watched as the servants distributed glasses to all of his guests. "Before we adjourn to dinner," he said in a carrying voice, "I have an announcement. Rose, if you please?"

As Rose made her way through the crowd of guests, Lucien glanced between Fiona and Alexandra. His aunt's expression was one of complete bafflement, as though she simply couldn't reconcile Alexandra's reappearance with the pending marriage announcement. He looked forward to explaining things to her.

Rose reached his side, and he took her hand and kissed it. "My friends, many of you know that my cousin arrived in London under less-than-happy circumstances. Tonight, though, we all find ourselves full of joy."

Fiona stepped forward, already accepting congratulations from the wags she'd adopted as her cronies. He'd warned her about spreading the news before it had been announced, and she'd ignored him. He and Robert and now Monmouth could protect themselves and the ladies—Fiona was on her own. If Robert chose to help her regain a modicum of dignity, that was his prerogative. Personally, Lucien would have been perfectly happy to leave her for the crows.

"I have the very great joy of announcing," he continued, "that my cousin, Rose Delacroix, is to be married. And I am equally pleased to inform all of you that her husband-to-be is my good friend Robert Ellis, Lord Belton. Robert, Rose, my congratulations."

Robert joined them at the front of the room. Amidst the loud applause and congratulations, Lucien thought he detected a shriek of fury, but he wasn't certain if he'd actually heard it, or if he'd just expected it so strongly that he'd imagined it. When Fiona emerged from the crowd, charging him like a mad bull, he slipped Rose's hand into Robert's and led the angry bovine into the adjoining sitting room.

"This will not do!" Fiona bellowed, red-faced.

He closed the door. "I think it does quite well myself."

"You will not get away with this! People know the truth about you and my daughter."

"Apparently several people were misled," he returned calmly, beginning to enjoy himself.

"I won't have it! Lady Welkins and I will see that . . . whore of yours ruined tomorrow if you don't go back out there right now and tell everyone you were joking—that *you* are marrying Rose."

He closed the distance between them. "Robert is marrying Rose, because they both wish it."

"You don't care about what they want, Lucien."

"Yes, I do. And if you say anything against either of them, you will find me *very* annoyed."

Fiona backed away a step. "Don't you threaten me."

He narrowed his eyes. "Have I threatened you? As I recall, it was you making the threats. And that will stop now—especially with Alexandra. She's done nothing to you. In fact, you owe her your thanks."

"My thanks? That—"

"Enough!" he snapped. "I wouldn't have married Rose, regardless. Miss Gallant made her enough of a lady to take a place in society."

"She is to be a countess!"

"She is to be a viscountess," he returned. The woman was a one-note song, and out of tune to begin with. "With a very generous dowry." Lucien took another step closer. "And understand this, Aunt: Alexandra Gallant is reconciled with the Duke of Monmouth. You and Lady Welkins will keep your idiotic speculations to yourselves, or His Grace and I will see the two of you in Australia. Is that clear?"

For a long moment she glared at him. "You are evil!" she finally shouted. "You are exactly like your wretched father."

He bowed. "That, Aunt Fiona, remains to be seen."

"I don't need to see anything further. I know." With that, she stalked back out to the drawing room.

Lucien let her have the last word. He would rather see her angry with him than with Alexandra or Rose. As he strolled back to his guests, he allowed himself a moment of self-satisfaction. He'd seen Rose engaged to the titled gentleman of her choice, he'd thwarted his aunt's clumsy attempts at blackmail, and he'd seen Alexandra protected from all further rumor and innuendo. Quite a night's work, if he did say so himself.

Several times during the meal he tried to catch Alexandra's eye, but she seemed completely occupied with amusing Rose and Robert and the dinner guests on either side of her. Even Monmouth received a smile and a gentle jest. Lucien frowned—Alexandra appeared *too* calm and content. She was putting on an act. He'd seen it before, at Rose's first public outing, when she'd been angry and miserable. She was far too skilled to allow it to show, but he knew.

Of course, it was entirely possible that *he* was overreacting. Despite his plotting, he really hadn't expected everything to go so smoothly. As he began to convince himself that she was becoming reconciled to the reunion, though, she glanced down the table at him. He'd seen icicles warmer than the expression in her eyes.

The dinner proceeded flawlessly, but he ceased to care. Fiona no doubt continued to fume, but as the elderly females she'd invited piled on the praise and congratulations at her daughter's catch, she mellowed a little. He was delighted when they all decided that he was Lucifer himself, and that she and Rose were lucky to have so narrowly escaped his clutches.

As the guests finally began to leave for the evening, he kept most of his attention on Alexandra, to be certain she didn't try to slip away while he wasn't looking. When she finally turned to stalk up the stairs, he was ready. "Miss Gallant," he said sharply.

She hesitated, then stopped and looked down at him. "Yes, my lord?"

"In my office, if you please."

Her lips compressed; she smoothed her skirts and returned downstairs. She headed down the foyer, and a moment later his office door slammed.

"You keep her out of trouble," the duke said, and motioned for his hat and coat. "I won't go out of my way for her again."

Lucien looked at him. "So you've resolved your differences?"

"What differences? I'm here to keep the damned gossips at bay until you marry her and get her out of London."

"Ah." Of his guests, only Robert remained, chatting quietly in the morning room with Rose. "I believe I need another moment or two of your time."

"Make an appointment with my man. I'm meeting the prime minister at nine in the morning."

Lucien stepped forward, blocking the duke's path, while Wimbole shut the front door. "Just a moment," he repeated calmly, and gestured toward his office.

"I have no time for such nonsense."

"Make some, then," Lucien returned, unmoving.

"Impertinent ruffian," the duke blustered, but strode down the hallway.

Lucien pulled the door open for him, and followed him inside. Alexandra stood behind his desk, her clenched fists resting against the smooth mahogany surface. "What is it?" he asked her without preamble, closing the door behind him.

"I have to admit," she said in a low, unsteady voice, "that the events of this evening took me completely by surprise."

"Bah," Monmouth snorted. "Don't thank me, because you can never repay me. Just be grateful that I care about my family's reputation, girl, because if I didn't, I'd happily see you in Aus—"

"I wasn't going to thank you," Alexandra snapped. "How dare you presume that I would ever ask anything from a poor excuse for a gentle—"

"Alexandra," Lucien broke in, "I asked your uncle to come tonight."

She came around the desk toward him. "I thought . . ." she began, then broke off.

"You thought what?"

"I thought you'd changed! Rose seemed so happy, and I thought you'd changed!"

Lucien narrowed his eyes. "I have changed—I think. I certainly spend more blasted time worrying about it than I ever did before."

"Then why is he here?" She jabbed her finger in Monmouth's direction.

"Why, indeed, you ungrateful—"

"Enough!" Lucien roared. "Monmouth, go."

"With pleasure." The duke stormed out of the office, slamming the door behind him.

"He came tonight because you were using him as an excuse," Lucien continued, watching her stalk between him and the fireplace.

"An excuse for what, pray tell?"

"An excuse for demanding your damned independence from everything. From me. Now you can't use him for that any longer."

"I don't need to use anything but you," she retorted, a tear running down one cheek. "You're the best reason not to marry you that I could possibly find."

"Just a damned minute," Lucien cut in, surprised by her venom.

"Take all the time you like. It won't change anything."

"You gave me a list—a *list*—of reasons you wouldn't marry me. I have resolved them, one by one. You have no reason to be angry with me for something you instigated."

"*I* instigated? How dare you, for your own convenience, bring the Duke of Monmouth here and blame it on me?"

"That doesn't make any blasted sense, Alexandra. We—"

"You had no right to try to force a reconciliation just because it suited you! Is that clear enough?"

Furious, Lucien stalked a circle around her. "I have done everything for you," he growled. "You worried over Rose's happiness. I made certain she would be happy. You feared your reputation would mean trouble for those around you if you stayed here. Your reputation is now repaired."

"My reputation is now conveniently swept under a rug so you can have your way. You still need an heir to keep Rose's children from inheriting, and you're still the same stupid Lucien Balfour who said love was only a socially acceptable synonym for fornication!"

"*I'm* stupid," he repeated. "*I'm* the idiot who tried to make you happy. For God's sake, since I met you, I don't even recognize myself in the mirror anymore! Now I go frolicking about trying to solve people's problems—and I *like* it!"

"I don't—"

"I'm not finished," he snarled. "I even quit smoking cigars, because I knew you didn't approve. You have changed me. You have made me a different man, and one I actually like better than the old one. My question for you, Alexandra, is where does it say that you get to have exactly everything you want?"

"I didn't ask you for anything. Don't expect me to compromise for something I never wanted."

"You did want it. You still do. You're just too damned stubborn to admit it." Breathing hard, Lucien glared at her as she glared back at him. "It's your turn to bend," he snapped. "I'll be upstairs if you want to find me."

Chapter 20

"I was not wrong!" Alexandra stamped about the small office. "I was not wrong! He had no right to do what he did!"

"Lex, I didn't say anything. You're arguing with yourself. Which may be helpful to you, but it's giving me a headache."

Alexandra stopped in front of the scarred oak desk and looked at the young woman seated behind it. "I'm sorry, Emma," she muttered, and then stomped her foot. "He just made me so angry!"

"So I gathered," Emma Grenville said dryly. Tucking a strand of her ever-straying auburn hair behind one ear, she stood and came around the desk. "Sit down," she ordered. "I will fetch you some tea." The headmistress bent down and ruffled Shakespeare's ears. "And Shakes needs a cookie."

Reluctantly Alexandra grinned. "I've been yelling so much, he's probably deaf."

"Sit."

"Yes, ma'am."

Petite and slender, with an irresistible pair of dimples that appeared when she laughed, Emma looked more like a wood sprite than the owner of a girls' school. At the same time, her air of calm unflappability and kindness made her seem older than her twenty-four years. Alexandra sighed and took a seat by the window as Emma slipped out to the small kitchen.

Outside the door she heard laughter, quickly quieted, as a group of Academy students headed to the main hall for dinner. The former monastery had always seemed a perfect place for a school, though the addition of society's daughters had forced several modifications to the old building. The windows added to the classrooms, the study, and the offices were only the most minor of the changes.

"Now," Emma said as she stepped back into the room, "I gather that you and Lord Kilcairn had an argument." She set the tea tray on her desk and took her seat again.

"Yes, we had an argument. But it was his fault." Alexandra scooted forward in her chair and poured each of them a cup of tea. Shakespeare eagerly received his cookie, and retreated under the desk to gnaw on it.

"Since when do you argue with your employers?"

"Since they're wrong." With a small sigh, she sat back and sipped her tea. She couldn't remember how many times she'd sat in this same elegant chair and poured out her troubles to Emma's aunt. It felt . . . comfortable to be back, except that she had hoped by this time not to have any more troubles. Yet here she was with the same old ones, bolstered by the new ones Lucien had provided her. "He locked me in his cellar, you know."

"He did? What a barbaric thing to do!"

"It wasn't even his primary wine cellar. Just the secondary one."

Emma's lips twitched. "So you're angry because Lord Kilcairn didn't lock you in the main wine cellar?"

"Of course not. Don't make fun."

"I wouldn't dream of it, Lex. Why would he lock you up anywhere?"

That very question continued to trouble her, even after three days of thinking about nothing else in a bumpy, cramped mail stage. She stood again and wandered to the window. "I'm sure I have no idea." Half a dozen cattle grazed on the far side of the Academy's duck pond, just visible through the small garden and scattering of elm trees. "But that's not even the worst of it."

Her friend leaned her chin in one hand. "I thought not."

"Yes. He threw a grand dinner party, and invited Uncle Monmouth. Without telling me."

"My goodness."

"He's an awful, wicked man, and I should never have accepted employment in his household."

"Is he a friend of your uncle's?"

"I'm certain he's not. He just tried to force a reconciliation, for his own convenience."

"Convenience?"

Alexandra smacked the windowsill hard enough to make her hand sting. "Don't even ask. I can't explain it."

"Lex," Emma said, "I'm glad you're here. I can most definitely use your assistance."

"But?" A tremor of uncertainty touched Alexandra. There always seemed to be an exception to any positive statement lately.

"But I have the Academy to think of now. We're—"

"I'm so sorry, then," Alexandra interrupted, tears beginning a cascade down her cheeks. There really was nowhere for her to go now.

"Let me finish, goose. We're an institution of learning, not a refuge for lovesick cellar escapees. I need to be sure you're going to stay."

"I am not lovesick!" Alexandra declared, wiping her eyes. "I told him I was leaving. He said that was fine with him, and so here I am."

Emma looked at her for a long moment. "Are you certain of that?"

Stifling the urge to do more stamping, Alexandra settled for crossing her arms. "Of course I am."

Her dark green eyes still holding her friend's, Emma slid open the top drawer of her desk. "You may wonder why I wasn't surprised at your delayed arrival from London." She lifted a folded paper from the drawer and slid it across the desk. "I received a letter the day before yesterday."

Abruptly suspicious, Alexandra strode across the room and snatched up the missive. Before she even reached it, she recognized the torn wax imprint that had sealed it. "*He* sent you a letter?" He'd said he would take care of informing Emma, but she hadn't thought he actually meant to do it. They'd been somewhat distracted during that conversation.

"I had to read it twice before I believed it was from the Earl of Kilcairn Abbey. It doesn't . . . sound like someone of his reputation."

With another nervous, excited shiver running through her, Alexandra unfolded the letter. " 'Miss Grenville,' " she read aloud, hearing Lucien's deep voice in her head, " 'As you know, Alexandra Gallant was until very recently a part of my household. I am aware that she has accepted a position to teach at your Academy, and while

I can hardly dispute your choice of instructor, I do find myself at odds with you over her departure.' "

"He's well educated, isn't he?" Emma commented, as Alexandra paused to take a breath.

"Extremely. He's the most voraciously curious individual I've ever encountered." She realized her comment sounded very like a compliment, and she cleared her throat to continue reading. " 'As you have probably noticed, I have already convinced Alexandra to remain in London for another few days.' " She lifted an eyebrow. "Ha. He has an odd definition of *convincing*. 'It is my fervent hope that she will choose to remain here permanently. Either—' "

"I don't think he meant permanently in the cellar," Emma supplied.

Alexandra favored her friend with a glare. " 'Either she or I will inform you further.' "

"He doesn't sound like someone planning to hurt you," the headmistress said quietly.

"Perhaps, but you can see from this how very arrogant he is."

"Hm. Read the last part," Emma suggested.

Alexandra made a face, but complied. " 'Miss Grenville, Alexandra has several times referred to you as her dearest friend. I can only express to you my supreme envy over that fact, and the hope that you and I shall meet one day soon. I have found Alexandra's friends to be exceptional, as I have found her detractors to be lacking in intelligence, humor, compassion, and every other quality I have come to admire so highly in your friend. Yours in anticipation of acquaintance, Lucien Balfour, Lord Kilcairn.' "

Slowly Alexandra took a seat. "Oh, my," she whispered. "He must have sent this to you days ago."

"It seems you've captured a rogue's heart, my dear."

She shook her head, rereading the last few sentences of his letter. "No, I haven't. It's only that he's very charming."

"And why would the Earl of Kilcairn Abbey attempt to charm me?"

"I . . . Well, he may have felt this way—or perhaps he thought he did—before his stupid dinner party. I know he doesn't feel like this any longer."

"Are you certain of—"

"Besides, admiring someone highly and being in love with her are two very different things, Emma. I admire Lord Liverpool, for instance, but I could hardly consider myself in love with him."

"You—"

"And he only wants to marry me because he's comfortable with me, and he can produce his heir with the least bit of inconvenience to himself."

Emma stood rather abruptly and snatched the letter back. "He wants to *marry* you? Lex, you never told me—"

"No!" she interrupted sharply. "I've worked too hard to give in and live my life on someone else's terms. Even his. Especially his. I'll take care of myself, and my own problems."

"You're arguing with yourself again." Emma returned the letter to her. "You know Lord Kilcairn far better than I ever will, Lex. I will take your word that he is plotting and arrogant and cares for no one but himself."

"Thank you."

Emma gestured Alexandra toward the door. "And you will teach dinner conversation and how to discuss literature without sounding like a bluestocking, starting tomorrow. We'll get you better settled on Monday."

Alexandra nodded as she and Shakespeare followed Emma to the dining hall. All she needed was something to occupy her. With her first class tomorrow, she would begin the task of forgetting Lucien Balfour.

"Forget her, then," Robert said, guiding his gelding among Hyde Park's trees. "You made an effort—a titanic effort—and nothing came of it. The end."

Lucien kicked Faust into a trot, not bothering to see if the viscount followed. His head ached, reminding him that he'd drunk far too much whiskey at Boodle's club last night. At least, though, his pounding skull gave him something else to fuel his foul temper without admitting how damned lost he felt without Alexandra Beatrice Gallant.

"Lucien, there are a hundred ladies in London who would happily agree to marry you."

"Not happily," he retorted, starting another wide loop around the deserted carriage track.

"Yes, happily. You're wealthy, handsome, and titled. Not many bachelors can claim all three."

"Don't try to placate me. I'm not in the mood."

"I've noticed. That's what I've been attempting to rectify."

Scowling, Lucien pulled up Faust. "Who was your second choice?" he asked, as the viscount drew even with him.

"My second choice for what?"

"For a wife. If I had intended on marrying Rose, or if she had refused you, whom would you be pursuing now?"

Robert shrugged. "I don't know. Lucy Halford, or maybe Charlotte Templeton," he mused. "But I've found Rose, and we are both exceedingly happy about it."

Lucien looked down at his gloved hands as he twisted the reins around and around his fingers. "For me," he said quietly, "there is no one else. She is . . . who I looked for, the entire time I was looking. Even before that."

"But she refused you," Robert said in a solemn voice. "So now you must look elsewhere." He hesitated, glancing about the nearly empty park. "She seemed a bit too . . . intractable, anyway. A wife can't support you if she's always disagreeing with everything you say."

Lucien shook himself and nudged the bay into motion again. "You've got it ass backwards, but I suppose it doesn't matter. She doesn't trust me—or my motivations, rather—and there's not much I can do about that unless I give away my title and everything that goes with it and become a chimney sweep. And I don't intend to do that."

"So you'll forget her and move on."

"I suppose I will. As soon as I forget how to breathe."

"Then I can just expect you to go about moping for the rest of eternity."

With a glare, Lucien kicked Faust into a gallop. "I'm not moping. I'm waiting. I told her it was her turn to give ground. She's a sensible female; she'll realize that I'm right, and that she's a fool to give me up to those hordes of lovely ladies who'd be so happy to marry me."

"And if she doesn't realize it?"

Robert might have been his own conscience; Lucien had been having the same conversation with himself since she'd stomped out of Balfour House a week ago. "She will."

"Well, taking turns giving ground and waiting for her to come back all sounds like a pile of nonsense to me,"

Robert retorted. "I think it you who's going to have to realize that."

"Perhaps."

As Lucien went about his meetings and dinners and social gatherings, though, he couldn't help puzzling over what he'd done wrong. Yes, he'd locked her away to keep from losing her, and he should never have let her out. And yes, he'd tricked her into a meeting with a relative she despised. But she'd helped him see the chains and walls he'd put around himself, and she'd practically forced him into reconciling with Rose. Why, then, had it worked on him and not on her?

The answer, or what he hoped was the right answer, finally came to him while he and Rose were discussing her dowry, along with the stipend he meant to settle on her so she would always have her own income, apart from Robert and apart from him.

"Lucien, that's too much," his cousin protested, blushing prettily. "You've given me far more than I'd hoped for already."

He ignored Mr. Mullins's agreeing nod and continued scratching out figures on the draft of the agreement. "Don't argue. I'm feeling generous."

Rose giggled. "I don't think Mama would agree."

"As long as she holds to her vow never to speak to me again, she can disagree all she likes. It's not for her, anyway. It's for you."

"Thank you." She leaned over and kissed him on the cheek.

Lucien sat still for a moment. He'd enjoyed the morning spent with his cousin; she was pleasant, even if she didn't present much of a challenge to his intellect. And she'd smiled and laughed and kissed him on the cheek.

Two months ago he would never have tolerated it; two

months ago he couldn't stand being in the same room with either of the Delacroix females. Rose had changed, obviously. She'd become more confident and less self-centered; a pale imitation of her tutor, but a definite improvement over the girl who'd first come to London swathed in pink taffeta.

And he'd changed, too—more than he'd realized. That was the problem, and the solution. *He* had changed. Alexandra hadn't. She still thought of herself in the same terms that she had for the past five years: that she had to stand alone against everything and everyone who threatened to take away her independence, and that the ground could fall from beneath her feet again at any moment if she dared to relax her guard.

Lucien stood. He needed to open her eyes, as she'd opened his. Not to love, because he knew, he sensed, that she loved him—but to herself.

"Cousin Lucien?" Rose asked, looking up at him with a concerned frown.

"Make the arrangements, Mr. Mullins," he said. "And when you've finished, see me in my office. We have one more matter to take care of."

Alexandra sat on the edge of her desk and looked into the fresh, naive faces of her students. She'd been one of them herself not so long ago, though there were times, like this afternoon, when she couldn't remember ever being so young.

"Well," she mused, "when someone expresses a view about a work of fiction, the commentary is generally thought to be that person's opinion."

"But that's what I said, Miss Gallant," Alison, one of the rosy-cheeked young ladies, protested. " 'In my opinion, Juliet should have listened to her parents.' "

"Miss Gallant is saying that you're being redundant, Alison," another of the girls piped up.

"You be quiet, Penelope Walters," Alison retorted.

Stifling an exasperated sigh, and grateful Emma had only given her a dozen of the young ladies to begin with, Alexandra stepped forward to restore order. "Now, now. Romeo and Juliet experienced enough bloodshed. We don't need to add to it."

The classroom door burst open and Jane Hantfeld, one of the Academy's older students, hurried past the desks to the windows at the far end of the room. Her face flushed with excitement, she barely spared the other girls a glance. "Oh, my goodness, look! You have to see this!"

"Miss Hantfeld," Alexandra chastised, too late to stop the stampede to the windows, "class is in session here."

"Who is he?" Alison asked, giggling. "He's so handsome."

"I like his horse," one of the younger girls chimed in.

"Who cares about his horse?"

Moving as nonchalantly as she could, Alexandra sidled over to the window—and stopped breathing.

Tall and powerful looking in a dark gray riding coat, Lucien Balfour sat on Faust at the Academy's gated entrance. As she watched, Emma reached him and scattered the gathered cluster of gawking girls. He tipped his hat, obviously introducing himself, and Emma said something in response.

As soon as she spoke, he dismounted and stepped forward to shake her hand. Alexandra drew a ragged breath. In his letter he'd said he looked forward to meeting Miss Grenville; from his reaction, he'd been sincere.

They were too blasted far away for her to be able to hear or even to interpret what they might be saying, though her students provided a lively commentary of their own. The consensus seemed to be that he was a wealthy nobleman, come to Miss Grenville's Academy in search of a bride. Alexandra clutched the windowsill to keep her fingers from trembling.

"Do you know who he is, Miss Gallant?" one of the girls asked. "Alison says he's a duke."

"He's an earl," she corrected, and cleared her throat as they all turned to look at her. "We have a lesson to finish, ladies."

"Ooh, you know him? Who is he? Tell us, Miss Gallant!"

Alexandra winced at the cacophony of questions and demands. "He is the Earl of Kilcairn Abbey, and he is undoubtedly lost. Shall we continue?"

"Oh, he's leaving," Jane moaned. "Dash it. I wanted him to come in and visit."

"So you could swoon into his arms?"

Alexandra felt nearly ready to swoon herself. She watched, unable to move or to look away, as he swung back up into the saddle, tipped his hat again, and trotted back toward the road. He'd come all this way, apparently to see her, and then left without doing so? Besides being hugely disappointed, she couldn't believe it of him. Lucien Balfour wouldn't go to this much effort for nothing.

"Miss Gallant, do you know him from London?"

She blinked and returned to her desk. "Yes. Now, back to the nonoffensive expression of opinions and point of view."

The girls reluctantly resumed the lesson, but Alexandra seemed to have completely lost her ability to form a coherent thought. What the devil was Lucien Balfour doing in Hampshire, much less at Miss Grenville's Academy?

A few moments later, her classroom door opened again. Emma Grenville leaned into the doorway and gestured at her. "May I speak with you for a moment, Miss Gallant?"

Alexandra stood too quickly, and grimaced at the resulting hushed commentary coming from her students. "Of course. Jane, please read the next sonnet. I'll be back in a moment."

She followed Emma a short distance down the hall. When Emma faced her, Alexandra tried to decipher the headmistress's expression, but Emma seemed as blasted unflappable as always.

"You saw our visitor, I presume?" she asked.

Alexandra nodded. "I have no idea why he would come here. I made my feelings quite clear to—"

"He's looking for you, Lex."

"He's . . . What did you tell him?"

"I told him you were here and in good health, and that I was not at liberty to allow him onto the Academy's grounds."

He was looking for her. Did that mean he still intended to convince her to marry him? Or had he come to Hampshire simply to be sure he had the last word? Or—

"Lex." Emma interrupted her thoughts, making her jump. "He will be back tomorrow at noon. You need to speak to him."

A flutter of pure terror ran down her spine. "But I don't know what—I have no idea what—"

"I am teaching young ladies propriety," the headmistress broke in again. "I can't have the notorious Earl of Kilcairn Abbey lurking on my doorstep." She leaned closer, humor touching her gaze. "It doesn't look well. And I'd lose most of my students."

Alexandra closed her eyes. "I know, I know. I never thought he would follow me here. I can't even guess why he's come."

"But he did come." Emma took her arm, and Alexandra opened her eyes again. "You have to resolve this."

She sighed. "Obviously, Emma, you've never been in love."

The headmistress smiled. "And obviously, Lex, you are in love."

Chapter 21

Lucien arrived at Miss Grenville's Academy a few minutes early.

He felt like a damned idiot waiting outside the front gates, a sinner banned from heaven, but Miss Emma Grenville had made it very clear that he was not to set foot inside the grounds. The old Lucien would have stormed the gates anyway, but today he didn't relish the thought of scores of young ladies screaming and fleeing and fainting before him.

As the time for his rendezvous came and went, though, he was beginning to contemplate a strategic incursion. And then his goddess appeared, walking up the long, curving drive. It felt like far more than a fortnight since he'd last seen her, and he had to stifle the sudden impulse to break down the gates, throw her over the saddle, and make off with her.

"Lucien," she said, as she reached the closed gates.

At least she hadn't decided to pretend they'd never been acquainted. "Alexandra." Belatedly he dismounted. He wanted to be as close to her as he could manage. "How is Shakespeare?"

She tilted her head a little. "My dog is well, thank you."

"Good. And how are you?"

"I'm well."

Lucien blew out his breath. This was fairly useless. He preferred the direct approach—and he knew she did, as well. "You have completely upset the order of my life," he said. "I didn't think anyone could do that."

"Is that what you came here to tell me—that I've ruined your life? What do you think you've—"

"I didn't say you'd ruined anything," he interrupted, scowling. Obviously he wasn't being direct enough. "You did *change* everything—the way I look at people, and at myself. And considering the magnitude of that task, you deserve congratulations. And my thanks."

She fiddled with a button on her pelisse, avoiding his gaze as he looked for a chink in her well-polished armor. "You're welcome, then. That was what you paid me for, though."

He shook his head. "I paid you so you wouldn't leave." Lucien reached through the gate's iron bars to touch her cheek. "I miss you."

Alexandra took an unsteady breath and backed away from his caress. "Of course you do. Now you have to go to the bother of finding someone else whose life you can play with."

Her defensiveness hadn't lessened a whit, but he understood it now. "No one else will let me play," he said softly, and smiled.

She blushed. "Stop that. What are you doing here?"

"You do still like me."

"It's a purely physical reaction. You're better off without me, anyway."

"I thought I was going to be the one apologizing," he

returned. "Come out of there and walk with me."

"No. Go away, Lucien."

"I feel like I'm trying to steal a nun away from a convent," he grumbled, watching her face for a glimpse of her usual humor.

Her lips twitched. "This used to be a monastery."

He leaned against the gate, his fingers curled around two of the vertical iron bars. "It's larger than the cellar, my dear, but you still seem to be trapped inside." Experimentally he rattled the bars. "At least come closer and kiss me."

She folded her arms. "Allow me to remind you that you *locked* me in the cellar. I am here by choice."

Lucien nodded. "You're here because you can't think of anywhere else to run."

"According to you and my dear uncle, I don't need to run any longer. I have his so-called support now."

"I apologize for setting you free into Monmouth's arms. But it had to be done."

"Why did it have to be done?"

"Because you wouldn't marry me if you had to rely on my support. Now you don't have to do that."

For a moment she looked at him, curiosity warring with her damned stubbornness. "You've left me other reasons to refuse you."

"Yes, I have. About those," he said, and with a nervous breath he hoped she didn't notice, he reached into his breast pocket to produce a folded piece of parchment. "I hope this will help to dispel them." He slid the paper through the bars.

She hesitated, then took it. "What is it?"

"Don't read it yet. Wait until this evening. When you're alone, preferably."

"All right." Alexandra gazed at it, then returned her

attention to him. "Do you intend to wait here all night, then?"

"No. I have to get back to London. Robert wants to wed Rose before the end of the Season, while everyone's still in town."

"Then this is good-bye again."

"I hope not," he murmured, wishing he could simply pull her into his arms and make her let go of everything that caused her to hold on to her stubborn independence. "I want you to marry me, Alexandra. But I won't ask you again. Read that. If you feel inclined to travel, I'll be at Balfour House until the tenth of August." He reached through the gate again, but she eluded his grasp. "The next time, Alexandra, you have to ask me." He smiled. "But I'll say yes."

A tear ran down her soft, smooth cheek. "I won't ask."

"I hope you will." He released the gate and backed toward Faust. "I'll see you soon."

Turning his back and riding away was the hardest thing he'd ever done. He wanted her—needed her—in his life. If she chose not to follow, he would at least know that he'd done everything he could. If that wasn't enough, if she didn't care for him as much as he cared for her . . . well, he'd have a lifetime to torture himself with those questions.

As he reached the first curve in the road, he looked over his shoulder toward the Academy's gates. She was gone.

Alexandra stuffed the parchment into the pocket of her pelisse and hurried back to the main building. It would never do for Lucien to see her standing at the gate and blubbering like an infant as he rode away.

She was crying so hard that she ran into Emma before she even noticed her friend lurking near the front doorway. "Oh! I'm sorry," she said raggedly, between sniffles.

Wordlessly Emma handed her a kerchief.

"Thank you." She blew her nose. "He's just impossible. I should never have gone out to see him."

"You ended it?"

"I ended it in London. He just didn't want to listen to me." A group of girls on their way out for their daily walk passed by them. "There was never any 'it,' anyway," she said more quietly, when they'd gone.

"Anyone watching the two of you would have trouble believing that. Why can't you simply admit that you care for him?"

Wiping her eyes again, Alexandra started up the stairs to her tiny private room, Emma on her heels. "I don't know. Because he expects me to, I suppose. He decides I'm going to fall in love with him, and so I do."

"And that's not the way it's supposed to be?"

"Oh, he's just so damned sure of himself."

A chorus of giggles rained down on them from the stair landing above. Wonderful. Now she was teaching profanity to her students.

Emma grimaced. "I know you're overwrought, Miss Gallant," she said in a carrying voice, "but didn't you mean to say 'dashed'?"

"Yes, I did, Miss Grenville. My apologies."

The headmistress tucked her arm around Alexandra's as they continued up the stairs. "At least it's over with," she stated. "And we have the recitals this afternoon to take your mind off your troubles."

"Yes, thank goodness," Alexandra muttered, though she was fairly certain that nothing was over with, and she knew the recitals wouldn't stop her thinking about Lucien for one blasted second.

She fidgeted all afternoon. Usually she enjoyed the weekly recitals, for some of the Academy's students played exceptionally well. Today, though, all she could think about was the piece of paper in her pocket, and Lucien saying he wouldn't pursue her any longer. That was precisely what she wanted, of course—no one trying to use her for his own ends, or judging her by someone else's actions.

If only she could stop thinking about him—about how much she enjoyed conversing with him, and how she longed for his kisses and his touch—she would realize how perfectly happy she was.

Of course, if she was so happy, she had no real reason to keep reaching into her pocket to touch the letter; and she certainly had no cause to wait and open the stupid thing exactly when and how he instructed. Twice during the recitals she pulled it free and started to unfold it. Both times she put it back, unopened.

As soon as Jane Hantfeld finished her rendition of Haydn, Alexandra stood. The sun had descended halfway through the western band of scattered trees; technically, that made it evening.

"Miss Gallant," Elizabeth Banks, one of the other instructors, said as she passed, "I do hope you will tell us about your mysterious earl at dinner tonight. All of the girls seem quite mad about him."

Alexandra paused. "I've something of a headache this evening. I think I'll forgo dinner. Please give my excuses to Miss Grenville."

No one would believe she had a headache, of course, and they would likely think she was in her bedchamber mooning over her lost love. Well, that was a fair enough description of what she had planned for the evening.

One of the staff had already brought Shakespeare his dinner, and he jumped up on the bed beside her as she lit her lamp and pulled the letter free. The terrier sniffed at it, then wagged his tail and barked.

"You recognize Lucien, don't you, Shakes?" she asked, scratching him behind the ears.

She unfolded the parchment. To her surprise it wasn't a personal letter, but rather some sort of legal document. A smaller piece of paper, folded inside the larger, dropped onto her lap. Alexandra turned her attention to it first.

"Alexandra," it said, in the same scrawling handwriting that characterized Emma's letter from the earl, "I believe even you will have to admit that you have only two reasons remaining for not wishing to marry me."

She took a breath. Why was he still bothering with her? She would have given up the attempt some time ago. The rest of the missive beckoned to her to keep going, so she read on.

"The first reason, as I recall, is that you are a convenient vessel on which I might get an heir and thwart Rose and Fiona from receiving an inheritance. I wish to state here for the record that you are not the least bit convenient." Alexandra stifled an unexpected smile. "The other half of that reasoning will hopefully be answered to your satisfaction by the accompanying addendum to my will. It states, in short, that whether I have offspring or not, Rose's children shall inherit my title and lands."

Alexandra stopped. "It's a joke," she said aloud. "It has to be a joke."

She grabbed the larger piece of paper and read through it once, and then a second time. Couched in legal terms and clauses, it nevertheless stated very clearly that Lucien Balfour, upon his death and regardless of any blood heirs, transferred all nonentailed titles and lands to Rose Delacroix and her heirs. A stipend of five thousand pounds a year for any and each of his own children and surviving spouse was all he held back from the Delacroix branch of the family.

"My God," she whispered, and with shaking fingers returned to the first letter.

"Your second and last remaining objection, I believe, was my belief in love—and more specifically, my lack of ability to love you. I think you already know the answer to that, Alexandra. I shan't debase either of us by protesting to the sun and the moon and the stars how very much I have come to love you, to desire you, and to need you in my life.

"I, then, have one question for you, for I cannot think of anything else that stands between us. Alexandra, do you love me?"

She closed her eyes for a long moment, then read the short signature. "Yours, Lucien."

A tear plopped onto the page before she even realized she was crying again. The Lord Kilcairn she'd met when she'd first gone to London would never have relinquished his inheritance to anyone, much less to Rose Delacroix. He had done it, though. That he had done it for her, she could scarcely believe.

Alexandra stood, pacing to the window and back while Shakespeare trotted along behind her. The will's amendment was signed by Lucien, and witnessed by Mr. Mullins, Lord Belton, and another solicitor. It was real; unmistakably and unfakably real.

She made another circuit of the room, the letter clenched in her fist. He'd done it again: made a point in such a grand fashion that she had no choice but to notice, consider, and explain it to herself. And of course, he'd done it by letter, so she didn't have the outlet of arguing with him about it.

With a strangled growl she flung the letter to the floor and stomped on it. Then she picked it up and smoothed it against her chest, because she'd never received anything so nice. She swore under her breath, glad there weren't any students around to overhear her.

"Look at me, Shakes. He's made me insane."

Shakespeare only wagged his tail. Sighing, she plunked down on the bed. Insane or not, she knew precisely what she wanted to do now. She wanted to rush back to London and punch him, and then throw herself into his arms and never let go. He'd done this for her, and he'd done it because he loved her. No other explanation fit.

"My goodness," she breathed, clutching the letter to her breast. Only one person's motivations remained a mystery, as they had for the past five years. And he was the reason she'd nearly lost Lucien.

"Lex?" Emma knocked at her door.

She started. "Come in."

The headmistress leaned into the doorway. "I came to ask if you were all right."

"I don't know whether I am or not." She chuckled, wondering whether she sounded as hysterical as she felt.

"I see." Emma shut the door. "What happened?"

"I finally learned a lesson, I think." Alexandra stood and dragged her trunk from under the bed. "I'm sorry, Emma. I have to—"

"Resign your position. After seeing the two of you together this morning, I can't say I'm surprised."

"After what I've put him through, though, I'm not

sure he'll really want me about. I'm such an idiot, you know."

"No, you're not. You're very lucky." Emma smiled. "And you're going back to London."

A warm, nervous, excited spark glowed to life in her heart. "Yes. But I have one stop to make before I see him again." She wanted—needed—one more explanation. And thanks to Lucien, she finally had the courage to demand it.

Alexandra took a deep breath, tightened her grip on Shakespeare's leash, and rapped on the massive oak double doors. The sound echoed and faded into the bowels of the house, and her heart hammered in the same nervous rhythm. A moment later the door swung open.

"Yes, miss?"

She looked at the hawk-nosed butler. "Please inform His Grace that Miss Gallant is here to see him."

He hesitated, then nodded. "This way, miss."

The mansion was enormous, perhaps even larger than Balfour House. The butler led her into the morning room and closed the door behind him as he vanished. Portraits of the duke and his two sons hung from one wall, along with a rendering of his late wife and several other, more distant, relations.

"What do you want?"

Alexandra kept her attention on the paintings as the duke's voice boomed into the room. "Why is there no portrait of my mother here?" she asked.

"She left the family. I thought you'd run off to Hampshire."

"You pushed her out of the family."

"Is that why you behave so poorly in my presence? Your mother taught you to dislike me, didn't she?"

She turned around. "Is that what you think?"

The Duke of Monmouth rolled his eyes. "I'm a busy man. You'd best get to whatever point you have. I don't have and I won't take the time to hand out lengthy explanations to minor relations."

His reply resoundingly answered one question. Lucien was nothing like her uncle. That was another apology she owed the earl. "I don't want an explanation," she said, her jaw clenched. "I want an apology."

"For choosing not to display a portrait of your mother? Nonsense!"

Alexandra looked at him. "You don't have any idea why I'm angry, do you, Uncle Monmouth?"

He strode to the writing desk and began rooting through the drawers. "I don't care why you're angry," he retorted. "I told you, I'm busy."

Far from being intimidated, Alexandra abruptly wanted to laugh. "You sound like a thespian who has only learned one line of a play—'don't bother me, I'm busy.' "

The duke rounded on her. "I will not be made a figure of ridicule. Is this how you show your gratitude? I went out of my way to publicly forgive your indiscretions, and in return you call me an actor? A poor actor, yet?"

"If you are so very busy, why did you go out of your way to forgive my indiscretions?"

"Bah. Kilcairn caught me at a weak moment."

"I see."

"No, you don't. And you've already made me regret taking you back into the family fold." He lifted out a ledger and slammed the desk door closed. "I suppose you want money now?"

"Good heavens," she muttered. "I don't want money.

All I ever wanted from you was an apology, as I just said."

"An apology? I told you, I will not have your mother's por—"

"Not for that," she interrupted sharply. "When my mother and father died, I asked you for money—only enough so I could settle their few debts. You refused. I had to sell most of Mama's jewelry and all of Papa's paintings just to see them decently buried."

"And how—"

"I'm not finished! I was completely alone after they died. And you did nothing—*nothing*—to demonstrate that you cared in the least whether I lived or died."

"Well, you lived. And now you seem determined to plague me at every turn."

For a long moment she was silent. Red-faced and blustering, her uncle still gave no indication that he realized he'd done anything wrong. Perhaps that was the most telling difference between him and Lucien: The earl took responsibility for his misdeeds. And lately he'd worked to correct them.

In addition, all of the slights and manipulations and barriers she'd fought against—all of them put there by the duke because he disliked her family so much—apparently she'd made them all up. Monmouth didn't hate her; he simply didn't care about her. "I only wanted a piece of your heart," she said slowly.

"Ha! My heart and my purse, you mean."

"No. You won't apologize, will you? Not even to the memory of my mother, your own sister."

"*She* married that damned painter, against my wishes. I don't owe her—or anyone else—an apology."

Abruptly her long, burning anger at him—at his whole side of the family—sputtered and died. She didn't want to be a part of this family. She'd found the family she wanted.

"Well then, Uncle, I am sorry," she said. "And I forgive you, because you obviously can't help being the heartless man you are. If you could help it, you wouldn't be such a fool." Alexandra turned for the door.

"I will not be insulted!" he bellowed at her back.

"Have you come back to beg for money, cousin?"

Alexandra paused. Virgil Retting stood on the landing, leaning over the railing to sneer at her. "Good day, Virgil," she said, and continued down the hall.

"You'll never get anything from us, you know, you strumpet."

That was enough of that. Squaring her shoulders, Alexandra slowly turned to face him again. "Virgil, I doubt you have the intelligence to understand me, but I'll give it a try anyway."

"How—"

"I don't like you," she interrupted. "You're a fool and a conceited idiot of no significance. If you were a pauper, you wouldn't have a friend to speak of. If you were a rat, I wouldn't feed you to a snake for fear of giving the serpent a sour stomach. Now, good-bye, and good riddance."

"How dare you!"

She walked down the hallway and out the front door, Shakespeare at her side. The hack she'd hired still waited in the street, and she gave him the next direction and climbed in. Her uncle might have been completely incapable of recognizing his own stupidity and of apologizing for it, but thankfully she was not.

"My lord, you must . . . amend this amendment," Mr. Mullins said, waving sheets of parchment in the air. Half of them escaped, and went flying about the garden like a miniature fleet of sails.

Lucien shook his head and resumed planing the cellar's new window frame. "No. One more word about it, and you'll be looking for other employment."

The solicitor scrambled to recover his paperwork. "But . . . it makes no sense!"

"Mr. Mullins, do not make me repeat myself."

"Yes, my lord. Of course. But what . . . what about this construction you're doing?" The solicitor gestured at the half-repaired window. "You have sufficient funds to hire a score of workers for Balfour House."

"I broke it, and I'll fix it." Eyeing Mr. Mullins, he returned to his task, daring the solicitor to contradict his lie. He couldn't very well explain that if he didn't keep himself occupied, he would go insane, or that by repairing the cellar window he felt some absurd connection to Alexandra.

It had been five days since he'd ridden away from Miss Grenville's Academy. If she'd left there immediately after reading his letter, she could have been in London by yesterday. Of course, as far as he knew, she might be still at the Academy teaching spoon etiquette.

Just in case she chose to come, though, he would be ready. The gold room's furnishings were back where they belonged, as were the other household objects she'd managed to acquire for her cellar dungeon—though if he had any say in the matter, she would be occupying the master chambers with him. He'd rented a house and servants for Rose and Fiona, so his damned aunt would be as far away from Alexandra as he could get her and still allow him to keep his word to Rose about assisting with the wedding.

In addition, he'd acquired a special marriage license

from the Archbishop of Canterbury. If Alexandra did return, he was not about to give her another opportunity to escape. That nagging "if" was the same reason he'd scarcely left the house since he'd arrived back in London. He wasn't about to risk missing her.

"Very well, my lord." The solicitor sighed. "I do hope you understand I have always had your best interests at heart."

Lucien glanced sideways at him. "That's why you're still here. At the moment, though, I'm beginning to find you annoying. Go fetch Vincent, will you?"

Mr. Mullins bowed. "At once, my lord."

Once the solicitor had vanished toward the stable, Lucien leaned the window frame against his makeshift worktable and sank down on the stone bench. He'd never really taken the time to notice what a lovely garden his gardeners kept for him. He'd been seeing quite a few things he'd missed before, and he thought he knew why: the jaded, cynical anger that had seemed such a part of him had faded and softened. If nothing else, he owed Alexandra for that.

"Did someone else escape your dungeon?"

Lucien whipped to his feet, his breath catching. Alexandra strolled into the garden, Shakespeare beside her. She wore the green patterned muslin he liked so much, and if not for the hesitant look in her eyes, he could almost have believed she'd just returned from a morning stroll.

"No," he said as coolly as he could manage. "I'm working at preventing future catastrophes."

"Ah. That's wise."

She continued toward him, and Lucien forced himself to stay where he was. He wanted to sweep her into his arms, but he'd told her the next move in this little chess game was hers, and he'd meant it. "It's self-preservation. If my next prisoner were to escape, I might find myself arrested."

Alexandra stopped her approach a scant few feet from him. "I . . . read your letter."

"Good."

"You can't do that. It's insane."

He lifted an eyebrow. "What's insane?"

"Cutting your own heirs off from their inheritance!"

"Oh, that."

Finally she stepped closer. "Yes, that. You've made your point, Lucien. I don't want future generations to suffer because I'm a stubborn idiot."

He wanted to ask if she meant *their* future generations, but he'd let her tell her news the way she chose to do so. "Is that all you came to tell me?"

She blushed, winding Shakespeare's leash around her hand. "No. I wanted . . . I wanted you to know that I took your advice."

As Lucien recalled, he'd given some rather foul advice in the recent past. "My advice?"

A tear ran down one cheek. Lucien tensed, his heart pounding. He would go after her if she turned to run, but ultimately if she wished to leave, he would have to let her do it.

"Yes," she whispered shakily. "I bent a little. I went to see my uncle."

It was more than he'd expected, but Alexandra had never been predictable. Unable to resist touching her, Lucien reached out and brushed the tear from her cheek. "And?"

To his further surprise, she gave a short, unsteady laugh. "He's an awful man." Alexandra took his hand, squeezing his fingers. "And not at all like you. I should never had said such an odious thing."

Lucien shrugged. "I've heard worse."

"No, you haven't. It's the worst insult I can think of, anyway." She shut her eyes for a moment. "This is so blasted difficult to say."

That sounded promising. He smiled. "I'm not the damned Spanish Inquisition." He continued gazing at her, noting the warmth of her hand, and the way the slight breeze caressed her golden sunburnt hair. As the silence lengthened, he chuckled. "You do have to say something eventually. It'll be dark in a few hours."

Alexandra nodded. Still gripping his fingers, she led him back to the stone bench. His heart pounding in a nervous rhythm he hoped she couldn't detect, he followed her.

"Sit," she instructed.

"I'm not one of your students, you know."

"Sit."

He complied, only to wonder what in damnation she was up to when she turned her back on him. All she did, though, was loop her dog's leash around the leg of his worktable and face him again.

For a long moment she stood there, gazing at him, before she returned to where he sat. He slid sideways to make room for her, then stopped, frozen, when she knelt at his feet.

"Don't do that," he said harshly, leaning down to lift her up again.

"It's all right. Just be quiet and listen for once, won't you?"

Lucien sat upright again. "Fine."

"Thank you." Alexandra took a deep breath, her lovely bosom heaving. "I want to apologize to you. You said and did some very—*very*—nice things for me, and I . . ." Another tear rolled down her cheek.

Good God, this was too much. He'd just wanted her to come to her senses, not to beg him for forgiveness for every real and imagined slight. He slid off the bench and knelt in front of her. "Stop it," he murmured.

"But you said—"

"Forget what I said. Just tell me your thoughts. They have always fascinated me no end."

"Don't jest."

He took both her hands in his. "I'm not. You are the most mesmerizing, fascinating, compelling, desirable woman I've ever met."

"I love you," she blurted, and then flung her arms around his neck and kissed him.

Lucien kissed her back, pulling her across his legs so he could feel the warmth of her against him. "I love you," he returned feelingly.

"Then I have a question to ask you," Alexandra continued, her voice shaking and tears flowing down her face.

"Yes?"

"Will you marry me, Lucien?"

He kissed her again, roughly. "I told you I would, Alexandra. Thank God you haven't completely come to your senses."

"I *have,* finally. Thanks to you." She ran her fingers along his jaw. "I think I just couldn't believe you would want me."

Lucien chuckled. "I locked you in the damned cellar, Alexandra. You were beginning to try my patience."

"You try mine all the time."

"And I hope to continue to do so."

She pushed a little away from him, though she kept

her hands wrapped tightly into his shirt. "You have to change your will."

"Are you certain? I want *you*, Alexandra. Nothing else matters."

"I understand that." She shook him. "You're very stubborn. Change it back the way it was, but make certain Rose and Fiona are provided for, as well."

"Already taken care of." Lucien kissed her again, wishing they were somewhere other than his garden, and that he hadn't already sent for Vincent. "I'll make you a bargain."

"What sort of bargain?"

"I'll put our heirs back into my will if you will marry me this afternoon."

Shock crossed her face. "What? How—"

"It's all arranged. Just in case you returned, of course."

"Do you have a pastor in the cellar?"

"I would, if I'd thought of it. Do you agree?"

Alexandra laughed, her turquoise eyes dancing. "Yes. For heaven's sake, yes, yes, yes! Marry me this instant."

Lucien pulled them both up, then swept her up to cradle her in his arms. "As you wish." He looked up as Vincent appeared. "Vincent, bring the coach around."

"Yes, my lord." The groom turned on his heel.

"Wait!" Alexandra called.

"What is it?" Lucien asked, wondering if he would have to kidnap her again to get her to the church, after all.

"Vincent, please see that Shakespeare is tended to. We will return shortly."

"Yes, Miss Gallant."

"Yes, Lady Kilcairn," Lucien corrected sternly.

The groom grinned and bowed. "Yes, Lady Kilcairn."

Alexandra eyed Lucien as he carried her toward the front steps. "Not quite yet, Lucien. Don't jinx anything."

"You're not getting away from me again, Alexandra."

She twined her arms around his neck. "I don't want to escape any longer," she whispered, then kissed him. "I'm home now."

He kissed her back. "And so am I."